For
Jim, John, Mary Catherine,
Jeanne, and Amy,
with love

LIFELINE

A JACK McMORROW MYSTERY

Praise for Gerry Boyle's *Lifeline*

"[Boyle's] style is poised and pointed..."
—*New York Times*

"Boyle, a Maine newspaper writer himself, makes McMorrow a credible crusader, equally comfortable in the quiet woods and small town courthouses. The narrative moves briskly as McMorrow eliminates several suspects on his way to a surprise solution."
—*Publishers Weekly*

"Stay healthy, McMorrow. You're fun to have around."
—*Washington Times*

Praise for Gerry Boyle's *Potshot*

"Fans of Robert B. Parker's Spenser will love McMorrow, a quintessential male who's tough, funny, macho, and intelligent."
—*Booklist*

LIFELINE

A JACK McMORROW MYSTERY

GERRY BOYLE

ISLANDPORT PRESS

LIFELINE

First Islandport edition/June 2015

Printing History
G. P. Putnam's Sons hardcover edition/1996
Berkley Prime Crime mass market edition/March 1997

ISBN: 978-1-939017-52-9
Library of Congress Control Number: 2014911183
Islandport Press
PO Box 10
Yarmouth, Maine 04096
www.islandportpress.com
books@islandportpress.com

Publisher: Dean Lunt
Cover Design: Tom Morgan, Blue Design
Interior Book Design: Teresa Lagrange, Islandport Press
Cover image courtesy of Blue Design

Printed in the USA

ACKNOWLEDGMENTS

Thanks go to Tom M., who knows homicide; to my friends and colleagues in the newspaper business, who still fight the good fight; and especially to Mary Marsh Grow, whose generous and meticulous assistance is, and will always be, appreciated.

INTRODUCTION

The day was winding down in district court. I'd been parked on a back bench, watching the parade of defendants: drunk drivers, petty thieves, a few inmates from the county jail, slouched in their orange jumpsuits and enjoying a field trip.

I was a newspaper columnist then, trolling the courtrooms, among other places, looking for a story to tell. Nothing had grabbed me that day, and I was about to move on when she stepped up.

If memory serves, she was about thirty-five, tallish, dark hair, and a long narrow face, with a stoic yet determined expression. The prosecutor said the woman was seeking a court order to protect her from abuse. The judge said something like, "What sort of abuse?" And the woman told him, then and there, in open court. The inmates sat up and the room went silent as she began.

It was a terribly sad story. Her boyfriend had assaulted her, threatened her, tried to rape her. He said if she told anyone he'd kill her. She was in court that day because he was, for the moment, in jail for another matter. It was safe.

The guy did some unspeakable things to the woman, but she was speaking of them anyway. That made the story sadder still. In front of a room full of strangers, most of them men, she told her story in unvarnished detail. She started at the beginning and kept going because nobody tried to stop her. When she was done the judge gave her the protection order, and she turned and walked through the gate in the rail and down the center aisle, all eyes on her, some no doubt luridly imagining what she'd just described.

The woman went to the court clerk's window and got her paperwork. When she went out the courthouse doors, I followed her. I caught up with her at her car and introduced myself. She listened to my pitch and the story hung in the air for a moment and then she said she'd do it. She agreed to be in the newspaper because she wasn't going to be afraid anymore. I hoped her courage wouldn't come back to haunt her.

We talked at length, and I wrote about her in the column that appeared in the newspaper the next day. We met a couple more times, as she wanted to keep me abreast of what was happening with her case.

The boyfriend, still in custody, was charged with additional crimes, though not the ones that she had described. He was sentenced to a few years in prison. The woman moved out of state at that point, but she wrote to me, and stayed with me long after—so much so that my encounter with her was the seed for this novel.

The fictional character is Donna Marchant, who goes to court to get protection from an abusive, bullying man. The prosecutor is unsympathetic, and the judge tells Donna to be more careful picking her boyfriends. Jack McMorrow, sitting at the rear of the courtroom, steps up. And when McMorrow steps up, he's all in.

He writes about Donna and then he tries to protect her. She has a beguiling innocence, despite her hardships. She likes watercolors, and paints along with an artist on TV. She tries to seduce McMorrow, and he tells her she deserves better. In the end, despite his best intentions, his attempt to help Donna Marchant comes up short.

Donna is a character I've thought of many times since *Lifeline* was first published. I think of her and her daughter, Adrianna, the first child character I had written at that point. And I sometimes think back to the moment when I was writing the climax to the novel.

I had a plan in my head and no intention of deviating from it, but then, at a crucial moment, an entirely different scenario appeared—one I hadn't imagined, one that didn't appear in any synopsis or outline. The words flowed through my fingers to the keyboard like I'd been taken over by a spirit, and the resolution was chilling, even to me. I remember sitting at the desk in my study as I finished the scene. I was stunned. Later I would hear that readers were, too.

I also think of *Lifeline* at other times—when I hear of yet another domestic violence murder, another woman terrorized. It's been ten years since that woman stood up in the courtroom, and sadly, this terrible problem is just as real and relevant as ever.

In my fictional world, Jack McMorrow is ready to strike back, with Clair Varney to back him up. Roxanne is there to counsel McMorrow when needed, waiting when he returns, bruised and bloodied from having fought the good fight.

I like to think there are real McMorrows out there. I know his fictional world is a much better place because of him.

—Gerry Boyle, March 2015

1

It was the low end of what had once been a pasture but now, like a field full of Hydras, was growing back into forest. Where teams of horses and then tractors had worked, there was an almost impassable tangle of poplar and spruce and blackberries and burdocks.

I had worked my way into the thicket just before dawn, when the woods were still blurred with mist. For a half hour, maybe longer, I had sat still on a rock that had been part of a wall that some Sisyphus, now long dead, had built where his field met the forest. I had heard chickadees. A redstart in the distance. Gulls calling as they wafted overhead on the way to the dump. And then a musical gurgle, high-pitched like a piccolo, coming from somewhere in the brush behind me.

Motionless, I waited, resisting the urge to turn around. The trilling call came closer and then there was a flutter to my left. I looked without turning my head and saw a small bird perched near the bottom of a poplar sapling, a couple of feet from the ground. It was a thrush, smaller than a wood thrush and more olive-colored, more drab. Its eyes were dark and wet. I held my breath as it flitted closer, from the poplar to the ground and then back up again.

As I exhaled silently, it began to call again, a series of soft, piping notes. And then there was a flash.

A missile-like shadow.

A barely audible *poof.*

"So, right in front of me, the hawk just picks this thrush off, just like that," I said. "I'm pretty sure it was a Swainson's thrush. But it might have been a Cooper's hawk or a sharp-shinned hawk. They look sort of the same."

I took a sip of ale.

"But it was this unbelievable moment. Sort of transcendent or something, you know? This thrush is there one second and then swish, the angel of death comes out of nowhere and the thrush isn't singing. It's having its heart picked out of its chest. I don't know. It was like, there was life right there. And wham, it's gone. Like a meteor dropping out of the sky and hitting you right in the head. Life's going along fine and a spear comes out of the darkness and skewers you. And you never even saw it coming."

I finished the ale in a long swallow.

"You want tea?" Roxanne said.

"No," I said. "I think I'll have another beer."

I got up from the table and brought my plate over to the counter. Roxanne's back was turned to me, and I squeezed her hip as I slid by to open the refrigerator door. It was the last can. I opened it as I went back to my chair. Roxanne snapped the lid on the coffeemaker and it started to hiss. I opened my field guide to where I had the page marked.

"Yeah, it says even experienced birders have trouble telling a Cooper's from a sharp-shinned. The sharp-shinned is smaller, but a male Cooper's is quite a bit smaller than the female. Cooper's, fourteen to twenty inches. Sharp-shinned, only ten to fourteen. So maybe it was a Cooper's. It seemed more than a foot long. God, you should have seen it, though. Not from you to me away. *Whoosh.*"

Roxanne poured her coffee and stood against the counter. The smell of hazelnut filled the big open room.

"It sounds like an interesting thing to see," Roxanne said. "Why don't you write an essay about it."

I shrugged. Sipped the ale.

"No, really," she said. "It sounds like something the *Globe* magazine might buy. Maybe the *Times*. I don't know. Sell it to *Maine Times*, but at least you'd be doing something with it."

"Why should I do something with it?"

"I don't know. Because you're a writer. A reporter. Jack, don't you want to get back into it? Somehow? Really. You can't just tromp around the woods and then come home and drink beer all night."

"Why not?" I said. "Thoreau did it."

"He drank beer?"

"They all drank beer back then."

"But he also wrote *Walden*," Roxanne said.

"So he was an overachiever."

"But, Jack, this is your life," she said, a hard edge creeping into her voice.

"Don't tell me that you've found my third-grade teacher. Mrs. McGillicuddy! You haven't changed a bit!"

"Jack."

I sipped the ale. Roxanne held her mug to her chest but did not sip her coffee.

"But I'm happy," I said. "This thing this morning was great. An epiphany or something."

"Great. Wonderful. But you should be creating something, too."

"Why?"

"Goddamn it," Roxanne said. "Because you're good at it. You're thirty-eight years old. You can't just retire. My God, are you going to go from the *New York Times* to nothing? Just stop? Retire to Prosperity, Maine. For the rest of your life?"

"I don't know. When I get real old, maybe I'll move to one of those places in Arizona. You know, the ones where they don't allow anybody under fifty?"

"Come on, Jack. I'm serious."

"So am I. When we're old, the last thing we'll need is a lot of youthful forty-nine-year-olds doing laps in the pool. We'll hate people who have their own teeth. All shiny and white and—"

"Goddamn it, Jack. You know what I think?"

"No, but I think I'm going to find out."

Roxanne glared at me. I closed the bird book.

"How many beers have you had?" she asked.

I looked at the table. There were three empty sixteen-ounce cans of Ballantine ale. A fourth that was a third gone.

"Two," I said. "Officer."

I grinned. Roxanne didn't.

"I think you're numbing yourself for some reason. To keep from having to go out again and give it your best shot."

"Thank you, Dr. Masterson, but I gave it my best shot. Sorry if I'm not being a high-enough roller for you."

"Jack, you know that's not true," Roxanne said, softening for a moment. "But you know I'm right. You may not like it, but I'm right."

I looked at her. Shorts. Sandals. A sleeveless denim blouse, undone to the third button.

"You know you're sexy when you're right?" I said.

"I know I'm sexy when I'm happy. And it doesn't make me happy to see you in this, I don't know, this state of hibernation."

"So either I do a five-part series on the plight of the middle class, or I sleep on the couch?"

Roxanne sagged.

"Oh, Jack. I don't want to fight. I know you were happy and I know how you love the woods. But are you happy like this? With only this?"

I eyed the green can of ale, ran a finger across the condensation on the silver top.

"That hawk really was beautiful," I said quietly. "And that thrush. I don't know. I feel like my eyes are just opening up."

"It's not enough, Jack," Roxanne said.

"For me or for you?"

"For us."

"Why do I feel like that's an exit line?"

"I don't know what it is," Roxanne said, blinking back tears. "I just know I have work to do."

She took her coffee and a bundle of folders and went up the stairs to the loft. I heard the bedsprings squeak, a sound that for months had been associated with our joy and pleasure, but now sounded like a gate that had just swung shut.

2

The *Kennebec Observer* offices were in an old brick building on the city's main drag. They offered a view, indeed, of the Kennebec River, which loitered in the distance, but mostly of downtown Kennebec, a cluttered, half-vacant jumble of shops and offices. The place looked as though it was in the grips of a long-standing economic malaise, one of the benefits of which was ample parking. I pulled the truck into a space directly in front of the newspaper, where an old man was allowing an old golden retriever to defecate on the sidewalk.

"Nice morning," I said, slamming the truck door shut.

Neither the man nor the dog appeared to have heard.

It was a nice morning. Cool and fresh and filled with the promise that marks early June. I'd spent it in the woods, listening to spring warblers, straining to catch glimpses of them as they fluttered and fell through the trees. Then, as the sun moved higher, I'd made my way back home, where Roxanne was still asleep and the house was quiet. I'd showered, put on khakis and my least-worn oxford cloth shirt, and grabbed a blazer and a half dozen newspapers from the stack in the back of the bedroom closet.

Now, on the sidewalk, I put the blazer on, dropping the papers in the process. I gathered them up, a few of the fruits of ten years' labor, yellowed reports of what had once, and only once, been news. The dog and the man still ignored me.

The sign in the foyer said the *Observer* newsroom was on the second floor, circulation and advertising on the first. There was allegedly an elevator, but I took the stairs, which were old and wooden and creaky. After two flights, I came to a door with a frosted-glass window. A sticker on the window said someone at one time had given to the United Way. Someone else had tried to scrape the sticker off, but the United Way had prevailed.

I opened the door and stepped out into the newsroom, startling a circle of men and women who were standing around a table, feeding on doughnuts. They looked at me as if I'd just stepped into the ladies' restroom.

"Good morning," I said. "I'm looking for Mr. Albert."

A pale, wizened man with glasses turned toward me. He was wearing a short-sleeved shirt that was two sizes too small, and his mouth held a chaw of honey dip. But he did the polite thing and pointed me to the end of the room.

"Thanks," I said.

Still chewing, he nodded.

The place was like most newsrooms I'd been in over the years, except smaller. I walked past small cardboard signs that had been stuck on the walls to designate the different departments. Sports had four desks. The Living department had three. News had five. On each desk was a beat-up computer that no doubt had taken the place of a beat-up typewriter. The desks were covered with newspapers and notebooks and page dummies. The plants were mostly dead.

I walked in the direction Mister Doughnut had pointed. When I got to the end of the room, I stopped. There was a clatter, then the muffled sound of a restroom hand dryer. I waited for a moment and a guy walked around the corner and almost bumped me in the chest.

"Mr. Albert?" I said.

"Jack McMorrow?" he said.

We shook hands. His was wet.

Albert was fifty, maybe a little older. A big, stoop-shouldered guy, he had a little bit of a paunch but not much. He was wearing a bright green tie with a pale green shirt and dark green slacks, both of which complemented his reddish face. It would have been a nice outfit for St. Patrick's Day, which was nine months away, but Albert, moving with the unhurried languor that is a sign of long-term, unchallenged authority, didn't seem to care.

I followed him to his office, which was a desk like the others but set off in the corner, behind a fake-paneled partition. Behind his chair there was a six-foot map of the state of Maine. As he stood in front of the map waiting for me to sit, Albert looked like a television weatherman who'd forgotten his pointer. "A low-pressure system will move in from the southwest . . ."

"So, Mr. McMorrow," Albert said when we'd both sat. "You want to do some court reporting?"

"I might," I said.

"You know it's only a part-time position?"

I nodded.

"Like the ad says. Two days a week," Albert said. "And I don't anticipate it growing into a full-time job, if that's what you're thinking."

"That's not what I was thinking," I said.

"This isn't a big-budget operation, you know," he went on. "I don't have money to throw around."

I tried to conceal my surprise.

"What's your circulation?" I asked.

"About nine thousand. Stays pretty steady. Six days a week, except for Christmas."

Nine thousand. I could just hear what my former colleagues would say about that. "You shouldn't deliver those papers. You should number them and sell them as a limited edition."

"So you brought some clips?" Albert said.

"Not exactly. I brought some papers."

I put the newspapers on his desk. There were four metro sections from the *Times*. My byline above the fold. Two copies of the *Androscoggin Review*. My byline on every story on the front page.

Albert picked the papers up, unfolded them, and began to read. As he read, he made a *hmmph* sound. He hmmphed four times, then put the papers down.

"So you're that Jack McMorrow," he said, looking me in the eye.

"I guess so," I said.

"The one from the weekly over in Androscoggin. Where those people got killed."

I nodded.

"That was a crazy business," Albert said.

"Yeah, it was."

"I read about that. The photographer got killed first, didn't he?"

"That's right," I said.

He gave me a long look, then picked up a section of the *Times*. The story was about a night riding with an ambulance in the Bronx. Four overdoses. A shooting. Two stabbings. A pretty teenage girl slashed across the face with a razor. A couple of heart attacks. An infant, the mother of whom spoke only a Hmong dialect. The baby had severe diarrhea and dehydration. She was followed by a drunk homeless man, run over because he was passed out in the middle of the Grand Concourse.

An average night, the ambulance people had said.

"Jesus," Albert said, putting the paper down. "I don't know how people can live like that. Animals. So, Mr. McMorrow. What brings you to Kennebec, Maine?"

"Needed a change, I guess," I said.

"So you ran the weekly in Androscoggin."

"Yup."

"And you've been freelancing since then, you said."

"Some," I said.

"And you're living out in Prosperity?"

"Right."

"Got family up here?"

"Nope."

"Leave a family down in New York?"

"No," I said.

"Married?"

"No."

"Divorced?"

I hesitated.

"No, and my underwear size is thirty-four, boxers. Shirt, sixteen and a half. I brush twice a day, but I don't floss as often as I should."

Albert looked at me. I smiled. He didn't. He picked up one of my papers.

"Well, you know Kennebec isn't New York City."

"I noticed," I said.

"And district court in Kennebec isn't like something in the Bronx there. I see you covered a murder trial. You won't get anything that exciting in district court."

"A kid got shot in an argument over a thirty-eight-hundred-dollar crack deal. It wasn't all that exciting."

Albert was scanning the story.

"He end up getting convicted?"

"Sort of. Manslaughter. He shot the guy in the face with a three-fifty-seven, but I guess he didn't mean to kill him."

"So what happened?" Albert said again.

"Plea bargain," I said.

He put the paper down, shaking his head.

"You sure you aren't overqualified for this job, Mr. McMorrow?"

"Depends on what the job is."

"Report on what goes on in court. Who the people are and what they did. What their fines and sentences are. Spell the names right and use middle initials. We have a lot of people around here with similar names. Tom Jones the punk gets convicted of drunk driving and Tom Jones the lawyer calls up and chews my ass out 'cause people think it was him."

"So I'll say Tom Jones the drunk punk, not Tom Jones the drunk lawyer," I said.

Albert gave me the long look again. There was the sound of marching in the aisle behind me. I turned. It was Mister Doughnut, carrying an empty coffeepot. He gave me the quick once-over and headed for the bathroom to refill.

I waited while Albert looked down at my newspapers, then turned toward the window. The view was of a big brick mill, now used as a warehouse. It had nice classical lines, but plywood plugged half the windows. Beside the mill were rows of tenement houses that had been built for the mill workers who'd come down the Kennebec from Quebec, or walked in from their farms. Beyond the houses there were wooded hills, pale spring green against the searing blue sky.

Albert frowned as if he'd seen something he didn't like, then turned back to me.

"If you're willing, I'm willing," he said. "But I don't want any trouble."

"Trouble?"

"I like stories written by my reporters. Not about them."

"Likewise."

"Like this stuff at the weekly. I don't need that."

"I didn't either," I said.

"Just so we understand each other," Albert said.

"In time," I said.

He gave me the look again.

Albert got up from the desk and walked to the corner of the partition. He was a big man, one of those flabby guys who still have residual strength. There was football in his distant past.

"Charlene," he called. "I need one of those laptops."

I heard heels clack off into the distance.

Albert walked to his desk and sat on the edge of it. I got up from my chair.

"So what was it like to work for the *New York Times?*" he said suddenly.

"Probably a lot like working here," I said. "Except bigger. Reporters are reporters, you know?"

"When I first got out of J school, I wanted to be a foreign correspondent. You know any of those guys?"

"Some," I said.

"That must be something," Albert said.

"Not that much different," I said. "The actual reporting, I mean. But then they get the foreign stuff in their blood. Some of them can't come home. Can't adjust to it. Get to be nomads."

"You ever do any of that?"

"No," I said. "I stayed in New York mostly. New York and New Jersey."

"You liked the city stuff better than the foreign?"

"I didn't say that. It wasn't always up to me."

Albert picked up the *Times* again. Flipped it back onto the desk.

"So why are you here, McMorrow?" he asked again.

"To get a job covering Fourth District Court in the town of Kennebec. Like it said in the ad. Two days a week. Salary negotiable."

"Yeah, we'll pay you what we can. With your experience, say eighty bucks a day."

"Sounds good."

"When can you start? Court's held Tuesdays and Thursdays."

"I'll go tomorrow," I said.

Charlene walked in and handed him a plastic case. She was one of the women from the doughnut circle—forties, matronly, obviously nosy. She smiled at me, and I grinned back.

"Going to be joining us?" Charlene said brightly.

"Beginning to look that way," I said.

"Good for you," she said, and gave me a mischievous look that seemed to imply I didn't know what I was in for. She probably was right.

Charlene walked out. Albert slowly pulled the computer out of the case, as though he were unsheathing a very sharp knife. The computer was a Tandy, from RadioShack. An old one.

"Ever use one of these?" he asked.

"Once upon a time," I said.

"You can write your story here or wherever. Then shoot it into our system. Some of our people come in and use the phone here because it takes a few tries sometimes. Saves calling back and forth. Deadline for the court report is eight p.m."

"Fine."

"So leave your Social Security number with Charlene. Her desk is up by the door," Albert said.

He handed over the computer and my newspapers and we shook hands again. His hand had dried.

"See you tomorrow," Albert said.

I nodded and started for the hallway.

"Mr. McMorrow," Albert said.

I turned.

"There an arrest warrant waiting for you in New York or what?"

He smiled. Just barely.

3

Roxanne left at six thirty for a meeting before school. A sophomore boy had punched a teacher and, as a result, Roxanne had been assigned as his social worker. He was six one and weighed two hundred pounds. Roxanne's job was to help him rechannel his anger. I offered to go with her and bring a baseball bat, but she said no.

"Sometimes the old ways are best," I said, standing in the driveway in my boxers.

"So bring back public executions," Roxanne said from the car.

"You laugh," I said.

"At somebody in the yard in his underwear," she said.

I moved to the window and leaned in.

"You know you were right," I said.

"About what?" she said, her hands on the wheel.

"About me getting back into it."

"I hope so. I don't want you to think I'm some old nag."

"Not at all," I said. "And you know what you are when you're right?"

She looked puzzled for a moment. I reached into the car and grabbed her thigh.

"God, Jack," Roxanne said, pushing my arm away and grinning. "But I'll be waiting for you when you get home."

"Naked?"

"With bells on."

"I love it when you talk kinky," I said, and she kissed me and drove away.

But even as I waved and smiled, something told me that this particular brush fire had been knocked down but not extinguished. Even if it were out, another would flare up. There was something smoldering between me and Roxanne, and for the first time in a long time, it wasn't strictly passion.

I thought this in the driveway, and then it came back to me again as I sat in the fourth row from the front at Fourth District Court. It was eleven thirty and my back hurt and my stomach was growling. The judge, a small woman who looked tough as dried sinew, had walked in, sat down, and then a bailiff had handed her a note and she'd walked back out. We, the people, had waited another hour and a half, and I'd thought about Roxanne and then the bailiff had banged through the door again.

"All rise," he said, and the thirty or so men and women had hauled themselves up from the hard benches like reluctant churchgoers; then, after the judge had settled into her chair, they'd flopped back down again.

I flopped too.

It was the first session, just getting under way. The judge had been tied up all morning for an emergency Human Services custody hearing, which they'd held in the other courtroom. I'd watched as the social workers hustled the kid, a bewildered-looking boy no older than eight, into the courtroom. After almost two hours, they'd hustled him back out like a protected witness, a diminutive rock star. It was a celebrity that no doubt had been hard-earned and was destined to be short-lived.

So now we waited.

The lawyers, men and women in an odd assortment of suits and tweed jackets, leaned against the railing up front and chatted, ignoring the huddled masses behind them. In front of me, a young guy stretched his muscled arms out on the back of the bench, showing a crude tattoo on his right forearm that said BORN TO BE BAD.

An icebreaker in the nursing home someday.

Next to him was an older man wearing a dark blue uniform. His face was brown and weathered, with fissures like something on the bottom of a dried-up clay riverbed. There was a woman with him, maybe twenty and quite heavy, whom I presumed to be his daughter. She leaned over and whispered to him and he reached in his shirt pocket and took out a cigarette, which he gave her. She got up and eased her way along the row toward the door, hunching low as if the courtroom were a movie theater and she didn't want to block anyone's view.

Not that there was much of one.

The room was done in blond wood paneling, which was warped and faded. There were two flags, United States and Maine, one at each end of the judge's bench, and they were faded too. On the wall to the left was a dusty print of George Washington. It was crooked, giving George an impish look. He stared across the room at a long line of framed photographs of past judges, all men, all grim, as if their years on the bench had left them with no hope for humanity. Their photographs were black-and-white, except for the one at the end of the line, which was in garish color. That judge had blue eyes and pink cheeks that made his colleagues look like stiffs.

Which was what I was, after two hours on the hard pew. I hadn't taken a single note, but I was ready. Jack McMorrow, veteran reporter, at your service. All I needed was a story.

The bailiff talked to the judge in courtroom whispers and the judge, in a black polyester robe, sat back in her big leatherette chair.

She sat, and we sat, and then she picked up a piece of paper and said she was going to call the docket.

"I am Judge Marlene Dorsett," she said, "and I'm going to call the names on the docket. If you hear your name, please stand and tell me."

"Yeah, I'll tell you," the tattooed guy sneered under his breath.

"Dale Mulcahey," the judge said.

"Here, Your Honor," the tattooed guy called politely.

I choked back a chuckle. The guy turned around and scowled. I smiled back sweetly.

The roll call continued, like the first day of school. The defendants stood awkwardly, holding baseball caps in front of them, tough guys temporarily humbled. A young woman was there with her mother and they both stood, as if their case would be won on solidarity alone. An old man in green work clothes stood slowly and painfully and asked if his name had been called.

"What's your name?" the judge asked, her list in front of her.

"What?" the man said.

"Your name, sir."

"What?" he asked again.

A bailiff marched down.

"What'd she say?" the man said loudly.

"What's your name, sir?" the bailiff barked into the man's ear.

"Reny," the man said, as the audience snickered. "Reginald Reny."

The judge glared. The snickering stopped. The judge examined her list.

"Mr. Reny, your case will be heard shortly," the judge said.

"What?" the man said.

"Sit down," the bailiff called into the man's ear.

"Okay," the man said. "You don't have to get all wound up about it."

The audience tittered. I opened my notebook to the first blank page and waited.

At that moment, the lobby door opened with a boom and a woman strode in. She was very big, almost masculine, but very blonde and carefully groomed, like a linebacker in meticulous drag. As she approached, the lawyers watched her deferentially. She dropped a stack of books and papers on the table and turned to the audience, scanning the faces. When she came to mine she paused, as if trying to place me. I stared back, and she turned to the judge.

"Are you ready, Miss Tate?" the judge said.

"All set, Your Honor," Miss Tate said. "Let's do it."

And so they did. One by one, the cases were called. One by one, the defendants came out of the rows and walked to the podium in front of the judge.

"This is a change of plea, Your Honor," Miss Tate would say.

"Is that true?" the judge would ask.

"Yes, Your Honor," the lawyer would say. The defendant would stand passive and mute.

"Sir, you had pleaded not guilty to a charge of operating under the influence of intoxicating liquor. You've decided to change your plea?"

"Yes," they said, one after another.

"To what?" they were asked.

"Guilty," they said.

"And you're giving up your right to a jury trial?"

A nudge from the lawyer.

"Yes."

"You've decided to do this on your own? Nobody's telling you to do this?"

Another nudge.

"Yes, Your Honor."

After which the judge would ask Miss Tate to recount the circumstances of the case.

"On Thursday, April 12, at seven thirty p.m., the defendant was observed driving in an erratic manner on Main Street. He was stopped by the officer and a manual dexterity test was performed. He was believed to be under the influence and was arrested and taken to the Kennebec Police Department, where a breath test was administered."

"What was the test result?"

"Point zero eight, Your Honor. It was borderline, but with the defendant's inability to perform even the simplest dexterity test, the officer felt there was more than enough evidence to support a charge of operating under the influence."

"Do you have anything to say, sir?"

"No, Your Honor," the defendant would say sheepishly.

"Is there a recommended sentence?"

"Yes, Your Honor," Miss Tate would say. "This is a second offense, Your Honor. We would ask the court to impose the minimum three-day jail sentence but a thousand-dollar fine."

"Is that your understanding, sir?"

"Yes, ma'am."

"How much of that fine can you pay today?"

"Fifty."

"And the balance?"

"I don't know, Your Honor," the defense attorney would put in. "He's working, but he has a previous fine to pay and a sizable child-support obligation, and I—"

"Your Honor," Miss Tate would interrupt. "The defendant does have a steady income. I would suggest one hundred dollars a month for the next ten months. If he gives up beer and cigarettes, that will pay half the fine right there."

"A thousand-dollar fine, then," the judge would say. "Fifty today and a hundred a month for ten months. The additional fifty to be applied to court costs. You may see the clerk at the window. Bailiff."

"Now?" the defendant would ask, but the bailiff would already be propelling him toward the door.

"Next," the judge would say.

It was swift justice, relentless as an assembly line. It didn't break down until a little after two o'clock, when a lawyer, a young woman, said she hadn't had time to confer with her client. The judge glared. Miss Tate threw her hands up in disgust. The judge called a five-minute recess and we all filed out, like good little school kids.

In this case the playground was the parking lot outside the front door. There was an old metal trash can chained to a pole, but the pavement was covered with layers of cigarette butts, like a midden built by chain-smokers. I followed everyone else out, and they all lit up.

Smoking doesn't cause cancer, I thought. It causes misdemeanors.

I stood there with nothing to do, like a recovered alcoholic at a cocktail party. My notebook in my back pocket, I stood with my back to the door and, like everybody else, gazed silently across the parking lot at the river, quiet and relentless.

"Those seats are tough on the back," I said, sidling up to the guy next to me.

He was twenty-five, maybe, tall and thin, with bad skin and a worse mustache. His hair was long and his T-shirt, which commemorated a rock band's world tour, had yellow stains under the arms. Perhaps it had been warm and he had carried the amps.

I looked at him. He glanced back and moved away. Next time I'd bring some of those chocolate cigarettes.

The class was becoming restive as the end of recess approached. I wondered if they rang a bell. If not, perhaps we should have synchronized our watches.

I stood and looked at the river and the empty brick mill that rose from the water at the opposite shore like some giant monument to the forces of decay, the cruel vagaries of economic change, the intrinsic boom-and-bust nature of a free-market economy. I thought of mentioning this to the next guy who came within striking distance but thought better of it.

"Time to go back in?" I said.

"Yup," he said.

He was older than the first guy and his shirt was cleaner. It was plain green, with MAINTENANCE written in small white script over a pocket in which a pack of cigarettes bulged. Pausing in front of the door, he took a last drag and flicked his cigarette thirty feet, hitting the side of a parked car. I followed him inside and we stood and waited for the bailiff to open the courtroom door.

"Who's this Tate lady?" I said.

He looked at me. "The DA," he said.

"People sure roll over for her."

"If you don't you'd best be ready to get screwed but good," he said, looking straight ahead. "You cross her, that bitch'll have your ass in a sling."

"That why everybody pleads?"

"You don't, you'll be friggin' sorry."

"What if you're not guilty?" I said.

The guy looked at me.

"Got nothin' to do with it," he said, and the door banged open and we all filed in. When the maintenance man sat down, I sat beside him.

The rest of the afternoon was more of the same. They filed up to Miss Tate like cattle. She loaded the gun and the judge pulled the trigger, bleeding them dry. When they said "Guilty," the maintenance man turned to me and raised his eyebrows.

"They're smart," he said.

"But where do they get the money for these fines?" I whispered. He shrugged.

"Beg, borrow, or steal," he said. "I know a guy broke into a house and stole a TV, VCR, whole bunch of shit. Another guy I know stole it from his mother-in-law."

"Stealing to stay out of jail?"

"Can't think of a better reason," he said, and five minutes later walked up and heard his charge: driving without car insurance.

"Guilty," he said.

"We would ask the court to impose a two-hundred-dollar fine," Miss Tate said.

The court did. The guy left. He nodded at me on the way by.

By this time, it was three thirty-five. There were four people left in the courtroom, including me, and I had a notebook full of nothing. When I'd covered municipal courts in the past, the idea had been to pick the most interesting case, the most dramatic testimony. Watch as the cases rolled by and pluck the standout off the conveyor belt.

I flipped through the pages. Nothing jumped out. Nothing even flinched.

The kid Mulcahey had gotten two days and four hundred dollars for driving after suspension. The big girl with the cigarettes had been fined a hundred dollars for shoplifting sweatpants. The old man, Reny, had his driver's license yanked for ninety days for driving without insurance, taillights, and a rear bumper. So what was I supposed to write for the *Observer*? Give them the court results? Joe Schmo, fined two hundred bucks for driving without insurance. Jane Doe, whacked for four hundred for driving without a license. This newspaper recommended by four out of five physicians.

For insomnia.

And the last three cases were assembly line. Driving after suspension. Giving alcohol to minors. Miss Tate didn't even recount the specifics of the case. How old were the kids? How drunk did they get? No matter. The plea was guilty. The fine was three hundred and fifty dollars.

What had I gotten myself into? Roxanne, start packing.

The last guy called up was bagged for passing a school bus that had its flashing lights on. As he laid himself down at Miss Tate's feet, I heard one of the bailiffs, an older guy, talking to the other one, who was younger.

"All done with the pleas?"

"That's it," the younger guy said. "Except for one protection order."

"Oh, jeez," the older guy said. "It'd be nice to get out of here early one of these days. I get out right at four, I can still get in a quick nine holes."

"I'd like to get in a quickie, myself," the younger guy leered, and then the door swung open.

It was two women, one young and thin and blonde, one older and heavier, with reddish hair tied back. The red-haired one was well-dressed, wearing a white tailored blouse. Her face was grim but resolute. The blonde woman looked weary and haggard. As they stood there, a clerk came in and turned on the tape recorder next to the judge's bench.

The two women hesitated, then sat down in the next row directly in front of me, holding pocketbooks on their laps. The blonde woman's hair was short and she was wearing big gold hoop earrings. She took the left one out, pulled at her ear, and then put it back in, probing for the hole. Her nails were done in dark pink. Her blouse was turquoise and loose, and I could see that her bra strap was turquoise, too, but a shade lighter. She had just reached up to adjust it when the judge called her name.

"Miss Donna Marchant," the judge said.

The red-haired woman gave the blonde woman a sisterly touch on the shoulder. The blonde woman got up from the seat, put her pocketbook down, seemed to take a deep breath, and walked to the front of the room. Glancing at me, the red-haired woman pulled the pocketbook closer.

"Miss Marchant," the judge said, looking down at the form. "You're asking this court for protection from abuse from one Jeffrey Tanner. Is Mr. Tanner your husband?"

"No, he's my boyfriend. Was my boyfriend."

"But you had been living together."

"Yes," the blonde woman said, her voice small and high and quavering.

"With your daughter."

"Yes."

"But Mr. Tanner is not your daughter's father," the judge said, letting the words hang in summary judgment.

"No," the blonde woman said. "He's not."

"So tell the court, Miss Marchant. Or is it Mrs. Marchant?"

"It's Miss."

"All right, Miss."

She paused.

"Tell the Court why it is you feel you need protection from Mr. Tanner."

The blonde woman tilted her head back and an arm went up and wiped her eyes.

"Because of this," she said, and with the red-haired woman, the bailiffs, Miss Tate, the judge, and me all looking on, she reached to her waist and yanked up her blouse.

4

"Oh, Jesus," Miss Tate said.

"Miss Marchant!" the judge gasped.

"Tell 'em, Donna," the red-haired woman called out from her seat. "Tell 'em what that bastard did to you."

The judge banged her gavel. I scribbled frantically in my notebook. When I looked up, Donna had lowered her blouse. She was starting to cry, and her shoulders were thin like a child's.

"Miss Marchant, this is a court of law of the State of Maine," the judge said. "I could find you in contempt."

"What about him?" the red-haired woman called out. "What are you going to do about him?"

The older bailiff trotted down the aisle, a big finger pointing.

"You'll be out of here, you say one more word," he said, his eyes narrow with anger.

"That's my sister," the red-haired woman said.

The gavel banged. Donna stood there. Miss Tate looked at her disdainfully. The red-haired woman slouched back in her seat. I flipped the page in my notebook.

"Miss Marchant," the judge said. "If you feel compelled to display yourself again, will you please tell the court so that it may rule as to whether it is necessary for your case? Now, as long as you've treated the court to this spectacle, perhaps you could tell us what you purport those marks on your chest and torso to be."

"Bruises," Donna said timidly. "And one's a bite."

The bailiffs stood with their arms folded across their chests. Miss Tate turned away, rolling her eyes as if the whole episode were in terribly bad taste.

"A bite?" the judge said slowly.

"Yeah. He bit me. He beat on me and he bit me."

"Mr. Tanner?"

"Yes."

"When did this happen?"

"Three days ago. What's today, Tuesday?"

"Yes," the judge said.

"It was Saturday night."

"And I presume that this was done in anger and not with some other, how should we say, amorous motivation."

"Well, yeah, it was anger," Donna said, not getting it. "He came over and he said I wasn't leaving him and I told him to leave and he wouldn't and I said I was gonna call the cops and he tried to pull the phone out of my hand and I wouldn't let go, so he hit me. It was when we fell down that he bit me."

The judge gave Donna a long look.

"And did you file a complaint with the police?"

"I called them," Donna said.

"Did they arrest Mr. Tanner?"

"He was gone."

"He left the scene?"

"Yeah," Donna said. "He got in his truck and took off. And he ran over my daughter's bike, also."

"So what did the police say?"

"They said they'd arrest him for domestic assault."

"Have they?"

"I don't know. I don't think so. I don't think they can find him."

The judge turned to Miss Tate.

"Is there an officer here to testify about this?"

"No, Your Honor," Miss Tate said wearily. "You know how they come in on these things. No warning whatsoever. I did not have prior notification so that an officer could be present."

She began gathering up folders and papers from her table.

"I didn't know I needed an appointment, Your Honor," Donna said. "I just don't think he has any right to treat me like this, and I don't want him coming 'round anymore. It isn't healthy for my daughter, either."

The judge looked at Miss Tate, who had her books and files gathered up, holding them in her arms as if the bell were about to ring. Donna stood there and waited, like a schoolgirl called before the principal. Donna's sister glowered in her seat.

"I'm going to issue this order, Miss Marchant," the judge said suddenly. "It will say that Mr. Tanner cannot come on your premises. If he does, he will be arrested. He cannot call you on the telephone, or visit you at your job, assuming you have one. This order will remain in effect for thirty days, at which point a hearing will be held at which Mr. Tanner will have an opportunity to give his side of the story. If the court finds cause, the order will remain in effect."

She paused.

"Thank you, Your Honor," Donna said.

"Two more things," the judge said, starting to gather up her papers. "One, I will not tolerate any more of these displays in my courtroom.

Two, I would suggest that in the future, you pick your paramours more carefully. This court is adjourned."

She went through the double doors. Miss Tate exited stage left. Donna, her eyes swollen, turned back to her sister. I finished scribbling. For the first time, Donna and her sister noticed me.

"Are you from the police or something?" the red-haired woman asked me.

"No," I said. "I'm a reporter."

"Oh, my God," Donna said, and bolted for the door. The red-haired woman followed her, and I brought up the rear. We went through the lobby, which was empty, and out into the parking lot. Twenty feet from the door, where the cigarette butts started to thin out, Donna stopped and put her hands up to her face. The sister put an arm around her.

I stopped five feet behind them and paused, then circled in front of them and stopped again.

"I didn't mean to upset you," I said. "But this is what I do. I'm supposed to cover the courts."

"You're going to put my name in the paper?" Donna said weakly.

"You do and we'll sue," her sister snarled. "We'll own that paper."

Lucky you, I thought. Don't spend all the assets in one place.

"I didn't say I was going to put your name in the paper. I just want to talk to you."

"About what?" the sister demanded, her arm still around Donna's shoulder.

"About what you were talking about in court. Is this the first time you've had to go to court for something like this?"

It was the crucial moment. If they told me to take a hike, I was stuck with half a story. If they answered this question, more than likely they'd answer the next one, and the one after that.

They hesitated. I waited.

"No," Donna said, dabbing at her eyes with her finger. "I've been here before."

"About this guy?"

"Yeah," she said. "And once for my husband."

"Did they do anything about it?"

"I got a protection order."

"Was this a violation? This assault?"

"No. I let it expire. I guess he knew that."

"Did your husband beat you too?"

"Not as much. He mostly screamed at me. Called me names. He was always cutting me down. It was worse than getting hit, really."

As she spoke, I reached for the notebook in my back pocket. I pulled it out slowly, like a doctor reaching for a syringe. No abrupt moves that might scare the patient.

"My name's Jack McMorrow," I said.

"What are you going to do with this?" the sister said, her eyes carefully made-up and narrowed with suspicion.

"I'd like to write about what happened in court."

"What if we don't want you to?"

"Anything that happens in that courtroom is public."

"Her name?" the sister said.

"Yeah. But that doesn't mean I'd use it."

I looked at Donna. Her eyes were deep and dark and sunk in shadowed hollows. She'd endured a lot of pain.

"I don't want to victimize you any more," I said. "I just think that what happened in there is important. I'm sorry you had to stand up there and talk about that sort of thing in front of all those people."

She smiled, but just barely, just for a second.

"That? That's nothing," Donna said, looking at the dirty pavement. "The first time I went, the place was full. All these guys looking at you and laughing. Even the judge got pissed at them and told them to all shut up or she'd toss them out. They were quiet after that, but they were still there, you know? That's how I learned not to go first thing in the morning. You go late in the day, just before they close up, and there's usually nobody there."

"Was it me, or did it seem like the prosecutor there and the judge weren't very sympathetic?"

"Miss Tate?" Donna said. "I tried calling her once about this and she wouldn't even return my phone calls. I came in and they said she was in a conference. I mean, what kind of joke is that? She too high and mighty to talk to me?"

I jotted in my notebook.

"You don't have to talk to him," her sister said, still vigilant.

"You gonna put my name in the paper?" Donna asked.

"Not if you don't want me to."

"No. I've got a kid, you know? A four-year-old kid. It'd be like putting her name in the paper, too."

"You don't want this guy to see it?"

"Oh, Christ, he'll see it. Screw him. I hope he does see it. I hope he comes right over and I'll call Lenny and he'll arrest the son of a bitch. I hope he resists and they have to mace the shit out of him."

"Who's Lenny?" I asked.

"The policeman," the sister said. "He does her neighborhood."

"Which neighborhood's that?"

"The North End," Donna said. "Peavey Street."

"This Lenny a good guy?"

"Real good," Donna said. "I've known him since I was a little kid. He said he'd break Jeff's arms if the law'd let him."

"The law frowns on things like that," I said.

"Yeah. While she gets beaten, over and over," the sister said. "Where's the law then?"

"I don't know."

"You see the marks on her?"

"No," I said.

"Well, they aren't pretty. And a man who'd do that to a woman. I mean, she weighs a hundred pounds soaking wet. Jeff's what? Six one, one-ninety?"

Donna nodded.

"A very big bully," I said.

"A piece of shit," the sister said. "I mean, he bit her, the bastard."

"How did that happen?" I said, scribbling blindly in my notebook.

"I was on top of him," Donna said. "Well, it started with—he had me by the shoulders, you know? And he tried to kind of throw me across the room, but I hung on to him and we both landed on the floor and his head was underneath my stomach and he bit me to get me off of him."

"Nice," I said.

"Broke the skin and everything. Right at my waist."

She started to reach for her blouse, then stopped.

"Listen, what'd you say your name is?" her sister said.

"Jack McMorrow," I said. "What's yours?"

"Marcia," she said. "I'm her older sister. You're not gonna put her name in the paper, are you?"

"No."

"Well, you better not. When will this be in the paper?"

"Maybe tomorrow," I said.

"Tomorrow?" Marcia said, as if the project should require further research. "Well, listen. I don't want my name in the paper either, Mr. McMorrow. You live here in town?"

"Nope. Out in Prosperity."

"You got a number where we can get you?"

I hesitated for a moment, then pictured them picking up the phone in the *Observer* newsroom. "McMorrow. Never heard of him."

I scribbled my home number on a piece of paper and tore it from my notebook. I held it out, and Donna took it.

"Listen, hon," Marcia said to her. "I gotta run. Randy is gonna be home. You need anything, you call me. And if that son of a bitch calls, just hang up. If he comes over, call the cops and keep the doors locked."

She turned to me.

"You better treat her right," Marcia said.

"I don't think you have to worry."

"You hurt her, you better start worrying," she said.

No need for Officer Lenny. She'd break my arms herself.

Marcia leaned over and gave Donna a hug and, without another word to me, walked to a new maroon Buick with a white top. She started the motor, slammed the car into gear, and spun gravel as she left the lot, headed up the block toward Main Street.

Donna and I stood there in an awkward silence, like kids on a first date.

"So you need anything else?" she said, reaching into a small black pocketbook for her keys.

"Do you have a few more minutes?"

"I have to pick up my daughter. She's staying with my neighbor."

"But that's not Jeff's daughter. He's not going to try to snatch her or anything, is he?"

"Snatch her?"

Donna laughed, and for the first time I noticed that her voice was sort of soft and pretty.

"Even when things were good between us, he didn't want her around. The guy never grew up, you know? Thirty-one going on sixteen. All he wanted to do was party, and—"

She stopped.

"Anyway, Adrianna was always in the way," Donna said.

"That's a pretty name."

"Thanks."

"Unusual."

"Yeah," Donna said. "It was this girl on *The Young and the Restless*. She was only on, like, four shows, and then she got written out. Went on a trip or something. But I always liked the name."

I looked at her.

"How old are you?" I asked.

"Twenty-two."

"How long were you married?"

"Too long," Donna said.

"How long's that?"

"Three years."

"How old were you when you got married?" I asked, still jotting.

"Not old enough."

"How old is that?"

"Eighteen. I was a kid, and he was this cool older guy. And he seemed to love me. It wore off."

"But you hung in there."

"Nobody likes to admit they've done something that stupid. So you pretend to the outside world that everything's okay."

"But three years is a long time."

"Tell me about it," Donna said, picking at the pavement with the toe of her white flat shoe. "It seemed like twenty-three."

"And then you got involved with Jeff?"

"What can I say? Good-looking guys all turn out to be jerks."

She caught herself.

"No offense," Donna said.

"I'm flattered."

She blushed. I smiled. There was something naive about her. Something plaintive.

"Listen," she said, looking up at me with those dark bruised eyes. "Don't get me in any more trouble, okay?"

"That's not what I want to do," I said.

No promises. No guarantees.

"Well, take it easy," Donna said.

"Is there a phone number where I can reach you? If I have a question?"

Donna looked at my notebook and considered.

"Yeah, I guess. It's 879-0909. Don't give it to anybody else, okay?"

"No," I said. "I won't."

"Bye," she said, and walked to a beat-up blue Chevy Chevette with one primer-black door. She was thin and, in another life, might have been a model or something. In another very different life.

The car started with a big puff of smoke, like something from a magic act. Donna gave me a little wave and pulled out of the lot. I stood there for a moment, writing in my notebook.

"*The guy never grew up, you know? Thirty-one going on sixteen. All he wanted to do was party and—*"

I heard voices behind me and turned. The older bailiff was standing outside the double doors of the courthouse, jingling his keys. He said, "Have a good night now" in a loud voice, and two of the court clerks came out, teetering on high heels and carrying shopping bags. They went to the right, toward the other side of the lot, where cars were backed against a blank brick wall. The bailiff still stood there and then Miss Tate came out the door, a battered brown leather valise held in front of her.

"Have a good night now," the bailiff said again.

"You, too," Miss Tate said, and started across the parking lot toward me. I glanced over my shoulder and saw that there was one car left in that section of the lot, a sleek black Pontiac parked next to my beat-up mostly red Toyota pickup.

Miss Tate rode them hard in court, rode home in style.

She was twenty feet away when she looked up and stopped. Behind her, the bailiff watched.

"Hello," I said.

"Who are you?" Miss Tate said, moving closer.

"Jack McMorrow."

"You were in court today, but I've never seen you before."

"First time in your courtroom," I said, smiling.

"You screw up, or are you just a peeper?" she said.

"I'm a reporter," I said.

She stopped again, this time four feet in front of my face.

"For who?"

"The *Observer*."

"Since when?"

"Since today."

"Doing what?"

"Covering Fourth District Court," I said.

"Well, you should have come and talked to me," Miss Tate said.

"Why's that?"

"Because we can set it up so you get the results. That's the way we do it here. You stop by and get the results. I give you the highlights. God, you don't have to sit there all day."

"I didn't mind."

"The novelty will wear off, I promise you. You ever do this anywhere else?"

"Some," I said.

"Where?" Miss Tate asked, wariness creeping into her voice. The bailiff still watched from the door. It looked as if he had his hand on his gun.

"Here and there. Different places. I used to work for the weekly in Androscoggin."

"Where else?" she said, pressing on the way experienced interrogators do.

"Other papers out of state."

"Like what?"

"Oh, I don't know. *Hartford Courant. Providence Journal.*"

"You cover criminal courts for those papers?"

"On occasion," I said.

"Where'd you do it last? Before you came here, I mean."

"*New York Times,*" I said.

"Huh," Miss Tate said. She paused.

"And you're working for our local rag?"

"I don't consider it a rag," I said.

"It isn't the *New York Times.*"

"People keep telling me that, as if I should be surprised."

"So what are you doing here? Was it Jack McMorrow?"

"Yeah. And I'm covering Fourth District Court," I said. "I think I'll enjoy it."

"I hope so," Miss Tate said. "Next session is Thursday. Stop by my office and I'll have all the results for you."

"That's okay. I can get them myself."

She looked at me. I grinned.

"We'll see," Miss Tate said.

"I guess we will," I said.

I held out my hand, and she took it and gave it a squeeze. Her hand was thick and fleshy and cold as dry ice.

5

I sat in the truck and ate a tuna submarine sandwich that I'd bought at a pizza shop on Main Street. The shop had video games in which people were kicked and punched and maimed. The machines beeped even when no one was being killed, but other than that the place was dead quiet. The sallow-faced girl behind the counter heard my order, made my sandwich, took my money, and gave me my change, all without looking me in the eye.

But the sandwich wasn't bad, with real Greek olives instead of the stuff out of a can. I parked on a side street and ate it in big bites between sips of black coffee. When I was done, I balled up the paper wrapper and flipped it through the open back window into the bed of the truck. When I went to the Prosperity dump, I took a broom and a shovel.

After I finished the coffee, I got the little laptop out of its vinyl case and flipped it on. The screen was tiny but the batteries seemed good. I turned and put my feet up on the seat and my back against the door. With the computer on my lap, I started to write.

> KENNEBEC—*In Fourth District Court Tuesday, a woman bared her torso to show bruises she hoped would convince Judge Marlene Dorsett to issue a protection order against her estranged boyfriend.*

> *The woman, who is 22 and lives in Kennebec's North End, claimed the bruises and a bite mark were the results of an altercation Saturday night in which her boyfriend punched her and tried to throw her across a room in her apartment.*

I paused. Scrolled the words up and down. A couple of kids rode by on bikes and looked at me. I pondered. If I didn't identify Donna, which I could justify because she was alleged to have been the victim of an assault, how should I describe Jeff? I knew the name but not much more. And if the cops couldn't find him, chances were I wouldn't be able to contact him for comment. Certainly not before my eight o'clock deadline.

I flipped the pages of my notebook, trying to decipher my scrawl.

> *Dorsett issued the protective order after being told that Kennebec police were seeking the woman's boyfriend and planned to charge him with domestic assault in connection with the incident.*
>
> *The judge warned the woman, who appeared in court without counsel, that she should ask for permission before removing any clothing to show evidence of assault.*
>
> *In an interview outside the courthouse after Dorsett's ruling, the woman said it was the second time she had sought a protection-from-abuse order against her former boyfriend.*
>
> *The last order had expired at the time of the alleged assault, she said. In this incident, the boyfriend bit her on the abdomen, leaving teeth marks, the woman said.*
>
> *"I was on top of him," she said. "Well, it started with—he had me by the shoulders, you know? And he tried to kind of throw me across the room, but I hung on to him and we both landed on the floor and his head was underneath my stomach and he bit me to get me off him."*
>
> *Assistant District Attorney—*

I stopped. I hadn't asked her first name, damn it. Jack McMorrow, go back to Reporting 101 for a refresher. I'd have to look it up in the *Observer* files. I kept going.

> *Tate said her office was unable to have the investigating officer present because the woman did not contact the district attorney's office prior to coming to court to request the order.*
>
> *In other court business, Craig T. Mansett, 34, of 12 Adelard Street, Kennebec, pleaded guilty to a charge of operating under the influence of intoxicating liquor May 3 on Elm Street in Kennebec. Mansett was sentenced to three days in the county jail and fined $1,000.*
>
> *Cheryl R. Pooler, 22, of County Road, Kennebec, was fined $400 after pleading guilty to a charge of attempted theft. According to court testimony, the theft occurred at the Kennebec Kmart April 10. Pooler admitted to attempting to steal four cassette tapes and assorted makeup, valued at $79.*

And so on and so forth, a sixteen-inch story, maybe. I finished it up as the light was fading and the old woman on the porch across the street was about to call the police. Man loitering with computer. But, Officer, I can explain.

As the woman stared I started the truck and drove across town to the *Observer* building. Once again, there was a parking space right out front. I pulled in, shut off the motor, and scuffed a newspaper over the empty beer cans on the floor. I had a reputation to preserve.

The advertising and circulation office was closed and dark. I went up the stairs, which weren't much lighter, and walked out into the newsroom. And the *Observer* newsroom was jumping. It felt good.

I walked up the aisle, unnoticed by the reporters and editors who were bent over their terminals. A woman in Sports had her neck crooked against her phone, taking scores. The guy next to her, maybe twenty-five and tall and stooped, with that big-kid look you see in all good sportswriters, was pounding the keyboard like a jazz percussionist. In the news aisle, a fiftyish woman with an unlit cigarette behind her ear let out a howl.

"Aaaahhh," she shouted to no one in particular. "This guy doesn't need an editor. He needs a literacy volunteer. Oh, it is by divine intervention that this newspaper appears every morning."

No one seemed to hear her. I smiled.

For ten years this had been my world. A weekly in Rhode Island, right out of college. Right on to a mediumsize daily and then up the ladder, allowing myself a maximum of two years at each paper. Most places, I stayed a little over one. I was good and I was ambitious. And in the tournament that is the news business, I made the finals. The *New York Times*.

I reached the *Times* before I hit thirty, starting as a metro reporter. My mother first saw my byline in her nursing-home bed out on Long Island. My father missed it by six years. He'd read the *Times* most of his life, commuting into the city, and he died before his only son's name appeared in its venerable print.

That didn't seem fair, but life was like that.

He'd missed the aftermath, too. Jack McMorrow, rising star. Jack McMorrow trying out for an "About New York" metro column and getting passed over for the simple reason that the reporter who got it was better.

Jack McMorrow asked for assignment to London or Dublin or any place foreign and was turned down.

"You know the city," he was told. "You're steady. You're reliable."

The words that end the climb. The words that tell you to get out of the way because the stars are coming through. And they did: tough, young, smart as hell, confident beyond their years. So I got away, all right. I went to Maine and there was no looking back.

Or was there?

The newsroom brought it all back in a rush. The pounding on the keyboards. The faces pressed to the computer screens. The editors whirling from their desks.

"She says fifteen inches on the council advance," a guy with gold-rimmed glasses sputtered. "So what does she send? Twenty-three. Where am I supposed to put this?"

"That's why computers have kill buttons," the older woman snapped. "Control. Kill. No more problem."

She looked up.

"Can I help you?" she said.

"Yeah," I said. "I'm Jack McMorrow. I'm covering the court. Mr. Albert said to come in and file with this laptop."

"Oh," the woman said, loud enough to be heard across the room. "You're the hotshot from the *New York Times*. What the hell brings you to this dump?"

Hands froze on keyboards all around me. Eyes rose from screens. One of the sports guys got up and came around the partition for a look. My computer under my arm, I answered the editor's question.

"I don't know," I said. "Place doesn't look so bad to me."

She raised her eyebrows.

"Yeah, right," she said, then stood and held out her hand. "Catherine Plante. Like the things that grow. Chief copy editor and bottle scrubber. You know how to send with that antique?"

"It's been a while," I said.

"Of course it has. That's a museum piece you're working with. A collector's item. David. Get over here and help this guy out."

From behind me, a face appeared. A kid's face, round and eager, with a shock of black curly hair and an incongruous stubble of dark beard. His sleeves were rolled up.

"David Archambault," he said, holding his hand out.

"Jack McMorrow. I take it you know how to work this thing?"

"Surely do," he said. "Bring it right over here and we'll fire her up."

We went to his desk, ten feet up the row. It was covered with reporter's notebooks, notes scrawled on legal pads, empty cardboard coffee cups, a bag of potato chips spilled out on a faxed press release from the governor's office. David shoved the pile aside in one smooth movement. I put the computer in the space he'd cleared.

"So you used to be with the *Times*, huh?" David said, pulling the cord from the laptop. "Goddamn, I'd give my right arm. Both arms."

"Type with your toes?"

"I'd type with a pencil in my teeth to work for a paper like that. I'm giving myself eighteen months here, then I'm gonna go for a fifty-thousand-or-up paper."

"Why so long?"

David looked at me.

"You're being facetious?"

"Not really. We used to say that more than a year in one paper was death."

"Seriously."

"We were young and ambitious."

"So who isn't?" David said.

"You been here long?"

"Seven months. And my feet are itching bad."

"You don't like it here?" I asked.

"It's okay. It's a start."

"What do you like to write?"

"I don't know. Cop stuff," David said, punching the code into the laptop.

"Much of that here?"

"Diddly-shit. We run stories out front here that the *Times* wouldn't even report. I remember this one time, I think it was a couple of years ago. The *Times* did this story on all the murders that happened on New Year's Eve in New York City. There were, like, fourteen of them. They weren't even real stories. It was like a murder log."

"Yeah," I said. "New York can be a pretty brutal place."

"I'd love it," David said, his eyes glistening at the thought of all that murder and mayhem. "Christ, we get a murder here and it's this big deal."

I had to smile.

"Pretty sad, huh," I said.

"Goddamn pathetic," David said. "There. Your story's in the system."

"Thanks," I said.

"You really gonna cover the court here? I mean, I don't mean to butt in, but isn't that kind of beneath you?"

"We'll see."

"Yeah, well, I'd love to talk to you some more."

"Be glad to," I said, and gathered up the computer and wires, stuck them back in the case. I walked to Catherine Plante's desk and told her the story was in the system. She started to answer and then the phone rang and she made a gun with her finger and thumb and shot it, then picked up the receiver. David came up and stood beside me.

"Good to meet you, man," David said.

He shook my hand and looked into my eyes earnestly and ambitiously. I looked back and it was like looking into a mirror, back in time.

It was quarter to eight when I came out onto the sidewalk in front of the *Observer*. The downtown was deserted, but the newsstand up the block was still open. I walked up and got the second-to-last *Boston*

Globe off the rack. The little guy behind the counter, a wizened old man in a Red Sox T-shirt, took my dollar without speaking.

"The *Times* sold out?" I asked him.

"Went quick," he said. "Always does."

"How many do you get?"

"Six," the man said.

"Pretty popular, huh?"

"They're gone by eight thirty," he said.

I tucked the *Globe* under my arm and started for the door, then turned back. The old man was shoving cartons of cigarettes into the rectangular holes on the cigarette shelf behind the register.

"You know where Peavey Street is?" I asked him.

"You ain't from around here, are you?"

"No," I admitted.

The old man hesitated, as if he'd prefer to give directions to Peavey Street to someone who had lived in town for forty years and would, therefore, know exactly where Peavey Street was.

"Up Main to School Street. Follow School Street up about a mile and take a right. Past the billiard place. Peavey's on the left. You hit the railroad tracks, you've gone too far."

I thanked him and went back to the truck, putting the *Globe* on the passenger seat. The Toyota started with a whir and I drove slowly up the block, past shops that were closed for the night and more that were closed for good. I took a left and then another left and pulled into the one store that was open and busy.

It sold beer. I went in and bought a six-pack of Ballantine ale. The beer went beside the paper on the passenger seat. I drove back to Main Street and took a right, then followed the old man's directions to Peavey Street. I didn't hit the railroad tracks.

Peavey was a couple blocks long, one tier of houses up from the railroad tracks. The tracks ran along the river. The houses were divided into apartments, with outside stairways that hung like scaffolding on the sides of the buildings. From the top floors of the buildings, there probably was a river view. I doubted that it was ever advertised.

I drove the length of the street, slowly. There were kids playing Wiffle ball who didn't want to move. They stood and stared, daring me to run them over, until a guy crouched beside a dismantled motorcycle screamed something. They moved grudgingly. I drove fifty yards to the end of the street and turned around and came back.

They moved even more slowly.

I was looking for the blue Chevette with the black door, and it was on the return pass that I found it, parked in a driveway behind a Camaro with a green plastic tarp draped over its front end. The building was gray and nondescript. The first floor was dark, but there were lights showing on the second and third. I pulled over in front of the next house and looked back.

The third-floor windows showed bare walls, a Budweiser sign that lit up. In the windows on the second floor there were hanging pots, curtains with some sort of gauzy shades. As I watched, a child flitted past one window, then the other. Then a taller figure, a woman. I turned in the truck seat to look. The child flashed by the windows going the other way, the woman running after her. For a moment the windows were empty, and then the woman stopped in front of the nearest one, her hands on her hips.

It was Donna.

I watched her curiously and then, ten feet from the truck, a light came on in a window. The shade pulled back and a face stared out. Like an interrupted voyeur, I brought myself back to reality, started the truck, and drove away.

What was it about her? Certainly not her looks. Donna was thin and almost boyish, with narrow hips and shoulders. I didn't know much about her, except that she had hooked up with at least two dirtballs and didn't seem to deserve that fate. And I knew she had a bite mark on her belly.

It was a strange sort of intimacy, one that reporters experience every day, especially if they're good. A woman would tell me her life story. A week later, I would have forgotten her name.

But I hadn't forgotten Donna. There was something appealing about her, something naive and vulnerable and blindly optimistic. As I drove through the redbrick funnel that was downtown Kennebec, then over the bridge and east along the winding, tree-lined river, I thought of a guy I'd known who had been a *Times* correspondent in Bangkok.

His name was Harrison, his first name, and he'd told me that he'd had to resist the urge to save the Thai women he saw in brothels, on the streets. He said they brought out this primitive instinct in him.

"I didn't want to have sex with them," he'd said over beers one night. "I wanted to bring them to Long Island and show them dishwashers and garage-door openers. It just seemed so unfair."

Maybe it was like that with Donna. I just wanted to swoop in and save her, show her that she could live with a man who didn't hit her and call her names. She seemed like a good person. Why should she have to live like that? What did she do, apart from being born, to deserve this idiot who'd left bruises on her chest, teeth marks on her belly?

I shook my head. I was in the town of Albion, driving east, the glow of the setting sun lighting the rearview mirror. The road twisted between rocky pastures trimmed with lupine, past long dairy barns crammed with black-and-white Holsteins. I reached for a beer and twisted it loose, then put it between my legs and popped it open. It was pretty, forgotten country out here, thirty miles from Maine's gold coast, ten miles east of the interstate. I sipped the ale and flicked the radio on. The public radio announcer said the Pittsburgh Symphony was about to begin Mozart's *Requiem*. Roxanne was waiting for me at home.

For me, if not for Donna, life was good.

When I pulled onto the dump road in Prosperity twenty minutes later, I'd finished the ale. I slid the back window open and dropped the can into the truck bed, where it clinked and rolled. Coming over a rise, under the big oaks that lined the road, I spotted Roxanne's Subaru. I wondered how she'd done with the young and the violent. I hoped the glow she'd left with that morning had not subsided.

It hadn't.

She was sitting in the big chair by the back window. There was a bottle of chardonnay open on the counter, one glass poured. I put the beer and the paper on the counter and went in to see her. She was wearing a khaki skirt and her legs were up over the side of the chair.

"Hi," I said.

"Hey," she said. "I missed you."

"How'd it go with your young serial killer?"

"I don't want to talk about him."

"It didn't go well?"

"It went fine. I just don't want to talk about it."

"What do you want to talk about?" I said, leaning over to kiss her.

"Who said anything about talking?" Roxanne said, and her mouth opened and drew me in.

6

We moved to the bed silently, as if in a trance. Roxanne slipped out of her clothes, shedding several articles of clothing in a single swift movement. Women are able to do that. Men yank off their pants and socks clumsily, like city people shucking corn.

But then we were in the bed and there was only the sound of breathing and the squeak of the springs as we pulled each other closer. It was almost dark, but not quite, and I could see Roxanne's body in a filmy dusk. We kissed but didn't speak, and then for a few minutes lay still, running our hands over each other so that you could almost hear each caress. And then we were not so still and fell into a rhythm that was like a little chop slapping at the shore, and then it slowed and there was just Roxanne beside me, my hands on her hips, her breasts, her neck, her chin.

And the phone rang.

Neither of us made a move to answer it and it kept ringing, ten rings or more, so that we began to take on the rhythm of the rings, which made us laugh.

"We should have turned the answering machine on," Roxanne murmured. " 'We can't come to the phone right now. We're making love.' "

"I could answer it and turn it on."

"You turn me on," Roxanne said, smiling and kissing me.

And then we were gasping, and when the phone stopped ringing we bent into each other like rowers to their oars. Roxanne's legs were splayed over me, pressing.

And the phone rang again.

"Jesus," Roxanne said, backing off but still moving.

"I'm sure it's important," I said. "Maybe we won a weekend at a timeshare. Or a set of steak knives."

Roxanne kissed me on the temple, ran her lips over my hair. The phone kept ringing.

"You want to throw it out the window or should I?" she asked.

"You've got a better arm. Among other things."

"But you're closer."

"But if I get it, I'll have to leave you," I said.

"Enough said," Roxanne said, and reached to the bedside table, where she snatched the receiver in mid-ring.

"Hello," Roxanne said, trying to sound as if she'd just put down a dish towel.

"Yeah. May I ask who's calling?"

She held out the phone. Her hips went still.

"Somebody named Donna?" Roxanne said.

I frowned. Grabbed the receiver.

"Hello."

"Uh, hi," the voice on the phone said. "Mr. McMorrow?"

"Yeah."

"Yeah, well, this is Donna Marchant. We talked today. Outside the courthouse?"

"Right."

"I'm sorry to call you . . . at home, I mean. But I've got kind of a problem."

I sighed inwardly.

"And what's that?" I said.

Roxanne kissed my chest. Lapped at my phoneless ear.

"Well, you know that story you're going to write? The one about me in the court and everything."

Oh, that one, I thought.

"Yeah," I said.

"Well, my ex-boyfriend, Jeff, the guy I was telling you about? He found out about it and he was, like, really ripped at me for talking to you."

Roxanne stopped kissing me and let her head fall back on the pillow.

"How did he know about it?" I said.

"I guess I told him."

"I thought he wasn't supposed to have any contact with you?"

"Yeah, but he called up and he was, like, really drunk, and he started screaming at me and I told him about the story, I guess."

"So? I thought you didn't care what he thought about it."

"Well, I don't. I mean, I don't care, but he was really ripped, screaming and stuff, and I told him it didn't matter what he said, it was going to be in the paper anyway, and he said he'd kill me, and I said, 'Keep talking—you're digging a bigger hole for yourself,' and he said he'd kill you too."

"What?" I said.

Roxanne's hips slid away.

"Yeah, well, he talks like that when he's drinking a lot, and I'd just had it with him and I said, 'Yeah, right. The guy doesn't even live in town, he lives out in Prosperity or someplace,' and he said some really disgusting stuff, you filthy slut and stuff like that, and then he said he'd find you."

"Does he even know my name?"

"I told him," Donna said as Roxanne got up from the bed and picked her underpants up from the floor. "I mean, he didn't believe me when I said I went to court and I told him I got a protection order and he was like, right, you lying bitch. So I sort of mentioned your name as proof. I guess I shouldn't have."

"He would have seen it tomorrow, anyway."

"Tomorrow?"

"That's when the story's running."

"God. I mean, I just didn't think it would be so quick."

"So what about Jeff?"

"He, I don't know, he was crazy drunk, the way he gets sometimes. When he's drinking hard stuff, he's, like, right out there, you know?"

Roxanne had her skirt back on and was hooking her bra. She had a beautiful back.

I sighed, aloud this time.

"So he said he could find you," Donna said. "I mean, he said he was gonna find you. He was saying you were—we were together, you know?"

"Together?"

"You've got to know Jeff. He's got this crazy streak. Paranoid or something. Some guy would talk to me in a store or something. I mean, he had to talk to me. I was buying something and he worked there. And Jeff would say the guy was hitting on me. I'm like, 'I said ten words to the guy.' Four of them were 'How much is this?' But he's, like, nuts when he's like that."

"So what's the story?"

"He said he was gonna come and beat the shit out of you."

"Where? Out here?"

"He said he could find you."

"In Prosperity?"

"His uncle lives in Palermo. He's spent a lot of time out that way. Knows quite a few people. Half of 'em are in jail most of the time."

"So what's he gonna do?" I asked as Roxanne rattled dishes downstairs. "Drive around until he sees somebody he thinks is me?"

"He said he'd ask around and he'd find you."

"When?"

"He said he could find you tonight. He might've just gone and passed out, but I wouldn't count on it. When he goes on one of these, he does a lot of coke, too. Sometimes he's up three or four days. Him and his buddies call it going on a twister."

"That's nice. I'm glad he has buddies."

"Yeah, well they're all like him. Won't grow up. Four-wheel-drives and motorcycles. Like little boys with their toys."

I was on the edge of the bed, pulling on my boxers.

"So when did you talk to him?" I asked.

"I don't know. Maybe an hour ago. He was at Mac's. That's a bar."

"So he could have gotten in his truck and right now he could be knocking on doors out here, asking for Jack McMorrow."

"I don't know," Donna said sheepishly. "Maybe. He gets an idea and he's like, crazed. Won't get off it. I think it's the coke."

"Yeah, or maybe he's just plain nuts."

"That, too."

Downstairs, the television came on. From the loft, I could see Roxanne sit down on the couch. She crossed her beautiful legs. Damn, I thought.

"Does Jeff carry a gun?" I said.

"Not usually. But he does have a knife. The kind that goes on your belt? He doesn't go anywhere without it."

"American Express."

"What?"

"Never mind. Listen, you've got my number, Donna. If he calls up and says he's decided to join the priesthood or something, give me a ring."

"Okay," she said.

I thought for a second.

"He's not gonna come and hurt you, is he?"

"No," Donna said. "I took my daughter and we're at my sister's. He doesn't come here. My sister'd kill him. She told him. My brother-in-law, he's, like, this really big hunter, and he's got all these rifles. My sister told Jeff if he ever set foot on her property, she'd blow his head off. She would, too."

"We can only hope."

"What?"

"Nothing," I said.

Donna paused.

"So I just thought I'd tell you."

"Thanks."

"And I'm sorry, Mr. McMorrow."

"It's Jack."

"Sorry, Jack," Donna said.

"Don't worry about it," I said, worrying like hell.

"So I'll be talking to you."

"Yeah, right."

"Take it easy," she said.

"Oh, yeah," I said.

I hung up the phone and pulled on my jeans. I took a T-shirt out of the drawer and pulled it on and went down the stairs.

Roxanne was reading a magazine. She didn't look up.

"Sorry," I said.

"Who was that?" Roxanne said, still reading.

"Oh, some woman I met at court. She was there to get a protection order on her paranoid maniac boyfriend. She told him about talking to me and he said he's going to kill her and kill me. Maybe not in that order."

Roxanne looked up.

"So what's he going to do? Go to the newspaper and make a scene?"

I thought for a minute, trying to think of a benign way to put it.

"No, she told him I lived out here. In Prosperity, I mean. He said he'd come out here and find me."

"Would he really?"

"I don't know," I said. "I doubt it. Probably go in search of another eight-ball and forget I ever existed."

"Wouldn't it be a needle in a haystack?"

"She said he knows people out here. Has an uncle in Palermo or someplace."

"What's her name?"

"Who?"

"The woman who called."

"Donna."

"You gave her your number?"

"Probably shouldn't have. It was her sister—she has this vigilant, protective sister. She wanted to know where to reach me, and I could picture somebody at the paper saying they'd never heard of me. They'd think I was some weirdo or something. And it's hard. You're asking them to bare their souls and you hide behind this wall. I've always had trouble with that."

Roxanne had put the magazine down. It was a *Newsweek*. The new one. She looked worried.

"So you think this could be a problem?" she asked.

"I don't know," I said. "Probably not. These guys are ninety-nine percent talk."

Roxanne got up. I took her by the shoulders and kissed her gently. She kissed me once and stopped.

"You want tea?" she said.

"Yeah," I said. "Want to be on my toes for Willie the wife beater."

"And we need to talk," Roxanne said.

There was something ominous in her voice, in her walk.

Roxanne got mugs from the cupboard, lit the burner under the kettle. I went to the front window and looked out. It was a moonless night, a good night to stand out in the yard and look at the stars.

With a gun.

The kettle rattled and Roxanne took it off the burner and poured. She had instant coffee, milk and sugar. I had Twinings English Breakfast, black. She brought the mugs over and set them down on the table, which was made of stained and battered oak planks. The tea spilled and she wiped the wood with a dish towel. As if it mattered.

"There's something we need to talk about," she said, sitting down and crossing her legs again. It was hard to talk when she crossed her legs.

"You're pregnant," I said, sitting down beside her.

"No."

"You're not pregnant."

"No."

"No?" I said. "That means yes, and if the answer is yes, I volunteer to stay home while you work."

"Jack. This is serious."

"Okay, I'll give it to you in writing."

"Jack, I've been offered a job."

"But you just started with the school district."

"This job is in Portland."

"That is serious," I said.

And not funny, I thought.

"John called from Child Protective. He said Don Boulette is leaving. You remember Don?"

"No," I said.

"Well, he always had this massive caseload, and they want somebody to take it over rather than spreading it out among a whole bunch of people temporarily."

"Uh-huh."

"And I want to take the job."

"But I don't want to move," I said. "I like it here."

Roxanne looked at me and didn't smile. It started to sink in.

"You're leaving?" I said.

"I'll be back, Jack."

"Last time you left you went to Colorado and didn't come back for seven months."

"You didn't ask me to come back. You didn't even ask me to stay before I left, remember?"

"Temporary insanity. And fear. I'm sorry. You know that now, don't you?"

"Yes. And I love you. You know that."

"Yeah. And I love you."

She looked at me, her eyes deep and thoughtful.

"I do love you," Roxanne said. "That's why it was so important for us to make love tonight. And then your little friend called. But I wanted to make love because I'm not leaving you. It's just a job. It's more what I do than this school counseling. I'll work down there during the week. Maybe I'll get on a four-day week and that'll give us three days together. I'll come up. You can come down."

It sunk in deeper, like a knife blade.

"You're not planning on commuting?"

"Jack, it's an hour and a half. I can't do that. Besides . . ."

"Besides what?"

"I don't know, Jack. I love you and I want to be with you. I do. But I'm not sure what I'd do here."

"We'll do what we do. We make love a lot. I worship you and you laugh at my jokes. It's an even trade."

"But, Jack . . ."

"You've only been here four months. And the summer is coming. The garden'll come in and we'll explore around. You like Mary and Clair. They're right up the road."

"Jack, I'm not Mary. I can't just stay here and can vegetables."

"So we'll get a freezer."

"Jack, I'm serious," Roxanne said.

"Okay. No freezer. We'll eat out. Millie's Ridge View has great french fries and gravy. You've said so yourself."

Roxanne looked at me somberly.

"Jack, no."

I paused. Sipped my tea. It tasted harsh and acidic.

"Is it the drinking?" I said.

"Maybe. I don't know. Maybe not. I just don't want to see you waste your potential, all your talents."

"But doesn't it beat not seeing me at all?"

Roxanne put her mug on the table and turned to me. She took my hand and held it.

"We need different things," Roxanne said.

"We'll take up bowling. A couples' league. Get his-and-her Harleys. They make this gal's model, I heard. Has a makeup mirror and everything. And I'll get you a little carbine to go with my thirty-aught-six. We'll get hunting licenses."

"Jack, stop. I'm serious. We can make this work."

I paused.

"Of course we can," I said. "If your mind's made up."

"I think it is."

"So you want my advice, right? Well, Roxanne, I'd say you should consider taking that job. I mean, don't turn it down out of hand. Give it some careful thought. Weigh the pros and cons."

"I start Monday," Roxanne said.

"There must have been a lot of pros," I said.

"I love you," she said.

"I'm going to need to know that."

"I was trying to show you."

"When we were so rudely interrupted," I said.

"And now I'm exhausted. I've been up since five."

"Chatting with some maniac."

"They're everywhere, aren't they?" Roxanne said.

"Yeah," I said. "They are."

So Roxanne went back up the stairs to the loft. The bedsprings creaked again, but this time only once. I bagged the tea and got a beer from the refrigerator and sat in the big chair by the front window. After a few minutes, very few, I heard a clunk. Roxanne's book had hit the floor. I went to the bottom of the loft stairs and turned out the light. The house was in darkness. I finished that beer and went for another. I sipped it and listened to the bugs and the birds. It looked as if I was going to have a lot of time for the birds.

I felt as though my life, such as it was, was unraveling. Roxanne wasn't supposed to leave. She was supposed to stay and grow gray with me in the country. We'd hide away from the world in this little hamlet in the lost hills of Waldo County, Maine. We'd tromp around the woods, make love in little clearings in the pines. At night, we'd have a glass of wine, an ale or two, and then tea and then read, knowing that all we needed to be content was each other. Well, almost all.

Hey, but things didn't ever go the way they were planned. My day at the *Observer* was spent playing the washed-up major leaguer for the Single A club in Kennebec, Maine. I tried to do a simple story, and even that got complicated. All those years in New York City, I never got a scratch. One day on the job in Kennebec and some drunken, coked-out redneck said he was going to kill me. At the rate I was going, I'd be racking up two death threats a week. You could cover the drug trade for the *Miami Herald* and sleep better.

I sipped the beer. Listened to the rush of sound from the woods. A cacophony, really, from the swarming, rustling, writhing darkness. Bats, only lately evicted from our rafters, swooped close to the screen. There was a soft, murmuring hoot. A mourning dove disturbed on its roost. A billion stars flickering over this wilderness. A set of headlights that bumped down the road.

And stopped.

7

The truck was big and loud, with lights high off the ground. I heard at least two people, maybe three. The exhaust throbbed slowly and then there was a short rev and the truck started moving again, rolled ahead about fifty feet, and stopped. The motor quieted. The lights went out. Both doors opened but didn't shut.

I got up from the chair and stepped to the side of the window. I could hear footsteps on the gravel. The footsteps drew closer, then softened on the grass in front of the house.

"You think this is it?" a guy's voice said.

"The lady said an old red Toyota four-wheel-drive," another voice said. "There it is."

"Let's get him outside," a third voice said. "I don't need another B and E."

"You and your friggin' record," one of them said. "Friggin' wuss."

They were twenty feet from the front of the house. I stepped carefully to the closet, eased the latch up, and drew it open. From behind the jackets and coats, I took out the thirty-aught-six. Clair's Remington on long-term loan.

Outside, one of them called, "Hey."

I hurried to the kitchen and opened a cupboard. Pushed the Ajax and Windex aside and found the box of shells. Slid the top back and picked five out, jacking four into the magazine and one into the breech.

"Hey, writer man. Come on out," one of them was saying. "Come on out, you little writer pussy. Wanna talk to you."

I walked to the window and looked. The three of them were on the edge of the grass. The one in the middle was doing the talking.

"Reporter pussy. Come on out."

I heard Roxanne roll out of bed.

"Jack, what is it?" she whispered.

"Nothing," I said. "Stay up there and don't turn on any lights."

"Jack?"

"No lights. Stay there."

I walked to the door, eased it open. The door was to the right of the house. The thing that looked like a door in the center of the house was really a window. They were standing in front of it, like deranged carolers. I leaned the gun against the wall and stepped out onto the grass. I felt that rising tingle of fear, but they were like mean dogs. I couldn't let fear show.

"Car trouble, guys?" I said.

There were just the three of them. Assorted sizes, all within the big range. Jeans. T-shirts. Two beards. No guns in sight. At least one knife, showing on the middle guy's belt.

"You the reporter pussy?" the one in the middle said. He was bearded, with long dark hair.

"Yeah," I said. "And if you guys are some of those religious types, I'm really not interested. Not that I don't keep my own faith. I do. It's just that, well, I like to think that's between my God and—"

"What the hell are you talking about?"

"I'm just saying that, religion or no religion, I'd prefer that you come by at a more reasonable hour. And call first. Because I'm out a lot and I'd hate to have you drive all the way out here just to—"

"Shut the friggin' hell up."

He stood in the middle. The two bookends were at his side, looking amused.

"You're not here from the church?"

"Jesus Christ."

"Oh, you are here from the church."

"I'm here about Donna."

"Why, was she in an accident?"

"No, but you're gonna have one."

"Who are you?" I asked.

"It don't matter," he said.

"You're Jeff, and it doesn't matter. If you don't have religion, at least have decent grammar."

"He thinks he's friggin' funny," one of the bookends said.

I looked at him. His T-shirt advertised vodka. He looked as if he'd downed a pitcher of martinis with a two-gram chaser.

"I don't think I'm funny," I said. "I think it's funny that you're here. Funny odd. Not funny ha-ha."

"Listen, you son of a bitch," Jeff said, tilting his head back in a tough-guy look he'd seen in some video. "I don't know what the bitch told you, but you're not gonna put it in the paper. You're not gonna write one word. And that lying bitch is gonna learn that she ain't gonna go around town saying shit about me."

"What are you going to do? Bite her on the tum-tum again?"

He paused.

"She told you that?"

"She showed me that."

"That friggin' slut."

"The judge didn't think so," I said. "Neither will any of the other people who'll read the paper tomorrow."

"You're gonna call 'em up and tell 'em to stop the story."

"Too late. How 'bout I call the subscribers in the morning. All twelve thousand of them."

What better time to fudge circulation numbers.

"I'm gonna break your fingers," Jeff said.

"That's aggravated assault. You want to do a year inside?"

"Worth it."

"Easy for you to say," I said. "You don't have a future. You know, that's the problem with the criminal justice system. It levies punishments based on middle-class values. But the perpetrators often don't hold those values; therefore the penalty holds no punishment value at all. This is something our society must come to grips with if—"

"I'm gonna friggin' destroy you."

"Exactly," I said. "We must read the same journals."

Jeff took a step forward. He was wide-eyed but his eyes were glazed. Too many beers, too much cocaine. The bookends took a step forward too.

"Did you guys learn that with those footprints you stick on the floor?" I said.

They took another step. I tensed, heard my voice like it belonged to someone else.

"I didn't say Simon says," I said, and in the darkness to my left there was a movement.

"Jack, you want me to call the police?" Roxanne said.

The bearded bookend looked over.

"Oh, man," he said, grinning. "You can have this guy, boys. I'm gonna go chat with the babe. Oh, I bet you're not wearing anything under that, are you, honey? Let's just check and make sure."

He took two steps toward the door. I took three to the rifle, picked it up, and turned to where all three of them had stopped. Instantly.

"Go back in," I told Roxanne.

"I bet the reporter pussy don't even know what to do with that thing," the bearded guy said.

He took two more steps toward the door. And Roxanne. I pointed the rifle at the bookend's head, lifted it six inches, and fired. The gun roared like a howitzer. The bullet missed his head by three feet and headed for Belfast. The fear showed in his eyes.

"Beat it," I said.

Jeff was frozen, not even breathing.

I jacked out the empty cartridge and slid the bolt forward, then pointed the rifle at his head. Then I wheeled to my right and fired. The back window of the truck shattered before I'd stopped squeezing the trigger. I turned back to Jeff.

"That's for Donna," I said. "And me, too. I don't like bullies. Especially dumb ones. And you're dumb as a post."

"You're not always gonna have that gun, man," Jeff said.

"But I have it now. And that's all that matters. Go."

They went, backing away ten steps before turning their backs to me. The bookend without the beard held his hands up as he eased around me. They got in the truck and I could see the bearded bookend start to brush glass off the seat.

"Just get in the friggin' truck, man," the other one snapped. "Get in the friggin' truck."

Jeff started the motor with a defiant roar, backed it into the ditch, and then gunned it out. As he went by he looked at me, still standing by the house with the rifle cradled in my arms.

"It ain't over," he called.

"Isn't," I called back.

Roxanne was sitting at the kitchen table, her face white and taut, knees drawn up underneath her flannel nightgown.

"Did you call the police?" I said, jacking the three unused cartridges out on the table.

"Yeah."

"What'd they say?"

"She said it would be twenty minutes, at least. The deputies were on another call."

"Great. Remind me not to give Clair his gun back."

She looked at me, still pale, still wide-eyed. I picked up the cartridges, put the gun in the closet, and went to the kitchen counter and dropped the cartridges back in the box. I put the box back on the shelf behind the Ajax, then went to Roxanne, standing behind her chair with my arms around her neck. She didn't move. I waited.

"Do you think that was the right thing to do?" Roxanne asked softly.

"I don't know. It seemed like a good idea at the time. And I didn't feel like wrestling with them."

"Do you think that guy would have hurt me?"

"What do you think?"

"Would you have shot him if he'd kept coming toward me?"

"Probably," I said.

"Just like that?"

"No time to think about it. Maybe I would have fired one more over his head. Maybe not."

Roxanne was quiet. I could feel the pulse in her neck. It seemed too delicate, a dangerously fragile way to sustain her precious life.

"Sometimes you don't seem like the guy I met—what was it, almost three years ago?"

"I'm not," I said. "I've been assimilated."

"I'm serious. I feel sick. I mean, I could throw up right now. But you have this hardness to you. I know a lot of things have happened, but . . . I don't know. I don't know what to think."

"I was scared. I'm still scared. But I couldn't show it out there. They would have been on me like wolves."

I shrugged.

"It's a hard world sometimes," I said. "You know that. You, of all people."

Roxanne took my hand and held it to her lips, then put it on her chest.

"I know that, but I don't want it to make you hard, Jack," she said. "I don't want it to change you."

"Don't worry," I said. "It's all an act. Inside I really was scared to death. Really."

It seemed an odd thing to say in an attempt to be reassuring.

I kissed her cheek.

"I'm going to go to Portland in the morning," Roxanne said, so softly that it was almost a whisper. "I'm going to look for a place."

Now I was the one who felt sick.

"Need any money?" I said.

"No."

"Need any company?"

"No. I don't think so," she said. "What are you going to do?"

"That depends."

"On what?"

"On whether you're ever coming back, after this," I said.

She didn't reply.

It wasn't twenty minutes; it was thirty-five. I was sitting on the bumper of my truck when the cruiser's headlights peered toward me from down the road, and then the side spotlights flashed on. I walked over and met the car as it pulled up. The spotlight flicked off. A flashlight flicked on from the passenger window.

"You the guy wanted the subjects removed?"

"Yeah. But they're gone."

The deputy in the passenger seat was thin and young, with a long, narrow face. He didn't get out. The driver, heavier and older and balding, kept the car in drive, his foot on the brake.

"So what's going on?" the younger deputy said.

I looked down at him. The driver looked at his watch and took out a clipboard and wrote something down.

"Some guys from Kennebec. One of them didn't like me talking to his ex-girlfriend."

The young deputy's eyes glazed over, just barely, a ripple of disinterest.

"He beat her up and she went to court. I met her there and he didn't want me writing about her."

"Writing what?"

"For the newspaper. The paper in Kennebec. I'm working for them."

"What's your name, sir?"

"Jack McMorrow."

The older guy wrote that on his clipboard. The car was still in drive, his foot still planted on the brake pedal.

"So what happened here?"

"They made some vague threats."

"Then they left?"

I thought of the rifle and the explaining I'd have to do.

"Yeah," I said.

"Dispatcher said it was a lady that called," the thin deputy said.

"My friend. She was in the house."

He glanced toward the house.

"Where is she?"

"She went back to bed."

"So she's okay?"

"Yeah."

"So this is a domestic situation?"

"Yeah, and I think the woman in Kennebec, she could be in trouble if this guy gets hold of her. This guy could kill her."

"Where's she?"

"At her sister's. In Kennebec or someplace around there."

"Is that where this guy was going?"

"His name's Jeff. And, no, I don't think he'll bother her there."

The deputy behind the wheel yawned.

"Well, if I was you, I'd take this up with the Kennebec police, sir," the thin guy said. "Unless you want to file a complaint about the threats. You want to do that, I'd suggest you go to the S.O. in the morning. That's in Belfast."

I thought for a moment, shook my head no.

"Well, okay then, sir. If you have any more trouble, be sure to call. I'd talk to you more, but we have another call to respond to."

"The guy is really dangerous," I said. "He could hurt her."

"I don't doubt it, sir," the thin guy said, his voice flat and mechanical. "He's also drunk. Driving an older Chevy four-wheel-drive."

For the first time, the driver perked up and almost looked at me.

We slept close together but felt apart. I got up every couple of hours and went down and stood by the window. Outside was impenetrable darkness that later peeled back before the glow that rose in the east. The sun had just skimmed the trees when Roxanne got up and went to the shower, taking her clothes with her. That was not a good sign. Going to get her overnight bag was worse.

"I might stay with Kim in Cape Elizabeth. If I'm still looking at places and I feel too tired to drive back up."

"You don't have to work tomorrow?"

"I gave my notice. They said there was no point in continuing."

"Your young psycho is going to be disappointed."

"He'll cope," Roxanne said, folding a blouse and placing it in the leather bag.

"What about me?"

She looked up at me and smiled.

"You'll be fine," Roxanne said.

"What's the kid's name? Maybe I'll have him over for pizza. We'll get a video. Some horror thing."

"He's seen too many of those."

"Okay," I said. "I can see *The Sound of Music* one more time."

She grinned halfheartedly. I felt halfhearted too.

"This stinks," I said.

"Jack, I'll be back."

"Not all the way back."

"Jack," Roxanne said. "Last night, three hoodlums came here in the middle of the night. They wanted to beat you up and do who knows what to me. You took your rifle—it's yours, not Clair's, so don't try to tell me otherwise—and shot at them and into their truck. How do you expect me to feel?"

"Proud?" I said.

I smiled. Roxanne's terse expression crumbled into a smile and she shook her head.

"God, I love you. I don't know why sometimes, but I love you."

"I love you too," I said.

"Then why are things so crazy?" Roxanne said, zipping her bag. "Why are they? Why can't we just watch TV and sit around the house and be normal?"

"Because the road doesn't have cable?" I asked.

Roxanne shouldered her bag.

"I'll call you tonight," she said.

"Drive safely."

"You be careful."

"I won't fire until I see the whites of their eyes," I said.

"That's not funny," Roxanne said, and she kissed me on the cheek and walked down the stairs and out the door.

I stood there in my boxers until her car was out of sight. Then I stood there some more. Then I went and looked out back. Tree swallows were nesting in the boxes on the wall of the shed, and I watched them pitch and swoop, popping back out of the hole like paratroopers bailing out of a plane. There was a buzzing clatter and an English sparrow fluttered up to one of the birdhouses. A city bird invading my woods.

Even the bird world was going to hell.

I went to the kitchen, put water on for tea, and poured a bowl of raisin bran. I poured milk on it and glumly shoveled it into my mouth. I used to wonder what I'd done to deserve Roxanne. Now I wondered what I'd done to deserve losing her.

The kettle whistled. I got up to get a cup and tea bag. And the phone rang.

I looked at my watch. It was five past seven. I grabbed the phone.

"Hello," I said.

"Hello, may I please speak to Jack McMorrow?" a small voice said.

"This is Jack."

"Jack, this is Donna. Donna Marchant? The girl from the courtroom?"

"Hi," I said.

"Hey, I wanted to tell you I really like the article. Really. I mean, I got up first thing and my neighbor—she gets the paper—and I really liked it. I was like, 'God, somebody finally believed me,' you know? But I didn't expect to be right there on the top. I was practically the only one you wrote about."

I wasn't sure what to say.

"Yeah, well, I thought it was important," I said.

"Well, I wanted to thank you," Donna said.

"You don't have to."

"My sister called and she's all pissed off that you put it in about the bite mark."

"Kind of hard to write around it," I said.

"Yeah, well, I thought it was fine. Hey, that's what happened, right? But that's not the only reason why I'm calling. Jeff called too."

"Up bright and early, was he?"

"I don't think he'd been to bed yet."

"Probably got into a good book and couldn't put it down," I said.

"Yeah, well, he didn't call me, he called my neighbor. A different one from the one who gets the paper. He left a message on her machine, 'cause he, like, knows I know her."

"What'd he say?"

"He said I was dead. And you were dead, too. But he was gonna kill you first so I would know you were dead. He said some other things that weren't so nice."

"Thanks for only giving me the good news."

"No, I mean, like, this really gross stuff."

"And he left this message on an answering machine?"

"Uh-huh."

"A master criminal."

"If he had a brain, he'd be dangerous," Donna said.

"He isn't doing a bad job without one," I said.

8

Wednesdays and Fridays were my days to work out. At quarter to eight, I put on my workout outfit—jeans, boots, a T-shirt, an old blue chamois shirt—and went out to the truck. It was a bright blue day, vivid against the pastels of the spring woods, and I almost wondered if I hadn't dreamed what had happened the night before.

Then I walked out in the road and picked up a nugget of window glass.

I got in the truck and started the motor and pulled around to the shed door. I slid the door open and went inside and got my chain saw off the workbench. The saw, gas, chain oil, and a toolbox went in the back of the truck. I got back in the front and made sure my ear protectors were behind the seat. Putting the truck in four-wheel-drive, I pulled ahead, then stopped. I thought for a moment and then got out and trotted back to the house and then back outside.

The rifle went in the gun rack, the cartridges in the glove box.

I was ready. Jane Fonda, eat your heart out.

Clair and I called it hardwood aerobics. He was probably already out there, but he was a real Mainer and an ex-Marine to boot. I couldn't compete with that, so I didn't try.

I drove up the road to Clair's house and turned off before his barn. The path led past the barn, through a pasture and into a stand of maples, with second-growth stuff all through it. With the branches scraping the side of the truck, I drove up the road, following the ruts made by Clair's truck and tractor. The path went over a rise and back down to a small stream that ran during spring runoff but already was subsiding to a trickle. I lurched the truck through it, then back up the hill on the other side, the tires grabbing at the ruts. At the top of that rise, the path veered to the right past two big beeches and came out into a clearing that had once been an orchard. Clair's big Ford was parked on the far side.

I drove over and turned off the motor.

Clair looked up from his tailgate, where he was filing his saw.

"How are the flies?" I said.

"They're good. Eating a healthy breakfast. What you got that for? Rabbits?"

I glanced at the rifle.

"And squirrels," I said. "We'll make some pie."

"With that thing, you'll make squirrel burgers," Clair said. "You expecting trouble, or you just trying to impress the girls?"

"A little of both, I guess."

Clair went on filing, leaning with both elbows across the big Husqvarna. He'd already shucked his flannel shirt, and I could see the muscles stretched across his shoulders, rippling in his arms. Silver hair stuck out from underneath his baseball cap. He looked great for fifty-five. He looked great for twenty.

"You gonna explain or am I gonna have to drag it out of you?" Clair said.

I opened my tailgate and dragged out my saw, another Husqvarna, and my toolbox. The file was in the toolbox, along with wrenches, screwdrivers, a spare chain, and a spark plug, all of which Clair had showed me how to use. He liked to say I arrived on the dump road in pretty sorry shape, skinny and runty and not knowing how to shoot or saw wood. He called me his "project," and had taught me how to do both. His wife, Mary, said I was the son he never had. Clair said if he had a son, his genetic imprint alone would cause him to shoot straighter than me. But he allowed that I'd improved.

"I had some visitors last night who weren't what you would call friendly," I said, drawing the file across the first of the saw teeth.

"What time was this?"

"Around midnight, I think."

"I heard a couple of shots about then. Figured it was the Maynards out jacking. Almost got on the horn to John Philbrick, but then I decided to let me and him sleep."

"This was a different kind of varmint," I said.

"What kind's that?"

"Kind that doesn't like what you're going to write about them in the paper so they try to get the story killed."

"But don't go through the editorial desk," Clair said.

"They went right to the source."

Clair tossed his file in his toolbox and reached for his gas can.

"And what did the source do?" he asked.

"We talked and they weren't listening. Then one of them decided he was going to try something with Roxanne."

"She okay?" Clair said sharply.

"Yup."

"So what were the shots?"

"One just over one of their heads. One through the back window of their truck. I think it went out the driver's window, but that was open."

"I take it they weren't in the truck at the time."

"No, they were standing in my yard, being chatty."

Clair poured chain oil in the saw's reservoir.

"How were they after you shot off that bazooka?" he said.

"Whole different attitude. But this morning one of them said he was going to kill me."

"Forgets quick."

"Either that or he doesn't forget at all. He said he was going to kill me and then kill his girlfriend, but he was going to do me first so she'd know I was dead."

"And this boy's loose?"

"Like a cannon," I said, pouring gas in the gas tank.

"Who's his girlfriend?"

"A woman I met in court. I'm writing for the *Observer* now. Covering the court in Kennebec."

"I know," Clair said. "I read it this morning. That the girl?"

"Yup. And the guy is the guy who bit her."

"And he came out to see you."

"Right."

"How'd he know about you, if the story wasn't in the paper until today?"

"She told him about it."

We lifted the saws from the trucks and started walking toward the woods.

"The girl coming out to see you too?"

"She calls," I said.

"What's Roxanne think of that?"

"Not much," I said, stepping over a blowdown.

"How was she after this brouhaha last night?" Clair said.

"Not so good. She's moving to Portland."

Clair's face went somber. He looked at me, then stepped up to a big maple with a trunk a foot across. He fiddled with the choke on his saw.

"You have to work at finding trouble or does it just come naturally?"

"It finds me," I said.

"Well, sounds to me like you may have found it but good," Clair said. "Next time you have visitors, don't hesitate to invite me to the party."

He started his saw. It revved once, then sputtered and stalled.

"I mean that," Clair said, adjusting the choke. "Somebody who comes all the way out here over some little newspaper story isn't gonna just forget somebody blowing a window out of his truck."

"It wasn't that little," I said. "And the writing was clean and evocative. Didn't you think?"

Clair looked at me sideways.

"Sometimes I wonder about you," he said, pulling at the starter cord. His saw revved, the sound ripping the quiet of the morning. He leaned toward me and half shouted in my ear.

"And if I were you, I'd get Roxanne back. A girl like that comes along once in a lifetime. I married mine."

I smiled at him.

"End of free advice," Clair said, and put the saw to the tree, spewing a plume of flesh-white chips.

We cut for most of the morning, working our way into a hardwood stand that had some good-size maple and beech and, on the fringes, yellow birch. This was our firewood. I got five cords every year. Clair got ten, keeping six for himself and giving four to Mrs. Hazlett down the road, a widow with no children. He'd been doing it for years, cutting it, splitting it, delivering it. He was being neighborly. She paid him in blueberry pies.

I was along because Clair's wife, Mary, didn't want him to bleed to death in the woods if he had an accident working alone. It could happen, and every once in a while, somewhere in these Vacationland woods, it did. One misstep. One moment of inattention. Screw up while you were working in the woods and you couldn't fix it with a correction.

We worked without speaking, except to shout when we were ready to drop a tree. They slammed to the ground with a whump, branches that had been stretched high skyward suddenly tangled in the brush. It was sad and final and, every time, gave me pause. I felt as though we should have a moment of silence.

But there was no silence as we worked, sweat dripping from our faces. The roar of the saws was muffled by my ear protectors, Marine-issue headgear that was really intended to protect the ears of a shooter on a firing range. The way things were going they could be just the ticket.

As I worked, the events of the night replayed in my mind. There was something reckless and dangerous about Jeff, a disregard for his own life that would make him tough to deal with. Would he get away with leaving threats on an answering machine? Ultimately, no. Would it be too late for Donna or me, or even Roxanne? Hard to say. Justice at best is mostly too little, too late.

And there would be no hiding from the guy if he decided to come after me. Kennebec, with its three-block downtown, two tough bars, and one courthouse, was compact, shrunk like the *Observer* newsroom. Everything within arm's reach. It was like Jeff was the school bully and I had to stay on the playground. What had Donna's life been like, stuck with the guy in a bedroom?

I wondered what made a guy like that so angry at the world. Had he spent his whole life in a rage? What was it about women that frustrated him so much? What made him want to beat them into submission? See them as property, territory to be conquered and claimed and consumed?

"I bet you're not wearing anything under that, are you, honey?" the one guy had said.

The son of a bitch.

And now Roxanne was headed south, having seen the worst that central Maine had to offer. I don't want to can vegetables. I don't want to be threatened by some filthy pig in my own house. What made that guy think he had any right to even look at Roxanne, much less say what he had said, take even one step in her direction?

"Jack," Clair shouted. I was lost in thought, limbing the last pale-leafed branches from a birch. "Good enough."

I turned off the saw and pulled off the headgear. Clair walked back toward the yard and in a minute there was a clacking as he started his venerable John Deere, which rumbled up the track. He turned it around and backed an old handmade trailer toward the trees we'd cut into four-foot lengths. When a cord of wood had been stacked, he climbed up on the old tractor and clacked his way out of the woods, the logs lined up like bodies from a battlefield. I followed, swatting flies.

Clair parked the tractor near the trucks. I filled both saws with gas and oil and put my headgear back on and started cutting the wood right on the trailer. In an hour, all those big majestic trees had been reduced to chunks, like a whale chopped into slabs of blubber. We filled my truck and Clair's truck and put the saws and toolboxes and gas cans on top.

"Well, I guess that should do her," Clair said, wiping his forehead with a blue bandanna.

"Yessuh," I said.

Clair went to the cab of the Ford and opened a small plastic cooler and came back with two cold, wet bottles of Budweiser. He handed me one and we opened them and raised them in salute.

"To the god of the woods," Clair said.

"Amen," I said.

We drank in long cold gulps, standing in sweaty silence as the blackflies buzzed around our heads. Clair finished his beer and stuck the empty bottle in with the wood. I took a last swallow and did the same.

"Back to the ranch," Clair said.

He walked around to the front of his truck. I walked to mine. He opened his door and paused.

"Jack, I mean it about those Kennebec yahoos. You could get in over your head."

"I know," I said.

"This guy's got nothing to lose."

"I know that, too."

"And you don't shoot a gun at a man unless you mean it."

"I did," I said.

Clair climbed into the Ford and the motor rumbled.

"And you patch things up with Roxanne, or I'm gonna be some pissed," he said.

I grinned. Clair did too.

So I drove slowly home. The wood went in a pile behind the shed, to be stacked later. I went inside and peeled off my sweat-soaked shirt and took off my boots. There were wood chips worked into my socks, and my jeans smelled of oily exhaust. I dumped them in a pile and turned on the shower and stepped in.

When I got out, I heard a voice.

On the answering machine.

"Give me a call or stop in. We've got some things to talk about."

It was Albert. He did not sound pleased.

I got dressed in the house that now echoed with Roxanne's absence and got in the truck and headed for Kennebec. If nothing else, I could buy beer.

"I'm not sure where to start, McMorrow," Albert said. "You filed after I left, so I didn't see it until this morning. I don't know what to say, except what the hell is this?"

He had traded his green ensemble for a brown one. The day's *Observer* was spread out on his desk, open to an inside page of the first section. My story was at the top of the right-hand page, with a thirty-six-point, three-column head.

The story was circled in red. I didn't see a gold star.

"It's a story about what went on in court yesterday," I said, shifting in my chair. "You hired me to cover the courts."

"Yeah, but I expected you to report the results."

"The results aren't what went on."

"It's what we do," Albert said. "We report the dispositions, maybe provide some details about cases of particular interest. This is, like, I don't know, it isn't exactly a column, but it isn't exactly a story, either."

"Sure it is. It's the story of what went on in a public courtroom yesterday."

"Some of this didn't go on in the courtroom."

"What do you want me to do?" I said. "Conduct my interviews in the front row?"

"I didn't expect you to conduct interviews."

"Then you don't need a reporter. You need a stenographer. Hold down your costs and send a tape recorder."

Albert looked down at the paper and said nothing. Behind his head was Cumberland County. Behind the partition, something rustled. In the *Observer* newsroom, all walls had ears.

"I got a call from Linda Tate, the assistant DA, at home this morning," Albert said.

"Yeah?"

"She was not pleased."

"So what's the bad news?"

"I mean she was really not pleased," Albert said.

"It's not my job to please her."

"Yeah, well, we depend on her office for a lot of information. She can make our job pretty goddamn difficult."

"Putting out a newspaper is supposed to be difficult. If it's easy, you're not doing it right."

Albert gave me a hard look.

"That's what they taught you at the *New York Times*, huh?"

"They taught me that a good newspaper doesn't kiss anybody's ass."

"What are you trying to say, McMorrow?" Albert said coldly.

"Nothing. I'm just saying that when you cover a courtroom proceeding, you can't kowtow to the DA."

"Who said anything about kowtowing?"

I paused. Something rustled behind the partition again. Charlene walked by one way, then the other. I could hear David Archambault's voice. He was on the phone.

"Listen," I said. "That case was the highlight of the docket yesterday. A woman comes in and pulls her shirt half off to show the judge where some guy bit her. You don't want me to report that?"

"I just don't know that it has to be reported quite like this," Albert said. "Chasing the lady out in the parking lot."

"Reporters chase people. It's what we do."

"Not at this newspaper."

I started to say something, then held back.

"Listen, McMorrow, you're a good writer," Albert said.

"Thanks."

"We're lucky to have you here, though I have to admit, I think there must be a skeleton in your closet someplace."

"Every closet has at least one. Some are chock-full."

He looked at me. I looked right back.

"Tate made a good point, I thought," Albert went on. "She said, 'Why single out this case?' She said it isn't fair to the alleged perpetrator, who hasn't been convicted as yet. I mean, these are just allegations."

"What do you think? She bit her own belly?"

"Well, no—"

"And God almighty, if we waited for convictions to cover cases, we'd never cover another trial again. We wouldn't report arrests. You do cover arrests here, don't you?"

"Yeah," Albert said. "But we do it without making a ruckus about every little case that comes along."

"I don't consider a woman being bitten and beaten and terrorized a little case."

"Oh, come on, McMorrow. Guys have been whacking their wives around for as long as there've been wives. That's reality."

"Right," I said, and I stood and reached over his desk and put my finger on my story.

"And that's reality too," I said.

"Reality is a DA who can make our lives miserable."

"Maybe we should do a story on that. My take on Tate is that she runs that courtroom like her own little fiefdom."

"It is her own little fiefdom," Albert said. He paused.

"And this is mine," he said slowly, with just a hint of a threat. "So tone it down a little, will you?"

I looked at him.

"That was toned down," I said.

Albert's phone rang, like the bell at ringside. He picked it up and I left.

As I walked through the newsroom, Charlene looked up from the desk and gave me a shy, knowing smile. Archambault, still on the phone, gave me a thumbs-up.

9

Roxanne didn't come home that night. She left a message that she was staying in Cape Elizabeth with her social worker friend, Kim. I slept alone and not very well, then got up and drove into Kennebec as a steady rain fell. The truck whirred down through the hills and pastures, past old farmhouses sinking into the ground, barns with their ridgepoles snapped, crumbling mementos from a time when hard work was its own reward.

It was a long time ago.

There were trailers and ranch houses and, every once in a while, a big monstrous new house with gates and gold-painted eagles, built by somebody with money and a subscription to *House Beautiful.* And finally there was the Kennebec River, black in the rain, and then I was on the bridge looking across at the houses that were all jammed together. It seemed odd in this sprawling, empty state, as if the town were some sort of refugee camp, the fences of which had only lately come down, and the weary residents had decided it wasn't worth trying to escape.

I pulled off the bridge and headed up Elm Street to the courthouse, following a woman on a bicycle with bags of empty cans tied to the back, one on each side. She crossed into the courthouse parking lot and I pulled in behind. She got off her bike and started digging in the metal trash can for empties. I dug in the rubble on the seat of the truck for a pen.

It was arraignment day and there was a blue paddy wagon pulled up to the courthouse door. Beside the paddy wagon, a cluster of defendants stood and smoked, peering out from under their sodden baseball caps. I threaded my way through them, stopping by the trash can.

"The back of that red Toyota is full of cans," I said. "Help yourself."

She turned and looked at me. Her face was almost handsome, with tanned smooth skin and not very many teeth. She said nothing, then headed for the truck.

Inside it was a full house, lawyers and defendants milling in the lobby as though it were intermission at some crazy opera. I went to the bulletin board by the soda machine and looked at the docket list. It was long. A woman in for bouncing seventeen checks. A guy charged with cruelty to animals. Several simple assaults. Kids caught with beer. Kids caught driving with beer. Kids caught driving drunk after drinking the beer. Several people caught driving after their licenses had been taken away for driving drunk.

A commercial for Prohibition.

I turned from the board and looked around the room. People were chatting in clumps. Lawyers to their blue-jeaned clients. Girls and guys to other girls and guys, as if arraignment day were some sort of reform-school reunion. In the corner five or six cops, state, Kennebec, and county, were joking around. With them were a couple of detectives or probation officers. To tell them apart, I'd have to pat them down.

In New York, everybody was armed. In quaint little Kennebec, the probation guys carried wallets under their three-season sport coats.

I watched for a minute, looked at my watch. Then I went and leaned against the counter and a clerk came up behind me.

"Are you here to pay a fine?" she said.

"No," I said. "I'm here to pay my dues."

I smiled.

"Just kidding," I said. She looked puzzled.

It was nine twenty-five, five minutes until the courtroom doors would open. With Jeff in mind, I stood and waited, my back to the wall.

And Donna came out of the DA's office. Crying.

I hesitated for a second. Saw the cops part for her and look at each other and shrug. She was dressed in jeans and a light blue sweatshirt and running shoes, and she was holding her lips together as if to keep a sob from spilling out.

Donna headed for the door and I followed. She slipped through the smokers and was halfway across the parking lot when I caught up with her.

"Donna," I said.

She half turned.

"Oh," Donna said. "I tried to call you, but you weren't home."

"What's the matter?"

"It didn't work."

"What didn't?"

"The whole thing. None of it. The going to court. Talking to you. Getting the protection thing. The story in the paper. None of it means shit."

She wiped her eyes and then dug in her pocketbook for a cigarette.

"Why?" I said. "What happened?"

"Jeff came to the house," Donna said, her voice quavering for a moment, then settling. "It was, like, three in the morning and he was drunk and wired and he's pounding on the door and yelling and he scares my daughter half to death."

"Did you call the cops?"

"Yeah. But he's saying he's gonna kill me and kill you 'cause nobody takes a shot at him when he's not armed. And I'm a bitch and a slut and all this and it went on and on. I felt so bad for the neighbors. They've got, like, four little kids, and this other guy, he works graveyard at the bakery, and this lady's home alone and Jeff's screaming and yelling."

"So was he there when the cops came?"

"Oh, yeah. And they arrested him. But he's meek and mild for them. I'm saying, 'Go ahead. Be a tough guy with them.' There's, like, three cops there and I was hoping he'd take a swing at one of 'em, but he's like Mr. Boy Scout."

She finished that cigarette and seemed calmer.

"And they arrested him?"

"Yeah," Donna said. "For three friggin' hours. He bailed at seven forty-five this morning. Two hundred bucks, cash. He's out, goddamn it. He's out. Where's the protection in that? How am I supposed to sleep? What about my little girl? What if he takes her? What if he takes my little girl?"

She bit her lip, then started to cry. The tears welled up and she wiped her eyes and her makeup smeared, leaving a long black streak across her right cheekbone.

I stood there awkwardly, not sure how, or if, to console her. The smokers were watching, glad for the distraction. Then the bailiff opened the door and told them court was starting and they went inside. I looked to the door, then back to Donna.

"You gonna be all right to drive?" I said.

"My car wouldn't start," she said. "I'm walking."

"Where's your daughter?"

"My sister came and got her this morning. When the cops were there. When we'd fight, she'd always call Auntie Marcia. She knows the number. It's like, 'When in doubt, call Auntie Marcia.' "

"So you walked down here?"

"To see the DA."

"Assistant DA, you mean. The DA's in Augusta."

"Whatever. That lady there. I wanted to tell her what happened, you know? See if I could get Jeff's bail upped or something. I mean, the guy is gonna hurt me."

"What'd she say?"

"Nothing. She wouldn't talk to me. She was right there behind this door and she wouldn't talk to me. It's like. 'You're trash. Go away.' I sat there for a half hour and then this secretary, she tells me they need the room for the lawyers and stuff and I have to leave. I'm like, 'Yeah, what's more important than this? Is my life nothing at all?' Who else am I supposed to talk to?"

Donna started to cry again. When she cried, her head shook. When her head shook, her earrings, big hoops with turquoise beads, shook too. She seemed very small and very frail and deserving of more than this.

"You want a ride someplace?" I asked.

"No. I don't know. Maybe to my sister's. I need to get my daughter."

"It's the red truck," I said.

Donna walked to the truck and I opened the door for her, clearing off the seat and tossing the newspapers and cardboard coffee cups on to the floor. She got in and held her pocketbook, which was small and made of black leather, on her lap, which was thin and narrow. I got in on the other side and started the truck. The tape in the player started too. It was Audubon Society birdcalls: spring warblers.

"I like birds," I explained.

"What, like in cages and stuff?" Donna asked.

"No, in the woods. You know, bird-watching."

She looked at me curiously but said nothing.

Donna gave the directions. South through the downtown and out the main drag and over another bridge. We went past a school and a big apartment complex and took a right at a country store. A half-mile out, in what had been a farmer's pasture, was Marcia's house, a neat brick-red ranch with a neat brick-red garage. There was a pickup with a camper in the driveway. Behind the truck was a trailer with two snowmobiles on it, wrapped tightly with tarps.

"Lots of toys," I said as we pulled up.

'That's Randy's thing. He works, like, sixty hours a week at the mill in Skowhegan. They've got snow machines, a boat. A new truck plus that one just for the camper."

"So your daughter likes it here?"

"More than her own house, sometimes," Donna said. "Marcia and Randy never fight."

"They have kids?"

"No. They want to but they can't. And Randy won't adopt, so that's it. Adrianna's their kid, really. They love her and she loves them."

I was parked in front of the house. A curtain moved and a small blonde girl was in the window, waving madly. Donna looked up and smiled.

"Hi, honey," she called, and then her face froze and she said, "Oh, Jesus."

The truck was bigger in the daylight. It came down the street toward us in a burst of noise, then made a U-turn and pulled up and cut me off. The back window was taped with plastic.

Jeff got down from the cab. I got out of my tiny Toyota, sticking my keys in my pocket. Donna bolted across the lawn for the house.

"Hey, scumbag," Jeff said, walking toward me, ignoring her. "Where's your rifle?"

"Under the seat," I lied. "Where's your friends?"

"Home," he said. "That makes us even, right?"

"I don't know. How were your SATs?"

He got within six feet of me and stopped. His eyes were bleary, and I could smell alcohol already.

"Rum," I said.

"Cuervo Gold," Jeff said.

"You like to go down in style, huh?"

"Who says I'm going down?"

"You just got arrested. Twice in one day, there won't be any bail."

"That's my problem."

"You got that right," I said.

I opened the truck door. Jeff lunged out and kicked it shut. He stood there, hands by his sides, swaying slightly. He was a little shorter than me but wider at the shoulders and hips. His boots were unlaced and his denim shirt was half-buttoned. He was good-looking, with high cheekbones and deep-set dark eyes, just handsome enough to be arrogant. A gold chain showed against his hairy chest.

"My grandmother had a necklace just like that," I said. "And these faux pearl earrings. Clip-ons because, of course, this was before body piercing was en vogue. She shopped at Bloomies. People say it's pricey, but if you shop the sales . . ."

"Shut up."

"That's not nice."

"Shut up."

"I heard you the first time," I said.

"I don't think you did, or you wouldn't be poking my girlfriend."

"She's not your girlfriend and I'm not poking her."

"I say you are," Jeff said, inching forward, getting up on the balls of his feet. "I say that slut was all over you. I say you had your—"

I moved first, I had to, coming off the line like a tackle and putting my shoulder into his chin and neck. I had the momentum and I drove him back against the side of his truck and got my left forearm up under his neck. He was bent back over the bed of the truck and he reached in with his right arm and grabbed a piece of pipe. Before he swung it, I punched him twice in the throat, once in the eyes, and once in the side of the head near the ear.

Maybe I could win on points.

The pipe came up and hit me in the back of the head, but I was so close to his body that he couldn't get weight behind the swings. It jarred me loose and I spun away from him, ripping his shirt and chain and swinging him against the hood of my truck. He staggered for just a second, and I jumped onto the truck and him and pressed his head back as far as I could.

His legs went off the ground and I dug the keys out of my back pocket and raised the jagged metal high over his face.

"Drop it," I said, panting through clenched teeth.

Jeff grunted and swung the pipe and hit me in the back of the head again, this time harder. He swung again and it made a clank against my skull and there was a black flash and I slammed the keys as hard as I could against his mouth.

He said, "Ohhh," and blood spurted from his lips. I raised the keys again and then there was a scrape of gravel and a blip of a siren and a voice on a PA that said, "Police. On the ground. Get on the ground. Get on the ground now!"

"So he says you came at him without provocation," the cop said from the front seat of the cruiser.

"He said that? Provocation's a big word for him."

"That's my word. He said he was just talking to you and you came at him."

The cop was Donna's friend, Officer Lenny. I'd read his name tag and was surprised to see that Lenny was his last name. His first name was William, and he was sitting in the driver's seat of the Chevy cruiser with a clipboard on his lap, writing with a chrome Cross pen. The radio coughed and he reached over and turned it down. The ambulance with Jeff in it pulled away

"Poor baby," Lenny said. "Just stalling so he doesn't have to go to jail. Now tell me what happened."

"He had a pipe," I said. "He was drunk and pissed-off because I wrote about his girlfriend and her appearance in court, where she came to get a protection order. He's threatened to kill her and he's threatened to kill me, and in my opinion he's a bail risk. He came out to my house last night and threatened me."

"Where's that?"

"Prosperity."

"He didn't assault you?"

I hesitated.

"It didn't get to that," I said. "This time he came at me with a pipe, swung first without any sort of provocation, and I pushed him away to defend myself. I had my keys in my hand, and when he was hitting me on the head with the pipe I was forced to use my keys as a weapon."

"That's not what he says," Lenny said.

"Who you gonna believe?" I said.

"I'm gonna let the DA's office worry about that."

Lenny wrote, and I watched him. He was in his early fifties, had a military precision about him, and seemed to take his job very seriously. My gut said he was a good man and a good cop. My gut had been wrong before, but not often.

"Never should have let him out," Lenny said suddenly. "Guys like that get full of booze and drugs and it's just a matter of time. I believe he'll hurt her if they keep giving him more chances."

"Tell the judge that."

"I will. But I want you to tell me more about your connection to all this."

"Isn't much of one. I met Donna a couple of days ago. At court Tuesday. I just started covering the court for the *Observer*. I wrote about her coming to court and he saw it. He came after her and came after me. Today she was at the courthouse trying to talk to Tate about the whole thing, and she was upset. She didn't have a car, so I offered her a ride out here to pick up her kid."

Lenny scribbled, his face inscrutable.

"You involved in a relationship with her?" he asked without looking up from his clipboard.

I looked at him.

"No. I just met her. I've talked to her twice. And I've got somebody else. I mean, no."

Lenny still didn't look up.

"Maybe it's none of my business, but I'm gonna say it anyway. You'd be wise to keep your distance from things like this, Mr. McMorrow. They have a way of sucking you in, especially if you're the type who thinks he can save the world."

"You think I'm that type?"

"I've seen it before," Lenny said.

"I told you. I was just giving her a ride. The guy came at me. I didn't have any choice."

He looked at me in the rearview mirror. I couldn't see his mouth, but his eyes seemed to grin.

"Right," Lenny said. "And if you're smart, you won't get in any deeper. A word to the wise, my friend."

"Thanks, I think."

I got out of the cruiser, and my head swirled and ached. Lenny got out too. He handed me the clipboard and I signed the statement form on the bottom. The door of the house opened and Donna came out, while Marcia stood in the doorway with Adrianna and watched. Donna walked across the lawn and Lenny got back in the cruiser.

"You might want to stay here with your sister," Lenny said to her through the window. "I can't guarantee that he won't be out again."

Donna nodded. She had redone her eyes and put on lipstick, which was pink. I felt a sharp spasm of pain and I grimaced and put my hand to the back of my head, where I could feel the scabbed-over scrapes.

"Whoa," I said.

Donna reached out and held my arm with both hands.

"You okay?" she said. "Why don't you come in and sit down?"

Lenny looked at me and his eyes grinned again.

"Word to the wise," he said, and put the cruiser in gear and pulled away.

"Come on in," Donna said, and she looked up at me, this time letting her gaze linger. She was so small, so blonde, and her eyes were so big and dark.

"Maybe a cold drink," I heard myself say, and Donna walked me across the lawn, still holding me by the arm.

There was a microwave on the counter, next to a food processor and a twelve-cup coffeemaker. Everything was shiny and new, like a display at Montgomery Ward. There was a two-week menu on the almond-colored refrigerator, which had an icemaker in the door. On the menu I could make out the words "American chop suey" and "Pepper steak."

"Diet Pepsi or regular?" Donna said.

"Water would be fine."

She held a glass to the door and filled it, then put it down in front of me on the kitchen table. Adrianna came in with a stuffed dog in her arms. She was wearing pink pants with flowers on them. Her hair was curly and blonde like a wreath and she was brown-eyed like her mother.

"This is Shaggy," she said.

"Hello, Shaggy," I said. "Pleased to meet you."

"Shaggy is pleased to meet you too," Adrianna said, then looked up at me.

"What's your name?"

"Jack."

"Like the beanstalk?" she asked.

"Yeah. Like the beanstalk."

"Go ahead now, honey," Donna said. "Go and play."

"You ever climb a beanstalk?" Adrianna asked, frisking around the kitchen with the dog.

"No," I said. "But I'd like to. You have any magic beans?"

"I'll ask Aunt Marcia," she said.

She trotted off. Donna sat down next to me.

"I'm sorry you had to get all caught up in this," she said.

I shrugged.

"What can you do?" I said.

"How's your head?"

"It aches."

"Maybe you should've gone to the hospital."

"Nah," I said. "I have to get back to work. I've missed the morning session."

"What will you do?"

"Wing it."

I smiled.

"I'm really sorry," Donna said, and she reached out and patted my arm, letting the last pat linger.

I got up from the table. Marcia came in with Adrianna, holding her against her legs.

"We don't have any magic beans, Jack," Adrianna said in a tiny voice. "Aunt Marcia says we're all out. Can you get some at the store, Aunt Marcia?"

"Sure, honey," Marcia said in a gentle tone I hadn't heard from her before.

She looked up at me and didn't seem gentle at all.

"So what are you going to do?" I asked Donna.

"Hope they keep him in, I guess."

"I'll talk to Tate, if you want."

"Thanks," Donna said.

"You can both stay here," Marcia interrupted, still holding Adrianna to her.

"I need my own life," Donna said.

"How 'bout I keep Adrianna for tonight?" Marcia said.

"No, she needs to be in her own bed, I think. Don't you, honey?"

"I want to stay here," Adrianna said.

I moved toward the door. Donna went to get Adrianna and the little girl bolted down the hall. I let myself out and Marcia followed me all the way to the truck. I got to the driver's door and stopped.

"She doesn't need another enabler," she said.

"Pardon me?"

"Another enabler. That's all these guys are. That's all she is to them. Donnie, her husband, was useless. Jeff is a goddamn psycho. She gets involved with these guys because she drinks."

"I'm surprised to hear that," I said. "I didn't think it would be that simple."

"Well, I'm telling you for her sake, not yours. Hers and the baby's. Back off."

I looked at her. What did I look like, I thought—a cruiser of singles bars?

"I don't have to back off," I said. "I'm already backed off. I was never backed in. Really. I have somebody at home. I'm just trying to do my job."

"Well, go do it. I'm sorry about what happened today, but we don't need any more of your help. That baby needs a normal life."

"Which you'll gladly provide?" I said.

"What's that mean?" Marcia asked, adding even more chill to her voice.

"I don't know. Just that you seem to get along well with Adrianna."

"I'm practically her mother," Marcia said. "What that child has seen in her life . . . I just try to give her some stability, you know?"

"She's lucky to have you."

"And I'm telling you to stay away and let my sister get back on her own two feet. She doesn't need another man in her life."

"And I don't need another woman in mine," I said.

I thought for a moment, then threw one out.

"Or a child," I said.

Marcia almost snapped her chain.

"Don't come near her," she hissed. "That little girl is my—I'd do anything for that little girl. Anything. So stay away."

"She's your what?" I said.

"My life," Marcia said. "You go and don't come back. And don't go near that baby or my sister."

"You're your sister's keeper?"

"Go, and leave us alone," Marcia said. "Or you'll—"

"I'll what?"

"Regret it, Mr. McMorrow. Go."

10

So I went, getting back to court at eleven thirty. The bailiff gave me the evil eye but let me in when there was a break. I sat in the back row with an empty stomach and a screaming headache. Worse than that, something in Donna had stirred something in me, and I didn't feel good about that at all.

Roxanne wouldn't feel good about it either.

The judge was a white-haired man this time, very calm and placid and slow. After a few minutes, one of the probation guys slipped in and sat at the end of the row beside me. He was fortyish, small and wiry, and had a smile-creased face that looked as if he'd long been bemused by human nature.

I asked him the judge's name.

"Poulin," he said. "Nice guy. Too nice."

"This your beat?" I asked.

"Tuesdays and Thursdays," he said. "Mondays and Wednesdays in Augusta. Every other Friday in Waterville. It's controlled chaos. Who are you?"

"McMorrow. Jack McMorrow."

"Oh, Jesus, you're McMorrow. You've got this place stirred up. I thought Tate was going to put a warrant out for your arrest."

"Why?"

"Because this court hasn't had a real reporter here in . . . I don't know. Maybe they never have. You know what you ought to write about?"

"What?" I said.

"The goddamn plea bargains she hands out. She has some guy ought to be in the slammer and she gives him a suspended sentence, friggin' two years' probation. Hey, I don't have time to chase any more of these guys. I've got a hundred and ninety-three clients. Right now. Today. I've got rapists and arsonists and all these badass types I see once a month. It's a joke. It is."

"So why doesn't she go for jail time?"

"Because these guys aren't going to go for a plea with jail. They'll get a lawyer and go to trial and take their chances. And there's a chance they'll win."

"And Tate will lose."

"You got it."

"So she plays it safe."

"At the public's expense. We've got loonies running the streets. You wouldn't believe who's walking around out there. I mean, I'm their probation officer and I don't have the goddamn foggiest notion where they are."

"What's your name?" I said.

"Doesn't matter. You want a good one? There was this guy in here this morning. John DeSoto. A goddamn career criminal. I've had him on for most of the last twenty years. Guy is here for assaulting his neighbor. Some bullshit argument. He hit the guy in the face with a shovel. A shovel. Cops have him for aggravated, and by the time Tate gets the case in here, it's been pleaded down to simple assault. Thirty days suspended and a two-hundred-dollar fine plus restitution for the guy's medical bills. But this guy couldn't pay a parking ticket. Doesn't have a pot to piss in. The cop was ripped."

"Why doesn't he do something about it?" I asked.

"Because you cross Tate and you'll never get a conviction again. You get on her shit list, you' re finished."

"What kind of way is that to run a prosecutor's office?"

"Tate's way," he said. "I heard the victim was really ripped about it. He had half his teeth knocked out or some such thing. You should talk to him."

"I'd like to."

"John DeSoto," he said. "Go ask the clerk to give you a printout of his record here. They have to give it to you."

Right then, a woman pleaded guilty to theft. She hadn't returned a rented car. She looked as though she'd have trouble spelling *rental*, much less reading the fine print. It was her third offense and she got probation. My source followed her out the door.

When the court recessed for lunch I went to the clerk, an efficient prison-matronly woman.

I asked for a printout of DeSoto's convictions and she looked put-upon, but printed it out for me anyway. Rapunzel could have reached the ground from the tower window with it. I stuffed the sheaf of paper in my pocket and waited for my probation buddy, who was helping the car-rental wizard fill out a form. When he'd given up, I walked over.

"I need a victim," I said.

He smiled. "You gonna be here?"

"All day."

"I'll get you a name," he said.

"Thanks," I said, and I walked out the door through the smokers and went in search of something to eat.

Lunch was from the pizza shop with the nasty video games. I ate in the truck and listened to the news on public radio. None of it was good, so I turned it off and sat and watched the trucks and cars lurch through the traffic light. I had enough bad news of my own.

I had Jeff, who would be putting a contract out on me from jail. Marcia, who hated my guts and wanted to be a mother. Donna, who didn't hate my guts enough, and was a mother, but was mucking it up. And then there was Albert, who was already kicking himself for allowing a reporter to work at his newspaper. And old Miss Tate, who was going to be on the phone to the newspaper tomorrow morning, too. Whose idea was this anyway?

It was Roxanne's, and she was gone, or going. Something to look forward to after a day in the trenches.

So I ate and went back and waited and, sure enough, the probation guy got me the name, slipping it to me in the courtroom early in the afternoon. I waited for a recess and went to the pay phone in the hall.

The name was Limington, first name Paul, and he lived in Kennebec's south end. I called directory assistance and it went through, and in two minutes Limington's phone was ringing and a man answered.

"Mr. Limington," I said, pronouncing it like the citrus fruit.

"Limington," he said, as in *limb*, the thing that the citrus fruit grows on. I asked him about this DeSoto guy and what had happened. An argument over a parking space outside their apartment house, Limington said. The result was seven lost teeth, a wired jaw, and thirty-three stitches in his mouth.

"So what did you think of the deal?" I said.

"I think it friggin' sucks," Limington said. He pronounced it *shucks*.

"Why's that?" I prompted, the phone propped under my chin, pen on the pad.

" 'Cause you couldn't squeeze a nickel out of that son of a bitch with a vise. I got no insurance. Collection people on the phone all day. That's who I thought you were."

"No, just a reporter."

"And you're gonna write an article about this?"

"Thinking about it."

"Well, put this in your article. The system sucks. The DA lady there, she sucks. Treated me like I was a friggin' criminal, you know? Hey, did I hit myself in the face with a goddamn shovel? I'm the goddamn victim, you know?"

"I know," I said.

"I gotta go," Limington said. "My face hurts."

His face. My head. This was quite a town.

So I spent the rest of the afternoon in the courtroom, where the defendants filed past like milk bottles on a conveyor belt. Big and imposing and dressed in an expensive blue suit, Tate looked at the defendants with distaste, like a queen eyeing her serfs. Sometimes Tate barely looked up as some guy in dirty jeans and boots with grease-mottled hands said that he understood the charges against him and his rights, too.

As if he had any.

I waited and finally the last defendant, a kid up for illegal possession of wine coolers, had held his hand out to be slapped. He left and it was just me and Tate and the judge. He left, hearing a scotch and water calling. That left me and Tate, who turned and gave me a long, cold stare.

She jerked her head toward the lobby.

"In my office," Tate said.

She didn't hold the door.

Her inner office door was closed when I walked in. I knocked twice, hard, and heard Tate say "Come in."

I did.

She was sitting behind a big oak desk, smoking a cigarette. She had big hands and a wide mouth. The mouth blew smoke.

"I thought it was against the law to smoke in a public building," I said.

"This isn't a public building," Tate said. "It's my building. Sit down."

I sat and did a quick scan of her desk. The usual pens and pencils. A big black volume of Maine statutes. Legal pads and manila folders. A framed photograph of an obese orange-and-white cat.

"Nice cat," I said. "It must pack it away. Had it a long time?"

"I'm going to ask the questions. What the hell do you think you're doing?"

"Sitting here, trying to be polite."

"What planet did you drop off of?" Tate said. "You're here one day and you're making trouble. What's your problem?"

"I don't have one. I'm just doing my job."

"And you're gonna make it harder for me to do mine."

"Which is what?" I said.

"Keeping these scroats moving."

"That's it?"

"Yup," Tate said. "Shovel 'em in. Shovel 'em out."

"How do you keep your idealism?"

"I don't have time for wisecracks, McMorrow."

"Why? Mittens waiting for supper?"

"Listen, chump," Tate said, pointing her finger and cigarette in the direction of my face. "This is my courtroom, and I don't want some reporter getting it all fouled up."

"Running pretty smooth, huh?"

"Better than anything you saw in New York."

"Dante's Inferno ran better than New York courts," I said. "What's your excuse?"

"What do you care?"

"I just think people should be treated with a little respect."

"You haven't been dealing with this scum for fifteen years."

"If you think of them that way, what are you doing here?"

Tate didn't answer, but she didn't look away. I didn't look away either. Finally, Tate stubbed out her cigarette and blinked.

"Listen, McMorrow. I want the news from this court reported the way it's always been."

"It hasn't been reported."

"It's been reported fine."

"So why did the story about Donna Marchant get you so pissed off?" I asked.

"Because it was sensational and it cast this office in an unfavorable light."

"What's that mean in English?"

"It made me look bad. The next thing you know, I'll have some goddamn rape group out there with signs."

"They should be out there. They should be in the courtroom when you make somebody like Donna Marchant feel like some slut. Today you wouldn't even see her."

"What? You in her pants too, McMorrow?"

"Nope. But I was in the courtroom. You thought it was some joke."

"I've seen a thousand Donna Marchants over the years. They bat their big eyes and wiggle their little butts and then when the guy sobers up and tosses them out of bed, they come here crying."

"That's why her boyfriend was arrested today for threatening to kill her, and me?"

"You are screwing her," Tate said. "Is that what got you tossed out of New York? Bedding your sources?"

"Yeah, right."

I looked around. The place had as much personality as a thirty-five-dollar motel room.

"You have court twice a week, right?"

Tate nodded.

"What do you do the rest of the time?"

"Prepare cases."

I smiled.

"Not bad for government work," I said.

"And I intend to keep it that way," Tate said.

"Don't blame you."

"I give you two weeks, McMorrow."

"I'll see that two weeks and raise you six months," I said. "And while I have you here, I've got a couple questions. The plea bargain for John DeSoto. Do you think there's any chance that DeSoto will come up with the money to pay Mr. Limington's medical bills? Were you aware that Mr. Limington didn't approve of this plea bargain? Did you even consult him about this? Do you ever consult victims before proposing a sentence some victims might consider lenient?"

I took out my pad and pen and waited.

"One week, McMorrow," Tate said.

"Is that a no comment?"

"You got it."

I got up from my chair and put my pad in my back pants pocket, my pen in my shirt. I went to the door and opened it.

"Say hi to Mittens for me," I said. "I think I can hear his stomach growling."

"One week tops," Tate said.

The story was written in the truck again, this time in the alley behind the *Observer* office. I parked opposite the back door, behind a Dumpster. When the story was done, read, and reread, I sat behind the wheel and waited. I watched pigeons rustle to their roosts under the black brick eaves. Said hello to two guys on bicycles who dove headfirst into the Dumpster, looking for bottles. Listened to the news and the Cleveland Symphony. The symphony was playing Schubert. When Albert came out the back door, I turned Schubert off and went upstairs.

For the *Observer*, things were hopping. There had been a bad car accident north of town. Three people had been killed. The wrecked truck was filled with beer bottles, most of them empty.

David Archambault was doing the story. Catherine Plante was on the desk. They were arguing. Following David's example, I sent my story into the system, then went to Plante's desk and stood with my computer under my arm and watched.

"I've got to get more families," Archambault was saying.

"I don't think it's necessary," Plante said from her chair. "You've got one. The sister-in-law. We don't want to seem like we're harassing these people."

"It's not harassing," Archambault said, jumping up from his terminal. "It makes the story more human. You know. That these guys were more than statistics."

"Yeah. They were drunks. The good news is that they didn't hit anybody else. When do we get the blood alcohol on the driver?"

"Too late for tonight," Archambault said. "But don't change the subject, Catherine. I want another hour to try to get some more family stuff. Give me 'til nine o'clock."

"I don't know," Plante said. "I've got late meetings up the wazoo. I'd like to get this one in the can."

She looked up at me.

"What would you do, McMorrow?"

I shrugged. They both were waiting.

"Is this your strongest story?" I said.

"Hell, yes," Plante said. "Leading the page."

"Which page?" I asked.

"Page one," she said. "What do you think this is? The *New York Times*?"

I smiled. Archambault looked up at me expectantly.

"I'd give the accident story your best shot. I don't know, but one sister-in-law for three people dead doesn't sound like enough. Were the dead people from the same family?"

"No," Archambault said. "Old friends. Drinking buddies."

"You go to their bar?"

"No."

"Their neighborhood?"

He shook his head no.

"When did this happen?" I asked.

Plante scanned the screen.

"Eleven thirty-three this morning."

"Got off to a slow start, didn't you?" I said.

"This goddamn paper's in a coma," Archambault snapped. "I could have done that. I could have gone to the bar. Albert says to stay by the phone and get the cop's report. I could have done all kinds of things at a real newspaper."

Plante looked at the screen, then at her watch.

"You've got an hour," she said.

Archambault was stuffing a notebook in his pocket, pumped up like a rookie coming off the bench in a championship game. Nothing like a nice tragedy to get the adrenaline pumping.

"Thanks, Jack," he said on the way by me. "Hey, that story about the woman in court was dynamite. Excellent stuff. I gotta buy you a beer."

And he was gone.

Plante looked up at me. "If I'm late to press, it's your ass," she said.

"Take a chunk. Everybody else has."

She scrolled up.

"Court. McMorrow. Here it is. You know your first contribution almost got me fired?"

"Sorry about that," I said.

"I hope this one's a little easier on Albert and his ulcer."

She punched a couple of buttons and her eyes narrowed as she read.

"Oh, Jesus," Plante said. "How long are you gonna keep this up, McMorrow?"

"Depends on who you ask," I said.

"Oh, baby," she said, still eyeing the screen. "The shit's gonna hit the fan."

11

—✄—

Roxanne's Subaru wagon was parked by the shed. She was inside, standing by the stove. When I came through the door, she turned and the sight of her took me aback. I walked over and put my arms around her.

She pressed against me.

"Hi, baby," Roxanne whispered. "I missed you."

"I missed you too."

We kissed gently and I leaned back and looked at her, then hugged her again.

"I brought you a present," she said.

"You are a present," I said.

Roxanne peeled off me and went to the refrigerator. She opened the door and reached in and came out with a bottle of Samuel Smith's Nut Brown Ale.

"Your brew. In moderation," she said.

"As long as I can have you to excess."

"You'll end up in a twelve-step program."

"Twelve steps up the ladder to the loft," I said.

"You're slipping," Roxanne said. "There are only eleven."

I went to the drawer and got an opener for the ale. I'd taken one sip, standing at the counter, when I felt Roxanne's arms slip around me. She kissed my neck and my ear, and her forearm brushed my bumps and I winced.

"What's that?" Roxanne said, feeling a lump.

"Nothing," I said. "I bumped myself shaving."

"What?"

"It's a long story," I said. "And I don't want to tell it now."

And then I turned around and she kissed some more of me.

"You smell like smoke, too," she murmured.

"The original Marlboro man. Pretty sexy, huh?"

"Pretty gross," Roxanne said. "I think you're going to need a shower."

"Too bad."

"Terribly inconvenient," she said.

"And I had my heart set on watching a little tube," I said.

"Watch all you want. Tomorrow."

So we took a shower, with the beer by the sink and a glass of Bordeaux by the beer, part of Roxanne's red phase. The shower lasted until the water got cold, which was mercifully soon. I took my Sam Smith's and Roxanne took her Bordeaux and we went up the stairs, counting them as we went.

She was right. There were eleven.

We made love fiercely, not talking, just breathing. The bed slammed and banged and the sheets and comforter flew off and I think we would have flown off, too, if we hadn't gripped each other so tightly. And then we were still, collapsed on our backs like marathoners across the finish line.

"You got the bed all sweaty," Roxanne said.

"You did."

"No way."

"Whatever," I said. "I'm just glad it's on your side."

"Wait a minute. You're on my side."

"While you were gone, I switched. I like this side better now."

"But I was only gone one night," Roxanne said.

"It seemed like an eternity."

We were quiet and it was cooler and I leaned down and found the comforter on the floor and pulled it over us. I lay back and could feel Roxanne's breasts, hips, and legs against me. She'd be beautiful to a blind man, I thought.

"So," I said. "Was that hello or good-bye?"

"I don't know. Depends on how you look at it."

"When are you leaving?"

"I thought maybe you'd help me move tomorrow."

"So this was a bribe?"

"A kickback," Roxanne said, and laughed to herself.

"I don't get it," I said.

"That's because you're so thick. Or at least you were."

"That's awful, Rox. You should be ashamed."

"Does that mean you won't move me?"

"I thought I had," I said.

"I felt the earth move," Roxanne mugged, reaching for her wine. "Of course, the way this house is built, it doesn't take much."

"Okay, Miss Fancy Pants. What kind of house did you get?"

"A condo on the harbor. Two bedrooms."

"That's a waste."

"Jack, be quiet. I'm telling you my story. Two bedrooms. A deck overlooking the water. A nice kitchen. Lots of windows. I can see the sun come up over Casco Bay."

"Any birds?"

"I'm sure there are gulls and ducks and stuff."

"Spoken like a true ornithologist."

"And it comes with a boat dock thingy."

"A slip, you mean?"

"Right."

"But you don't have a boat."

"That's okay. The guy next door has a forty-foot sailboat. He invited me to come on a sail sometime."

"Don't tell me," I said, finishing my ale. "His name is Biff. Or Kipper."

"It's Skip," Roxanne said.

I snorted.

"And another thing," I said. "It's widely known that those guys with forty-foot boats are compensating for shortcomings in other areas."

"Jack, come on. You have a canoe."

"Exactly," I said.

So we slept just like that, together again, once again. I didn't awaken until the room was filled with light, and then I turned over to make sure the previous night hadn't been a dream. Roxanne was there, her hair spread on the pillow. I kissed her on the cheek, looked at her again, then got up and put on a pair of boxers.

It was six fifteen. The birds were up and at 'em out back, and I stopped by the door and closed my eyes and listened. That cardinal. Chickadees and nuthatches and a hairy woodpecker. A redstart. Tree swallows chittering. Blue jays and a crow. A warbler I still couldn't identify. Maybe a pine warbler.

In serious birding, where most sightings are by sound, I had a long way to go. But it looked as if I'd be having more time.

I put water on for tea and looked around the house. A lot of the stuff would be going: Roxanne's books, her Bonnie Raitt tapes, which I grumbled about but would miss. Her dresses in the closet and shoes on the floor. I would very much miss her dresses in the closet. Maybe she'd leave one or two.

The kettle rattled and whistled. I grabbed it, but I heard Roxanne stir. There was a creak, and her head poked up over the railing. Her hair was disheveled and she was beautiful.

"Good morning," Roxanne said.

"Hi, there," I said. "Didn't mean to wake you."

"That's okay. God almighty, what did you do to my hair?"

"Rich ladies pay hundreds of dollars to have their hair look like that."

"Yeah, and they pay to have their noses pierced too," Roxanne said, and disappeared back into the bed.

"That's where I draw the line," I said.

I made her coffee, real coffee from Costa Rica. The smell lured her down the eleven steps. She was wearing one of my T-shirts, and I watched her walk down each step.

"I hope short hemlines come back," I said.

"They are back," Roxanne said, "and don't try to tell me you haven't noticed."

We sat at the table and had English muffins and jam and orange juice. I was hungry, and Roxanne was too, and we were halfway through the meal before we really talked.

"So how was the *Observer* yesterday?" Roxanne asked, getting up to get more coffee.

"Hunky-dory," I said. "I waited until the editor left to file my story."

"He doesn't like your work?"

"He'd rather be printing wedding invitations than a newspaper. The guy's a wimp. Likes the waters calm."

"And you make waves?"

"That's what a reporter does."

"I'm sorry it isn't working out," Roxanne said. "I feel like I got you into this."

"It's okay. It really is. It's sort of interesting. I get a kick out of a couple of the people in the newsroom. There's this kid, David. He's just like me, fifteen years ago. And some of the court stuff has been pretty good."

"You're seeing my people."

"On their best behavior."

Roxanne sipped her coffee. Hesitated.

"So what's with the bump on your head?" she said.

I sipped. Considered how to phrase it.

"I ran into our buddy from the yard."

"Where?"

"His girlfriend's sister's house."

"What were you doing there?" Roxanne asked.

"Giving Donna Marchant a ride home."

Roxanne's eyebrows rose, just a millimeter.

"She was in court and she didn't have a car because it wouldn't start and she needed to go pick up her little girl. I got there and he was waiting. For her, I guess."

"So he hit you?"

"A couple of times. Not very hard."

"So what happened?" Roxanne asked.

"I don't know. We wrestled around a little and the cops came."

"They took him to jail, I hope."

"Yeah," I said. "Well, after the hospital."

"The hospital?"

"He cut his mouth a little."

Roxanne looked at me knowingly.

"On what?" she said.

"On my car keys."

She got up from the table, shaking her head.

"But he had a piece of pipe," I said as she climbed the stairs. "What was I supposed to do?"

"Jack," Roxanne said, looking down at me from the top of the stairs. "I just don't know anymore."

So the packing was an even more somber affair than it could have been before our talk. We walked around the house, selecting items one by one like a couple getting divorced. I had to keep reminding myself that we were not. I had to keep telling myself.

I put rack sides on my truck and we loaded it up to the top with boxes and two chairs and a bookshelf and a bicycle and six pairs of Roxanne's skis. When it was full, I tied it down with clothesline. It was a beautiful day, which was good because I didn't have a tarp.

Roxanne's car filled fast, even with the seats folded down. By ten o'clock we were pretty much done and I was ready for a beer but settled for a Diet Coke. There were two in the refrigerator and Roxanne had one and I had the other. I gulped mine and went back outside to give the load a last check. As I stood on the bumper, I heard the phone ring inside. It rang twice, and after a minute or so Roxanne came out.

"It's for you," she said coldly. "It's your friend. Your friend Donna. She sounds very nice. She asked if I was your wife."

"Did you tell her you were my girlfriend?"

"No," Roxanne said. "I didn't tell her anything."

She went to her car, though there was nothing to do there. I went inside and picked up the phone from the table.

"Hello, Donna," I said.

"Jack," Donna said, her voice soft and familiar. "How are you feeling?"

"Fine."

"How's your head?"

"Good," I said. "Better. How are you?"

"Okay. I'm home."

She said it as if I had been there. I flinched, remembering that I had been there. I'd seen her in the window.

"But Jack, Jeff is out."

"Out of what?"

"Out of jail."

"What?"

"The DA lady set his bail at three hundred bucks. He saw the judge this afternoon and bang, he was gone."

"Assault and violation of a probation order is three hundred bucks?"

"I guess it was this time," Donna said.

I give you one week, Tate had said. It hadn't taken her long to start the countdown.

"How'd you find out?" I said.

"Marcia called to see when he was going to be in court. The clerk said he'd come and gone. So Marcia's offered to take Adrianna for a while. Until things settle down."

"When's that? In time for her high school graduation?"

"Jack."

Donna said it like we were accomplices, almost intimate. A ménage à trois with a maniac. I could understand why Roxanne was chilly.

She came in and set her Coke can on the counter, then walked back outside without looking at me.

"I've got to go," I said.

"With your girlfriend?" Donna said. Her voice was wistful.

"Yeah," I said.

I heard Roxanne's car door slam.

"I've really got to go. Take care of yourself. You going to your sister's too?"

"I don't know," Donna said. "I don't want him to think he can chase me out of my own house, you know what I'm saying? Marcia says he's just a big control freak. Like my ex-husband. They want to run every part of your life, you know? My ex used to tell me what to wear, what not to wear. That's too short, on and on. It's the same thing as Jeff, when you think about it."

"You're right. Listen, can I call you back?"

"You don't have to. I just wanted you to know Jeff was out. I mean, he's gonna be looking for you. I know him."

"Yeah, well. He knows where to find me. And you too. Listen, I'll call you tomorrow, see if you've heard anything. How you're doing."

"I'd like that," Donna said.

Outside, Roxanne started her car.

"Bye," I said.

"Bye," Donna said, somehow making that single syllable hang in the air.

"Damn," I said, and hurried outside.

"I'll follow you," I told Roxanne.

"Okay," she said, and pulled out and started down the road.

I went to the truck and opened the door, then paused and went back inside the house. By the time I'd grabbed the shells and the rifle and stuck them behind the truck seat, Roxanne's car was out of sight. It wasn't until I was halfway to Albion that I caught up.

The condo was a town house, 22 Harbor Way. There were ten cedar-shingled town houses, lined up like overgrown cabanas. They were identical except for the cars parked out front, which were similarly small and foreign and new. When I backed my old truck up to Roxanne's door, I could almost hear the dead bolts sliding home.

This was on the South Portland side of Portland harbor. Across the water, four or five office towers gleamed above the city's redbrick past. The people who worked in those towers lived in places like this. Their boats were worth more than my house.

I got out and stretched, and Roxanne, who'd gotten ahead of me when we'd gotten into Portland, came out of the front door. She was smiling and pretty and trotted down the walk.

She was happy here. In spite of me.

"Leave it and come in," Roxanne said. "I'll give you the tour."

I followed her inside and onto the carpet. The place was new and white and the carpet was dark green. The condo had a first floor and a second floor and big windows on both floors that looked out on the harbor and the slips and the sailboats, the masts of which bristled like a forest of dead trees.

"It's nice," I said. "Except I'd spend all my time watching the ships go by."

"It's nice at night, too," Roxanne said. "I came down with Kim and looked. The lights of the skyline and everything."

"Yeah. I'll bet it's pretty."

"Well, you'll find out," she said. "Hey, there's Skip."

Roxanne slid the big window open and stepped out onto the deck. The air was cool and smelled of the ocean. The deck was pressure-treated wood. A guy stepping off an enormous sailboat, the biggest on this particular block, saw Roxanne and waved. She waved too, and he started up the dock.

I had a sudden urge to go home.

"He's really nice," Roxanne said.

"You would be, too, if you'd made your fortune smuggling drugs."

"Jack."

We waited as Skip skipped along. He was tall and tanned and blond, wearing khaki shorts, deck shoes, and a T-shirt. When he came up the stairs to the deck, he stuck his aviators on top of his head and held out his hand.

"Skip Hendsbee," he said, handsome as a soap star.

"Jack McMorrow," I said.

"I live next door."

"I heard. Nice place."

"It isn't bad. Mostly it's a place to keep yon vessel. A boatyard with housing."

Skip turned to Roxanne.

"You need some help?" he asked Roxanne.

"I'm sure we wouldn't turn it down," she said. "Would we, Jack?" I smiled.

"Wouldn't think of it," I lied.

So like a smiling clerk in divorce court, Skipper helped us unload the truck. He was cheerful and fairly strong for a guy with looks. In no time at all, the jumbled mess in the truck was a jumbled mess in Roxanne's hall.

"I'll be right back," Skipper said, and he trotted out the door and down the dock to his boat. When he came back, it was with three slippery cold Heinekens. He handed them out, then opened each one with a Swiss Army Knife he kept on his belt. The knife had more utensils than my kitchen. The belt was blue with red sailboats. His T-shirt commemorated a LASER REGATTA.

"Salud," Skipper said, holding up his bottle.

"Cheers," Roxanne said.

I lifted my bottle and smiled and took a long pull. Roxanne wet her lips. Skipper took a sip. I felt as if I'd taken a wrong turn and ended up at a wine-tasting.

"So, Jack," Skip said, turning his looks my way. "Roxanne tells me you're a journalist. Where'd you work, the *New York Times?*"

"Yeah," I said.

"How'd you end up . . . where is it? Prosperity?"

"Just lucky, I guess."

"After Roxanne told me, I had to get out my atlas and look it up. I thought she was kidding me. Prosperity, Maine."

"No, it's a real place," I said.

A lot more real than this, I thought.

"So, you sail?" Skip said, having exhausted the topic of journalism and life in rural Maine in two sentences.

"No, I went out in a Sunfish once when I was a kid and the thing flipped over and the do-jigger on the mast hit me in the head. I still have a scar."

I smiled at him. Roxanne gave me a kick-under-the-table look.

"So," I said, looking at Skip's shirt. "You play computer games?"

He looked at his shirt too. And laughed.

"No, Jack," Skipper said. "A Laser is a kind of sailboat. Small one. I race them sometimes. It's a change of pace from the *Queen Mary* out there."

"Is it forty feet long, your boat?" Roxanne said.

"Actually, it's forty-one feet," he said. "But I've been looking around for something a little bigger."

I looked at Roxanne and grinned. She glared back.

"I have a canoe," I said.

"Hey, that's great," Skipper said. "I know people who use a sixteen-foot Old Town for a dinghy. Put it right up on the deck. You can load that thing right up, too. It's amazing."

"I use a dinghy to get out to my canoe," I said.

Skipper sniffed his beer for a few more minutes and then shook my hand again and went down to polish the brass or something. He was barely out of earshot when Roxanne turned to me.

"What was that all about?" she said.

"What was what all about?"

"Giving him a hard time like that. He's a nice guy, just being neighborly, and you're playing these games. What's the matter with you?"

"Nothing. Where's his wife?"

"He isn't married."

"Where's his girlfriend?"

"He said he just broke up with his lover."

"Why?" I said. "She kept getting between him and the mirror?"

"Jack."

I put my empty bottle down on the counter.

"I don't know. There's just something presumptuous about people like that. It just rubs me the wrong way."

Roxanne stood in the empty kitchen, hands on her hips.

"What do you mean, people like that? Is he supposed to apologize because he's got money? Some people are successful. This is America. They get money for that. They can't help it."

"What does he do? Covers for preppie romance novels?"

"Jack. What are you—jealous?"

"No," I said. "I just don't like guys who carry pictures of themselves in their wallets."

"God almighty. He was being nice. He liked you."

"He thinks I'm not a threat to him. But he hasn't seen me with my makeup on."

"Jack, why are you doing this?"

"Doing what?"

"I don't know. Cutting yourself off. Being so cynical. It's like you'd rather be off wrestling in the gutter someplace with some . . . I don't know, some filthy scumbag."

"I don't think Biff would want to wrestle me. Maybe he'd wrestle with you."

Roxanne whirled away from me and started pulling boxes off the pile.

"There's no need to continue this conversation," she said, striding by me. "I don't know what's wrong. I don't know what's going on with you, I don't know what's going on with your little friend."

"She's not a friend. She's an acquaintance."

"Yeah, right. Who'd like to acquaint you right into the sack. Who's she kidding? You think I can't tell? I could tell by her voice this morning. 'Is Jack there?' Women like that are as transparent as . . . as transparent as their goddamn sleazy underwear."

"Roxanne."

She stopped in front of the sink with her back to me. Her head dropped and then her shoulders started to shake and I heard a sob. I went and put my arm around her shoulder.

"Hey, it's all right," I said. And then I said it again.

"It's not, Jack," Roxanne sobbed. "It's not all right. I'm afraid. I'm afraid I'm going to lose you. We're going to lose us."

"No, we won't. We're okay. It's just . . . I don't know. I've got to figure some things out."

"I'm trying to help you. I thought I was trying to help you."

"You are."

"But I can't stay up there in the woods all my life," Roxanne said, turning to me. "I just can't."

"I don't expect you to."

"And these people. Do you want to live this way? I go to work and I see people and their sad situations, but then I come home and leave it behind. But all this? Shooting at people? It's crazy."

"I didn't invite them."

"But you do, Jack," Roxanne said. "I don't know how, but somehow you do. And I can't live like that, but I love you so much I can't live without you."

She put her hands over her face and sobbed. "I just don't know what to do."

I put my hand on her shoulder.

"I love you. So we'll just do what we're doing," I said. "Some people work on different coasts and do it. We can do this, right? We'll get some dinner in the Old Port and come back and just sit and look at the lights, okay?"

Roxanne shook her head. Dropped her hands and looked at me.

"No, Jack, this is more than that. I need to think. I think I need to be alone."

I took my hand off her shoulder.

"And maybe you do, too," Roxanne said. "Maybe you'd be better off by yourself for a couple of days. It might be good for you."

"Okay," I said. "I'll call you."

"I don't get a phone until Monday."

"I'll call you Monday."

"Okay," she said.

So that was the plan, I guessed. Roxanne would stay and I would go. She would stay at 22 Harbor Way, with Skipper next door and the lights of the big city shining in her window. I'd go home to Prosperity, have a couple of beers, and climb into bed with a good book.

And a loaded gun.

12

—⁓—

Fifty yards in on the dump road, I pulled over and shut off the lights. The Toyota idled quietly as I got out and pulled the seat forward. I slid the Remington out and dug on the floor in the dark for the cartridge box. When I found it, I opened it on the seat and slid five cartridges out. Four for the magazine, one for the chamber. And I was ready.

When in Rome . . .

I put the headlights back on until I reached my road. I turned right, got my bearings, and turned the lights off again, easing my way along in second gear. Two hundred yards from the house, I slowed and put it in first. On the downhill grade, I slipped the truck into neutral and let it roll silently. I turned off the motor. When the truck rolled to a stop, I got out and eased the door closed but didn't latch it. I took the rifle with me.

It was very dark and very quiet but not silent. The cooling motor ticked behind me, and ahead, in the brush along the road, things flitted and rustled. A bat skimmed the road and rose over my head.

I walked slowly, the rifle at my side, pointed at the ground. Every ten steps, I stopped and listened. There were just the woods noises. I kept walking.

If Jeff had come, he wouldn't park the truck in the road this time. He'd probably pull it into the woods, out of sight. Or maybe somebody would drop him off, and he'd wait in the woods for me to pull in. I wondered if I should have left the truck out on the dump road and walked the whole way in. I wondered if he had seen my lights. I walked on. Then waited. Then walked.

The house was dark, as we'd left it. There were no cars or trucks out front. I stopped short of the yard and waited, then backtracked thirty feet and stepped off the road into the woods.

In the woods, it was damp and thick with vines and poison ivy. My boot caught and I tripped and grabbed a branch. The rifle caught too, and I eased it out of the branches almost noiselessly. Then I crouched and peered out of the brush at the house. Nothing moved except the mosquitoes in my face. I counted to fifty in spite of them and then stood slowly and walked ten more feet.

More mosquitoes, homing in on my body heat like missiles. Still I didn't slap. And when I brushed, I did it slowly. I rose slowly, too, and moved to my right again, between the poplars. I held the rifle high as I squeezed my torso between two trunks.

A muzzle pressed against the back of my neck.

"Don't even breathe," a voice said.

An arm reached from behind me and took the rifle out of my hand. I saw a hand, an arm. Even in the dim light, I made out a tattoo. *Semper Fi.*

"Clair?" I said.

"Jack? Damn, I thought this rifle felt familiar."

The muzzle ended its cold kiss. I turned slowly and felt a bead of sweat trickle down my spine like a pinball. Clair was wearing a Red Sox hat, a dark sweater, and a rifle. He lowered the rifle to his side.

"What are you doing out here?" I said.

"Trying to figure out why somebody would park a truck down the road, then go creeping around the woods with a gun."

"You saw me?"

"From the front of my barn. I was looking at the stars. Nice dark night for it. Then I saw lights, then no lights, then just a dome light, on for a second."

"So you thought—"

"I thought your friend was back."

"So you came down to see," I said. "But how did you get behind me?"

Clair smiled.

"Your tax dollars at work," he said.

"I thought I was being pretty quiet."

"Like a foraging grizzly."

"Thanks," I said. "See anybody else in your travels?"

"Nope," Clair said. "But we can circle back, sort of check the perimeter."

"And then check under the beds."

"You can do that while I'm getting a beer from your refrigerator."

"You sure you trust me?" I said.

"Sure," Clair said. "Your beer's always nice and cold."

We made a wide arc, thirty yards back in the woods, ten yards apart. Clair slipped silently through the trees like a wraith. I crunched along as though I were walking on broken glass.

"I think I owe grizzlies an apology," Clair said softly when we emerged in the clearing on the other side of the house.

"I can't help it if I grew up in the city."

We went to the house and stopped and listened. I opened the front door and flicked the lights on. The living room was empty. And the kitchen. And the loft. When I came down the stairs, Clair was coming in from the shed.

"I've got to get my truck," I said.

"I'll grab a couple beers."

"You don't want to come?"

"Can't hold your hand all the time," Clair said.

I pulled the truck up to the house, backed it into the dooryard, and locked it and came in. Clair had poured two Ballantine Ales into tall glasses. He said he'd only drink out of a can if he was out in the field. As in battle, not farmer's.

The Remington went by the door, still loaded. Clair's Mauser went by the door, too.

"You know, this stuff kind of grows on you," he said, reading the Ballantine can.

"I've noticed," I said.

"Don't go off the deep end now that Roxanne's not here to keep you in line."

I tried to think of something funny to say, but couldn't.

"I won't," I said.

I got up and went to the cupboard and took out a box of stoned-wheat crackers and some peppered cheese. The knives were in the block, and I took the biggest one out. While I was up, I got two more beers from the refrigerator. I brought the beer to the table, then went back for the crackers and cheese. On the way by, I punched the answering machine. It hissed, then beeped.

"Jack, this is Donna. I . . . I just felt like talking to you. Please call me. I'm at my house. Bye . . . Oh yeah, the number is 879-0909. Thanks. I mean, thanks for everything."

The voice was soft and either slurred or sexy, or both. Clair looked at me as I sat down.

"This why Roxanne left?"

"No. I wish it were that simple. No, this just made the morning a little rough."

"Aggressive little lady, isn't she?"

"Oh, I don't know. She's just got kind of a crummy life. I talked to her in a nice way, I guess, and she's not used to that."

"Or if she is, she never knows when the weather's gonna change and the guy's gonna start slugging her again," Clair said. "What a shame. She's got a kid, right?"

"Little girl. She's probably seen enough to last a lifetime."

"Problem is, kids grow up with this stuff and they end up repeating it."

"Yeah," I said. "Pretty little kid, too."

"How 'bout the mother?"

"Attractive, I guess."

"She interested in you?" Clair asked.

"Roxanne thinks so. I didn't, but now I'm beginning to wonder."

I emptied my glass and opened the second can. Clair took a swallow and sliced a piece of cheese and put it on a cracker. He had big hands that made the cracker and cheese look a little absurd, as if he were drinking from a bone-china teacup, pinkie extended thusly. He ate the cracker and cheese in one bite.

"Don't screw it up, Jack," he said when he finished chewing.

"What? Roxanne, or the rest of this mess?"

"Either. Both. What made you want to tromp around the woods with a loaded gun?"

"Same thing that made you want to tromp around the woods with a loaded gun."

"But I tromp better than you do," Clair said.

"But it's my fight."

"Which you may not be able to win alone."

"I'm beginning to wonder about that, too. The DA in Kennebec let Jeff out today."

"What was he in for?"

"Coming after Donna. Running into me instead."

"Head-on?" Clair asked.

"Oh, yeah."

"Who was left standing?"

I allowed myself a brief smile.

"I was," I said.

"And now he'll come back after you with a vengeance," Clair said.

"Hence the tromping."

Clair took off his Red Sox hat and ran his hand through his hair. The hand was tanned against the silver.

"Thing about these kinds of fights, any kind of fight, is things have a way of escalating," Clair said. "Going in, you've got to be willing to do whatever it takes to win. There's no halfway."

"You learned that one the hard way."

"Yup. They let us tromp around the jungle, but they didn't let us do much more. All those boys, all those sons and fathers. All dead, and now we're selling them Pepsi. Never should have happened. Never should have started."

"Maybe this never should have happened either," I said.

"Too late now."

"Assuming I'm not going to run."

"I can't see you running."

"Nope," I said. "Not yet."

Clair was quiet for a minute, then got up from the table, leaving his second beer unopened.

"Just as well Roxanne's gone," he said.

"Maybe," I said, and Clair took his rifle and went out the door.

I drank my beer and Clair's too, and then forced myself from the chair. The cans went in the paper bag by the sink. I took that bag and three more full ones from the shed and put them inside the doors, two in front, two in back. Then I took the rifle, still loaded, and climbed the loft stairs. The rifle went on the floor beside the bed. I took off my boots and jeans and slid under the sheet. It was so dark that I could barely see the ceiling over my head, but I could hear the sound of a nighthawk, screeching as it dropped through the sky in a desperate attempt to keep its young and itself alive.

The stuff of life.

In the morning, the rifle and the beer cans were still there. I pulled on my pants and moved the front bags and went outside and the truck was still there too. No bullet holes. No threatening notes. No bombs underneath.

That I could see.

I went back inside and started for the phone to call Roxanne, but then remembered she wouldn't have a phone until Monday. I thought of writing her a letter, but it was Saturday, and a letter wouldn't get there until Monday. I thought of driving back down to see her, and was still thinking of it, when I hit the answering-machine button again.

"Jack, this is Donna. I . . . I just felt like talking to you. Please call me. I'm at my house. Bye . . . Oh yeah, the number is 879-0909. Thanks. I mean, thanks for everything."

I picked up the receiver, then put it back down. Stood there for a moment.

I wanted to know more about Tate. I wanted to know if she'd heard from Jeff. I wanted to know if he was in town, what he was saying.

But if I called, it would be for none of those reasons. It would be because part of me wanted to talk to Donna, to hear that soft, musical voice.

I shook myself and walked away. On the way to the bathroom, I pulled off my T-shirt. In the bathroom, I slid my jeans and boxers off and flipped on the shower. I stood under the water as if to wash something off myself. And it wasn't grime.

It was a day for action. Any action. I did all the dishes and swept all the floors. I bundled the pile of newspapers and stuck them out in the shed. I put the bags of cans out there, too, and then I was hungry for breakfast. The cupboard was pretty bare and so was the refrigerator. I decided to drive to Kennebec to go shopping.

The coupons went in my pocket. The rifle, unloaded, went in the rack.

I drove out onto the dump road, swerving to avoid two crows and a dead porcupine that were along the edge of the road. The porcupine had been hit by a car or truck during the night. The crows were pecking away in their shiny black suits.

It started to drizzle when I was driving through downtown Albion. I slowed for the traffic at the general store, then sped up on the other side of town. In fifteen minutes, the woods and fields and farms dwindled, and then there were subdivisions and then neighborhoods and then the tenements of Kennebec, elbow to elbow, overlooking the rock-lined trough of the river.

Civilization.

I drove across the bridge, past the empty mills and the crumbling concrete pylons that stood along the riverbank, holding up nothing. The river rolled along relentlessly, unmoved by the town's decline. I didn't give it much thought, either. I had other things on my mind.

After the bridge I turned off and headed north along the river, to a fork that led to a tedious stretch of used car lots, pizza shops, and auto-parts stores, none of which had been in business long, nor would they be in business much longer. That strip was to the left. The shopping center with the supermarket was at the end of the strip. I took a right.

The road made a long circle, past a railroad yard and overgrown empty lots. I took one right, then another onto School Street, where there was no school, and onto Peavey, where there likely was no Peavey.

Just a Donna.

The kids weren't playing Wiffle ball, but the yellow bat lay in a puddle in the gutter. The guy had taken the wheels off the motorcycle and left it up on concrete blocks, where it looked dismembered. The green tarp was still draped over the front end of the Camaro like a shroud. And Donna's Chevette was parked in the driveway.

I pulled over to the curb and stopped.

It was a little after nine on a Saturday morning, yet the street was deserted, a silent testimony to television. I got out of the truck and walked to the front door of the building. There were three unpainted steps and a rough two-by-four railing. I stepped to the door, which was new and cheap, and turned the knob, half hoping it would be locked.

It opened and I went inside.

The door opened to a hallway, which was dark and smelled of cat urine. There was a pink plastic cat-litter tray on the floor to the left, but the cat had missed. There was a paper package of cat food, too, but it was in shreds.

I went up the stairs slowly, as if Jeff might be around the corner. He wasn't, though there was a hole in the drywall, waist high and a foot across. Maybe he'd taken his anger out on the building instead of Donna. Just that once.

The window on the second-floor landing had curtains and a broken pane. A plaque propped on the windowsill told people to MAKE A GOOD DAY. There was a doll carriage in the corner. It was missing a wheel, and a dad to fix it.

I waited for a moment but then was afraid that Donna would come out or in and find me standing in her hallway like a pervert. I knocked and heard nothing. I was feeling relieved when the door opened.

"Oh, hi," Donna said, smiling. "You didn't have to come right over."

"I was up this way anyway. And you'd called but I hadn't called back, so . . ."

"Come in. You'll have to excuse the mess, but Adrianna has been over to Marcia's and I decided to, like, go through her stuff and sort it out. I want to move out of here, and I'm not moving with all this stuff."

Actually, there wasn't much of a mess, nor was there much stuff. There were stacks of children's clothing on a metal kitchen table in the front room, which wasn't the kitchen. There were a few stacks on the floor. Donna went to pick them up. She was wearing cutoff denim shorts. Very short. When she bent over, I looked the other way.

"You want coffee?" Donna said, putting the clothes down and turning back to me. She seemed excited, even buoyant.

"Sure," I said.

"It's instant. Jeff smashed the coffeemaker. No loss for him, you know? He only drinks beer and vodka. So, whoosh. Everything on the counter onto the floor. I was making cookies with Adrianna and I had a jar of molasses. Smash. Broken glass and molasses all over the floor. What a mess, you know? I was cleaning for two days."

She was in the kitchen, which was at the rear of the apartment, two rooms from the door. I hesitated, then followed her in. She was kneeling on the counter, reaching down a new jar of coffee. Her feet were bare and the soles of her feet were pale gray.

"When did this happen?"

She jumped down and went to the sink and filled a saucepan with water.

"The molasses?" she said, moving to the stove. "Oh, that must've been a couple of months ago. He was drunk and pretty strung out on coke and he came home after, like, three days straight of partying, and he just started in on me. You this, you that. He didn't hit me or anything that time, but Adrianna was all upset because she'd made this special cookie for a little friend of hers. Jason. And the cookie was on the counter and it got smashed. She was really bummed out. She called Marcia, like she does, and she was, like, 'Jeffrey smashed my cookie for Jason and I can't make another one.' "

"Nice guy, Jeffrey. What did Marcia do?"

"She did what she always does. She was here in, like, five minutes. She took Adrianna home and Jeff was passed out on the bed. I got to clean up."

Donna opened the cupboard above the stove and started to sort through packages.

"Would you like a cookie or something? I mean, I don't really have—"

"No, thanks."

The water started to hiss, and there we were. Donna's hair looked damp, as if she'd just had a shower. She didn't have makeup on and she looked prettier that way, with a spray of freckles across the bridge of her nose. Her shirt was sleeveless like the one she'd worn to court, except it was rose instead of turquoise.

She smiled awkwardly.

"I feel sort of silly, calling you and you come over here like it's this urgent thing or whatever."

"That's okay."

" 'Cause it isn't. I mean, this is gonna sound funny, but I just wanted to talk to you about all this stuff that's going on. You're a reporter and you see this kind of thing, all kinds of things, I suppose. I mean, I just . . . I don't know what I'm trying to say."

"I think I understand," I said.

"Do you? I mean, I thought you could . . . Listen, the water's boiling. I'll get this and we can sit down or whatever. Do you have time? I mean—"

"Sure," I said.

So we took our coffee and went to the living room, which was the room with the table and clothes. There were an old couch and a big chair with a tapestry sort of thing tossed over it. I sat on the couch beside a pile of clothes. Donna moved a stack of clothes and sat in the chair. From the couch, I could see through a door to the bedroom. The bed had a mirrored headboard. I looked away again.

"Jeff got sprung, huh?" I said.

"Yeah, it was really strange. Lenny, the cop I know, he said he couldn't believe it. I mean, this guy is dangerous. You know that. And he's out in, like, four hours. Three hundred bucks. What kind of bail is that for somebody who's threatening to kill people?"

"Not much of one."

"I guess. I mean, this Tate knew he'd tried to punch you out. And this protection order is like nothing to him. Might as well be written on toilet paper."

"Has he been here since he got out?"

"No, but I didn't expect him right away," Donna said.

She sipped her coffee.

"I know this guy and there's, like, a pattern to it. He goes on these binges. It's at the tail end of the binge that he comes after me. It's like he's been working his way up to, you know, whatever it is that's boiling inside him. Since he's been into the coke it's been worse, 'cause he keeps drinking but he doesn't get tired, you know?"

"So he has more energy to come here and beat you up?"

"Or smash the place. In fairness to him, it's more often that he smashes the place."

"Fairness to him?" I said. "Donna, what are you doing with this guy? Normal people don't do this kind of thing. You don't have to put up with this."

"I know. I mean, Marcia's been telling me to get counseling, get away from him. And what it's done to Adrianna."

"How did you end up with him, if you don't mind my asking? And your husband? Why these guys?"

Donna gave a little snort and looked away.

"I don't know. I've thought about that. Part of me can't believe I'm telling you all this, but you're easy to talk to. And you seem to care."

"I do."

"I believe you. So I don't know. This isn't for the paper, is it?"

"No. I'm not working today. Do you work?"

"No. I get support and AFDC. Donnie wouldn't let me work. He said I'd screw around behind his back. Jeff wouldn't take care of Adrianna, so I couldn't work then, either."

"He didn't have a job?"

"Well, sometimes. He used to drive a wrecker, but he kept losing his license. Now he's a junker—when he works at all, I mean."

"Junker?"

"Yeah. He goes around with this buddy of his and picks up old cars and stuff and brings them to Augusta. They melt them down or something. For the metal."

"You could work now?"

"I'm gonna as soon as all this is settled. All this Jeff stuff, I mean. You know where I'd like to work?"

"Where?"

"A greenhouse. You know. Plants and flowers and stuff. I've always loved plants."

I looked around the room. There weren't any.

"Yeah, I know," Donna said.

"Don't tell me. Jeff smashed them."

"Every single one. I'm gonna get some more. Sometime."

Donna crossed her legs and leaned forward.

"You don't know my sister that well, but the two of us—I'm the screw-up, you know? I mean, she was my big sister and she did everything right. We didn't have much. My mother stitched shirts piecework, so we didn't have this la-di-da background. And Marcia goes to college. Gets a scholarship. Marcia marries a guy with a trade. He's a millwright. She's sort of like an accountant, but not really a CPA or whatever it is. Works at home on this computer and everything. Does people's taxes and stuff, and here I am, like, this loser. So I guess I kind of rebelled. I figured, I can't beat her anyway. I'm not gonna try."

"So you got married?"

"I partied a lot. I don't drink much anymore. Once in a while I get into it. When I kind of lose it. So I got pregnant in high school. Married Donnie and it was, like, a disaster right from the start. Donnie looked down on me, you know? I mean, when I was pregnant it was like it was my fault or something. And then he started just cutting me down all the time. Still does. We fight over support for my daughter. Well, it wasn't all the time at first."

"Why'd you stay with him then?"

"Same reason I stayed with Jeff. I figured I could fix it. Make him love me, you know? And I didn't want everybody to know—my mother was alive when I was married to Donnie—I didn't want everybody to know I screwed this one up too."

"Did your mother die recently?"

"Ma died . . . it'll be three years in August."

"So she knew Adrianna?"

"A little. The last few months she was all drugged up, so she didn't know much. My father, he split when I was a baby. Your folks alive?"

"No," I said. "They've been gone twelve, thirteen years."

"Did you like 'em?"

"Very much."

"They liked their son the reporter?"

"Yeah. But my dad died when I was just getting into it. My mother lived longer, so she knew."

"That's good. That she knew, I mean. Brothers and sisters?"

"Nope."

"Were you a rich kid?"

I paused.

"No. My dad studied beetles. In a museum, mostly. Taught in a college in New York."

"Nice guy?"

"Very nice. Quiet. Never said much when I screwed up."

"I can't picture that," Donna said, looking at me closely.

"Yeah, well, I was pretty wild for a time. I worked hard to make up for it later. Worked night and day for ten years."

Donna looked puzzled.

"But he was dead?"

"I thought if I did well enough, somehow he'd know anyway," I said. "Like you not telling your mother, I guess."

"I didn't tell anybody," Donna said. "As long as I didn't do anything about it, it was my secret."

"Like being a prisoner, wasn't it?"

"Yup. But I had Adrianna in there with me. That kept me going."

She leaned forward and I could see that her chest was thin too, with her breastbone tight against her skin, the skin very white on the slope of her breasts.

"Could you excuse me for a second, Jack?" Donna said.

She got up and went toward the kitchen, then took a left. I heard the door close. The bathroom.

I got up and looked around. The only books in sight were for children. There was a rack of movie videotapes by the television. I glanced at the titles, which were mostly Disney, then took a couple of steps into a little hall, almost an alcove.

There was a metal footlocker set on two red milk crates. Propped on top of the footlocker was small piece of plywood. Tacked to the plywood was a piece of paper. The piece of paper was a painting. A watercolor portrait of Adrianna.

It wasn't bad. Odd, but not bad.

The painting was done in a primitive sort of style, sort of flat. But the eyes were deeper and the expression was real and childlike. The whole thing had sort of a faint fuchsia tint.

I looked behind me and listened, then reached behind the board. There were other paintings stacked there. Another Adrianna. One of the living room. One of the street, seen from the living-room window. All of them had the same lavender cast. I was flipping through them again when there was a knock on the door.

Then two more knocks. No Donna. Three more. Still no Donna. I thought for a second, then walked through the room and opened the door.

There was a guy standing there. Light gray cowboy boots and jeans. A cream-colored short-sleeved shirt and a bad blue tie. A phony tan and a nasty scowl.

"Hi," I said.

"Who the hell are you?"

"Who the hell's asking?"

"None of your goddamn business."

"Likewise, I'm sure," I said.

He started to say something, then caught himself. I stood there with my hand on the door.

"Where's Donna?"

"Who wants to know?"

"Her goddamn ex-husband," the guy said. "Now get the bitch."

"You really ought to get something for that misogyny before it spreads. Maybe an ointment or something—"

"What? Listen. I don't know who you are, pal, but tell her to get out of the sack, 'cause I got something important to talk to her about."

"But she already has a vacuum cleaner," I said. I gave him my best grin.

"What the—I don't have time for games. I got business to attend to. Consider yourself lucky."

"If you're leaving, I already do."

He gave me his best threatening look. I smiled.

"Tell Donna to call me. Today, numb nuts. That bitch isn't gonna bleed me dry for one little kid. Tell her to call me."

"No."

"What?"

I shut the door. There was a moment of silence and then the sound of his boots tip-tapping down the stairs.

As I turned away from the door, Donna came into the room. She had makeup on, and when she moved by me, I could smell perfume.

"Who was that?" she said.

"Your ex-husband. I don't think he liked me."

"Donnie doesn't like anybody. Except himself. Did he want me to call him?"

"Yeah, but I wouldn't. He isn't a nice person. What's he do?"

"He sells cars. I guess he's pretty good at it, 'cause he makes good money. Drives this Jeep that sells for, like, thirty thousand bucks."

She went to the front window and knelt on the couch and looked out. "There it goes."

She turned and slid off the couch.

"And he bitches about me buying Adrianna Nikes. Donnie's worse than Jeff in some ways. He's sneakier. And he looks good to somebody who doesn't know him, you know? I used to think that nobody would believe me if I told them what he was really like."

Donna sat down in the chair. She crossed her legs. Her shorts seemed shorter. I stood.

"I didn't know you painted," I said. "I saw them over there. While I was waiting."

Donna blushed.

"I didn't mean to be nosy."

"Oh, no. I mean, that's okay. I just . . . I don't know. It's kind of silly, I guess."

"No, it isn't. They're very nice. The one of Adrianna was very good. You have your own style."

"Yeah, right," Donna said, looking away.

"Have you painted for a long time?"

"No, I mean, I don't know what you mean by long. A few months. I've done lots of them, but most of them are gone."

"Where'd they go?"

"Jeff and Donnie. They hated it. Donnie just sort of made me feel silly, but Jeff used to rip them up when he went nuts."

"Why didn't they like them?"

Donna sniffed.

"Because they were mine," she said. "That's all. It was something that was mine."

"And they didn't want you to have anything that was yours?"

"Nope. But I kept painting. Me and Adrianna would get out our paints and paper. That's how I started, with Adrianna. She had her little paint set. You know the ones with the little squares. We'd share. Coloring, she calls it. We'd watch this guy on TV who has this art show. Mr. Mike. It's for grown-ups, but she—"

Donna caught herself.

"You don't want to hear all this," she said.

"Sure I do. I liked them. They're good. They have this purplish mood to them."

She grinned.

"Oh, God, I can't believe you noticed that."

"Oh?"

"The purple, I mean," Donna said. "I just tried to do what he said on the TV, you know? He mixes the colors and stuff. I didn't have all the fancy paints and stuff, but I'd try to do what he said. So I went along and everything came out kind of purplish, but I figured, hey, what do I know about painting? Then one day we had a bad day and Jeff smacked the TV or something and it went all haywire and so I had to adjust everything again. And I start doing all the buttons and I get it so it looks pretty good and when the show comes on, guess what?"

"What?" I said.

"No purple," Donna said. "It was the television."

She laughed, and it was a pretty girlish little laugh. She even gave her knee a little slap. I grinned and went to sit on the couch. When I did, a stack of clothes tumbled onto the floor. When I moved to pick them up, Donna came over to help. I was crouched on the floor and Donna knelt beside me, very close. When the clothes were picked up, she sat on the couch. I stood again.

"You don't have to do this," I said.

"What?"

She looked up at me, open and vulnerable and childlike.

"This. It's not what you need. It's not what your daughter needs."

Donna didn't say anything.

"You need to stand alone for a while. You don't need somebody else. You need to get rid of these guys. Not need any guy at all."

The anticipation slowly drained from her face.

"I mean it, Donna. I was wrong to come here. I think you're attractive. I feel, I don't know. It's just wrong for you. It's absolutely the worst thing for you. And for me."

Behind the makeup, she sagged.

"Your girlfriend. The woman on the phone. That's a permanent thing, huh?"

"They should all be permanent things," I said. "That's the idea. Mate for life. Like wild geese."

"So what's so great about her? Is she gorgeous or something?"

"Yeah, but that's not really it."

"So what is it?"

"She's honest," I said.

"With you?"

"And with herself. She's brutally honest with herself."

Donna got up from the couch, then stood there in the middle of the room as if she weren't sure where to go. She turned toward the window.

"Oh, God, that old hag is watching me again. Get a life, will ya?" Donna turned back. With tears in her eyes.

"Yeah, well, some of us aren't so lucky, Jack. I see these women and their husbands and they're sending them flowers and having anniversaries and their pictures in the paper and you can just tell by looking at them that they're so together and then I think, 'Why can't I have that?' What's wrong with me? Why should I take it in the face every time I try, you know? Why should I have . . . Why should I have complete shit for luck?"

Her voice cracked.

"But you have to make your luck sometimes," I said gently. "Don't put yourself at the mercy of these people. Don't let anybody get you in that position again. You don't need these people. You don't deserve them. You deserve better, and your daughter deserves better too."

She looked at me. Her face was hard, her eyes shining with tears.

"I thought you might be better, Jack."

"I'm not better," I said. "I'm just different."

She looked at me and the tears spilled from her right eye. At that moment the phone rang, jarring as a fire horn. I grabbed it.

"Yeah."

"Who is this?"

"Shut up," I said.

"Get Donna."

"No."

"Listen. You tell that worthless slut that she's got the IRS on me now. If she thinks she's gonna ruin me, she's wrong. I work hard for what I've got and she isn't gonna take it away. If she doesn't understand that, I'll make her understand. You got that, numb nuts?"

I sighed.

"I hate people like you," I said, and I hung up.

13

—ɱ—

I felt like hell and deserved worse. I sat in the truck for a minute and watched the rain. To be brutally honest with myself, I'd been intrigued by her. Her funny mix of toughness and innocence. Her naïveté and forwardness. It wasn't fair to play games with Donna. It wasn't fair to Roxanne.

God, what had I been thinking?

I turned the key and started the truck. A boy had come out and picked up the bat and crossed the street in front of me. As I waited for him to saunter past, a fancy Ford pickup approached. Marcia was in the driver's seat, Adrianna beside her.

Adrianna waved and smiled. Marcia glared and pointed her finger at me. I nodded and drove away.

I'd let Donna explain this one.

It was almost ten o'clock and I hadn't eaten. Even if I had, eating was better than going back to Prosperity and waiting for Jeff. Besides, I didn't feel like tromping around the perimeter in the rain.

I drove two blocks up and took a right onto the main drag. There was a store with a lunch counter up ahead. I'd stopped there for coffee once and the milk had been sour. What better way to continue this day.

The store was right on the sidewalk, with concrete steps and a steel railing that set it apart from the other old frame houses on the street. I parked by the side of the building, on which someone had spray-painted obscenities. Nobody had tried to paint over them.

I went inside. There was an old man at the counter, and as I sat down, he didn't look up. I waited and finally there was a rustle from the next room, where the videos were lined up on wooden racks. Through the doorway, a small bald man came through the colored tinsel that separated the video room from an alcove with a sign that said ADULTS ONLY! I'd written the guy off as a pervert when he came over and poured me a cup of coffee.

"Milk?" he said.

"No," I said.

The coffee was very hot and very strong and probably acted as life support for the old guy to my right. I was scanning the plastic menu on the wall in front of me for something I could eat when the old man erupted into speech.

"Gimme one of those muffins," he croaked, and the small bald man took an English muffin from a bag and lathered it with melted margarine with a plastic brush. I could see black specks in the margarine. I decided to pass.

But the first cup of coffee wasn't bad. The second came unsolicited. I was halfway through it when a blue uniform settled onto the stool to my left.

"Mr. McMorrow," a voice said.

I turned.

"Officer Lenny," I said.

"How's Donna?"

"What?"

"How's Donna?" Lenny said, turning to me with a half smile. "I saw your truck outside her house."

"Keeping an eye on the place?"

"Trying to. In between the other crap. This morning, I spent twenty minutes getting a bat out of an old lady's kitchen. For this, I went to the academy."

"To protect and to serve," I said.

"That's serve, not servant."

"A fine line."

"That we keep crossing," Lenny said. "But that doesn't answer my question."

"How's Donna?"

"Yeah."

The small bald man banged a cup down in front of Lenny and filled it. I waited as Lenny took a sip and grimaced.

"Good as ever," he said.

"Yup."

"So?"

"Donna's okay," I said. "Considering they won't keep that psycho in jail."

"That stunk. Off the record, I didn't think Tate would do that. She's unpredictable, but the guy is a clear risk."

"That's the idea, I think."

"The thing is, he'll probably come after you first," Lenny said.

"That makes me feel better."

"Thought it would."

He shifted on his stool and his gun belt creaked.

"You did a pretty good job on his mouth. They had to put a bunch of stitches in his lip."

"He would've needed more than stitches if he'd taken me down," I said.

"So you made the first move?"

I shrugged.

"You've got my statement."

"You're not like the reporters we get here," Lenny said between sips.

"That good or bad?"

"I don't know. That was a good article on the plea bargains over there. I'm surprised they printed it in that chickenshit rag."

"I caught them napping," I said.

"So when do they give you the boot?"

"I don't know. They may keep me. I'm a good speller."

"So's a computer with a spell-checker."

"Don't tell them that," I said.

Lenny drank his coffee. The small bald man came over and poured me a third cup. Lenny held his cup out and got a refill, too. The old man was putting ketchup on his English muffin. It looked like blood.

"So you're not doing anything to hurt Donna, are you?" Lenny asked suddenly.

I looked at him. He seemed to want an answer.

"Not that I know of," I said.

" 'Cause I'd hate to see her hurt anymore."

"So shoot her boyfriend."

"I've come close," Lenny said. "Let me tell you."

"You've known her a long time?"

"Ever since she married old pretty boy Donnie there. The first time I got called to her place—and this is off the record—he'd piled all her clothes on the bed and poured gasoline on them. Said he was gonna put a match to the whole mess."

"I thought he was the nonviolent one?"

"He is. I mean, he isn't the type to just beat on somebody, not like Jeff there. Jeff's a raging-bull type, but he'll come right at you. The first time we came to the place for him beating Donna up, I emptied a can of Mace in his face. Had to whack him a couple of times after that to keep him down. Strong goddamn boy."

"I noticed," I said.

"But Donnie, he's a different story. Meaner. Kind who'll hire somebody to burn your house down. He'd find ways to hurt that girl that you couldn't see. Like wrecking her clothes. One time he locked her out in the hall, nothin' on but her underpants. Friggin' January."

"Liked to humiliate her, you mean. She told me he was worse than Jeff in some ways."

"In some ways," Lenny said.

"And you don't want me to be number three?"

He sipped his coffee and looked straight ahead.

"I don't want you to get hurt, for one thing. These boys both play rough. And I don't want her hurt, either."

"You're a little late, aren't you?" I said.

"I do my best with the laws we've got to work with."

"Which don't amount to squat."

"I don't disagree with you there. If it were up to me, both of those guys would be sitting in prison right now. If she were my daughter, they'd have laid a hand on her just once."

"You have a daughter?" I asked.

"Yeah," Lenny said. "Same age. She's got a good job. She teaches special ed in Portland. Decent husband. Nice little baby."

"Donna had to settle for one out of three."

Lenny finished his coffee. The small bald man had vanished, and Lenny left a dollar bill by his mug. He looked at me and I decided I liked him, this grandfather and protector of the law-abiding public.

"But you know what I like about her?" Lenny said, easing himself and his equipment off the stool. "She keeps trying. She keeps that little girl dressed nice. She hasn't given up. So I don't mean to harass you or anything. I just want to ask you not to do anything that'll hurt her. I'd appreciate it."

He gave me a long, knowing look.

"She deserves a break, you know?"

"I know," I said. "She deserves more than that."

So I gave Donna the best break I could think of. I got my groceries and a case of Ballantine and loaded them into the front of the truck. And then I went home.

There was no one on the road near the house, no one under the beds. I hit the answering machine and it told me that David Archambault had called and wanted to buy me a beer. Networking. A woman whose name I didn't catch had called to offer me a credit card through a bank in Delaware.

Roxanne hadn't called at all.

I made a tuna salad sandwich, with Colman's mustard and a chunk of cheese. As I ate I considered having a Ballantine, but then the sun broke out and the day seemed more pure and I decided to take the high ground, which was ice water.

When I'd finished my lunch, I put the dishes in the sink and lathered some Avon Skin So Soft on my hands and arms and face. Then I grabbed my binoculars and headed for the one place that seemed safe.

The woods.

There was a tote road out back that I had used with Clair. I followed it through the second-growth scrub that bordered the yard and then up into the bigger stuff: birch and maples, oaks and beech. The blackflies were thick and hungry, and the Avon Skin So Soft seemed to infuriate them, so that instead of biting, they swarmed around my eyes and mouth. I flicked them away and kept walking.

The tote road ended on top of a long ridge that ran east and west a half mile behind the house. I moved along the ridge for a few hundred yards, picking my way between ash and arborvitae. When I could see the tops of dead trees in the distance to the north, I turned off the ridge and started down.

After fifteen minutes or so, the hardwood thickened with spruce and pine and then the softwood took over. I slipped between the stands, crossed a small stream by walking on a fallen yellow birch. In the silt by the bank, there were raccoon tracks and the single-file tracks of a fox. I kept going, continuing to head downhill, veering only when the blackberry brambles became impassable.

A half mile from the ridge, the softwoods thinned too, and I broke through their last line and looked out on an expanse of swamp. There were marsh grass and cattails, and thick brambles where marsh wrens broke cover and then disappeared. But what brought me here were the trees that stood in the brackish water, acres of them, all tall and silvery and dead.

This had been lowland forest, but at some point the highway had been raised and improved and the stream that flowed through here had been blocked. The water backed up and rose, the trees died, and here I was, Jack McMorrow, famous journalist, in search of the rare pileated woodpecker.

Well, they weren't all that rare. Just elusive, and I'd only had glimpses of the big black-and-white birds. Both times that I'd seen them, they'd been flying into the woods from this end of the swamp. I figured the dead trees were prime nesting sites and this was peak nesting season. The plan was to sit on the edge of the swamp at a point where I could see up and down the open area along the shore. If they came through here, I'd get a quick look. If I was very quiet, maybe a long one.

So I sat on a spruce blowdown and waited, binoculars on my lap. The blackflies converged like crows on a carcass, and remaining reasonably still took all the willpower I could muster. Through the cloud of flies, I saw several marsh wrens and what I took to be several swamp sparrows. Tree and barn swallows swooped by and red-winged blackbirds chirred from the marsh grass. A cedar waxwing swung from the brambles behind me. A flicker called out in the swamp, and for a second I thought it was a pileated.

Close but no cigar.

I waited an hour, sitting on the trunk until my buttocks screamed. There were clubs in New York where people paid a lot of money to have their backsides made to feel like this. To think that in the wilds of Maine I got it for nothing.

So with this bargain in mind, I sat some more. All around me was a sultry murmur. I looked out on the marsh, the flies and birds and bugs. Suddenly the trees reminded me of the masts behind Roxanne's place, which reminded me of Roxanne, whom I'd been thinking about all day but didn't want to admit it.

Why did I throw away the thing that was most precious to me? Why did I hold at arm's length what I wanted more than anything to embrace? Why did I risk doing something that would hurt Roxanne more than anything when hurting her was the last thing I wanted to do? Why did I more and more ride so close to the edge?

Donna didn't deserve to live her life with these domineering pigs. Did Roxanne deserve to live her life with me?

Warning shots in the middle of the night. Maybe they were a warning to her, too.

I sat for a while and came up with no answers. I thought about Donna and her appeal and couldn't find an answer to that one, either. I was still searching when there was a *kuk-kuk-kuk* from the woods to my left. I sat still and waited and there was another *kuk-kuk-kuk* and then a flash of black and white, undulating out of the line of spruces onto the swamp. It was a pileated, a male, and it landed on a trunk fifty feet in front of me and corkscrewed its way down.

I smiled, and just one thought flashed through my mind: If only Roxanne could be with me to see this.

I raised my binoculars to my eyes and watched the big crow-size bird as it worked its way across the swamp. When it disappeared, I got up and made my way through the woods and back home, where the message light was flashing on the machine telepathically.

"I was outside today and this big heron thing flew over and I wanted you with me," Roxanne said. "I'll be at Paul's in Camden at six. I don't want to eat alone."

Camden was forty-five minutes and several light-years from Prosperity. I took a shower and had a Ballantine and was out of the house by four. There was a chance that Roxanne, for the first time in her life, would be early.

But she wasn't. I sat at the bar and had another ale, a Sam Smith's. The bartender who served it looked as if she'd just stepped off Skipper's forty-footer. She was wearing a khaki skirt and a white polo shirt that accentuated her cocoa tan. She was very pretty, but she was not anywhere near as pretty as Roxanne.

"Sail in?" she said, flashing a nice smile and teeth from a catalog.

"No, I drove," I said, smiling back.

"From where?" she said.

"Prosperity."

"Where's that?"

"About twenty-five miles from here."

"Up the coast?" she asked.

"No," I said. "Inland."

"Oh. You mean twenty-five miles away from the coast?" She looked mildly horrified.

"The heart of darkness," I said.

"What?" she said.

"The name's Kurtz. Nice to meet you."

She smiled again, but only at half power this time. A couple came in and sat at the other end of the bar, and the bartender fled in their direction.

The sad state, I thought, of American education.

At five thirty I had my second ale, a Shipyard, delivered promptly but with trepidation. I sipped it and listened to two silver-haired guys talk about the engineering of the new Jaguar versus the engineering of the old. Then they complained about the summer tourist traffic, which made it difficult to get up and down Route 1 no matter which Jaguar you drove.

"So how long are you up?" one fellow asked the other.

"I'm flying back to Philly for a meeting on Friday," the second guy said.

"Duty calls?"

"Have to go kick a little butt."

The second silver-haired guy chuckled to himself. Corporate macho. He noticed me and turned and nodded, and I nodded back but didn't say anything. I wasn't there for them. I was there for one reason, and at five minutes before six, she walked in.

Their silver-haired heads turned.

Roxanne kissed me once on the lips, very quickly, and sat beside me at the bar and held my hand. Very tightly.

I looked at her and squeezed her hand back and beamed. She was wearing a white sleeveless cotton dress with a pale coral sweater over her shoulders. Her shining dark hair was in a French braid, which she knew I liked. She leaned over and kissed me again.

She knew I liked that too.

"We're not very good at this," I said.

"No," Roxanne said. "I needed you. I needed to see you."

"We'll end up meeting at rest areas."

"Where we won't rest."

"And we'll get arrested on morals charges," I said.

"And lose our jobs," she said.

"But I barely have one."

"Oh, yeah," Roxanne said. "Well, then, you'll have to take the fall."

"Only if you fall on top of me."

"That can be arranged," she said.

Roxanne had the house Chablis because it was quicker, and the sooner it was served, the sooner the bartender would go away. I had another ale, and when the maître d' called, "Masterson?," we took our glasses to the table. The table looked out on the harbor; I looked out on Roxanne.

We sat for a minute and beamed at each other some more, but then the waiter came, which forced us to speak. I ordered shrimp cocktail and Roxanne said that would be fine for her too. The waiter went away and we held hands under the table.

"I really had to see you," Roxanne said. "I had no choice. I hope you don't feel like I'm jerking you around."

"Are you kidding?"

"Yes."

"I knew it," I said. "You can't fool an old fooler."

"I wouldn't try."

"So are you coming back?"

Roxanne paused.

"No," she said. "Did you think I would?"

"No," I said. "I just thought I'd ask. This is fine."

"It's nice, isn't it? It's like a date."

"But how do I drive you home?" I said.

"You don't," Roxanne said. "We go parking."

"Your car or mine?"

"Is there a gun in yours?"

"Yeah, but it isn't loaded."

"And you call yourself a man," Roxanne said.

The shrimp came and I ate my three and one of Roxanne's. The sauce was good, but it really didn't matter. I would have dipped them in ketchup to be with her. When I was done, I took Roxanne's hand again.

"So what did you do today?" I asked.

"I unpacked. Got settled in. Went to the supermarket and bought some food. When the sun came out in the afternoon, I went out on the deck and read the newspaper. And I fell asleep in the lounge chair."

"Be careful with the sun."

"The newspaper was over my face. How 'bout you?"

"I didn't read the paper."

"What did you do?"

I thought for a moment. Thought some more.

"Well, this afternoon I went out in the woods. Way back to that swamp that I told you about. I wanted to see a pileated woodpecker and I saw lots of birds and then, finally, after an hour, zoom, this male comes out of the woods and lands right in front of me. They're huge. I mean, for woodpeckers. It was great. I wished you were there."

"I wish I had been," Roxanne said. "We could have found a nice little clearing and communed with nature."

"Without binoculars?"

"Right."

Roxanne smiled. The waiter, a match for the bartender, came over and asked if I wanted another ale. I said yes, I'd have one more. Roxanne said she was all set for wine.

"What did you do this morning?" she asked, smiling and pulling the sweater over her shoulders.

I hesitated. The waiter came back and asked if we wanted to order. I said yes. Roxanne said sure, and I looked at her.

"Broiled salmon," she said. "Baked potato and a spinach salad with vinaigrette dressing."

"The same," I said.

The waiter left. Roxanne waited.

"I went into town," I said. "To get groceries."

"Mr. Domestic."

I smiled. Took a deep breath.

"And I stopped and saw Donna," I said.

Roxanne looked stunned. Her face sagged and the lights went out in her eyes.

"She called again. And I was right over that way. I wanted to know more about Jeff getting out, whether she'd seen him. I know you don't want to hear that, but it's what I did."

Roxanne was silent. The wine in her glass was absolutely still.

"I like her," I said. "I feel sorry for her. And we have something in common. A hundred-and-eighty-pound psycho says he wants both of us dead. She said Tate bailed him for three hundred bucks. He was out in four hours."

Roxanne said nothing. Her fingernails traced tiny circles on the base of her wineglass.

"Did she try to seduce you?" she said quietly, still looking down.

"No," I said. "Not really. She went and put on makeup. If I'd asked her to dinner, she probably would have gone."

"But you didn't know you'd be having dinner with me."

"Yes, I did. If not tonight, tomorrow. If not tomorrow, the day after that. What God has joined, let no man or woman split asunder."

"Jack McMorrow, Bible thumper."

"It's true," I said. "Some things are permanent. We're one of them."

"Did you tell her that?" Roxanne asked.

"More or less. But she didn't really mean any harm. She's just had terrible luck, I think. She's reaching out for something normal."

"Somebody to hold her up."

"I told her that too."

"Did she understand?"

"I think so," I said. "But she's not used to being on her own. These guys never let her be on her own. She never had any independence. No life. Except for her little girl. She's got a very nice little girl."

"Domineering, insecure, threatened men," Roxanne said, fingering the stem of her glass. "They keep women down, under their thumbs, because they fear that they'll lose their power over them. It's everywhere you look. Like an aristocracy losing its grip."

"Everywhere?"

Roxanne smiled.

"Not everywhere," she said.

She sipped her wine. I sipped my ale. We looked at each other. Roxanne kept me pinned with her gaze.

"So you think you'll see Donna again?" she asked.

"I don't know. Maybe in court. I worry about her."

"Why?"

"Because Jeff is nuts. Very violent. Self-destructive. The only good thing is that he isn't devious. Not sneaking around. He'll come after you, but he'll let you see him coming. Then there's her ex-husband. He came while I was there. I opened the door and he let loose."

"On you?"

"On her. Some child-support thing. I was in the way, so I caught some of it. I was talking to one of the cops, real nice guy, Lenny, that's his last name, and he said this other guy, Donnie, is really more dangerous than Jeff."

"That's encouraging."

"Why do women get hooked up with guys like this?" I asked.

"People get hooked up for all the wrong reasons," Roxanne said. "Love is blind and your eyes open later."

"You still like what you see?"

"I love what I see. I've told you that."

"Still?"

"Still."

"What did we do to deserve this?"

"We didn't do anything," Roxanne said. "We were lucky."

"And Donna wasn't."

"But she can change that. And I'd be willing to talk to her. There are all kinds of support groups and counselors."

"That's assuming she can get away from the men in her life."

"Which is assuming a lot?" Roxanne asked.

"It's assuming a real lot."

"What about the man in my life getting away from the men in her life?"

"That may be assuming a lot, too," I said.

So we ate salmon and talked and then went outside and sat in Roxanne's car like high school kids on a date. Roxanne invited me to her place, but I had another date—with Clair at six a.m., bring your own Husqvarna. If I didn't show up, he'd cut alone. If anything happened to him it would be my fault, and I couldn't live with that. Some things took priority over being with Roxanne. Not many, but some.

We said a long good-bye on a dark street in Camden. When a town police cruiser swung by for a second look, we figured it was time to part.

I drove inland smiling to myself, glad that I'd dodged Jeff's fists and Donna's legs and had landed in Roxanne's arms. I made my way on darkened roads, past darkened houses where people slept wrapped in each other's arms. When I turned off the dump road, my house was in darkness too. I took the rifle off the rack, loaded it, and went inside to see if anybody had been eating my porridge.

They weren't in the kitchen. Or the shed. Or in the bathroom or under the bed. There were no messages on the machine. I left it on and went back up to the loft, where I undressed in the dark, put the rifle on the floor, climbed in, and was out cold.

Until the banging started.

I opened my eyes and pitched out of the bed and went down the stairs, bleary and unarmed, to see who was pounding on the door.

It was Clair. He had a rolled-up section of newspaper in his hand.

"What time is it?" I said.

"Five fifteen."

"You said six."

"You've got to see this," Clair said.

"See what?"

He unrolled the *Maine Sunday Telegram*. Held it out to show the front of the state news section, bottom right. His big finger pointed to a small story. Boxed.

"Oh, my God," I said. "Oh, my God."

"And Jack," Clair said. "You've got to look at your truck."

14

I didn't look. I didn't move. I stood there and read and reread the story, hoping it would disappear. It didn't.

The headline said KENNEBEC WOMAN FOUND DEAD. The story said details were sketchy. They did not seem sketchy to me.

> *A Kennebec woman was killed late Saturday night.*
>
> *Police identified the woman as Donna Marchant, 22, of Peavey Street, Kennebec. According to a dispatcher at the Kennebec Police Department, Marchant's body was discovered in her apartment shortly before 10 p.m. by a relative, who then alerted authorities.*
>
> *Police are treating the death as suspicious, according to spokesman Peter Santori. Late Sunday night, the state police mobile crime lab was at the scene. The cause of death was under investigation, police said.*

I stood there in my boxers, the newspaper held out in front of me. My breath came in short pulls. My stomach felt as if it had been sucked inside out.

"I'm sorry, Jack," Clair said.

He put his hand on my shoulder. I felt unsteady.

"I can't believe it. I just talked to her. Yesterday. What day was that? Saturday. That's last night. She died last night. I talked to her in the morning. She was fine. I mean, she was fine. Just standing there. I mean, God. I can't believe this."

"You see your truck?" Clair said.

I shook my head no. I walked over slowly, in my bare feet. Clair walked beside me.

When I'd come home I'd pulled into the yard, then, after scanning the house with the headlights, backed out and backed in again, training the lights on the woods across the road. The truck was where I had left it. I walked to the driver's door and stopped.

Someone had driven a hunting knife through the windshield in front of the steering wheel. Impaled on the knife was a black-and-white cat. Scrawled across the windshield in the cat's blood were two words: DEAD MEAT.

I looked at the cat. Its tongue was sticking out and its eyes were open. Dried blood stained the white fur on its chin. It was wearing a clear plastic flea collar. For a second I thought I'd vomit. Then the feeling passed.

"We've got to call the cops," I said.

"Let's go in," Clair said.

I walked weakly to the door, then looked back at the truck. I still had the newspaper in my hand, and I opened it and there was the story again. It hadn't changed. I hadn't awakened in a sweat. It was all real. Donna was dead.

Clair stood near me as I dialed the number. The Kennebec dispatcher sounded weary, until I identified myself. I could hear voices in the background, and then she covered the receiver and I heard her muffled voice say, "It's McMorrow. Who wants to take it?"

There was a pause. Then a click. Then a guy on the phone.

"This is Detective LaCharelle. Can I help you?"

"This is Jack McMorrow. I just saw the paper. I knew Donna Marchant, and I saw her just yesterday. I think I need to talk to you."

"You're on our list, Mr. McMorrow. We'd like to talk to you, ASAP. Where are you?"

"My house. Prosperity."

"How soon can you get here?"

"Well, ordinarily twenty-five minutes. Half hour. But I've got a problem."

"What's that, Mr. McMorrow?" LaCharelle said.

"Somebody jammed a knife through the windshield of my truck."

"When?"

"Sometime during the night," I said.

"Can somebody drive you in?" LaCharelle said.

"I guess. But it isn't just that."

"What is it, then?"

"There's a cat on the knife too. Dead. A dead cat. And a message in the cat's blood."

"Saying what?" LaCharelle said.

"Dead meat," I said.

"Frig it. We'll come get you. Don't touch the truck."

"I won't."

"Or the cat," he said.

The trooper was there in twenty minutes. A detective in a half hour. It seemed like an eternity.

I sat in the chair by the back window and waited for them. Clair asked if I wanted a drink. I said no. He asked if I wanted coffee or tea, and I said no again.

"Sad business," Clair said, staring out the window at nothing.

"Yeah," I said.

"But don't blame yourself for this."

"How can I not?" I said.

As I sat, my mind raced from one fact to another, one worse than the last. I had picked Donna out. I had plucked her from the passing faces in district court. I had selected her because I wanted a good story. I had wanted something somebody would read. I had wanted the readers of the *Kennebec Observer* to see that story and say, "Jack McMorrow. Who is this guy? Did you read this story about the girl in the courtroom?"

So I had struck, gliding after Donna like an assassin. I had followed her into the parking lot. I had adeptly negotiated my way around her vigilant sister. I had talked Donna out of her reticence.

I was very good at talking people out of their reticence. I was one of the best.

And I had proceeded even though I had liked her. I had written my little story for this little paper, heedless of the consequences. For me, there were no consequences. There was only an eight o'clock deadline. I hadn't looked beyond that. I really hadn't considered the consequences at all.

So Donna, the anonymous victim of two abusive men, had become the not-so-anonymous victim of two abusive men. Or maybe three. Ensnared as she was by these animals, I had held her up for her small, closed world to see: Squirming. Punished. Baring her lacerated belly to strangers.

Great stuff, Archambault at the paper had said.

Oh, yeah. Great stuff.

So now Donna was dead. With her modest dreams. Her little girl. Her paintings. Her purple paintings. Jesus, God almighty. What had I done?

Her daughter was alone now. Her mommy was gone. Because of Jack McMorrow, her mommy was gone. Because of Jack McMorrow, Adrianna would never see her mother again. Never hear her voice. Never snuggle with her in bed. Never sit across from her at a table. Never hold her hand. Never. Never. Never. Never. Round and round in my head it all went.

"Oh, damn," I groaned.

Clair touched me on the shoulder.

"They're here," he said.

The trooper was getting out of her cruiser, which bristled with lights. She had reddish hair that she'd stuffed into a blue Smokey the Bear hat. I pulled on a pair of jeans and a T-shirt and came out of the house with Clair. She looked at me sternly.

"Mr. McMorrow?" she said.

"Yeah," I said.

"I'm going to have to impound this vehicle, sir. And I'd like you to stay here. One of the detectives will be here in a few minutes. They've asked me to ask you not to leave the premises."

"I won't," I said.

The detective's car was like the cruiser, except brown, without the lights. Two middle-aged men got out, one very big, one not so big. Neither looked as though he would take much guff.

They looked at the truck and the cat. The big detective bent down and looked inside the driver's door to where the knife protruded six inches through the glass. He didn't react, didn't say anything except to the trooper.

"Haul it," he said. "Augusta."

The trooper nodded and walked to her car. The short detective was peering at the cat.

"Mr. McMorrow," the big detective said.

"Yeah," I said.

"I'm Detective Kelly. State police. Detective LaCharelle asked me to ask you if you would come into Kennebec with us."

"Sure," I said.

"It'll just be easier. We've got a few people working on this one, and it's easier to bring you to them."

"Fine."

"Somebody will give you a ride back."

"Okay," I said.

The big detective looked at Clair.

"Who are you, sir?" he said.

"Clair Varney."

"Did you know the deceased?"

"No," Clair said.

"Just what he read about her in the paper," I said.

The detective looked at me.

"We're ready when you are, Mr. McMorrow," he said.

"Okay," I said. "Just let me put on some shoes."

I put on a clean polo shirt, too and sat in the backseat. The detectives sat up front. We left Clair with the trooper. As we pulled out, I wished I'd cleaned the beer cans out from under the seat of the truck. We rode in silence, out onto Route 137, west through the farms and woods of Albion. When we rode through Albion village, cars were pulling up to the small white Baptist church. A couple of kids stared at me as we went by.

The detectives talked about gardening and woodchucks they had shot for eating broccoli and cabbage seedlings. One had used his nine-millimeter. The other had used a .22. At night, they rototilled the firing range.

We drove and then they talked about the Red Sox, who they thought were off to a good start.

"You a Sox fan, Mr. McMorrow?" the shorter detective said, looking in the rearview mirror.

"No," I said. "I was raised on the Yankees."

"Child abuse," he said, and smiled.

"We don't mean to ignore you, Mr. McMorrow," Kelly said. "It's just that we don't want to have you answer our questions now and then have to repeat yourself when we get to the PD. So hang loose another ten minutes and I promise you, you won't be ignored."

And I wasn't.

The room was behind the police station, which was at the rear of the Kennebec Municipal Building. The shorter guy opened the door and I went in. There were maps on the walls and a list done in marker that said REQUIREMENTS FOR SHORELAND ZONE.

The murder of Donna Marchant had evicted the planning board.

Two guys in sports jackets got up from their chairs and pulled one out for me. Nobody shook hands. We all sat down.

"Thanks for coming, Mr. McMorrow," a heavy red-faced man said. "I'm LaCharelle. You've met these officers. Kelly and Lister. This is Detective Noel."

A very young, very handsome guy nodded. I nodded back.

"So tell me about your truck," LaCharelle began.

"Somebody stabbed the windshield with a big knife," I said. "The knife had a cat impaled on it."

"Your cat?"

"No," I said.

"Recognize it?" he said.

"No."

"Why would somebody do that?"

"To annoy me, I guess."

"Why would they want to annoy you?" LaCharelle said.

"I don't know. Maybe because I annoyed them."

"Like who?"

I hesitated. All four detectives watched me.

"Donna Marchant's boyfriend. Jeff Tanner. I wrote a story for the *Observer* about her. Didn't use her name, but it was about how she went to court to get a protection order. How the guy had been abusing her. Allegedly. He didn't like it."

"Did he threaten to do something like this?"

"Not specifically. Tried to punch me out, though."

"And what happened?" LaCharelle asked.

I noticed he had broken blood vessels in his nose.

"He got a little hurt," I said.

The handsome detective looked up from his legal pad.

"Who else?" LaCharelle said.

"Donna's ex-husband, maybe."

"Donnie?"

"Yeah."

"How did you know him?"

"He came by while I was there," I said.

"What did he say?" LaCharelle said.

Same tone of voice. No emotion.

"He wanted to talk to Donna. He was mad. Some child-support thing."

"Why would he be mad at you?"

"I don't know," I said. "Maybe because I kicked him out."

"Why'd you do that?" LaCharelle said.

"He was using vulgar language. Toward Donna, I mean. Calling her names. Generally belligerent. Bad attitude."

"When was this?"

It was Kelly talking. I could see LaCharelle lean back and watch.

"Yesterday," I said. "Morning."

"Where?"

"At her apartment."

"What were you doing there?" Kelly asked, an edge creeping into his voice.

"Talking to Donna."

"Were you interviewing her?"

"No. Just talking."

"She invited you over?" Kelly said.

"Not exactly. Well, she did earlier. But I sort of just stopped by."

"On Peavey Street."

"Yeah," I said.

"Had you been there before?"

I hesitated again. Their detective ears practically pricked forward.

"Not inside," I said.

"What's that mean?"

"It means I'd been by the place before. But I didn't go inside."

"But you went inside yesterday?" Kelly asked.

"Yup."

"How long did you stay?"

"I don't know. Fifteen minutes. Maybe a little longer."

"What time was this?"

"Around nine. A little after."

"Are you married, Mr. McMorrow?"

It was Noel. The baton had been passed again.

"No, I'm not."

"Girlfriend?"

"Yeah."

"She live with you?"

"Sometimes."

"She living with you now?" Noel asked.

His face was hard. He didn't look so young.

"Not at the moment."

"So you're single?"

"No. She had to move to Portland. She got a job there. I saw her yesterday. After I saw Donna."

Noel's eyebrows crinkled slightly. Knowingly. He stared at me.

"Did you have sexual relations with Donna Marchant yesterday during your visit?" he asked.

"No," I said.

"So you talked."

"Right."

"About what?"

"About her. Her life. Her situation, I guess you could call it."

"For an article?"

"No. Just to talk. I got to know her a little and I liked her, and I felt like I sort of owed her."

"For what?"

"For talking to me for the first story. It was sort of hard, even though I didn't use her name. You see, she came to district court—"

"We read it, Mr. McMorrow. Very tear-jerking stuff."

It was Lister. He was short and his hair was greasy and he was wearing a navy-blue blazer with dandruff epaulettes.

"So why did you owe her?"

"Because her boyfriend, Tanner, didn't like the story. The fact that she talked to me, I guess. He came after me a couple times. I'm sure it didn't make things easier for her."

"Apparently not," Lister said.

I met his eyes. He met mine back.

"So what was Donna Marchant doing when you left her?" he said.

"I don't know. Just sitting there, I guess. She was waiting for her sister to bring her daughter home. Donna's daughter, I mean."

"Where was she?"

"Staying overnight at Marcia's. She does that a lot."

"So you left?" Lister asked.

"Yeah. As I pulled out, Marcia was pulling in."

"Did you talk to her?"

"No," I said.

I hesitated again. It got their attention, again.

"She doesn't care much for me," I said.

"Why not?" Lister said.

"She thought I'd hurt her sister. Not physically, I mean. Through the publicity."

"Do you think you did?"

It was LaCharelle.

"I don't know," I said. "I didn't intend to. I don't know. I just don't know."

So it went on from there. They wanted to know what I did when I got home and I told them about pileated woodpeckers. They wanted to know where I met Roxanne and I told them about the restaurant in Camden. They wanted to know what I did after the restaurant and I told them about sitting in the car with Roxanne. They wanted to know Roxanne's address and phone number and I gave them her address, but said she'd just moved and I didn't have her phone number yet. They gave me that impassive look that cops get when they think someone is lying, but they didn't say anything.

I asked them when I could have my truck back and they said they didn't know. They offered me a ride home, but I said I'd stay in town and try to rent a car.

I left and walked down the hall to the bathroom. I was sitting in the stall when the door banged open and two sets of police shoes shuffled by and stopped at the urinals.

"I told Joyce a week and we're outta here," a voice said.

"Boyfriend's gonna be a long-timer," said the other.

It was Kelly and Lister.

"You think the reporter was doing her?" Kelly said.

"Who knows? I wouldn't've kicked her out of bed," Lister said.

"That little slider? Don't you have any standards?"

"Yeah, and they get lower all the time. She had all her teeth, right?"

"Haven't seen the ME's report," Kelly said. "When it comes in, I'll check for you. How'd you do up at Moosehead?"

"A couple of salmon. Nice fish," Lister said, and then they flushed almost in unison. The sinks ran and then they shuffled to the door.

"So you would've called this little chippie up for a date, huh?" Kelly said. "You are hard up. You know, you gotta be careful these days. . . ."

The door closed. I sat.

Little chippie. Little slider. Donna deserved better than this.

Outside, the sky was a vivid blue, like a freshly painted bathroom wall. It was a little before nine and still cool, and even the river, roiled and swirling as it passed the empty mills, looked clean and inviting. That the day could begin so beautifully seemed like one more affront to add to Donna's long list.

I stood there for a minute and tried to get my bearings. A pickup rumbled past and the young girl driving looked at me as though I'd just been bailed. Then there was a long stretch with no traffic at all, just the empty river and the empty street.

They may not have been religious in Kennebec, but they took their day of rest seriously.

I walked around the Municipal Building, through a parking lot, and cut through an alley that came out on Main Street by a restaurant, which was closed. I broke into a trot. If Roxanne were to be awakened at nine on a Sunday morning with this news, I wanted it to be me on the phone, not a state police detective.

So I went up Main Street, past stores that were closed and dark. In front of a florist's shop, someone had broken an ornamental tree during the night, snapping it off three feet from the base. They had left an empty twelve-pack of Bud as compensation. Fair trade.

I went up two blocks before I spotted a pay phone, in the brick entryway to a bank. The phone book had been yanked off the chain, but the phone worked. I dialed directory assistance on the chance that Roxanne's phone had been put in early. The woman on the phone looked. It hadn't. I cursed.

For a minute, I just stood there. A skinny bearded guy trudged by with a grocery bag of empty bottles and stared at me. I'd seen him in court, had watched him plead to indecent exposure. He nodded, and I nodded back. We were simpatico. And I needed a ride home.

I had turned down the cops' offer of a ride. I figured I'd have to rent a car anyway, wherever it was in Kennebec that you did that. If the phone book had been there, I would have looked it up. Instead, I called the police department and said I was new in town and needed to rent a car cheap. The dispatcher asked if I needed it that day and I said yes, which was no lie. She gave me a number to call, which I did. The place was a Gulf station out toward the interstate. I walked.

The rental was a brown Olds Omega with 113,000 miles on the odometer and almost as many cigarette butts on the floor. I took it for a week and the guy at the service station said it probably would run that long. If it didn't, he had a tow truck. He gave me his home number.

I rattled across town, feeling anonymous but not anonymous enough. When I pulled around the corner onto Peavey Street, I could see that every kid within ten blocks was gathered in front of Donna's building. They were riding their bikes in the street in tight circles, then returning to the knot of children like pigeons fluttering back to roost. The bunch of kids was between two police cruisers, one state, one Kennebec. There were two unmarked cars and a state police van in the driveway. The dooryard was blocked with yellow police-line tape.

I was fourth in line in the caravan of oglers. I drove by and stopped.

The kids were giddy, the way children get when they're confronted by a tragedy that is not their own. I stood behind them as they wheeled back and forth.

"I heard the little kid found her," a boy in a Raiders baseball caps was saying. "She musta, like, freaked. You remember her. That little kid who used to watch us out the window? She had this funny name, like Madrianna or—"

"Adrianna," I said. "What's funny about that?"

He turned and looked at me.

"It's a pretty name," I said.

His buddies turned and looked at me too, their caps turned around backward.

"Right?" I said.

"Whatever you say," the first kid said, then wheeled off down the street.

The other kids were quiet after that, watching the door. The police radios rasped in the cruisers. An old couple stopped across the street and stared.

"What's going on?" the old man called over to me. I didn't answer.

"Some lady got killed," one of the boys called back.

"It's the goddamn welfare," the old guy said. "Lets these people sit around and drink and smoke dope and kill each other. We'll probably have to pay for her goddamn funeral."

I had turned to go when someone called my name.

"Jack. Hey, Jack."

It was Archambault, getting out of a beat-up green Toyota sedan. He had a reporter's notebook in his hand and he slammed the door and loped over to me.

"Hey, I can't believe I found you here," Archambault said. "I've been trying you all morning at home. I was headed out there. You're gonna find, like, ninety-three messages on your machine."

"Saying what?" I said, still walking toward my car.

"Saying I need to talk to you. Man, Albert called me this morning. It was, like, six o'clock. I'm going, 'What the hell?' He says, 'There's been a murder.' I say, 'Where?' He says, 'Right here in town.' They found the body last night and we didn't even know about it. Not that we could have done anything even if we'd been here. Except it would have been nice to get a shot of the body coming out on the stretcher."

I looked at him.

"Nice," I said, still walking.

"Yeah, I couldn't believe it was the same girl you'd talked to in court there. I didn't know that until one of the cops told me. I went out and got a *Telegram* and I was reading it at the doughnut shop and one of the cops came in and he was like, 'You know who that was, don't you?' I said, 'Donna something.' He said, 'That's the one who took her shirt off in court. The one your new guy wrote about.' "

"She didn't take it off," I said. "She just lifted it up to show her stomach."

"Right," Archambault said.

We were at the car. I opened the door.

"Hey, I thought you had a truck," Archambault said.

"It's . . . broken down," I said.

"Oh. Well, listen. Let's go get a cup of coffee. I've got to write this, and I figured I'd do the girl as a sidebar. You know, what she was like. Her problems with her boyfriends. Interview the family and all that."

"Go to it."

"Yeah, so we can go and have coffee and talk about her. I mean, all I know is what I read in your story. So I need to know what she was really like, what her life was like. She had a kid, right?"

"I don't think so," I said, still holding the door open.

"Didn't your story say that? She had a little girl or something. Yeah. It was a girl, and I remember that the kid would call for help when her mom and the boyfriend started slugging it out."

"No, I mean I don't think I want to talk about it."

Archambault looked puzzled.

"What do you mean? You want to meet a little later?"

"No," I said. "I don't want to talk about it at all."

"You're shitting me," he said.

"Nope."

Archambault stood there, notebook still in his hand.

"Well, why not? This is a great story. Girl goes to court for a protection order 'cause her boyfriend is beating on her and, like, three days later, she gets it. I mean, this is great stuff."

"I suppose," I said.

"And you knew her, right? You can tell me more about her, what she was like when she went to court. Did she want to talk about it, or did you have to persuade her? Was she really afraid of this guy? I mean, did she predict that this scumbag was gonna off her one of these days? And the little rug rat. How's she gonna feel about this? That's got to be pretty traumatic, having your mother killed."

"Got to be," I said.

I let the door fall closed.

"So what's the problem?" Archambault said.

I thought for a moment.

"Off the record, she's not a rug rat," I said. "She's a little girl. And it isn't 'pretty traumatic' to lose your mother like this. It's devastating and tragic. A woman dying like this is sad and tragic, too. And Donna wasn't a girl, she was a woman. And it is a good story, but I don't want to be a part of it. Any more than I already am."

I opened the door again. Archambault looked stunned. A couple of the bicycle kids rode by and eyed us curiously.

"Off the record?" Archambault said. "Then what are you saying on the record?"

"Nothing."

"Nothing?"

"*Nada. Rien.* No comment."

"You're stiffing me?" he asked.

"I guess so."

"Jack, I thought you'd help me out. All this *New York Times* stuff. Goddamn, what would you do if you were me?"

"The same thing you're doing."

"So I don't get it, McMorrow," Archambault said.

"I guess I'm just not you anymore," I said.

I got in the car and pulled the door shut. Archambault was standing there in the street, his notebook hanging at his side. His eyes were narrowed and he was staring at me, a burning cold stare. The cub reporter had claws.

"Something's screwy here, McMorrow," he said. "Were you poking her or something?"

I started the motor. It coughed and the belts squealed.

"People around here have dirty minds," I said.

"Maybe the cops will talk about you, McMorrow," Archambault said.

"Tell 'em I said hello."

I put the Olds in drive and drove.

But to where? I drove through Kennebec, past a big stone Catholic church where Mass was getting out and gray-haired people were crossing the street. I almost stopped and went in, but inched along in the church traffic instead. It was as if stopping would mean I would have to confront what I had done. And I didn't want to do that yet.

So I drove, south along the Kennebec River, past the dignified old homes, the trailers—some hopeful, some desperate—the flimsy little businesses that sucked each breath as if they were on life support. I followed the river to Augusta and swung east on Route 3, heading in the general direction of Prosperity and home. But I passed the sign for Prosperity and continued east, then cut off on a side road and wound my way south. The roads were narrow and potholed and led to lost little villages whose reasons for existence were indecipherable.

I was trying to elude something, outrun myself on these twisting paths through the woods. Finally, I couldn't run anymore, and somewhere past the village of Jefferson I let the car clatter to a halt on the gravel shoulder. There was nobody around, just woods and the road and the bugs and birds, and I shut off the motor and sat there and grieved for Donna Marchant and for her daughter, and maybe even for myself. I sat there for a long time, with the trapped blackflies buzzing against the inside of the car windows, and then I wiped my unshaven face with my hand and rubbed my eyes, where tears had dried and left salt.

That left one, and only one, next step, which was to go back and finish what I'd started.

15

—∿—

Roxanne called at 11:13 p.m. on the digital clock. She said she'd been watching the news. A small part of the news had been about Donna. She'd gone next door to Skip's to use the phone.

"Jack, I'm so sorry," she said. "I could have come up. I went shopping and then I was cleaning this place when I should have been there for you."

"I'm okay," I said. "There really isn't anything you could do."

"Well, I am sorry. I'm very sorry. I'm sorry for her. I'm sorry for you."

"Thanks."

"I'll come right now if you want me to."

"That's silly. I'm going to bed. You've got to get up and go to work tomorrow. Some of us need to make a living."

"What are you going to do?" Roxanne asked softly.

"I don't know. Have another beer. That's my long-range plan."

"Have you talked to the police?"

"They talked to me."

"Do they think her boyfriend did it?"

"I don't know," I said. "They didn't tell me. I think a couple of them would like to think I did it."

"My God."

"But that's only their little pipe dream."

"I hope so," Roxanne said. "So do you think it was the boyfriend? It had to be, right?"

"We'll find out," I said.

There was a long silence.

"What do you mean, we?" Roxanne said.

I paused.

"We. All of us. Us guys. Opposite of they."

"I don't think you meant that, Jack."

"Why's that?"

"Jack, you can't beat on yourself for this. And you can't think that you can do something the police can't. Not with this."

"So I just go on and find my next victim?" I said. "Business as usual?"

"If that's what you consider your business."

"I can't do that. I've got to finish this."

"The police will finish it for you," Roxanne said, urgency creeping into her voice.

"And what if they don't? What if they can't? What if they can't get a conviction? What if they can't make an arrest?"

"Then you'll have to accept that."

"I can't," I said. "I started this. I'm part of it. I may be the one who got her killed."

"You have to let it be, Jack. You have to."

"Can't do it."

"Goddamn it, Jack McMorrow. Just do it. I do it. I do it every day. I spend every day scratching the surface of this mess. I can't save the whole world. And it's only because I can accept that that I can have any hope of saving my little piece of it. I can help fifty people a little. Or burn up for one kid, one family."

"But you're more rational than me. More disciplined. You were raised by those scientists."

"They were research biologists," Roxanne said. "Your dad studied bugs. It's the same."

"Then how did we turn out so different?"

"We're not different," she said. "You just don't know when to quit."

"Yes I do. And in this case, it's not time yet."

"I'll be up this week," Roxanne said.

"Stay down there."

"Nope."

"I don't want you here right now," I said.

"You can't always get what you want," she said.

"But you get what you need? Thank you, Mick."

"Jack. I don't want anything to happen to you."

"Likewise, I'm sure."

"Jack. Be serious."

"Roxanne," I said. "I am serious. I've never, ever been more serious."

"I'm afraid you're going to get hurt this time. Your luck's going to run out."

"Like Donna's? She had to be in court that day. She had to be the only interesting case on the docket. She had to be nice enough to talk to me. She had to—"

"Jack, stop it. It's part of your job. Think of all the people you've helped over the years. What are you going to do? Just quit? Report nothing so that nobody will get hurt? It goes with the territory. You know that."

I thought for a moment.

"One time in New York, I interviewed this gang kid. This was years ago, when gangs were just starting to take off. Wouldn't be news at all today. So I talk to this kid and about a week later they find him in a playground with a bullet in the back of his head. Nice kid. Very charming. Very handsome."

I paused.

"And you know why they killed him?"

Roxanne didn't answer.

"Because they thought I was a cop. Somebody saw him talking to me and they thought I was a cop and he was a rat."

"So what did you do?"

"I took a day off."

"And then what?"

"I came back, and when the cops arrested two kids for killing him, I wrote about that."

"So get back on the horse this time too, Jack," Roxanne said.

"Yup."

"You have to."

"I know. I will. But this time nobody was mistaking me for a cop."

"Jack."

"I know."

"I love you," Roxanne said.

"Thanks. I'll call you tomorrow. Take care of yourself. Take good care of yourself."

"You do the same."

"Always do," I said. "Goes with the job."

"Jack," she said, but I hung up the phone.

I didn't sleep well that night. I had dreams of Donna and Roxanne and they were talking and they knew each other. And then Donna was trying to kiss me and Roxanne was watching and I was immobile, like a bug in amber, unable to cry out or resist.

And then I woke up. At quarter of three. Four thirty. Six fifteen.

"Hey, Bones. Out of the sack. Day's half shot."

I peered up at the ceiling.

"I've gotta get you outta bed too?" Clair said. "Need a goddamn servant in this place, but then you'd both sleep like goddamn woodchucks in January. They could hear you snoring at the Knox store."

The layers peeled away. The dreams. Donna. Donna dead.

"It's Monday," I called, pulling myself to the edge of the bed. "Were we supposed to cut Monday?"

"We are now. You got other plans?"

I couldn't think of any. I couldn't think of anything.

"Then let's go. Haul your skinny city-slicker butt out of that bed and put some clothes on. The truck's running."

So I did. Then I groggily descended the loft stairs.

Clair handed me my boots.

"Let's go. I've got coffee in the truck. Mary made lunch. There's trees waiting."

I pulled on my boots, brushed my teeth, and picked up my rifle. My saw and gas and oil went in the back of the big Ford. The rifle went in the rack. Right under Clair's.

"Varmint hunting?" I asked, sitting back in the seat.

"You never know when they're gonna pop up," Clair said.

So that's how Clair accomplished what Roxanne hadn't. Distracted me from Donna. Kept my hands busy and my mind idle. We cut all morning, loading the trailer over and over and hauling it out to the tote road with Clair's tractor. We ate at ten, sitting on a log and wolfing down tuna and cheese on big thick slices of Mary's homemade whole wheat. Clair didn't mention Donna, and I didn't either. We listened to the birds. Talked about deer and the Red Sox. Clair said he hoped his grandkids would be Red Sox fans, even though they wouldn't be raised in New England.

And when the talk and work didn't distract, the blackflies did.

The morning passed quickly, in the rasp of saws, the fountains of fleshy wood chips. We cut oak and beech and stacked it in four-foot lengths in the yard. The stack got bigger as I worked faster to keep the demons at bay. Finally, at midafternoon, I pushed too hard and hung up an oak that was a foot in diameter. When I tried to free it, cutting at head level, the tree sagged and clamped the saw blade in the cut, hard and fast. I shut off the motor. Cursed the tree. The saw. The bugs. The woods.

And myself. Loudest of all.

Clair appeared behind me.

"You're too emotional," he said quietly.

"To cut wood?"

"Yup. And to do what I think you're going to do."

"Which is?"

"Get involved in this thing with this girl."

"Hard not to get emotional about a woman getting killed," I said.

"There's a time for emotions, and this isn't one of them. If you're going to push it."

"I am," I said.

"Then get ahold of yourself. No emotion. Just intellect and execution. Emotion gets in the way of both."

"That what you told your Marines?"

"Yessir," Clair said, reaching up and tugging at my dangling saw.

"Did it work?"

"Increased the odds."

"Of what?"

"Accomplishing your objective. Coming home alive."

I waved blackflies away from my face.

"But this isn't Vietnam," I said.

Clair fiddled with his chain saw.

"You've got one casualty already," he said.

"Maybe more?"

"Why not? Whoever it is has killed one person. After that, it gets easier. What's one more?"

It was still in the woods. The air had stopped moving.

"So what's your advice?"

"Go slow," Clair said.

"And?"

"Identify your objective. Know what you want to accomplish before you go running off."

"I want to see that whoever killed Donna gets caught," I said.

"So do a lot of other people," Clair said.

"Their motivation is different."

"That's what I'm afraid of," he said.

Clair reached for the pull cord on his saw.

"But if you get in over your head, you tell me. It isn't easy to fight a war alone."

I nodded.

"Stand back now," he said, starting his saw and stepping up to the overhanging limb. "When this thing comes loose, you don't want to be in the way."

"I never am," I murmured, the words drowned out by the roar of the Husqvarna. "Goes with the job."

We finished at three, with no more talk. I was hot and sweaty and smelled like chain-saw exhaust. When I got home, I peeled off my socks and jeans and T-shirt and got in the shower. The rifle leaned against the sink, went with me when I went upstairs to get dressed. When I came back down, I paused. I felt as if I'd forgotten something. It was Monday. Court was Tuesday. I didn't write for the paper today.

The paper.

I was dressed and in the car in under a minute. Parked in front of the Knox General Store in seven.

It was the lead of the paper, six columns across the top of page one. There was a photo of Donna's building, with an arrow pointing to her front window. Inset into the copy was a head shot of Donna that could have come from her high school yearbook. She wasn't as thin. Her blonde hair was done in long wavy curls. Even the eyes were different: big and wide, as I knew them, but more hopeful.

Sitting behind the wheel, I started to read the story.

"That son of a bitch," I said.

Archambault had the basics up high. Donna had been found by her sister, Marcia Dickey of Kennebec. Police weren't releasing the cause of death, the position of the body, or any other information that might hamper their investigation. They wouldn't say whether they had any suspects.

That out of the way, Archambault had keyed on Donna as a past victim of an allegedly abusive boyfriend. He'd backed that up by noting her court appearance, and had quoted from the statement Donna had given when she had gone in for her protection order.

> *He punched me and shoved me and this was in front of my daughter, which I don't think is right. And then he knocked me down and jumped on me and hurt my wrist and when I ended up on top of him, he bit me on the stomach to get me off of him and it broke the skin. I don't think this is proper for my daughter to see, her mother bitten on the stomach and being assaulted and screamed at. He also was very drunk and on drugs.*

Archambault quoted a state police spokesman as declining to comment on whether Jeffrey Tanner was considered a suspect in the slaying.

And then there was this kicker.

> *Marchant was recently featured in an Observer Fourth District Court report by Jack McMorrow, a part-time reporter recently hired by the newspaper. McMorrow reported on Marchant's appearance in court last week, when the Kennebec woman, according to police, removed her shirt in the courtroom to show alleged bite marks on her abdomen.*
>
> *Sources close to the investigation said McMorrow continued to associate with Marchant after the story was published. One source said police questioned McMorrow Sunday about the slaying. Police declined to say whether McMorrow could shed any light on the circumstances leading to the murder, nor did they say whether it is believed that the newspaper story led to Marchant's death.*
>
> *McMorrow, contacted at the murder scene Sunday, declined comment, saying, "I don't want to be a part of it any more than I already am."*

That little bastard. That little son of a bitch. That little weaselly son of a bitch.

I scanned the story for anything libelous. There wasn't anything flagrant, just a lot of little things, all pushing toward the legal limit.

"Nor did they say whether it is believed that the newspaper story led to Marchant's death."

It was the oldest trick in the world. Insert a statement in a story by bringing it up yourself and having it denied. Nor did they say whether McMorrow is a suspected serial killer from Mississippi. Or was recently released from a New York State penitentiary, where he served nine years for second-degree murder for the killing of his third wife.

And using my off-the-record comment? Well, I should have known better. Archambault never agreed that my statements would be off the record. Even if he had, it would be my word against his. Tough luck, McMorrow. Next time keep your mouth shut.

I tossed the paper on the seat. Picked it up and tossed it down again. That little bastard. This was his revenge. A story that, solely by implication, left the impression that, while I wasn't a suspect, I was entangled in this murder somehow. At best, my story had caused it.

Worst of all, it wasn't far from the truth.

What I had feared was now public fact. What I had been haunted by in the dark of night was now broadcast to the public in broad daylight.

That little bastard.

I drove back home, feeling as if I should slide lower in my seat. Had Clair read this before he roused me? Did he come get me because he didn't want me to read it? Was he trying to tell me that he was still with me, that he was still on my side?

If so, that made two of us.

When I got back, the answering machine was blinking. I grabbed it, hoping it was Roxanne, but it was Albert, sounding gruff, asking me to call him back. The second call was from a young woman who eagerly identified herself as Janet McCall of Channel 3 News in Bangor. She asked me to call back too.

I didn't.

But I did call Albert. Charlene answered in the newsroom, turning cold when she realized it was me. She said Albert was in a meeting, but she was sure he'd want to talk to me.

I waited. He did.

"McMorrow," Albert said.

"Albert," I said.

"I thought I told you I didn't want stories about my reporters."

"You did. But I guess you didn't tell your other reporters."

"What the hell's going on?"

"I don't know. I wrote about a woman who was being abused," I said. "Now she's a woman who was murdered. It's a common progression."

"Fine, but how'd you get mixed up in it? Cops questioning you and all that. What the hell kind of representation is that for this newspaper?"

"I knew her, briefly. I saw her the day she was killed. In the morning. Briefly. The cops are talking to anybody who might know anything about it, you know? If she'd seen the milkman, they'd be talking to him, too."

"And by the sounds of it, I know what she'd be doing with the milkman," Albert said.

"Now, that's not true. She'd been with two men in six years. It wasn't her fault they were both slime."

"The story only talked about one. Two, counting you."

"So talk to the reporter."

"But you were in there pretty prominently."

"Talk to your reporter about that, too," I said.

"Well, I don't think we'll be able to use you anymore, McMorrow," Albert said.

"Why not?"

"I don't see how you can report on the courts when you're in the cases."

"I'm not in the cases. I had information about a woman who was killed. I called the cops. I mean, come on. I went to them. The only reason I knew her was because I was doing my job. Covering the court the way it should be covered."

Albert paused.

"But do you think your story got her killed?"

It was my turn to pause. I wondered if Albert had been talking to his lawyer.

"I have no way of knowing that," I said. "I just know there's no reason to bump me off this beat."

"I'm talking about bumping you entirely."

"I know that too."

He hesitated.

"All right, but we'll take it day by day," Albert said.

"You and me both," I said.

He didn't say anything.

The rest of the afternoon I took hour by hour. I left the answering machine on and sat on the back deck with the rifle and a six-pack of Ballantine. After each can of ale, I went in and called directory assistance to see if Roxanne's phone had been installed. It hadn't. Not at four, or five, or six. By eight the bugs were out, and I stayed out with them. Later, the stars came out and I stayed out with them too, wondering where Donna was, whether she was anywhere, whether my parents were out there somewhere too. And then I fell asleep under the stars, numbed by the ale, stretched out on a chaise lounge with a chamois shirt wrapped around me. I awoke at four, chilled and damp with dew, staring up at a starless cloudy sky. I staggered inside and saw the red light blinking in the dark. I hit it.

"Jack, it's me. It's eleven thirty. Where are you? They didn't put in the phone. I'm calling from a friend's. I'm going home and . . . and I just want you to know that I love you and I'm worried about you. I'll call you from work tomorrow. Baby, I'm praying that you're okay."

Roxanne was praying for me. Things were getting serious.

16

—∿—

The courthouse smoking area was packed Tuesday morning. I walked through, in the doors, stopped at the middle of the room, and looked around.

"McMorrow," a voice boomed.

I turned around. So did anybody who had read Monday's paper. I was a walking, breathing literacy test.

It was Tate, standing in the door of her outer office.

"Come here," she said.

"As long as you ask so nicely," I said.

Tate turned and went into her inner sanctum. I followed. The secretary looked at me as though I were Charles Manson. Then looked away.

I walked in, and Tate was already sitting behind her desk.

"Close the door," she said.

"When did you drop out of finishing school? Never heard of the word *please*?"

"Just close it."

I pushed the door shut. Took three steps to the desk and picked up the framed photograph of the fat orange-and-white cat.

"How's Fluffy? Those diet pills working?"

"Put it down."

Tate said it like it was the last warning before shoot to kill. I gave the cat a long, assessing look and put the picture back on the desk.

"I can't believe you're here. I can only think that it's in your capacity as witness to felonies and associate of known criminals."

"Makes it sound like I hang around with mobsters."

"Maybe you did, for all I know. It hasn't taken you long to seek out the lowlifes around here."

"Oh, yeah? Like who?"

"Jeff Tanner. Donna Marchant. That illustrious gentleman who didn't like his plea bargain."

"You think Donna was a lowlife?"

"Her life speaks for itself. She may have been cute, but she was a loser."

"Does that make you a winner?" I said.

"Yup."

"In the small-pond Olympics, you mean."

Tate gave me a look.

"You don't know who you're dealing with, do you?"

"Yeah, I do. Fluffy's mommy."

"You don't get wise with me, McMorrow. Not here."

"You want to meet later for a drink? We could talk."

Tate put her hand down on the desk, hard. Her fingers were splayed, her nails dark pink and blunt.

"No, McMorrow, we'll talk now. We're going to talk about how it's totally inappropriate for you to be working in this courtroom."

"Funny, people say the same thing about you."

"But they have no say."

"You have no say," I said. "The paper could hire Jack the Ripper as a reporter if it wanted to."

"But it wouldn't. Because I'd be all over my friend Albert. And I'm gonna be all over him about you."

"Why? Because I said your cat was chubby?"

"Because you don't get it, McMorrow. There's a pecking order here, and you don't get it. You're not learning. And you're a suspect in a murder. Or maybe the cause of one. Maybe if you hadn't shown up here, Donna Marchant would still be alive."

Tate smiled. She had very large teeth and red fleshy gums.

"And maybe if you had shown just the least bit of sympathy for Donna Marchant, she'd be alive," I said. "If you hadn't let her psycho boyfriend out for three hundred bucks. If you hadn't treated her like dirt every time she walked in here."

There was a rumble in the lobby.

"I've got to get into the courtroom," Tate said, getting up.

"Some justice to miscarry?"

"You just don't get it, McMorrow. I'm going to have to teach you."

"Too late," I said.

Tate stood close to me, so close I could smell her perfume, see the pores in her nose.

"You know what they call a reporter without a paper?" she asked, suddenly smiling.

"No, what?"

She leaned closer, and I could smell her coffee breath.

"A gelding," Tate said. "See you in court."

I was the last one in before the bailiff closed the door. I sat in the fourth row back, on the left. The guy to my right was in his fifties, going on eighty-five. He was small and withered by alcohol and had urinated in his pants. The rest of the crowd was comparatively upstanding, at least at first glance.

The first hour was the plea parade. Hats in hand, they walked up and had their audience with the judge, while Tate herself meted out the sentences. It was like watching them hand out diplomas at a high school graduation, and I was starting to droop when my friend from probation sat down.

"How's the news business?" he whispered.

"Peachy," I said.

"You've sure got this town stirred up."

"I've had help," I said.

We sat and watched, and then a name was called and a guy came in wearing an orange jail jumpsuit. He was big and rangy and had salt-and-pepper hair pulled back in a ponytail. A young muscle-bound deputy stayed a step behind him.

"Alphonse Danny Leaman," the probation guy said. "Criminal extraordinaire. He just got out, like, three weeks ago. In for drugs. Fairly big cocaine dealer down in Waterville at one time. But Alphonse is just a little too crazy. He always gets caught."

"Three weeks out and he's already heading back?"

"Got drunk, which he isn't supposed to do, in a bar where he isn't supposed to go. They got him driving, which he isn't supposed to do, and they found him with a pocketful of Quaaludes and all this other stuff. Schedule Z drugs. He tried to punch out the cop who stopped him. Some twenty-year-old kid who couldn't weigh a hundred and forty pounds. Look at this guy. This guy is dangerous."

He shook his head.

"So he'll be going back inside?"

"Most likely. Can you believe that? Three weeks and back in, to bleed more money out of the taxpayers. Yes, it's a wonderful system."

The probation guy got up. Alphonse's court-appointed lawyer looked afraid of his client but still managed to squeak out a not-guilty plea. The deputy led Alphonse out, like a pit bull on a chain. I wouldn't want to meet him in a dark alley, but for today's lead, he would do just fine.

So I had the top to the story; all I had to do was write it.

I sat there until almost four o'clock, catching Tate's glares and returning them with smiles. When court adjourned, I followed her into the lobby and started to ask about Alphonse and what she would be recommending for a sentence.

"No comment, McMorrow," Tate said, and walked into her office and shut the door.

"So be that way," I said, and walked across the lobby to the clerk's window. A young woman approached and stood in front of me without speaking.

"Alphonse Leaman. I need all his convictions and arrests. Anything you've got in that computer. I'm Jack—"

"I know who you are," the woman said, turning to a keyboard. She punched the name and the screen filled up. Then she hit print and three pages oozed from a laser printer at her elbow.

"Thanks," I said as she tossed the pages on the counter in front of me.

The word was still hanging there as she turned her back and walked away.

"So be that way," I said. Everyone else was.

At the *Observer* office, I was shunned like a wayward Amish. When I walked into the newsroom, heads sank to the keyboards as if in prayer. I walked down the aisle to the news desk, and only my kindred spirit Catherine Plante looked up.

And then she looked back down.

I paused and kept walking. Archambault's light was on but he wasn't at his desk, which probably was a good thing. With Tate on my ass, I didn't need an assault charge. Or disorderly conduct. Or one single parking ticket.

So I kept walking. Albert was on the phone, looking grim. I went out into the hallway to find Charlene and ask her if they had a file on Alphonse. I was standing there when she came out of the restroom. Charlene started.

"Hi, Charlene," I said.

She turned and started down the hall.

"I need a file. Alphonse Leaman. I need it right away."

Charlene turned abruptly and came back. She walked past me and into the morgue. I heard file doors clang, then Charlene was back. She handed me a manila folder, holding it out at arm's length as if it were an envelope full of excrement.

"Fast service," I said, taking the folder. "And no small talk to bog things down."

"I don't have anything to say. Except we didn't expect to see you here again after what happened to that little girl."

"She wasn't so little."

"Well, I think it's a shame," Charlene said coldly, finally looking me in the eye. "I wonder how you can live with yourself."

"Same way I always have," I said.

"You must have lost your conscience a long time ago."

"It's my conscience that keeps me going."

"Well, I don't see how you can just wash your hands of this whole thing so easily."

"They're not washed, and there's nothing easy about it," I said. "Unless maybe if you're watching from the sidelines."

Charlene arched an eyebrow and walked away. I stood there for a moment and then walked through the door and down the stairs, ready to file this story by phone. And then I turned around.

I sat at a computer terminal in the middle of the newsroom, surrounded by silence. For approximately an hour, I wrote my story about Alphonse Leaman and his inability to obey the law, even for short periods of time. I called the arresting officer and he called me back, perhaps out of curiosity. But he answered my questions and I finished my story two hours before deadline.

I assigned it to the city desk with two taps of the keys, then stood up and stuffed my notebook back in my pocket.

"At ease, everyone," I said. "You are now free to continue your conversations."

They looked up but still didn't talk.

So from a silent newsroom, I could go home to a silent house. Instead, I drove the Oldsmobile around Kennebec. I stopped and bought a tuna sandwich and ate it in an empty parking lot on Main Street. Then I headed up the street to the north end, dodging kids and circling the dreary treeless blocks until I spotted a police cruiser. I followed it back out to Main and down to Dunkin' Donuts, where I pulled in beside it.

Lenny got out.

"I thought that looked like you," he said, closing his door. "How long they gonna keep your truck?"

"Until they find next of kin for the cat," I said.

We went in and sat on stools, around the corner toward the back. Lenny said he liked to sit there because he could see everybody come in. Many he knew. Some he wanted to see. Some he'd recently arrested and didn't want behind his back.

"So you sure it's okay to be seen with me?" I said.

"After fourteen years, I decide who I'll be seen with."

"Those state guys made me feel like a criminal."

"That's their job," Lenny said.

The waitress came. She called Lenny "honey." He had coffee with cream and two sugars. I had mine black and she didn't call me anything.

"So you're still going to talk to me?" I said when she'd bustled off.

"Why not?"

"After Donna?"

"I don't think you meant to hurt her," Lenny said. "What happened to her could have happened next week or next month. It was a long time building."

"So why do those guys act like I'm a suspect?"

"They just have to try to rattle you. See if you're lying about anything."

"What'd they decide?"

"I don't know. They didn't tell me."

"What do you think?" I said.

Lenny sipped his coffee and watched the windows.

"I haven't changed my opinion. People are such bad liars, you know? It keeps up my faith in humanity sometimes. That people, even scumbags, find it so hard to not tell the truth."

I fingered my cup, which was dirty.

"So do they think it was Jeff?" I said. "Off the record. Way off."

"He's number one. Donnie is number two. You were supposed to be number three, but I think you're off the list. If anything, you're a long, long shot."

"Thanks."

"Don't mention it."

I hesitated.

"How'd she die?" I said.

Lenny sipped. Absently fingered the squelch knob on his radio.

"I haven't heard, really. Talk is that she had some bumps and bruises but nothing that looked like it'd kill her outright. I heard the sister walked in and found her. She grabbed the little girl and dialed 911. They were waiting outside when the first unit got there."

"The sister loves that little girl. So Adrianna was there for it. Was Donna strangled or something?"

"Not that I've heard, but I haven't heard much. They're keeping it pretty hush-hush."

"They pick Jeff up yet?"

"Yup. He says he was there earlier, but she was fine when he left. He went drinking, back to The Mansion on Elm Street. He says she must've drunk herself into a coma or something. I guess she was hitting the whiskey pretty good that night."

I thought of Donna, with her makeup and perfume, legs tucked up on the couch. If I had kissed her, would she be alive? If I had held her, would she still be here? Had the right thing been the wrong thing?

"She was nice," I said.

"Yeah. She tried hard," Lenny said. "She just didn't get many good cards dealt to her."

"The ex? Donnie?"

"He says he hadn't seen her in weeks. Both released after questioning. One of 'em probably lying. I'd say Mr. Tanner's in deep shit."

"So what do the detectives do now?" I asked.

"Keep asking questions. That's all they really can do. Go around and talk to people. Keep people talking because lying doesn't get any easier. Especially if more pieces of the puzzle get uncovered, you know? You uncover a piece here, a piece there, and hope somebody's story unravels. This'll probably be one of those."

"So the idea is to keep them talking?"

"Confront them with new facts. Keep them talking and hope somebody cracks."

The waitress came back with the pot. Lenny put his hand over his mug. I did the same and she smiled and went down the row, like a gardener watering seedlings.

"So it isn't like television," I said.

"Nothing like television," Lenny said.

"No murderer caught before the hour is up."

"Sometimes no murderer at all. You know how many unsolved murders there are in this state?"

"How many?" I asked.

"I don't know, but a lot. Twenty. Thirty. They've got three or four fresh homicides going down in Portland right now. And it isn't like they have five hundred people to throw at these things. This isn't New York."

"So they keep telling me."

Lenny shifted on his stool, pulled at the radio on his belt.

"No, if something doesn't shake loose in this one in the next . . . I don't know, week or so, then it's gonna be a long haul."

"Before justice is served?" I said.

"If it is. No guarantees. You know that."

"Yeah, I do," I said. "Now more than ever."

17

—ᴍ—

There were three messages when I got back to Prosperity, all from Roxanne. Two were from the Human Services office in Portland. One was from her apartment, complete with phone number.

I called it. Roxanne answered. There was a man's voice in the background.

"Who's that?" I said.

"Oh, that's just Skip."

"Just Skip? What's he doing?"

"Talking. To Miranda."

"Who's Miranda?"

"From the office. She lives in Scarborough. She stopped on the way home. You'd like her. She's talking boats with Skip. I guess she and her husband have a boat. Not as big as Skip's."

"Things are tough all over," I said.

"Yeah, well, I tried to call you last night."

"I was outside."

"At eleven thirty?"

"There were good stars."

"How are you doing?" Roxanne asked.

"Okay, I guess. Trying to adjust to my new role as long-shot murder suspect."

"Jack, the police were here today. I mean, not here. At the office. Two of them."

I wasn't surprised.

"I hope that wasn't a problem for you."

"Oh, no. We've got cops coming in and out of the office all the time. They're just not usually there to talk about us."

"And that's what they wanted? To talk about us?"

"Where we went. When we got there. When we left. They were very nice. One was kind of short and the other guy was sort of dim. But very good-looking."

"Got him where he is today," I said. "Token handsome homicide cop."

There was a burst of laughter in the background.

"Are we on speakerphone? That wasn't that funny."

"What? No. That's just Skip and Miranda. He's really very funny."

"I'm glad for him. Is the name of his boat really the *Queen Mary*?"

"Yeah. It's a long story."

"You can tell me when you come home."

"Home there or home here?" Roxanne asked.

"Home is here, isn't it?"

"Home is wherever we're together," she said, more quietly. "Do you need me soon?"

"I need you right now."

"How 'bout tomorrow after work?"

"No," I said. "Not yet."

"When?"

"I don't know."

"When will you know?"

"I don't know that, either."

"I'm here for you, you know," Roxanne said.

"And that's where I want you to stay for me."

"While you do what?"

"I'm not sure," I said.

"I'm not sure you're telling me everything."

"I don't know much. That's the problem."

"Please take care of yourself, Jack."

"No problem there," I said. "All kinds of people are looking out for me."

In the background, I could hear Skip laugh.

I woke up alone, with a phoebe calling from somewhere out behind the house. There were two of them, and they were nesting behind the shed. I fought off the urge to spend the morning watching them and made myself shower and shave.

Look out for any activity that requires new clothes, Thoreau wrote. I was becoming wary of any activity that required me to bathe.

I put on jeans and a faded blue T-shirt. Outside it was foggy, bordering on drizzle, so I put on a denim jacket, also faded. I chose work boots over sneakers, because where I was going they didn't jog or play tennis. I put the rifle in the trunk for the same reason.

The first stop was the Albion General Store. I bought an *Observer* and a *Boston Globe*, a day old. On page one of the *Observer*, below the fold, was a short David Archambault story that quoted police as saying there were no new leads in the Donna Marchant case. It said they still hadn't released the cause of death, that funeral services would be private. The rest of the story was background. It was short and didn't jump, even with all the padding.

Archambault hadn't come up with anything new. Maybe the story the day before had been beginner's luck.

I turned to page two and there was Alphonse, his troubles laid out for the world to see. He'd be celebrity of the week on the cell block. No need to thank me.

I skimmed the story and it appeared to have been left intact, probably because of short-staffing on the *Observer* rewrite desk. I opened the *Globe* sports, and it was mostly Red Sox stuff. But then, even Yankee fans had to know their enemy. And I had to know mine.

I drove to Kennebec in the fog, hitting the wiper switch every few seconds. As I drove, I thought of Clair saying I was too emotional for this sort of battle. I also thought of his offer of help, and wondered if it meant more than just being there to tell me to calm down and stay home. I wondered if I'd have to take him up on it.

So as I approached Kennebec, dreary in the mist, I took a deep breath. No emotion. Cool and calm. Figure out what you want to accomplish and the best way to accomplish it. I wanted to know who killed Donna. I wanted to help make sure that person, Jeff or Donnie or whoever it was, hanged for it. I had to help finish this business I had started.

Cool and calm.

I crossed the bridge just after a flight of ghoulish black cormorants, winging their way upstream. Off the bridge, I took a right and headed up along the brooding river. Five minutes later, I slowed as I passed Donna's building. Around the next corner, halfway up the block, I pulled over and stopped.

In my early days in New York, a homicide detective named Heneghan had explained his craft to me. He'd said the body was ground zero. The investigation moved out from there in widening circles, as if the dead guy had been dropped in a pool of water. Sometimes he had been. Sometimes he had just been shot and left on the street.

First you did the scene, Heneghan had said. Then you did the canvass. Heneghan was doing a canvass in SoHo when we first met. I was doing a canvass too, for a *Times* story on a sort of famous artist fellow who'd been stabbed to death in his loft.

"It isn't that I have anything against you personally," Heneghan had said. "It's just that you keep getting in the way."

I'd told him it was my job to be in the way.

It still was.

I got out of the car and started up the block, walking slowly and eyeing the houses, which were small and looked dirty, as if the rain were water from a muddy stream.

At the corner, there was a store. The sign said JANE'S MARKET AND REDEMPTION. I wondered if, when you went in for a six-pack, Jane also would save your soul.

But I didn't stop. I walked up the block, eyeing Donna's building from a distance. It was three stories, with five electrical entrances on the wall by the driveway. That meant five apartments, though I doubted they were all occupied. The building, like the neighborhood and the town, had seen better days.

I walked by the front door, where the yellow police tape hung in the rain like a macabre garland. On the other side of the house, the dismantled motorcycle was still propped on a concrete block. The Camaro was still there, but Donna's Chevette was gone. Probably rooming with my truck.

A couple of houses up, I turned and looked back. I'd have to check Donna's building and the building to its left, which was separated by the width of the driveway. Looking up, I remembered Donna's comment about the "old hag" who had been watching her. I scanned the windows of the building next door and wondered which one was the old woman's.

"Get a life," Donna had said. Maybe the old woman had seen somebody take one.

I went in the side door of Donna's building, up the landing by the driveway. These were the back stairs, dark and narrow and smelling of cats and cigarettes and stale beer. I stumbled over a bag of empty bottles but caught it before they spilled out. After the clinking there was silence, then the faint sound of a television. I kept going up the stairs, stopping every few steps to listen. At the second floor, I stopped and put my ear to Donna's back door. The only sound was my breathing. I kept going.

At the third floor, there was a dirty window with a sill sprinkled with dead flies. There were work boots lined up on the floor. Big ones. I stood for a moment and listened. This was the television. Somebody with big boots was watching cartoons. I steeled myself and knocked.

I had to knock three times. Finally there was a clatter and a shuffle and the door was yanked open with a shudder. I smelled bacon and marijuana.

"What?" the guy said.

"Hi, I'm Jack McMorrow. I'm a reporter, and I'm talking to people about what happened downstairs. Got a sec?"

"What?" the guy said again.

He was young and big, maybe six two and early twenties, with a roll of flab that showed under his T-shirt. His eyes were half shut, vaguely focused and rimmed with pink.

The guy was very stoned.

"Did I wake you?" I said politely.

"What? No. I just got home from work. Well, I didn't just get home. I get home at seven. I was eating, is all."

"Where do you work?"

"Arno Baking."

"What do you do there?"

"I . . . I run the mixer. You know, put in the ingredients. Last night I did raisin bread. You know, you got to mix in all the raisins?"

"And what's your name?"

"Ron," he said.

"I suppose the police have talked to you."

"Oh, yeah. The police. They came, I think it was a couple of times. Hey, I'm sorry about the girl. I mean, she was real nice. The kid was real nice too. I told the officers that. Too bad, really. No need for this around here."

Ron paused. He was wearing jeans and white socks. The white socks were dirty. Inside the apartment, cartoon characters were talking in nasal voices.

"So I don't mean to make you go through this again, but can you tell me anything about the girl or that night or whatever?"

"The night it happened?" he said.

No, the night before Christmas, I thought.

"Right," I said.

"I was working."

"So you didn't hear anything unusual or anything?"

"Umm, I don't know. I wasn't here."

"Before you left?"

"Well, I don't know. She and him were fighting, but that's not unusual."

"Him?"

"Her boyfriend. I don't know. It's none of my business, but they was always fighting. I didn't say nothing or anything. I mean, what am I gonna say? Hey, man, be nice to each other?"

"What could you hear?"

"Oh, yelling and stuff. I could hear her yelling and him yelling. And her crying. Sometimes she just yelled, but this time she was crying, too."

"So what did you do?"

"What did I do?" Ron said.

"Yeah. Did you call the cops?"

"No. I mean, it wasn't like they were killing each other or anything."

I looked at him. He didn't catch himself.

"So what did you do?"

"I turned it up."

"Turned what up?"

"The TV. I was watching it, so I turned it up."

"What were you watching?"

"This movie. But I couldn't hear it."

"Because of the crying?"

"Yeah, but then it stopped."

"The crying?"

"Yeah."

"So what did you do?"

"I turned it back down."

"What?" I said.

"The TV," Ron said. "I didn't want to, like, bother anybody."

"What time did it stop?"

"What?"

"The crying."

"Oh," Ron said. "I don't know. Before I went to work."

"What time's that?"

"I have to be there for ten forty."

"And it stopped before that?"

"Yeah, 'cause I turned the TV back down."

"Right. So did you hear anything after things quieted down?" I asked.

"Where?"

"In Donna's apartment."

"Oh, no. Not really. I mean, I don't remember much. The kid rattling around, maybe. She was up, like, too late for her age, you know? When I was little, we had to be in bed by seven thirty. That little girl, she's up when I go to work. I'm getting in my car, she's, like, up in the window waving to me. I'm, like, what are you doing up? Go to bed. You gotta grow. Kids don't grow if they don't get enough rest. They end up little and skinny. Rest is important for a kid, you know. I mean, their cells are dividing all the time."

I paused. Ron's eyes narrowed even more. Whatever he was smoking, it was still kicking in.

"So you heard noise down there after the crying and yelling stopped?"

"Yeah."

"Did you hear anybody leave?"

"Umm, not that I remember."

"But the yelling and crying stopped and then there were just normal noises?"

"Yeah. I mean, I don't know what you mean by normal. There were, I think, dishes and stuff. Those kind of noises. You know that little kid can do the dishes? I thought that was pretty good. Little kid like that. Maybe her mother helps her with the knives, the sharp ones. Yeah, she probably helped her with the knives. She seemed nice. They both did. The kid still living there? No, I suppose she'd have to leave, right? She go with the sister?"

"I think so," I said. "So you told the police all this?"

"Yeah. I guess. I mean, I told somebody about them fighting all the time and everything. But, umm, I thought you were the police?"

"No, I'm a reporter."

Ron stood and thought about that for a moment, the new information struggling to break through the buzzing in his head.

"Oh," he said. "Well, then, aren't you supposed to be, like, writing all this stuff down?"

I tapped the side of my head.

"Photographic," I said.

In widening circles, the canvass continued.

There was no answer on the first floor, and when I cupped my hands over my face and looked in a window, I could see wrappers and paper, strewn on the counter and the kitchen floor as if a hungry animal had ransacked the place. I knocked on the back door again, but there was no sound inside.

The animal was out.

I opened the back door and stepped out onto the steps. A Kennebec cruiser pulled up out front, passing the end of the driveway. When it was out of sight, I walked down the steps and across the driveway to the next building. There was a door out back. Beside it, black metal mailboxes were hung like dubious trophies of tenancy, proof that people paid money to live there. I opened the door and went in.

A white cat slipped out, brushing my legs. I stepped on broken glass and it stuck in the wooden floor, next to a plastic trash can from which the cat had been feeding. I went up the stairs so I wouldn't be blamed for the mess.

This building was bigger than Donna's, with doors at each landing that led to some sort of central hallway. I let myself into the hallway on the third floor and stopped and listened in the dim light. I could hear music, country-western. A baby crying. I could smell coffee and, more faintly, bacon. I walked down the hallway as though I were sneaking into somebody's bedroom at night. At the end of the hallway, there was a beat-up stroller. I wondered who had hauled it up all those stairs. I knocked to find out.

The door popped open. A young woman, childishly young, looked at me suspiciously. She was heavy, like a kid who ate potato chips instead of playing sports. There was a chubby kid in her arms, a fat-cheeked baby boy with a dirty face. The kid was holding a bottle.

Probably taking after his daddy.

"Yeah?" the woman said, her hand ready on the doorknob.

"I'm Jack McMorrow. I was wondering if I could ask you—"

"I already talked to you guys. So if you don't mind, I got things I gotta do. Like change dirty—"

"I'm not a cop."

"What are you, then?"

"A reporter."

"Christ," the woman said, and slammed the door shut.

This wasn't going to take as long as I thought.

I knocked one more time, but the woman didn't answer. As I waited, I could hear the baby screech inside. No comment. I walked down the hall and found another door that looked like an entrance to an apartment. I knocked and waited. Knocked and waited some more. Finally, I turned the knob slowly and eased the door open. The room was big and dingy and empty.

There was a TV cable dangling from the wall, a crushed Budweiser can in the middle of the floor. I walked in and saw that the adjacent room was empty too, the wall-to-wall carpet the same filthy green. I stepped into that room and it was hot and stuffy. There were faded stickers on the window—Big Bird, Oscar, Spider-Man. I looked out at Donna's building, her front right window one floor down. The window where she had stood in tears. I let myself out and went downstairs.

The second-floor hallway was identical but with a faint, foreign odor. Soap.

I walked down the hall and counted three doors. I tapped on one and waited. Tapped again. There was no sound, so I turned the knob and pulled. And stared into a closet, with a broom and a mop and bucket. Recently used.

As I closed the closet door, another door opened behind me.

"Can I help you?" a woman's voice said.

I turned and grinned.

"Looking for the apartments," I said.

"Oh?" the woman said.

She was in her early sixties, short and stocky, wearing blue sweatpants and a gray sweatshirt. Perhaps I'd interrupted her television workout.

"Yeah," I said, moving toward her. "I'm Jack McMorrow. I'm from the *Observer*, and I'm talking to people in the building about what happened—"

"Didn't see nothin'," the woman said. "Didn't hear nothin'. Just know what I read in the newspaper. And I don't want to be in it."

The door clicked closed.

I stood there like somebody who'd been turned down for a dance. The Jack McMorrow charm; it hadn't faded a bit.

The hallway was quiet. I could hear the country-western music from upstairs, the little boy still crying. I wondered if the woman in sweatpants was old enough to be considered a hag. I pictured Donna as she had said it, that the old hag was watching her. She had been looking across, not up or down. The woman in sweats was on the wrong side of the hall, but this apartment was empty.

I started for the stairs, then turned back. There were two doors past the closet, six feet apart, one with a lock, one without. I knocked on the one with a lock and waited. Nothing. I stepped over to the door without a lock and tapped on that too. Still nothing. I turned the knob. It was dark inside. An umbrella and a pair of old white sneakers. Another door, with light showing through the jamb.

I left the outer door open and moved forward. Hesitated, my arm up, then knocked. Two taps. Two more. I waited and listened. Still waited. Then I heard a toilet flush somewhere inside. I knocked again. There were footsteps, then a rush of light as the door opened.

I blinked. A very short old woman peered out.

"May I help you?" she said.

Her accent was very French.

"I hope so," I said. "My name is Jack McMorrow."

The door did not slam shut.

18

I sat on a faded blue wing chair with pink-and-white crocheted things on the arms. She sat on the couch, which was also blue and also had the pink-and-white crocheted things on the arms. Even the television, an old console, was draped with a crocheted strip, like a small, narrow afghan.

She had asked to see identification, so I'd given her my driver's license, my *Times* ID, even my card from the New York Public Library. She peered at each of them, then peered up at me.

"Okay, okay," she said finally, and invited me to take a seat.

"This place is a mess. I'm sorry," the woman said. "I didn't expect company."

The room was small and scoured.

"Sorry not to give you any warning."

"That's okay. Hey, you can't go around sending out invitations, right? Huh? You gotta write your stories. I saw the one about that poor little missy over there. You didn't put her name in there, but I read that, I knew right away. The sister and all that? I said, 'That's her.' Oh, her sister was there a lot. Good thing for that little girl, huh?"

She was short but square, her hair done in a tight perm, makeup all in place. Her feet barely touched the floor from her position on the couch, and she was wearing stockings with light gray soft leather shoes and beige slacks. Her hands were folded on her lap.

Only a distraught young woman could call her a hag.

"So you knew Donna?" I asked.

"Oh, did I know her? Well, yes. I knew her. I've lived here for eleven years. I know a lot of them. I see them move in. I see them move out. I see them have their boyfriends, their babies, eh? That little girl, she has one long row to hoe, I'll tell you."

"Because of the boyfriend?"

"Oh, yeah, some boyfriend. I could hear them, you know. In the summer, with the windows open? Eh, Christ. I hear them when they're all, you know, lovey-dovey. I turn on the television. I don't need to hear all that huffing and puffing, a woman my age. But it didn't last long. Then they were fighting most of the time. I call the police and they come and things are quiet, then one night later, two nights later, he's drunk again and he's screaming at her, hitting her. I call the police again. I don't give my name. I just say, 'Fifteen Peavey. He's hitting her again.' And I hang up."

"This went on a lot?" I asked.

"Oh, yeah. He was a drinker, this guy. I had a brother was a drinker. Nicest guy until he got the liquor in him. Then the fights. Eh, bucksaw, he'd come home all cut up. Jekyll and what's his name there."

"Hyde."

"Right. This guy, her boyfriend there, he'd be drinking, oh, he had a temper. And you know the worst of it?"

"What?"

"That poor little girl, the baby. She'd have to listen to all that and then the sister would come and take her. Sister should've just kept her, I always said."

"Who did you say that to?" I asked.

"To myself. I don't get involved in other people's problems. I worked in the cotton mill for thirty-eight years. Spinning room. Eh, those girls would talk and talk about everybody else's problems. Give all this free advice. You tell him this. You tell him that. Just liked to keep things stirred up. Like a soap, huh? Better than TV, you know. I say, people's joys are their own. Their problems are their own. Stay out of other people's business."

"Good philosophy."

"Sure it is."

"So you'd call the police but you wouldn't talk to Donna."

"No. What am I gonna do for her, you know? Say 'Get rid of that bum'? She knows that. She had that sister there. She hated that boyfriend. She must've told her."

I thought for a moment.

"So did you call the police that night?"

"No, I did not. And you know why?"

"Why?"

"Because I was watching my program and I had it turned up, 'cause of the baby upstairs, he was crying and crying. Then I turn the program off and I can hear her crying, the girl, I mean, and I'm not calling because it wasn't so bad. It was bad, but it wasn't so bad yet, you know? When I turned up the television, I mean. Then I turned my program off and I could hear that it was getting bad, him drunk and not supposed to be there from what I understand. And then I'm sitting in the window and then I see him leaving out the side door and walking off through the alley, the rat. Good place for him, eh? So I can see Donna, I call her 'missy,' and she's drinking and crying and the little girl is up and then the sister pulls up in that big truck thing she drives."

"So it was all set."

"I thought so," she said.

"What time was this?"

"Well, my program was almost over, so it was before nine. I watch that *National Geographic*, you know? The places they go, it's unbelievable."

"So Marcia came before nine?"

"Marcia?"

"The sister. Her name's Marcia."

"Yeah, she came. So I said, everything's all set. He's gone. She's there. The sister. She's coming and going."

"Yeah," I said. "I guess she's the one who found her. When she was dead, I mean."

"Now isn't that a pity. 'Cause she took care of that little girl."

"Which one?"

"The sister, I mean," the woman said. "And, of course, the little girl, she was like another mother to that little one. So it was good she got her out of there."

"Out?"

"Oh, yeah. She took her home. I saw them leaving. The little girl, she has this bunny thing. I think it's a bunny. Maybe it's a puppy, eh? But she came out with that, in her little nightie. Such a cute little thing. Awful thing for her to go through. But you know, maybe it's better this way. She's young enough, the little one, maybe she'll come through it. Sometimes these little ones, they're tougher than you think, eh?"

"Yes, they are sometimes. What time did they go?"

"Oh, I don't know. They was coming and going. The sister came once and then she left, okay. And then she comes again and got the little girl and then she came back again."

"Without the girl?" I asked.

"Oh, yeah. Well, it was after ten o'clock. That little one, she must've been asleep, don't you think? Hey, but let me tell you. I see these kids running the streets all hours. When I was a little girl, you didn't leave the house after supper. You had work to do, help Mama with the dishes. The washings. These kids got too much time on their hands. Devil's workshop, eh?"

"So Marcia left her home at her house. Marcia's, I mean. The last time?"

"The little girl? Yeah, I guess. Good thing, too. 'Cause two minutes after that the police come screaming down the street. I said to myself, 'God almighty, you'd think somebody'd been murdered.' Well, how was I to know? I felt bad, eh? 'Cause that's what already happened."

"And how long before that did Marcia come and get the little girl?"

"How long? Eh, I don't sit here with a clock in front of me. I don't know. *Geographic* was over. And then I watched the news for an hour. I don't know why. People killing each other now. They'll be killing each other long after I'm gone. So what do I care?"

I smiled.

"So I watched that news there, so that's ten. It was a while after that, 'cause I made a cup of tea and I sat down again. You're old, you don't sleep, you know?"

"So she came after ten and got her. And then she came back a little while after that and then the cops came."

"I guess so. Yeah."

"And she came one time before she got the girl. And she left alone."

"Right. So I thought everything was okay. I mean, she used to come a lot. They'd fight, I guess, and the little missy would get on the phone and call big sister to come over and help her. Take the baby. Thank the Lord that sister's there now, eh? What'd happen to that little girl? Go to some state home probably. Poor little thing. She'll be okay now, eh?"

"I hope so," I said.

I stirred in my chair.

"So you guess the boyfriend must've come back down the alley?"

"Must've, but I didn't see him. I wouldn't, if he was sneaking around in the dark. I saw the sister coming and going. God, she loves that little girl like she's her own. Good thing, too, now that this happened. Hey, I say prayers every night for that little one. Fifty Hail Marys."

"That's nice of you."

"*Rien.* Nothing."

She shook her head. I reached for my notebook, took out a pen.

"So, I'm sorry but I don't think I caught your name."

"You didn't, 'cause I didn't give it."

I looked up. Her face had masked over.

"Hey, I don't want my name in the paper," she said.

"Well, what about everything we've been talking about?"

"That's just talking. It doesn't count for the newspaper until you start writing it in your little pad there, right? My name in the paper, that's all I need. It's like I told the policeman there, the detective. I don't want you dragging me into court. I told him, I said, 'Young man, just stop right there if you think you're going to get me into a courtroom.' I mind my own business. I've got my pension and my Social Security. I get my cab over to the groceries. I get my hair done. I get to church, eh? I just want to be left alone."

"What did the detective say?"

She looked indignant.

"Well, he didn't say much, eh? What could he say? He said, 'Well, we may need you.' I said, 'Solve your own murder. You don't need some old lady. You know who did it.' He said, 'Yeah, we know, but we still have to prove it in court.' I said, 'Well, go right ahead, but leave me out of it.' "

"Did he tell you about subpoenas and all that?" I asked.

"No, I hustled him right out of here."

"When was this?"

"This was Sunday, right after I got back from Mass. He said he'd come back, but I haven't seen him. I told him and I'll tell you. I'll tell you what I saw, but leave me out of it. My name in the paper. Eh, Christ, all I need, eh, stuck all over the front page."

I got up and put my notebook back in my pocket.

"I'm sorry I can't help you with your story, but that's the way I feel."

"That's okay," I said. "You've been a lot of help."

"When's this story going to run in the paper?" she asked.

"Couldn't tell you."

"That's up to the editor?"

"Something like that," I said.

So Jeff had been there and then he'd left, on foot. When he'd left, Donna was still walking and talking, by the sounds of things. So what did he do? Go and drink some more. Stew some more. Cadge some money for some coke and let it fire up the furnace of his anger and resentment. Then walk back, through the alleys and side streets, letting himself in the side door, sneaking up the back stairs. Bullying Donna for the last time. Finding her alone.

Walking down the dim stairway, I wondered why Marcia hadn't taken Adrianna the first time. Did they argue? Did Donna resent this woman mothering her daughter? Did she refuse to lend out her prize possession this time? What did they talk about, that last time? Would

Marcia tell me? Would she talk to me at all? Maybe I'd give her a try. What could she do? Call the cops?

At the bottom of the stairs I looked at the mailboxes on the wall. One was O'Malley, scrawled in big letters with a red marker. Two had no names at all. One had four names, with two crossed out. Fathers to the crying babies? Another had neatly embossed plastic tape: Desrosiers.

Miss Desrosiers, I thought. *Merci beaucoup—à bientôt.* And on I went on my appointed rounds.

I couldn't find anyone else in the old woman's building, so I hit the two houses directly across the street. One was white and well kept, with a black spiked fence around it and alarm-company warnings on the windows. I opened the black-spiked gate, climbed the porch stairs, and rang the bell. The place was ordered and neat, with green indoor-outdoor carpeting on the porch floor. Its owners were off earning its keep. I took their name off the small plastic card by the door, writing it in my notebook.

Next door was a dump: peeling aquamarine paint, a plastic bag of trash torn open on the porch, music blaring from someplace inside. I would have knocked, but the doors were slung open.

On the first floor, two young guys and two young women were sitting around a table in the kitchen. There were bowls on the table, half full of cereal that had turned the milk pale pink. Little kids' shoes and clothes were scattered on the floor, as if there had just been an abduction.

Wherever the kids were, they weren't watching public television.

I tapped on the doorjamb and they all looked up. Two of the guys were working on morning beers. The women, barefoot in their dungaree shorts, were smoking and drinking coffee. They all listened impassively as I made my pitch, as if I were selling religion. Then one of the guys, small and thin, baseball cap on backward over long hair, pointed a dirty hand toward the door.

"Out," he said.

"You didn't know Donna?" I said.

"Out," he said again.

"Not even by sight?"

"Go."

"What, the paper spelled your name wrong in the police blotter?" I asked.

"Hit the road," the other guy said.

"Don't tell me. You have to get ready for work. But don't you hate putting on a tie sometimes? Don't you wish that just once, I mean just once, you could just say the hell with it and sit around all day drinking beer?"

The two guys got up from the table. But in that telling, pivotal moment, I didn't retreat. They didn't advance.

One for the good guys. I grinned.

"Later, people," I said. "Call me if you get a conscience."

I turned and went out the open door and down the steps. It was still raining, an earnest drizzle that turned the street black and oily. I paused on the sidewalk, then, as I started for the next house, heard a car roll up behind me and stop. A door popped.

"Hey, Jack," a voice called.

I turned. Archambault came around the front of his Toyota.

"Jack, we need to talk."

I looked at him. He stopped in front of me, his notebook in his hand, collar turned up on his dungaree jacket.

"I need to explain. Apologize, I mean. You probably weren't too happy being in that story."

I didn't respond.

"But Albert asked if I'd talked to you. I said, 'Yeah, but it wasn't really on the record.' He said he didn't care, he wasn't going to have his reporters keeping secrets about a murder. He gave me, like, an ultimatum. I had no choice."

I didn't believe him.

"Fine," I said. "But burning people's a bad habit. Comes back to haunt you."

"You're right," Archambault said. "And I wouldn't have, if I'd had a choice. Hey, what are you doing down here, anyway?"

"Just walking."

"Yeah, well, I thought I'd talk to some of the neighbors. Do kind of a profile on Donna, what her life was like here. I tried calling the sister, but there wasn't any answer. Have you seen her?"

I shook my head.

"Yeah, well, I guess I'll get started," Archambault said.

He looked around dubiously.

"Think anybody's around?"

"Oh, yeah," I said.

I looked back toward the house where the girls and boys had been so hospitable.

"The people in there wanted to talk. Couldn't shut 'em up. I told them I wasn't doing the story but I'd be sure to tell the guy who was."

"Are they home now?" Archambault said eagerly.

"Yup. Nice bunch, too," I said. "Tell 'em Jack sent you."

When I reached the corner by the store, Archambault was bounding up the steps of the house, notebook held out in front of him like flowers for a date. I smiled to myself for the first time in a long time, and headed for the car.

The sweet satisfaction that is vengeance.

But other than that, what did I have? I mulled it over as I drove across town, the car's wipers beating arrhythmically.

A stoned guy said he heard Donna and somebody, presumably Jeff, fighting. Then there were normal noises from the apartment, like dishes clinking. Would Jeff kill Donna in a rage and then do the dishes? Maybe if he'd killed her with a glass or a dinner plate. Or if there were blood and guts all over the place and he had to clean them up. But Lenny said he thought there was no obvious cause of death, no wounds or massive trauma, as they say. So who was tidying up? Was Donna dead by then?

The old woman said she hadn't called the police because the fighting wasn't that bad. Then Jeff went out the side door and, sometime not long after nine, Marcia pulled in. The old woman had seen Jeff leave, and Marcia come and go. What did Marcia see? What did Donna tell her in that last conversation? Had she taken Adrianna then? The woman said no. Not the first time. Then if the fighting was over, why did she come back? How was Marcia sleeping, with no arrest made, a murderer still trotting around town?

Marcia's house looked empty when I pulled up. I knocked on the aluminum screen door, then stepped down and walked over to the picture window. Cupping my hands over my eyes, I peered through the glass.

The living room was empty and dark. The other rooms were dark too. I walked over by the garage. The camper and snowmobiles were still there, but the other trucks were gone. I tried the garage door and it was locked. The side door to the house was locked too. A spider had spun a web over the glass of the storm door.

So they'd been gone for a while. But where had they gone in the middle of a murder investigation? And where was Adrianna?

I stood for a moment, then walked back to the car. I was about to get back in when a car pulled into the driveway of the next house up the road. I walked over and up their driveway and knocked. A guy pushed the aluminum door open. Forties. Stocky. Square, clean face.

"Hi, I'm a friend of Randy and Marcia's. You know if they're away or coming back?"

He looked at me closely.

"Who are you?"

"Jack McMorrow."

There was no recognition. So much for bylines.

"You know what happened?" the guy said confidentially. "With Marcia's sister?"

"Yeah, I do. I knew Donna, too. It's very sad."

"So they left for a while. You know. With the little kid and all."

"They go out of state or something?" I asked.

"No, Randy's still working. Took a couple days, I think, but he's got to go back. Hey, they just needed to get away. They had TV cameras over there the other morning. Goddamn media vultures."

I looked away.

"Goddamn scavengers, you know?"

"Yup," I said.

"So they had to get away. If they stop by to check the house or something, I'll tell them you were here. It's Jack, right? What, do you know Randy from the mill or something?"

"No, mostly I knew Marcia and Donna."

"You knew the sister? I didn't—I mean, I saw her a few times, dropping the kid off or whatever. Hey, I know the girl had her problems. But let me tell you, if she was my sister, this scumbag would have touched her once. One time, and let me tell you something, me and my brothers would have had him on his knees in the woods, begging for goddamn mercy. We'd have made him wish he'd never laid a finger on that little girl. See how tough he feels looking up the barrel of a 30-30, the son of a bitch."

"Not very," I said.

I didn't tell him I knew from experience.

"That's what's wrong with this goddamn country. The family's gone to hell. Used to be, you picked on one person, you had the whole clan climbing on your back. People looked out for each other. You got a sister?"

"No, I don't. No brothers, either."

"Well, if you did, wouldn't you kill any bastard who roughed her up? I mean, anybody who has any friggin' morals at all. Hey, but I don't mean to bad-mouth Randy. He's kind of laid-back, and it was just him alone, I guess."

He took a breath.

"So now she's gone, why don't these media people let her rest in peace, you know? Leave her be."

"I don't know. That's not what they're paid to do, I guess."

"No, they keep stirring things up, prying into people's business. I don't know how they can friggin' sleep at night."

"Probably isn't easy," I said, and I thanked him and he nodded and I walked back to the car.

It wouldn't be easy that night.

When I got home, I heated soup but didn't feel like eating. After I hadn't eaten, I went out into the sodden woods, but as I moved between the trees, I didn't hear birds. I heard Donna's voice.

I thought you might be better, Jack. I'd hoped you could help me. . . . I'd hoped you might be my ticket out. . . . I'd hoped you might be the one to deliver me from this mess. . . .

Deliver her? She was the story of the week, something to fill a little blank space on a page dummy. But it wasn't just that; Donna the casualty of journalism. It was Donna the casualty. It was Donna.

It was her hair. It was her looks, the naive hope for something better. It was her purple paintings, the little laugh when she'd told that story on herself, the spatter of freckles across her nose. It wasn't just the journalism thing, the subject of the story fed into the insatiable news mill. I could shrug that off or drink it off. This was Donna. She had broken through the wall, the professional facade. I had liked her. I had liked Donna very much.

This wasn't regret. This was grief.

So I walked in circles, thought in circles, too. The trail kept bringing me back to the same place, the same moment when I'd looked right into Donna's eager, hopeful face. Finally, I came home and sat down in the big chair by the window. It was quiet in the house, silent but for the hum of the refrigerator, and I sat for a long time. At four o'clock, I got up and got a beer and sat back down and sipped. At five I got up and got another one. The rifle was in the corner and the answering machine was on and all was unwell with the world.

At six fifteen the phone rang but I didn't answer it, and whoever it was hung up when the machine clicked on. Screw 'em, I thought. At seven, I was on my fourth beer and the phone rang again and the machine answered. There was breathing, then a click and the dial tone. At eight I got another beer and sat back down, heavily. I watched the light fade behind the trees and then I was dreaming: Donna and Roxanne in the same room. Donna sitting beside me and holding my hand and Roxanne glaring. Trying to explain but no words would come and Donna wouldn't let go. Donna leaning over to kiss me and a hand on my shoulder, holding me down . . .

"Jack," a voice said. "You're screwing up, my friend."

I looked up at Clair, standing over me. It was his big hand on my shoulder.

"Anybody could have walked in here and killed you," he said. "This isn't the time to get drunk."

"I'm not drunk. I'm tired."

"You've got a woman murdered," Clair went on. "A guy coming after you who's got nothing to lose. Somebody who drove a knife through your windshield in the middle of the night. And you're sitting here, swilling beer?"

"I wasn't swilling. I was pacing myself."

"Pacing yourself right into a grave."

"Oh, come on, Clair."

"Come on, nothing. That little girl probably decided to get drunk too. Look what happened to her."

"I know what happened to her," I said.

"Then what are you doing here, out cold with the doors open? An army could have marched in here."

"But Marines would have knocked."

"I'm totally serious, Jack," Clair said. "I am goddamn serious. It's time for you to be on your toes. If you were one of my soldiers, I'd drive you across the room. You've got to be sharp."

"I know."

"If you know, then do it."

Clair stood there as if he actually might slug me, just to make his point. But then the phone rang. I didn't get up.

"The secretary will get it," I said.

After four rings, the machine clicked and whirred and beeped.

"Hi, Jack."

It was Roxanne's voice. Soft and musical and bright.

"I just wanted to see how you were doing. Call me when you get home. I love you."

There was a pause.

"I really love you," she said. "Bye."

Clair looked at me.

"Do it for her if you won't do it for yourself. You want to feel sorry for yourself about this girl, save it for later. Think of somebody else. That woman on the phone there depends on you. Other people do too."

He paused.

"So don't let 'em down, Jack," Clair barked, and turned on his heel and walked to the door. He looked back at me, tall and erect and grim.

"Switch to coffee. Don't roll over and play dead, or you'll end up dead for real. Don't think it can't happen. And keep that goddamn weapon loaded and ready."

The door closed. There was no such thing as an ex-Marine.

19

Roxanne's phone had been busy. For hours. When I'd finally gotten through, a little after midnight, she'd just gone to sleep. Groggily, she told me she loved me, that she was talking to Jill in Colorado. I told her everything was fine, that I loved her and would call her Thursday.

A half truth. Maybe a third.

I woke up early, and felt as if there were a gauzy veil wrapped around my head. Too much beer. Too little sleep.

The sun was out and the morning was steamy, with branches and leaves dripping outside the window. I lurched out of bed and down the stairs and put on water for tea. Taking a peek out the front window, I saw that there was nothing impaled on my windshield.

Things were looking up.

I drank that cup of tea and then another and half of a third. I still felt like hell, but at least my heart was racing. If I couldn't be sharp, I could look wired. Jeff spent hundreds of dollars to feel just like this. No wonder he was irritable.

At eight, I was showered, dressed, and ready to go. I considered calling Roxanne again, but it was too late, in more ways than one.

The ride in was a good airing out, with lush woods, blue sky, and glimpses of a great blue heron and an osprey. I craned my neck under the windshield to follow the osprey, but it veered away over the tops of the spruces and dead crags, and I fought off the urge to pull the car over and chase after it and lose myself in the only place left that was pure and clean and full of wonder.

But I had promises to keep. At eight thirty, I kept one by standing in the lobby at Fourth District Court. I eyed the throng and a few people on the benches eyed me. I eyed them back. Looked at my watch. Felt for my notebook in the back pocket of my jeans.

"Good morning, Mr. McMorrow," a voice boomed. "We're honored by the presence of Jack McMorrow, ace reporter. Looking for a good story? Anybody have a story they want to tell Mr. McMorrow?"

Tate leered at me, then slapped me on the back with her big painted paw. Everyone in the place stopped and stared.

"Looking for anything in particular, McMorrow?" Tate went on, walking slowly by. "Nothing too juicy this morning, but you never know. Maybe somebody'll break down on the stand. How would that be, Mr. McMorrow? Good and juicy? I don't know, you've been finding some good stories in this little place. Writing those racy stories in the newspaper. Anybody going to do something racy today? Tell Mr. McMorrow here. He'll make you famous."

Tate glanced at me over her shoulder as she walked toward the clerk's window.

"Don't thank me," she said, and grinned again.

So much for being a fly on the wall. I was the centerpiece now. On display. I stood there nakedly for a moment and then followed a bunch of guys out the door. One of them held the door for me and I said, "Thanks," and then somebody was pushing me from behind, then still pushing, and there were hands on my shoulders and I was being guided to the left, boots catching at the backs of my sneakers. I turned to see who it was and saw only beards and hair and strangers.

We turned the corner and a hand forced my head down, while others clamped onto my arms. I said, "Hey," and "What the—," and then I was pitching forward, onto the floor of a car, my face pressing into trash and bottles, my hands behind me, and somebody sprawling on top of me, somebody who smelled like body odor and booze and cigarettes, a weight that crushed the breath out of me.

I started to scream and the motor started and the exhaust roared and we were moving. A hand grabbed me by the hair and pressed my face hard against the trash and cans and bottles, and something sharp sliced into my cheek and I was pressed down even harder, so my mouth couldn't open and no sound would come out.

The exhaust rumbled under my face and somebody whooped and somebody exclaimed, "Yes," and another voice said, "Smooth as silk, boys. We are in the wrong business."

"Let's see what business we're in," the guy on top of me said, and his hand dug into my back pocket, yanking out my wallet.

"Seven friggin' dollars," he said. "What is this?"

The hand let up and I lifted my face off the trash. It felt like my cheek was bleeding, and then there was a red droplet and then another and another. The car slowed, the rumble subsiding and then roaring again. I could hear other cars, a siren in the distance.

"Seven bucks, man," the guy above me said. "What're we gonna do with seven bucks?"

"He got a bank card?" the voice in the front said.

"Lemme see. Oh, baby. Two of 'em. We're in business again, ain't we, chump?"

"What bank?" another voice said.

"Citibank. Where the hell is that?"

I didn't say anything. Tried to place their voices. It wasn't Jeff. It wasn't Donnie. I couldn't place them. I had to keep them talking.

"Wait a minute. The other one is for Central Marine Savings. Which one's that?"

"Main Street. Past the fire station," the guy in the front said.

"I can't keep track of these goddamn things," the guy above me said.

"Deregulation," I said, speaking for the first time. "Mergers and buyouts. Turned the banking world on its ear."

"What the—? What are you talking about?" the guy above me said.

The other guy grabbed my arms and pushed them toward my neck. I grimaced but didn't make a sound. The car rumbled along. The driver turned on the radio. Top 40.

"Yuck," I said.

"Hey, shut the hell up, man," the guy above me said. "This guy is friggin' irking me, man."

"Yeah, we only need you to say one thing. That's the number for this card."

It was the other guy in the back. The driver was silent. We stopped in traffic and he turned the radio up louder. My face, sticky with blood, was starting to ache. The car rumbled and creaked and the brakes ground.

"Who owns this piece of crap?" I said.

A fist slammed into the back of my neck, numbing me.

"Don't hit him there, man," the guy above me said. "You'll friggin' paralyze the son of a bitch."

"Good, he owes me."

"He owes you a few hundred bucks, man. I ain't in this to whack the guy. I'm in it to get some cash and split."

"Yeah, well, he owes me."

"There's an echo in here," I said.

A boot against the back of my head.

"Shut the hell up," the guy with the fist said. "You owe me. You're lucky I don't friggin' put you in the river."

I was thinking. Who did I owe?

"Okay, start spitting numbers, dipshit," the guy above me said.

"Since you put it so nicely," I mumbled against the floor. "One, two, three, four, five, six, seven—"

The boot pushed and, a millisecond later, the fist again, hard against my back. I gasped.

"The friggin' number, you piece of shit," the other guy said behind me. He shifted and loosened his grip on my arms, and I yanked them under me and pushed myself up on my knees and elbows. They both started yelling and the driver said, "Jeez," and swerved and knees came down on my back and a boot on my head, but not before I twisted my head and looked up.

And saw a guy I didn't know. A guy I did.

Leaman.

"He seen me, the son of a bitch," Leaman said.

"Has seen me," I said between clenched teeth. "I can't stress enough the importance of good grammar if you are ever—"

He was on my back, punching me like a punching bag. I didn't feel pain, just flashes of sensation. My back. The back of my head. My ear. My forehead against the litter on the floor. The car revved up, as if the pace of the blows was somehow related to the flow of gas to the carburetor.

The punches were on the back of my head, and I felt something warm in my hair. Blood.

"Okay, okay," the guy above me said. "Don't friggin' knock him out. I ain't babysitting him all day. I just want to get the cash and dump this clown. There's a case of Jack and an eight ball waiting for me."

"Here's the bank," the driver said.

Leaman stopped punching.

"What's the number, McMorrow?" he said. "You owe me. Putting me out there in your goddamn article. My kids seen that, you son of a bitch. Wiseass newspaperman. How's it feel now, huh? Thought you made me look stupid, huh? Well, how's it feel?"

"The number," the guy above me said. "Four digits, right? Enter your personal identification number now. Just say the numbers, man."

"One, two, three, four," I said.

Leaman slammed the wind out of me.

"Maybe that's it," the driver said.

"No, nobody has one, two, three, four," the guy above me said. "He's playing goddamn games. Aren't you, McMorrow?"

I didn't say anything.

"Maybe that is it," the driver said. "Should I pull in?"

"No, you stupid nummy," the guy above me said. "He's got to be in front. They got cameras."

"Jeez, this is going all to hell," the driver said. "Let's dump him and this wreck and get the hell outta here."

"He's seen us," Leaman said.

"Much better," I murmured.

"So what're you gonna do? Whack him?"

"This sucks," the driver said.

"Keep going," Leaman said. "Down to the garage. We'll make this pussy talk."

"Does this gas gauge work?" the driver said.

"How the hell should I know?" the guy above me said.

"I hope not," the driver said. "I don't feel like taking him to get gas."

"The garage, you numb nuts," Leaman said. "The garage."

"Hey, I just wanted some blow," the driver said. "I ain't in for no—"

"Just drive," Leaman said. "God almighty. Does everything have to be this big goddamn deal?"

"Five, six, seven, eight," I said from the floor.

A foot jammed against my neck.

The garage wasn't far. I counted four minutes, maybe five. The car swung to the left and to the right, five or six times. We were loafing along, doing maybe twenty-five, when the car turned hard to the left and stopped. The driver got out and left the car running. He got back in and pulled ahead into near darkness. The door opened again and he walked behind the car and I heard doors bang shut and the place went black.

And a light went on, barely.

"Take off your belt," Leaman said.

"Why should I take off my belt," the guy above me said. "I like this—"

"Take it off and strap his goddamn wrists together. Just do it, for once."

I heard leather snap, then circle my wrists. One of them jerked the belt tight and I winced.

"You guys have been watching too much CNN," I said.

"Shut up," Leaman said. "Let's get him out."

They opened the door near my head and the driver came over and grabbed me by the armpits. They lifted me by the back of the jeans and shoved me forward and the driver pulled and I was piled out of the car and onto my face on a dirty concrete floor. I left a bloody stain.

"Now we can friggin' work on him," Leaman said. "I give him five minutes."

I rolled over and looked up. Leaman was wearing jeans and a dark green T-shirt. His hair was pulled back and his face was grim. The guy beside me in the car was shorter than Leaman and blond, his face bony and narrow and inbred looking. The driver was a chunky guy in his late twenties, with a round, soft face and a silly fringe of a beard. He looked doubtful. The car was an old Pontiac, primer black and rust.

"Hey, man," he said. "I ain't up for this. I didn't know you were—"

"I knew you'd wuss out," Leaman said. "But it's too late, champ. You're in."

"I ain't killing some guy. I thought this was gonna be a few quick bucks. I didn't—"

"Who said anything about killing anybody. Pick him up and bring him over to the hood."

The blond guy leaned over me and waited for the driver to step up. He did and they hoisted me to my feet, my hands behind me. I got my balance in a half second and kicked out and up, catching Leaman square in the groin, so hard that he was almost lifted off the ground.

"Aaahhhh," he said, and started to lunge toward me, but then crumpled, and I whirled toward the driver and he took a step back. The blond guy started to swing from my right, but without conviction, and I bulled past him and ran as fast as I could, shoulder down, into the wooden door.

It banged open a foot, maybe two, and I started screaming as loud as I could as I stumbled and slipped to my knees. Somebody grabbed me by the neck from behind and I bit the forearm hard and it slipped loose and I was moving forward again, digging like a running back, still shrieking and screaming. I got ten feet outside into the glaring sunshine, glimpsed junky houses, some sumac trees, before the blond guy tackled me from behind.

I fell forward and he jumped on top of me and got me by the neck again and I couldn't get my jaw down to bite and then somebody kicked me in the buttocks, the side, and I was sprawled with my face up just enough to see the driver run past me and out to the street without looking back.

"Get him back in," Leaman snarled, and I started screaming again and the blond guy hesitated. Then Leaman got me under the arms and dragged me along the ground, the blond guy following behind us, as I screamed like a banshee.

"We gotta get outta here," the blond guy said, but he was closing the doors and Leaman threw me up against the side of the car. He swung once and hit me in the mouth, the punch exploding in my head. I felt myself start to fold and the blond guy was saying, "We gotta get outta here, man," and then Leaman stuffed a bandanna into my mouth, opened the door, and shoved me in, bouncing my wallet off my chest. I was on my back on the floor in the backseat, and he leaned in and snatched his own belt off.

"You friggin' son of a bitch," Leaman breathed as he wrapped the belt around my ankles. "You friggin' son of a bitch."

Then he leaned over my face and spat once. I winced and he was out of the car, then back in, leaning over the driver's seat. He turned the key and the motor rumbled to life, but then he got out again and went around to all four doors, shoving the lock buttons down and slamming the doors shut.

One, two, three, four.

20

The light flooded in, but only for a moment, and then it was dark. I lay there on the floor and listened to the motor throb. How long did I have? When people put a hose in the window, how long did that take? I didn't have a hose, but the garage would be filled soon. How long?

Claustrophobia came over me in a choking wave, and I writhed and tried to scream behind the bandanna. There was no sound, just my gasps and the rumble from underneath me. I lay back and tried to think. I had to get the doors open. I had to get the bandanna out. I had to breathe.

I worked my tongue against the bottom of the ball of cloth, over and over like I was trying to get peanut butter off the roof of my mouth. The cloth didn't move, and then it seemed to be sliding farther back toward my throat and I gagged.

I forced myself to breathe through my nose.

Slowly.

Calmly.

I began working with my tongue again and gagged again. Worked some more and gagged again. Then I got my tongue farther behind the cloth, which was saturated now, and the bandanna pushed forward. Forward a little more. I could hear the exhaust rumbling underneath me and it was getting hotter in the car. I breathed deeply, in through my nose and out through my mouth, as if I were blowing out a candle.

The bandanna moved. I blew again. It moved some more. I blew again and again and again and the ball of cloth unfolded over my chin and I gasped for air.

But it wasn't air that I was breathing. The smell was noxious and the air already was burning. I threw my feet up onto the vinyl seat and used them to pull me up toward the door. When I was close enough, I kicked the door hard with both feet, like a mule. It didn't budge.

I kicked at the handles and the window crank broke off and fell onto the floor under my feet. I inched closer and kicked up under the door handle, but the door didn't open. I'd have to push with one foot and kick with the other, but they were strapped together. I slid the handle between my sneakers and pushed up and out. Up and out again. The door didn't open.

It was one of those doors that has to be unlocked to open. I rested for a moment, with the motor still thumping away, and then inched toward the door some more. When I was close enough, I heaved my feet up onto the bottom of the window. Inched them to the right until I felt the lock. Tried to squeeze it between my heels.

I missed. I missed again. I was beginning to feel weak. Nauseated. My face was throbbing. My feet felt leaden. I hefted them up again and worked them over until I felt the knob. Worked it between my sneakers. Pulled.

It slipped.

I was panicking. Why didn't the cops come? Why didn't somebody call them? Did they report that somebody was screaming and then the cops rolled through the neighborhood and found everything quiet? Deadly quiet?

I had to get out. I tried the knob again, but it slipped again. If I had more room behind it . . . If I could get the window down. Or out.

It was what prisoners did to police cruisers. The first kick sent jabbing pains through my heels and up my legs. The second did the same, and then the window cracked and then crumpled, folding over my feet. I pulled my feet back in and tiny cubes of glass sprinkled my face. Closing my eyes, I kicked one more time, then worked my feet around the lock button. Pulled and slipped. Pulled and slipped. Pulled and . . .

Click.

The door handle hooked between my feet. I inched it up until it wouldn't go up anymore and then pushed as hard as I could.

The door swung open.

But I was tired. I wanted to lie back and go to sleep. I wanted to take a rest. The fumes were working into my bloodstream. They were telling my brain to give up, to go to sleep forever.

I shouted, "No," but it came out a croak. I hooked my legs over the bottom of the door frame and pulled myself toward the opening. The motor coughed, then resumed its rhythmic rumble. *Blub, blub, blub, blub.* I had my legs out, then my feet on the floor of the garage. But my hands still were behind my back. I pushed up, but my torso only rose six inches. I fell back. Pushed again. Fell back again.

Finally, I gouged at the floor with my heels, dragging them along the concrete. I inched forward, literally. I was too groggy, too tired, but I dragged my feet again and again. And then my heel caught in a hole. A deep hole. It was as though I had hooked a winch cable to a tree. I pulled and my buttocks edged over the door frame, over and over some more, and I fell out of the car and onto the floor.

I got up and stagger-hopped toward the door, aiming for the crack of light. The doors opened in a blinding bang and I fell to my knees in the gravel and weeds, sucking deeply at the air like a gasping pump.

A white-haired man came by with a beagle on a leash. He walked over and the dog sniffed me as I lay there on the ground drinking in the air, my wrists and ankles still bound by the belts, the car still idling in the garage.

"You all right?" the man said.

"Just dandy," I said, raising myself to my knees. "Would you mind undoing—"

"This one of them kinky sex things?" the man asked.

"No, it's nothing like that. It's—"

" 'Cause there's kids in this neighborhood, you know what I'm saying? Bad enough with television. Don't need no weirdos tying each other up. How'd you get that blood all over your face?"

"Cut myself shaving," I said. "You mind undoing my hands here?"

"How do I know you don't have a gun?"

I looked at him. The beagle looked at me suspiciously.

"I don't have a gun," I said. "I'm not a weirdo. I'm a guy who's been abducted and robbed and left in this garage to die of asphyxiation. Didn't you hear me screaming?"

"Yeah, I heard that god-awful screeching."

"Did you call the cops?"

"Hell, no. If I called the cops every time I heard some crazy yelling in this neighborhood, I'd be on the phone half the day and most of the night. You wouldn't believe the goings-on."

"Sure I would," I said, still on my knees. "How 'bout you call the cops now."

"What should I tell 'em?"

"That there's a guy here who says he'll kill you if you don't call the cops. He'll take you by the throat and throttle you. He'll kill your dog and all its relatives."

"Easy there," the man said.

Just then, a window slid up on the second floor of the building to my right.

"What's going on, Marty?" an older woman called.

"Better call the cops," the man said. "One of them sex weirdos."

"You okay?" she asked him.

"Oh, yeah," he said. "I'm fine. And I'll keep an eye on this character."

"Don't get too close to him," the woman said. "Let the cops handle it."

And they did.

The first cruiser pulled up and a young woman got out. I told her I'd been robbed and she asked me for my ID. I said it was in the car in the garage, the one that was running. She went and shut off the car and came back with my wallet. I asked her if there was any money in it and she said no. Then I was robbed of seven dollars, I said.

She asked when this was. I said it was twenty minutes ago and she asked if I knew the assailants. I said I knew one, Alphonse Danny Leaman, and she got on her radio and requested an ambulance and reported an assault and robbery and said it might involve Leaman.

"You familiar with that subject?" someone radioed back.

"Negative," the young woman said.

"Just got out of Thomaston," the voice said. "Six foot two, over two hundred. Brownish, grayish hair with ponytail. Approach with caution. Known to be 10-32 with a knife. Got a name on the victim?"

"Last name, McMorrow," the young woman said. "First name, Jack."

"I'll be right there, drive time from Elm."

"Should I untie this guy?" she said.

"Oh, yeah," Lenny said. "Cut him loose."

He was there in two minutes, sliding his cruiser in the gravel as he pulled in. The ambulance was right behind him, and soon the lot was filled with neighbors and kids. The kids sat on their bikes and watched as the paramedics washed my cheek.

"Oh, yes," one of them said, dabbing at my cheek. "A nice deep slice. This a knife wound?"

"I don't think so," I said. "Maybe a piece of glass. I'm not sure."

"Gonna need some stitches. How 'bout a ride in?"

"No, thanks," I said. "I just need a ride back to my car."

"I'll take him," Lenny said.

"I'd get him in now," the paramedic said. "The sooner you get that stitched up, the less scarring you're gonna have. You might want to consider a plastic surgeon, because of the location."

"And maybe I'll have my tummy tucked, too," I said.

He smiled and finished taping a dressing over my face.

"All yours, Officer," he said.

"Let's roll," Lenny said.

He opened the back door and I climbed in. The cruiser eased out of the lot and we headed up the street, coming out on River Street, south of the downtown. As we pulled out, a red Toyota slowed and turned in.

Archambault.

"One of your colleagues," Lenny said. "You want to go back and talk to him?"

"No," I said. "Drive."

He did and, after a minute of polite silence, started in.

"So Leaman caught up with you, huh?"

"I was set up. Tate announced my arrival outside the courtroom with a megaphone. When I started out the door, these three guys hustled me around the corner and into that car. It was like Beirut."

"What'd they want?"

"Money. For booze and coke."

"How much they get?"

"Not much," I said. "Enough for a twelve-pack. They wanted to go to a bank machine, but we never got there."

"Why not?" Lenny said.

"I couldn't remember my number."

"And they took you to that garage to try to persuade you?"

"Yup."

"But they couldn't?"

"Nope."

"So what happened?"

"Leaman shoved me in the backseat all strapped up and left the motor running and the garage doors closed."

"Attempted murder?"

"Plea down to aggravated assault, maybe. That is, if Tate will prosecute it at all."

"She'll have to," Lenny said.

"From what I can tell, she doesn't have to do anything."

"There are limits."

"I used to think so," I said.

We pulled into the emergency entrance at Kennebec Regional Medical Center and parked beside an ambulance. Lenny opened the door for me and we went inside and I sat at a counter and told the reception person all about myself. He put this information into a computer so it could be called up next time I was abducted.

The cut took thirteen stitches. The doctor, a pleasant and efficient woman in her late forties, told me she'd done a tour as a medic in Vietnam. She asked if I wanted a plastic surgeon, and I said no. If she could sew soldiers back together, she could stitch me up, too.

"There will be some scarring," the doctor said, peering down at my face.

"Life is like that," I said. "This just happens to be on the outside."

She looked at me curiously.

"The police officer who brought me in here," I said. "Could you have somebody bring him in?"

"Are you in custody?" the doctor said.

"No, I just need to talk to him."

She looked at me again and then slipped through the curtain. A minute later, the curtain parted.

"Good as new," Lenny said.

"Archambault out there?"

"With his pencil sharpened."

"You tell him anything?"

"Said I hadn't completed my investigation."

"I don't want to talk to him. Is there another way out of this place?"

Lenny looked down the hall, away from the entrance.

"There's a sign way down there that says 'Exit.' "

"I'll meet you at the far end of the building," I said.

"You'll be the one with the bandage on his face, right?"

"But still smiling," I said.

"Attaboy," Lenny said, and then he was gone.

He picked me up and we drove back downtown. Lenny parked the cruiser behind the American Legion Hall and I gave him my statement. He wrote slowly and carefully.

"You know this will put Leaman away for a long time," Lenny said.

"If you can find him."

"Guy never should have been able to bail."

"That was no accident," I said. "It was a setup."

"Good luck proving it."

"She shouldn't be prosecuting this case. It really should be bumped into Superior Court."

"In a perfect world," Lenny said.

"Which this isn't," I said. "Not by a long shot."

"I'll need to talk to you."

"Likewise, I'm sure."

"About what?" Lenny said.

"About Donna. What's the latest?"

"Off the record?"

"Of course. Listen. Everything's off the record between us unless we agree otherwise."

"Okay," Lenny said. "Latest is that Jeff is headed for grand jury. Word I got is that she was asphyxiated and he admits to half-choking her."

"He told them that?"

"I guess he isn't much of a liar. It's too complex a process for his brain."

I thought for a moment. The old woman. Jeff leaving. Sounds of dishes.

"He still out?"

"Haven't arrested him yet. At least not as of this morning. You see the paper this morning?"

"Not yet."

"Your buddy there did an article on Donna. Made her out to be some kind of slut."

"That isn't true," I said.

"I know that," Lenny said.

"And this isn't much of an investigation."

"What do you want?"

"I don't know," I said. "I'm not sure. But they're not getting deep enough. They're just not getting at it."

"Well, I'm gonna need you about this little matter."

"Call my house in Prosperity and leave a message. I won't be hanging around the house a lot."

"Gonna be doing more reporting for the paper?" he asked.

"No, I'm not going to be doing that a lot either," I said.

Lenny gave me a ride back to my car. I drove around the block to Main Street and went through the drive-through at the bank for some cash. A lot of cash. The number was not one, two, three, four.

From there, I went up the block and stopped at the newsstand for a paper. I read it in the car, one eye squinting because of the bandage. The anesthetic was wearing off, and my face hurt. The story hurt more.

It was a profile of Donna, played high on page one, on the right side above the fold. There was no photo. Archambault had talked to Tate and the state police detectives. The rest was attributed to unnamed sources, "neighbors," and "longtime residents of the Peavey Street neighborhood."

You couldn't libel the dead, but this was close. Archambault implied that Donna was promiscuous, quoting an unnamed neighbor who was supposed to have said that men came and went at the apartment at all hours. The story said she'd had a series of relationships but didn't say she'd ever been married. It said Donna lived alone with her daughter and collected welfare and food stamps.

This was linked to a "longtime resident" who was quoted as saying the neighborhood had gone to hell when "people like her" moved in. The story implied that Donna's apartment was dirty. It said she often left her daughter with her sister. It said Donna "pulled off her blouse" in the courtroom at District Court. Tate said this had never happened before in all her years as a prosecutor.

It added up to a portrait of a woman who was sleazy, lazy, a drunk, and a lousy mother. It implied that she was morally corrupt and ethically loose. There was not one word in the story that showed any sympathy for Donna Marchant, any compassion, any attempt to get to know her.

The story was supercilious and disapproving. It said Donna Marchant deserved what she got.

And that wasn't true.

I put the paper down and sat there for a minute and stewed. Started the car and drove. Two blocks up, I pulled over and parked. Grabbed the laptop and went in the door at the *Observer* and up the stairs two at a time.

When I came through the door into the newsroom, Charlene was coming down the aisle. I didn't slow down and she got out of the way. Halfway across the room, I spotted Albert's head beyond his partition. When I turned the corner, he was easing himself into his chair.

"McMorrow," he said, startled. "What's this I hear about—"

"I won't be filing a story today."

"Well, I heard you were mixed up in some crazy thing and I'd already decided that—"

"I'm not filing because I'm quitting," I said.

I stood in front of his desk. He stood too.

"I didn't think it'd work out," Albert said. "You're just too much of a loose cannon, McMorrow."

"I'm not a loose cannon. The problem is that your paper is muzzled. The place has sold out, if it ever had anything to sell."

"Hey, wait a minute there—"

"And that story today on Donna Marchant was an abomination. I'd love to see if Archambault could actually produce any of these alleged sources. But the worst thing is, here you have this poor young woman who was killed, her daughter left with no mother at all, she was trying to get away from this abusive son of a bitch, and you do a story saying what a slut she was? What the hell is that?"

"I don't have to explain anything to you, McMorrow."

"And you can't. Because there's no way to explain it. Except as lazy, slipshod, fourth-rate journalism."

"Well, I'm sorry we can't all be the *New York Times*," Albert said. "But you listen to me, Mr. Hotshot—"

"You could try to be the *New York Times*," I said. "You just choose not to. This paper is a cowardly bully."

I turned on my heel and got around the corner of the partition before I realized I still had the laptop under my arm. I turned on my heel again, walked back to Albert's office, where he still was standing. Albert reached for the phone, as if to call Security. I dropped the computer on his desk and left again.

It would have been a better exit the first time.

21

I sat in the car on Main Street, my heart still pounding. I now had only one assignment, and it wasn't to cover the courts. It was to do Donna Marchant justice. Of some sort.

As I sat there, I considered exactly what it was that was wrong. It was like the whole thing had been trivialized. Donna had been stamped as trash. Jeff had been stamped a murderer, but not a real murderer. To be a real murderer, you have to take a life of consequence. Donna's life had been dismissed, written off. They might lock Jeff up for twenty years, but that wasn't enough if they didn't treat Donna with respect.

Feeling as if I'd just been cut loose, I started the car and drove up Main Street, onto Elm, took a left at a tire garage, and then down onto a street of big apartment blocks with wooden porches clinging to their fronts. On this glorious June day, feral kids were clinging to the porches. Mom was in front of the tube and Dad was on the run, dodging child support.

In this trough of domestic bliss was nestled The Mansion, Jeff's favorite haunt. The bar was on the first floor. Rooms for drugs and drunks and girls were conveniently located upstairs. A full-service resort, only forty-five minutes from Camden.

I pulled the Olds over in front of the apartment block next to the bar. A couple of guys were leaning against the wall next to the building's front door. One was thin like a cadaver, with a mangy beard. The other was heavier, with an eye patch and a Bud can half-wrapped in a paper bag.

The Pirates of Penzance.

"How ya doing?" I said.

The skinny one grunted.

I headed up the sidewalk. A barefoot toddler in diapers and a dirty white T-shirt scurried around the corner and came running toward me. I waited for the vigilant parent to follow. And waited some more. The kid disappeared, unattended, around the other corner of the building. I walked up to the open front door of The Mansion and went in.

It was one thirty and the bar was half full. I'd long ago learned that morning or early afternoon was the best time to visit places like this. The fighters hadn't shown up yet, or if they had, they were still moving slowly. In a place like The Mansion, that half-second advantage could save you your teeth.

I took an empty stool at the bar. The bartender, a woman with muscles on her arms and tattoos on her muscles, looked away from the television long enough to catch my eye.

"Bud," I said.

Tea was not on the menu.

The Bud was a longneck, thumped wordlessly on the scarred wooden bar. There were no glasses. The television show was an old sitcom, but nobody seemed to care. Nobody asked how I'd hurt my face.

I sipped the beer and it went down surprisingly easy. After three or four sips, I looked around.

To my left were a couple of young guys in jeans and dark T-shirts.

They were together, maybe laborers who had gotten off early and didn't want to go home. Beyond them was an old mummy of a man sitting in front of a shot and a beer. If he was still here at four, he wouldn't be sitting. In a year, he wouldn't be sitting anywhere.

On my right were three or four regulars, guys in their thirties. They talked to the bartender and, still staring at the television, she murmured unintelligible responses that apparently sufficed. These four were tougher than the others, leaner and stronger. Even sitting down, they had that hair-trigger stance, that tension that erupts into violence without warning.

I glanced at them. They glanced back. I was glad I hadn't worn oxford cloth and khakis.

When there was an inch left in my beer, the bartender lifted her head in my direction. I nodded and finished the last gulp. The second beer hit the bar before the empty.

"Thanks," I said.

"Yup," the bartender said.

I drank the second beer more slowly, and the four guys drank slowly too. One of them got up and went to the jukebox and plunked in a coin. The machine clicked and then the music blared, a barrage of heavy metal. The bartender turned up the television.

The music man sat down at the other end of the three, closer to me. I nodded to him and he nodded back. He was trying to make me. A drug cop? A liquor-enforcement cop? A guy looking to buy coke? A guy looking for a girl?

"How ya doing?" I said.

"Good," he said. "How 'bout yourself?"

"Fine."

"Been in here before?"

"Not during the day," I said.

"Extra thirsty today?"

He looked at me. The other three listened. The bartender, eyes on the TV, didn't miss a word.

"Hoping to meet up with somebody."

"Oh, yeah? Who's that?"

I lifted my beer and sipped. They waited.

"Jeff Tanner," I said. "You seen him?"

His face, taut and mustached with dark, narrow-set eyes, showed nothing.

"Friend of yours?"

I shrugged.

"Not really. I just need to talk to him."

"Why's that?"

"We knew this girl," I said.

"Oh, yeah? Who's that?"

"Donna Marchant."

This time his eyes flickered. The bartender turned slowly around to see me. The other three watched intently.

"The girl who got killed," I said. "You knew her?"

"I knew her," the bartender said. "What are you? A cop?"

"Nope. I just knew her a little."

"So what are you?" the bartender pressed.

"A friend of Donna's."

"So why you looking for Jeff?" the guy said.

"To talk," I said.

I realized that no one else in the bar was talking. Even the mummified man had turned to watch and listen.

"What do you want to talk to him about?" the bartender said.

"Donna," I said.

"What about her?" she said.

I took a sip of beer. The guy on my right was watching intently, like a stalking animal.

"I want to know if he killed her," I said.

"You think he's gonna tell you?" the guy blurted.

"He doesn't have to. I'll know by his eyes."

I looked at him and I didn't flinch. He looked back, not blinking. He understood.

"What if he says he did?" the guy said, more softly.

"I don't know. Play it by ear."

He thought for a moment.

"I know who you are," he said suddenly.

The rest of the bar watched and waited.

"Oh, yeah?"

"Yeah. You're the guy who smashed his mouth all up. Ain'tcha? He said his old lady was hooking up with some guy. From the newspaper or something. That you?"

I nodded.

"And you cut his mouth all up. Hit him with something."

I shrugged.

"He had a pipe."

"Yeah, you're the guy."

He got up from the stool slowly, his arms uncoiling from the bar. I sat still as he moved toward me. If he took me off the stool, I was done. I lifted my beer to my mouth, then put it back on the bar. He leaned close.

"Don't worry. He was no buddy of mine," the guy said. "But I ain't seen him. When I saw him all cut to shit, you know what I did?"

I shrugged. Waited. He let the silence hang.

"I laughed," he said.

In a different mood, at a different moment, he could take my head right off my shoulders. I tried to hold back a sigh of relief.

"So you think he took off?" I said.

"No, he's around. Old Jeffy wouldn't go too far. He's got a bit of a habit, you know?"

He put his finger to the side of his nose.

"And he's a sleaze. Kind of guy, somebody scores and there he is, sniffs it out. Always short on cash but long on nose. No. I laughed when I saw him all cut up. He didn't like it, but what was he gonna do? Take a swing at me?"

He reached out and put his hand on my shoulder. It felt like a steel clamp. The question was rhetorical.

I grinned slightly. He gave my shoulder a pat and nodded to the bartender. She put another Bud down in front of me.

"That's for giving me a good laugh, my friend," the guy said.

"Anytime," I said.

"Hey, what'd you do to your face?"

"A little cut," I said.

"Wrong end of that one?"

"Something like that," I said.

He smiled, turned away, and turned back.

"Hey, let me know what you find out?" he said.

I nodded, and felt a rivulet of sweat running down my back. He went back to his friends and their conversation, but I felt as if all the eyes were still on me. The bartender lit a cigarette and watched the television. I finished my beer and started on my freebie. The bartender turned away from the bar and lifted a case of empties off the floor. As she started for the back of the room, she caught my eye. I waited a respectable length of time and followed, going into the men's room first.

When I came out, she was waiting in the dimly lit hall.

"Foxy's," she said.

"What's that?"

"Foxy's. The porn place. If you're looking for Tanner."

"He goes there?" I asked.

"His nose isn't the only habit he has," she said.

"Okay."

"And if anybody asks, I never saw you. I knew Donna and she was a sweetheart. I'd kill him myself if I thought I could get away with it."

"I'm not planning on killing anybody."

"Well, that son of a bitch used her bad. It's about time he got it back. I swear, I'd do it if I could."

I looked into her eyes, big and black and brimming with hate and vengeance. And I believed her.

She went back to the bar. I counted to twenty and followed. The gang was all there except the mummified man, who was napping, his shrunken head on his arms and his withered arms on the bar. I put down a ten-dollar bill and headed for the door. My newfound friend gave me a farewell salute.

"You'll know by his eyes, man," the big guy said. "I like that."

It had been such a fun-filled day: Leaman, Albert, making new friends in the bar. A visit to a porn shop? Why stop when I was on a roll?

Foxy's was in the north end of town, in a back-street building that had been a working-class tenement. I'd driven by the place before, seen the guys disappear sheepishly through the door to do whatever it was they did behind the blacked-out windows and then other guys sheepishly come back out.

It seemed a strange compulsion. But it seemed stranger still on a radiant June day like this.

When I pulled up in front of the building, there were two cars in the lot and two more across the street. As I walked toward the door, it opened and a fortyish balding guy came out, squinting into the glare. He looked down at the ground as we passed, and I pushed the door open and slipped inside.

The door opened into a dimly lit room, with humming fluorescent lights in the ceiling and dirty rust-colored carpet on the floor. The walls were covered with movie packages that showed naked men and women frozen in grotesque parodies of passion. It was like an X-rated wax museum, but as I moved slowly across the room, something behind me stirred.

"Can I help you find anything?" a voice said.

I turned. There was a counter to the left of the door and a chubby kid behind the counter.

"Yeah, the way out," I said.

"Pardon me?"

"Just looking around," I said. ·

"Go right ahead," he said. "Those are our for-sale movies, the ones on the wall behind you. The rental movies are through that door. But the for-sale movies are a better buy. Almost the same price. Never been viewed."

He said it as if they might contain some kind of revelation, sleazy Dead Sea scrolls. I didn't think so.

I walked into the next room and it was more of the same. I scanned the walls, wondering who these people were, whether their parents knew what they did for a living. *My daughter, she's an actress. Out in California.*

I went back to the first room and the kid behind the counter looked up and smiled helpfully, giving my bandage only a fleeting glance. Nice job, I thought. A few years of this and you'll have one hell of a résumé.

There was a curtained doorway next to his counter, a display case of movies with numbers.

"What's that?" I asked.

"The viewing booths," he said. "Tokens are a quarter. Actually, you can use quarters or tokens. What they do is basically give you a minute and a half."

I pulled the curtain aside and looked down a dank, dark hallway. There were booths along one side, lined up like confessionals in a sewer. From somewhere in there came the sound of someone shrieking. I figured it was only a movie, but I wasn't sure.

"We buy back unused tokens," the kid said as I closed the curtain.

"That's okay," I said. "What I'm really wondering is if you know a friend of mine."

"Our clients are confidential."

"Oh, I know. But I'd really like to see this guy. I've been away for a few years and he moves so much, I can't find where he's living."

The kid looked at me.

"You a cop?"

"Nope. And this guy, I know he comes in here a lot. I've heard he's a very regular customer. Heck of a good guy. I'm sure you know him."

The kid waited. He was listening.

"His name's Jeff Tanner."

"You want to leave him a message, if an individual by that name comes in, I could give it to him," he said.

I smiled.

"I'm sort of hard to get ahold of. What I was hoping was to find out where he lived so I could just pop in and see him. How 'bout it? I'm gonna find him anyway. You can make some money on the situation, or I can give it to somebody else."

I took my wallet out of my back pocket and two twenties out of the wallet. I put one on the counter. The kid looked at it and sniffed. I put down the other.

"Confidential, of course," I said.

"One more," the kid said.

I dropped it on the other two. He scooped them up and slipped out of his chair and went to a computer terminal. Tapped a few keys and stared at the screen. As I waited, a balding guy brushed through the curtain and yanked the door open and left. The kid was scribbling on a piece of paper, which he then slid across the counter to me. I stuck it in my pocket.

"I never saw you," he said.

"How many addresses do you have?"

"Two," he said.

"Both of them on here?"

"No."

"Give me both. I'd also love to know if regular customers come here at a certain time of day, certain day of the week."

"One more," the kid said.

I put it down and he scooped it up.

"Usually weekdays. Between five and six."

"Thursdays?"

"Most days."

"Thanks," I said.

"Yeah, right," the kid said.

I went to the door and started to open it, and the glare of the afternoon sun flooded in.

"So who is it who's looking for him?" the kid said, back in his chair.

"His minister," I said. "He's strayed from the flock."

Both addresses were within walking distance, which may have been coincidence but I doubted it. Jeff liked his women subservient and one-dimensional. With Donna gone, he probably had gone back to his last girlfriend, who was inflatable with soft skin of genuine vinyl.

I left the car at Foxy's and walked. It was a nice day for a stroll, even on this tattered boulevard. I walked up the block, past the beat-up tenements, the tiny yards scuffed smooth by kids and cars and dog chains. A couple of mutts barked, but without conviction. A little girl with jelly on her face watched me from a porch and then scurried inside the open, screenless door. Another fifty yards up the street, a school bus pulled up, its brakes screeching. The door slammed open and five or six kids tumbled down the steps and onto the street. The girls were a little older than Donna's Adrianna and they were carrying jump ropes, coiled like lariats. The boys had baseball gloves. One of them turned back as the bus pulled away and gave one of his schoolmates the finger.

He needed a parent who would ground him for that. He needed a parent who would ground him. He needed a parent. I wondered how Tanner had tried to fill that role. I wondered if he had tried at all.

The first address was on Carter Street, which ran from Main to River. The number was 15C, at the far end. I walked past the open windows, the doors that spilled out onto the sidewalk. Number fifteen was a pink building set back from the street. There was a set of wooden stairs tacked to the side and a stoop on the front. I tried the stoop first, banging on the wooden door. I banged again. As I turned to leave, the curtain fluttered and I turned back. I caught a glimpse of an old woman, but then she disappeared. I banged again and the door shuddered open. The odor of an old woman billowed out.

"Hi, there," I said. "I'm looking for Jeff Tanner."

She was tiny, with a mustache and pale opaque eyes. Cataract gray. I reached for my wallet to get my ID.

"He ain't been here," the old woman said. "Like I told your pals. One hand don't know what the other hand's doing, I'd say."

"What pals are those?"

"The detectives. I told 'em. He ain't been here since the night they first picked him up. I told 'em and I'll tell you. You spooked him and he took off. You shoulda waited 'til you had your case and then pinched him and kept him in the can. What do they teach you in police school, anyway? How to drink coffee and eat doughnuts?"

I smiled.

"God almighty, I know more from watching television. Only now I mostly listen, 'cause of my eyes. What's that on your face, anyway?"

"A Band-Aid. So where was his apartment?"

"Upstairs. Only it wasn't just his. He lived there, if you could call it that, with another couple guys. Only they weren't there, either. Goddamn druggies, if you ask me. None of 'em went to work. That fella Jeff, he only been here a month, but I still don't know what he did for money. How do these guys buy groceries?"

"Maybe they don't," I said.

"Well, they live on something. That Tanner, he took my trash out one day. Strong buck. Usually the man next door does it, but he forgot or something and it was trash day, and I'm gonna be stuck with this garbage smelling for another week, and Tanner, he sees me and he comes over and he takes the bag and puts it out there. Polite and pleasant and everything."

"Really."

"That's why I was disappointed when I heard he killed that little girl. Not surprised, I'll tell you. These druggies don't know what they're doing half the time."

"Where did you hear that?" I asked her.

"At the hairdresser's," the woman said. "Her daughter, she's trouble, I think, but I don't say anything. She knows cops, too, and she said he was good as hung for it. Strangled her. Helps me with my trash, nice as pie, and then goes out and strangles some girl."

"Her name was Donna."

"Poor thing. She had a little girl, right?"

"Yeah," I said. "Her name is Adrianna. She's four."

"Well, ain't that a shame. Wonder what drove him over the edge? Usually it's one thing that makes these people snap. They go along and some little thing happens and bam, they lose it. Don't suppose it matters now. Won't bring that girl back."

"No, but it still matters. It matters a lot."

"Well, you would say that, doing what you do, wouldn't you?" the old woman said.

I thought of Donna. In court. In the parking lot. In the paper.

"Yeah," I said. "I would."

22

The second address was a lot like the first, except nobody answered the door at all. I waited a minute or two and then gave up, walking back to Foxy's and the car. I waited there for a half hour and saw three men slink into the place, two men slink out. They came and went alone. Jeff was not among them.

I decided to call it a day.

Before leaving town, I stopped for Ballantine ale. When I came out of the store, the car was dripping antifreeze. I decided to pretend I hadn't noticed. Maybe the car would pretend to run.

It was almost five thirty when I got home, driving down the dump road under the big green maples. I slowed as I approached the house and scanned the woods. I was looking for Jeff, his truck, Leaman and his buddies.

I didn't expect the state police.

But they were there, sitting in an unmarked car that was backed into an open space in the woods. It was Kelly and LaCharelle, and they both nodded at me as I rolled by. I kept going to the house and parked. They followed and pulled in behind me.

"Officers," I said, getting out of the car.

"Mr. McMorrow," Kelly said, closing the driver's door. "Long time no see."

"I've been around."

"So we've heard," LaCharelle said, walking up to me. "We need to talk."

"Come on in. I'd offer you an ale, but I suppose you're on duty."

"Story of our lives," Kelly said. "But you feel free."

I put the Ballantine on the kitchen table but left it in the bag. Kelly and LaCharelle scanned the place in that involuntary cop way and then leaned against the counter. I leaned, too.

"Mr. McMorrow, you've been busy," LaCharelle said, hitching at the gun under the back of his jacket.

"How's that?"

"Everywhere we go, you been there," Kelly said. "The pothead downstairs from Donna Marchant. The lady next door. Even at the bar."

"The Mansion," LaCharelle said.

"They said you'd been there. At least we figure it was you. Description fits. The way you handle yourself."

"How do I handle myself?"

"Kind of cocky, for a reporter," Kelly said.

"I prefer to think of it as quiet confidence," I said.

"Whatever," Kelly said. "I just wonder what you're working so hard on."

"A story about a murder. What do you want me to do? Wait for your press release?"

LaCharelle shifted to his other foot.

"Yeah, well, we stopped at the newspaper to try to find you," he said. "We talked to this Mr. Albert. He said you aren't even working for the paper anymore."

"Not that one."

"So who you gonna write this story for? The *New York Times*?" Kelly said.

"Maybe."

"What are you up to, McMorrow?" LaCharelle put in, his tone more confidential, more intimate. "I talked to the Kennebec cops. You've been connected to an assault, and Lenny there said you'd been hauled off by some local luminaries and beat up. They give you that cut on your face?"

I shrugged.

"Listen," Kelly said. "This isn't some goddamn game. And we're sick of you getting in the way all the time. I knock on a door and they say, 'I just told the other guy the whole story.' I say, 'What guy?' They say, 'The guy from the newspaper. At first I thought he was a cop.' You aren't impersonating a police officer, are you?"

I smiled.

"What good would that do me in a place like The Mansion?"

"What were you doing there?" Kelly said.

"Didn't they tell you?"

"Nope," LaCharelle said. "Like I said . . ."

"Cut the shit," Kelly said. "What's the connection to you and the victim? What's the connection to you and Tanner? We can nail him. We don't need your help. We don't—"

"Let him answer," LaCharelle broke in. "What is the connection between you and this Marchant woman?"

"I told you. I talked to her once, outside court. I wrote about her once. I talked to her again at her house. That's it."

"So what are you doing in this thing up to your eyebrows?" Kelly said. "She some squeeze you had?"

"No."

"So what is it?" Kelly said. "Why don't you just back the hell off?"

I didn't say anything.

"Let him answer," LaCharelle said.

"I am," Kelly said.

They both waited.

"I can't," I said.

"Can't what?" Kelly said.

"Can't just back off."

"Why the hell not?" he said. "It's none of your goddamn business. It's our goddamn business."

"You guys ought to work homicide in New York. Do a nice high-profile murder, with newspapers and TV and radio stations climbing all over you morning, noon, and night. You're spoiled."

"This isn't New York," Kelly said.

"No, he's changed the subject," LaCharelle said. "Shut up for a minute. McMorrow, now why can't you back off?"

I thought for a moment.

"Because I don't," I said. "Not anymore."

They looked at me.

"What is this bullshit?" Kelly said. "Listen, you know something about Marchant or Tanner or any of this that we don't know?"

"I don't think so."

"Well, you better friggin' know so," Kelly said. "And you sure as hell better not frig this up. 'Cause we will friggin' lock you up. And don't think I'm kidding."

"I don't."

"It's a homicide," he said. "No joke."

"What's the cause of death?" I said.

"What?" Kelly said.

"How'd she die? Nobody's released the official cause of death. I heard she'd died of asphyxiation. That true?"

"You're a nervy SOB, you know that?" Kelly said.

"What else you hear?" LaCharelle said.

"That there were no obvious signs of foul play. No cord around her neck or anything like that."

"No, but she was suffocated," LaCharelle said. "Bruises on the throat. Faint ones, but that isn't what killed her. Could have been a pillow, or even a hand."

"That for the record?"

LaCharelle thought.

"Sure," he said. "What are you going to do with it?"

"I don't know. Did the lady next door have anything to say?"

"You letting him ask all the questions?" Kelly sputtered.

"It's okay," LaCharelle said. "With all those kids, McMorrow? You could have a goddamn shotgun slaying next door and she wouldn't hear it."

So it wasn't Miss Desrosiers they'd talked to. I still had Jeff leaving and Donna doing dishes after he was gone.

They both straightened up and moved toward the door.

"Something doesn't add up about this, McMorrow," Kelly said. "So just stay out of the way. Whatever game you're playing, do it somewhere else."

"It's not a game," I said. "It's a woman's life. A man's life. A kid's life, too."

"Just so we understand each other," LaCharelle said.

"I think we do."

They pulled out of the dooryard and headed back out to the main road. I watched the cruiser, then went back to the table and got a Ballantine. I opened it and took a long lukewarm swallow. It would have tasted good boiled. I drained it, put one in the freezer, and opened a third. I had just sat back down when I heard tires in the yard again. I went to the front window.

Roxanne.

She came through the door and I got up and she threw her arms around me and held on tight. For a long time. A very long time.

Her face was buried in my shoulder and when it finally came up there was a hint of tears in her eyes.

"Your allergies kicking up?" I said, looking at her.

"I don't have allergies."

"Except to me."

"Don't say that," Roxanne said.

"All right, I won't."

"Don't even think it."

"I won't," I said, still holding her. "If you don't ask me what happened to my face."

"What happened to your face?"

"You weren't supposed to ask me."

"The deal's off, Jack. What the hell happened to your face?"

She reached up and gently touched the bandage.

"I got cut," I said.

"How bad?" Roxanne asked, her voice gentle too.

"Not too bad."

"What's not too bad?"

"A few stitches."

"How many's a few?"

"Relentless, aren't you," I said.

"Yes. How many's a few?"

"Several."

"Jack," Roxanne said.

Her fingernail slid under the tape on the side of the bandage. It peeled away easily.

"Oh, my God, Jack. Oh, you're going to have a scar."

"Not just another pretty face."

"What happened?"

Her eyes moved from my eyes to the cut, back and forth. Her eyes were deep and dark and beautiful. Her nose and mouth weren't bad either.

"I fell on a piece of glass. It was sort of an accident."

"Sort of?"

"They didn't mean it."

"Who's they?"

"The guys in the car," I said.

"What guys in what car?"

"It's a long story."

"I think I need a glass of wine," Roxanne said.

"But that'll mean letting go of me."

"Where's the corkscrew?" she said. "I brought a bottle of Merlot."

So Roxanne poured a glass of wine. I poured the Ballantine into a beer mug. We sat side by side on the bench on the deck. With one hand, Roxanne held her wineglass. With the other, she held my hand. We talked easily, as always. I told her about Leaman and his friends.

"So that's why you weren't supposed to come back yet," I said.

"That's why I did. I was worried about you. I am worried about you."

"I'm fine. But that isn't all."

"What else?" Roxanne said.

Her fingers were intertwined with mine. They were long and soft. Her legs were crossed under her skirt. They were long and soft too.

"I've been running around asking questions about Jeff and Donna. Then I quit the *Observer*."

"Why?"

"Because they did a story on Donna that made her out to be some worthless piece of garbage."

"And she wasn't."

"Not at all. She was a good person. She tried very hard in a lot of ways. She just didn't have a lot of luck. Good luck, I mean."

"Why didn't their story say that, then?" Roxanne asked.

"Because it was easier to fall back on the stereotype. Welfare. Boyfriends. Drinking. To know her you had to really look at her. They didn't bother. It's a very lazy, cowardly newspaper. I didn't want to be associated with it. I'm sorry I was."

I was quiet for a moment. Roxanne looked over at me.

"You shouldn't keep blaming yourself," she said. "Is that why you've been off on this mission?"

"I just need to know what happened."

"So you're doing some kind of penance."

"I don't know if I'd call it that," I said. "I just think I should see it through to the end. I liked her."

"No, it's a penance. And I can understand that, but it's wrong."

"Why's that?"

"I understand what you're doing, but I'm going to tell you how I have a problem with it," Roxanne said. "It's because it's this martyr thing."

"You think I cut my own face."

"Jack, I'm serious. You think you're to blame for Donna being killed. So you're going to throw yourself in the middle of this whole thing, put yourself in the line of fire. Half hoping you'll be hit, too."

"So what?" I said.

"I don't know, Jack. There's something self-indulgent about it. Dangerously self-indulgent. You wrote your article in good faith. It was a fair subject for commentary and you were trying to help. It didn't work out. So instead of going on to the next story, try to do some good for somebody else, you throw it all away."

I didn't say anything.

"It's like what I do, Jack," Roxanne said. "What if every time something went wrong with a client, I went on some crusade? If a child wasn't helped, if a child went from bad to worse, to drugs and the streets? What if I tried to help the child and failed? You know what I have to do?"

"No, what?"

"Go on to the next kid. The next family. Even though I don't want to. It would be easier to go off the deep end. A lot easier. But if I do that the other hundred and eighty-three clients are the ones who pay. I can't allow myself that luxury."

"But you don't get people killed," I said.

"Sure I do. I mean, I'm sure I do. I do it by not saving them. They just take a lot longer to die."

I thought for a moment. The phoebes fluttered by and lighted on a branch of a white ash. We were still. They flicked their flycatcher tails.

"Where'd you get all this cold common sense?" I said.

"From my mother. She's spent half her life feeling sorry for herself."

"So that cured you of it?"

"And keeps me from spending much time in Florida," Roxanne said. "I can't stand to watch her."

"What does she have to feel sorry for?"

"Not much. It's just this habit she can't break. I can't stand it."

"That's sad," I said. "So how are you going to stand me?"

"When?" Roxanne said.

"When I see this thing through right to the very end."

Roxanne sighed.

"Well, maybe I could help hasten the process," she said.

"You hasten my process."

"You're lucky I love you."

"That, too."

When the bugs got too bad, we moved from the bench to the house. We made a cold pasta salad and ate quietly, with candlelight. Roxanne talked about Skip and his boat, said that he was really becoming a good friend. She told me a few of her Human Services horror stories, then a couple more with tiny seed pearls of hope. She said she liked it, that she was enjoying being in the trenches again. I said I'd like to get her in the trenches again, and she shook her head in mock dismay. I put the dishes in the sink and she went to the bathroom. While she was gone, I took the rifle up to the loft and slid it under the bed.

Safe sex.

I lay on my back so that I wouldn't bump my stitches. Roxanne was gentle as a nurse and then not so gentle, her body moving above me in the shadows. And then she lay beside me and said she loved me even though I was as scarred as an old tomcat.

"But that's where the similarity ends," Roxanne whispered.

"That's right," I said, but even at that moment, I thought of Donna and wondered if I really was capable of straying.

"No," I said to myself.

"No what?" Roxanne said.

"No way," I said.

Roxanne left early the next morning. It was Friday and she had to be in Cumberland County District Court at nine for a custody hearing for some poor little kid who didn't get fed much, or often. Roxanne said she'd come back that night, that I needed her. I didn't disagree. We said good-bye and she held me again, briefly, and then I watched her from the window as she got in her car, adjusted her skirt and seat belt, and pulled out, her face already full of resolve.

She was tougher than me in a lot of ways. But I had more scars.

I turned from the window and the house already seemed empty. It occurred to me that I needed Roxanne more than I admitted, that this separation was not going to work out. Then I tried to see myself sitting on the deck at Roxanne's condo, waving to passing cabin cruisers. That would not work out either. I decided to think about something easier, like breakfast.

It was another warm sunny day, and I ate out on the bench. Toast with Mary Varney's homemade apple butter. Orange juice and Irish tea and the rifle leaning in the corner. I sat and sipped and then a shadow went over and I got a glimpse of a hawk, big with bands across the tail. It disappeared over the trees, heading in the direction of the marsh.

"Red-shouldered or broad-winged?" a voice said.

I turned.

"Red-shouldered, because the bands are dark," I said.

"When I was a kid, farmers around here used to shoot them on sight," Clair said. "It was all small farms around here then. They grew vegetables for canneries, had a few cows. It was a nice life and then it just disappeared."

"That's sort of a shame."

"Like a lot of things."

"You got that right," I said. "But then there's always Mary's apple butter to look forward to."

"Not if she gives it all to you," Clair said.

He stood on the edge of the deck and looked out at the woods. There were wood chips at the top of his boots and blotches of sweat on the back of his shirt.

"Don't tell me you've been cutting alone," I said.

"Just bucking up some wood right behind the house. If anything happened I'd have time to crawl in and draw up a will."

"I've been thinking along those lines myself."

"Strange doings in the big city?" Clair asked, still looking away.

"A little bit."

I told him about quitting the job. The bar and the porn shop. My ride with Leaman and his aides. I asked him if he wanted to see my stitches and he said no.

"Sounds like a full day," Clair said.

"I was ready for a beer."

"Where's this Leaman guy now?"

"Don't know."

"Don't you want to find out?"

"I suppose I'd better."

"Before he finds you. If you're all that stands between him and a twenty-year prison term, he might want to renew your acquaintance."

"We have a lot to talk about," I said, finishing my tea.

"I'd shoot him on sight."

"There's something to be said for the direct approach. And Roxanne's coming back. At least for the weekend."

"Come up to the house," Clair said. "Why don't you stay at the house? Mary'd like to cook for somebody besides me."

I thought of Leaman and Jeff. I wondered why I hadn't thought of them as much last night. It was all becoming too normal, and that was dangerous.

"Might take you up on that," I said.

"What are you going to do today?"

"Go into town and wander around."

"Must be nice," Clair said. "A man of leisure."

"It has its moments."

"So who should be here while you're off gallivanting?"

"Roxanne tonight. State cops might stop by. Last night it was detectives in an unmarked black Chevy. Leaman and his buddies had an old beater, loud exhaust, mostly primer black. This reporter kid, Archambault, he drives a beat-up red Toyota. I guess that's about it."

"I'll keep a weather eye out," Clair said.

"Don't shoot the Fuller Brush man."

"Just a warning shot over his head."

"Promise?" I said.

Clair went back to work and I did too, putting the rifle in the trunk and the cartridges in the glove box. It was eight thirty when I pulled into the parking lot behind the Kennebec police station, took a quick look around, and went inside. The dispatcher was peering at a computer screen. I knocked on the bulletproof glass and she didn't look up. I banged harder and she jumped. I smiled and asked for Officer Lenny.

"On the road," she said.

"North or south end?" I asked.

"South, out to the interstate. Is there anything I can help you with?"

"No," I said. "Unfortunately, no."

I went back out to the car. There was antifreeze on the ground under the front bumper, a small greenish puddle. I made a mental note to buy a gallon and top off the radiator. I made a mental note to ask the state cops about my truck, too.

The interstate ran along the west side of Kennebec's outskirts, through the last vestiges of dairy farms, past dreary prefab warehouses. There was a shopping center out there, a couple of car dealers. The road was pocked with mini-malls, where businesses came and went as they exhausted the demand for things like five-dollar T-shirts and cheap tools. But it was a long, straight stretch, and the cops sat and nabbed drivers as they sped from mini-mall to mini-mall in pursuit of one more piece of junk.

I figured I'd find Lenny here someplace, radar gun in hand. And I did, beside a sign for a water-bed store that was going out of business. I pulled in beside him. He motioned for me to come over and get in. I did.

"I just tried to call you," he said.

"What about?"

"We haven't found Leaman."

"Were you thinking he might speed by?" I said.

Lenny looked at me.

"Oh, we have to do this. A half hour a shift. But everybody's looking for him."

"Why doesn't that make me feel better?"

"This isn't going to make you feel better either. We found one of his old girlfriends. She said he told her he wasn't going back to prison, and if he did, he'd take you down first."

"Does that follow? Logically, I mean?"

"Not really," Lenny said. "But you've got to remember this isn't any rocket scientist we're dealing with here."

"But he has a doctorate in sociopathy. Should I be worried?"

"If you're the worrying type. Anybody at home to worry about?"

"Yeah, sometimes," I said. "You think he'd come all the way out to Prosperity?"

"Doubt it. But I wouldn't want to bet my life on it."

"Is that what you wanted to tell me?"

"Yeah," Lenny said.

"I had two state police detectives over last night. I should have asked them to stay."

"What'd they want?" Lenny said, perking up.

"To tell me to get out of the way. They said they could nail Jeff Tanner without me."

"Yeah, off the record, I heard they're really focusing on him now. I guess he admitted trying to choke her."

"So what are they waiting for?"

"I heard he says she was fine when he left. They're waiting for the ME's report on something. Time of death, I think. They'll work on him some more and he'll go away for a long time."

"Why not arrest him now?"

" 'Cause then he gets a lawyer. Right now he's just going around town shooting his mouth off. And he won't run. He's a homeboy too."

I looked out the window at the passing cars and trucks. Thought for a minute.

"What if he's telling the truth?" I said.

"What do you mean?"

"What if Donna *was* fine when he left? What if somebody else killed her after he left?"

"Hell of a coincidence. Two people trying to strangle the same woman on the same night?"

"But what if they did?"

"Then Jeff has to hope that the real murderer feels guilty and turns himself in."

"And that's a long shot," I said.

"Your theory is even longer."

"Maybe."

"And I thought you wanted to nail this guy."

"I do," I said. "I really do."

Our conversation killed the last of Lenny's half hour, and he sped off in the direction of town. He had my number, he said. He'd call if anything happened. I said I'd do the same. He said he hoped I heard from him first, and I think he meant it. I thought about that for a minute and then, when his cruiser was out of sight, I pulled out and went the other way.

I drove out to the shopping center by the interstate ramps, where the signs stood sixty feet high to lure unwary motorists off the highway. I turned in under the sign that said LINCOLN/MERCURY in ten-foot letters and pulled my heap around to the side of the building.

This was the only place in town where a car salesman, like Donnie, would be driving a thirty-thousand-dollar Jeep. The showroom was carpeted and dark, with country-western music coming from somewhere in the ceiling, and cars parked here and there with their doors open, trunks propped up like coffin lids. I felt as though I should kneel before one of the gleaming idols, but before I could, a young blond guy hurried from one of the little rooms off to the side, his hand out and his smile open wide, like an incision in his face.

"Hi there," he said.

"Hello," I said.

"Which of these cars can I interest you in?" he said, grinning madly. I turned toward the lot.

"That gray Lincoln out there, but I promised I'd talk to Donnie." His smile hung limply.

"Donnie. Oh, sure. Donnie is . . . Donnie is with somebody right now. If you'd like to look around a bit, he'll be—"

"Is that Lincoln unlocked?"

He looked.

"Should be. Yeah."

"I'll just sit myself down in there, then. Enjoy the leather."

"Oh, it's got that," Blondie said. "That automobile is loaded. And I mean loaded."

I smiled at the thought.

"I'll be out there."

"I'll send him right out."

I sat in the front passenger seat of the Lincoln and looked at all the buttons. There were many of them, and the seat was very comfortable. Not only that, but this car probably didn't drip antifreeze.

By the digital clock on the dash, I waited six minutes. The showroom door swung open behind me and then the driver's door. I opened the glove box and fiddled with the makeup mirror long enough for him to get in the car and close the door.

And then I turned and looked into Donnie's smiling face.

"How's the vacuum cleaner business?" I said.

23

—⚋—

Donnie's smile did a little flip and turned into a scowl.

"What are you doing here?"

"I'd scowl too if I had to wear that silly pink jacket," I said. "Let's go for a ride."

"What's this? Hey, I don't have time to waste on—"

"I know. You're very busy. There's a line fifty yards long of people who want to buy this thirty-eight-thousand-dollar car. And then there's me, who just wants to talk."

Donnie reached for the door handle.

"And if I don't get to talk, I'm going to go in and ask for the manager and demand to know why that salesman refused to talk to me about this car. And when you try to explain, he's going to say he wants his people to leave their screwed-up personal lives at home. And I'll say I'm going to go across the road and buy a Cadillac."

I looked away from him.

"Start this boat and let's go," I said.

Donnie paused for a moment and then slowly turned the key. The motor was out there somewhere, and it started softly. He put the car in gear and we went through the lot and out on the main drag. I pointed to the interstate ramp and he turned onto it, accelerating up onto the highway.

"This thing sure is quiet," I said. "How's the gas mileage?"

He pursed his lips.

"So talk," he said.

"You weren't too happy last time I saw you. You were angry and threatening. Of course, it was hard to take you seriously in those elevator cowboy boots."

"What do you want?"

"I want to continue that conversation we had. I believe you said something like, 'That bitch isn't going to bleed me dry.' Other things that might be construed as threatening to your ex-wife."

I looked at him.

"Construed by the police, I mean. The ones who are trying to decide who killed Donna."

"I had nothing to do with that. What the hell are you trying to pull? And who the hell—"

"I told you," I said. "I want to talk. About Donna."

"I got nothing to say about her."

"Not even to express your condolences? A little regret?"

"Who the hell—"

Donnie choked it back. Gave a disgusted little snort.

"What the hell do you want to know, anyway?"

"I just want to chat," I said as the car cruised along silently. "Did you talk to Donna after we met?"

"No, and she never called me back, either. If she got the message."

"She got the message. I told her some jerk had stopped by, but the good news was that he'd left."

"You got an attitude problem," Donnie said. "'I don't know what your problem is, but—"

"So you didn't see her?"

"Nope."

"You didn't call her?"

"No. I got other things to do, you know? I can't just chase her all day."

"Not anymore."

He stared straight ahead.

"So what were you going to do to her? You were pretty hot that day."

"Yeah, well, you'd be hot too. Goddamn state attached my wages. And then the goddamn IRS gets in on it. They want their piece, too. I mean, jeez. They're gonna destroy me for eighteen thousand bucks. Lien on my house. I'm gonna have to sell my boat, my snowmobiles, or something to get these guys off my back. I mean, for this one little kid."

"Doesn't seem fair, does it?"

"No, and you know what's—"

He caught himself. I grinned.

"So what were you gonna do about it?"

"To Donna, you mean? Wasn't anything I could do. Something happens to Donna, I still pay. Don't make no difference. As long as the kid is around, I have to pay."

"So what were you going to do about it?" I asked again.

"I don't know. Maybe nothing. Maybe I was just spouting off," Donnie said.

"Maybe you weren't."

"Listen, McMorrow, or whatever the hell your name is. I'm not some numbskull. I got a lot to lose if I get in trouble. Job, car, insurance."

"You won't need a car if you were the one."

I turned and watched him closely, especially the eyes.

"You think I'm gonna throw all this away on her? That bitch was nothing but trouble from the day—"

"Don't call her that," I said. "Don't call her that again."

"What are you gonna do about it?"

"I don't know. Something. Now, tell me what you were doing that night."

"Why should I?"

"Because I asked. Because maybe when I told the cops about you stopping by I didn't get into all the gory details. Maybe I need to go over it with them again."

The Lincoln sped across the bridge over the Kennebec River. I didn't look. I didn't take my eyes off Donnie's face.

"Myself and my girlfriend, we had dinner at my place, out on the lake. We went out on the boat, had a few drinks, whatever. Then came back and watched part of a movie."

"What movie?"

"*Lethal Weapon.* The second one."

"How was it?"

"Not bad. I mean, I like all that kind of stuff."

"What about your girlfriend? What's her name?"

"What's her name? Angie."

"She likes that kind of movie?"

"She don't care," Donnie said. "I mean, she's agreeable."

"Which is why you have her around."

He looked at me.

"One of the reasons," he said slowly. "She's a whole different ball game from Donna. I mean, whining about everything I did."

"Angie lets you call the shots, right?"

"Yeah," Donnie said, his hands on the wheel, rings on his fingers. "I mean, I got a right. I pay the bills. I got her driving a brand-new Jeep, power goddamn sunroof, CD, the works. She don't have to do nothing."

"Which is what you wanted Donna to do, right?"

"Right. But she had to get in my face about every little thing. I mean, who was she when I met her? Some little blonde who couldn't even keep a checkbook."

"So you married her."

"Hey, she was good in the—"

"Don't even say it," I said. "So you watched your movie with Angie and then you went to bed and that's all you did."

"Basically, yeah," Donnie said.

"And you didn't go to Donna's?"

"No way."

"And you didn't fight with her?"

"Hell, no."

"And you didn't kill her?"

Donnie looked at me.

"What do you think I am?" he said. "Stupid? You think I'm gonna throw all this away?"

I looked at him. He was serious. It was his best defense, and it was a good one. Donnie would not risk losing his Jeep with the CD player. He would not risk losing his boots and his phony tan and his gold chains and rings. He would not risk losing his Angie.

In that order.

I looked at him, then out of the window, where the trees were gliding by.

"Do you feel bad that she's dead?" I said.

Donnie shrugged.

"Sure," he said. "I mean, yeah. She wasn't making my life any easier, but what the hell. I didn't want her dead. I just wanted her out of my hair."

"Not to mention the devastating impact on your daughter."

"Oh, yeah," Donnie said. "Hey, they spent a lot of time together."

I looked at him, in his pallid attempt to show compassion.

"There's a crossover up here," I said. "Turn this thing around. Before I blow lunch on the leather."

Donnie drove back to the dealership, fast. He pulled the Lincoln up at the end of the lot, away from the showroom. I popped the door open.

"Listen," he said as I swung my legs out. "Don't you try to tie me to this, or you'll—"

"I'll what?" I said.

I swung back into the seat and closed the door.

Donnie looked at me. His mouth opened. And then it shut.

I got out of the car and walked away.

So Donnie was guilty of a lot of things. Of considering women to be accessories. Of being completely bereft of anything resembling paternal feelings toward his pretty little daughter. Of being materialistic and greedy and crass. Of having very bad taste in sport coats.

But he was not guilty of killing Donna.

I was convinced of that, and as I drove back into town I thought that maybe I could scratch him off my list. That Jeff had one more strike against him. That the answer isn't always the obvious one, but sometimes it is.

And then my mind skipped back to Donna and my story and her innocence in the midst of all this. Talking to me in a parking lot. Trusting me—trusting that I would not hurt her, when she had so little reason to trust anyone.

I was on top of him. Well, it started with . . . he had me by the shoulders, you know? And he tried to kind of throw me across the room, but I hung on to him and we both landed on the floor and his head was underneath my shoulder and he bit me to get me off him.

Don't hurt her, Marcia had said. Don't you hurt her.

I owed Donna. I guess I owed Marcia.

Back in town, I pulled into a mom-and-pop store and bought an *Observer* off the counter. I flipped through the first section until I found the police log. There I was, but only two paragraphs. The word *apparently* was used four times. It was reported that Officer Lenny had been unavailable for comment.

I owed him one too.

There was a twenty-inch story about some zoning dispute. An interminable piece of gush about an upcoming sidewalk sale sponsored by the Chamber of Commerce. A feature on a woman who had been reunited with her brother after forty-two years, complete with a photo of two middle-aged people hugging.

Archambault had written that story. He had not written about Donna. If he had skipped a day, maybe things were cooling off. Maybe Marcia had come home.

I drove across town and out into the subdivided hayfields. When I turned onto Marcia's road, I slowed. As I approached her house, I slowed some more.

From a distance, the house looked as deserted as last time. There were no cars or trucks in the driveway, nobody out in the yard. I made one pass and turned around in a driveway up the road. On the second pass, I slowed even more.

And thought I saw something move.

It was in one of the front windows. Just a flicker, a movement that could have been imagined. I drove two houses up and turned around again, then came back to Marcia's house and parked in the street out front. I sat in the car with the motor running and watched.

The windows were blank. The house was completely still. I shut off the motor and the car was still too.

And it moved again.

It was a shadow, a dark form, and it had passed in front of the same window, the one to the left of the front door. I watched for another minute, then got out of the car and walked slowly to the end of the driveway. I stopped there and stood and watched.

Nothing.

I walked up the driveway and then along the flagstones. At the concrete steps, I paused and then walked up and stood in front of the door. The cobwebs were gone. I knocked.

Nobody answered. I listened.

There was the sound of cars out on the main road. Crows from a distance. I knocked again.

Harder.

Then listened again.

Harder.

From somewhere inside came a faint sound. A television? A radio? Voices and then a barely audible sound of laughter.

This time I pounded. Waited. Pounded again. Waited again. Reached out to pound some more.

When the door rattled. And opened.

It was Marcia. Her eyes met mine through the window of the storm door. They were cold and her face was drawn and hard, her skin gray, her makeup unnaturally bright.

I waited as she fumbled with the catch on the storm door, then pushed it open just far enough to speak through the gap.

"Marcia. I didn't want to bother you. I just wanted to—"

"Haven't you done enough?" she said.

"Well, I did want to talk to you about—"

"Haven't you done enough?" she repeated, her voice flat and distant, the voice of someone exhausted by grief.

I felt almost stunned. I blamed myself for Donna, but now I realized that somehow I had hoped Marcia wouldn't blame me. That somehow there would be room for exoneration. She was an unlikely ally, but it was the unlikely ones that I needed.

"I'm sorry," I said. "I really am. I didn't intend for it to turn out this way."

"But it did, McMorrow," Marcia said wearily.

Her hand still was on the door latch. The room behind her was dark, the back blinds drawn.

"How's Adrianna doing?"

Marcia flinched. Pulled the door shut.

"Just go, McMorrow," she said, her voice muffled by the glass. "Don't come back."

"I didn't want to upset you. But I felt like I should come by. What would you have thought if I hadn't? I don't know. I felt like I should do that. And maybe this isn't the right time, but I wanted to ask you about that night. I've talked to some of the neighbors, and—"

The door was pushed open.

"You've talked to Donna's neighbors?"

"Yeah, and a couple of them were helpful. One woman saw Jeff leaving and sometime after that, Donna was still—"

"I'm gonna call the cops, McMorrow," Marcia growled, her voice soft and menacing. "And I'm going to tell them you're harassing me. And you're getting in their way. And if you ever come near me again, or come near my little girl, I'll kill you. If you come near my little girl, I swear to God I'll kill you."

Her eyes fixed on mine, and then both doors closed. First one and then the other.

I sat in the car and stared, Marcia's words running through my mind. Her haggard face.

I was a half mile down the road from her house, pulled into a rutted woods road. I'd gotten that far before I'd had to stop and try to sort this out. It wasn't sorting.

There had been no bluster in Marcia's threat. No anger, either. Just determination and this selfless resolve, like she was a cornered animal. A cornered animal with a baby.

If you ever come near my little girl . . .

But what had I done? I hadn't killed her sister. Even if she thought my story had indirectly caused Donna's death, what threat could I be to her or to Adrianna? How could I hurt Adrianna? By mucking up the investigation so that Jeff walked? Maybe. Was Adrianna a witness? If Jeff walked, would he come after Adrianna to silence her? But did she really think I could get in the way to the point that Jeff, or whoever it was, would go free?

Or whoever it was. I supposed that in Marcia's mind, there was no need for that caveat. And if that were the case, she wouldn't want any interference with the police.

But it was when she'd referred to Adrianna that her threat had been most vehement. "If you ever come near my little girl . . ."

Her little girl? True, Adrianna was Marcia's now. Donnie certainly wasn't going to petition for custody, not if it meant risking his perfect life with his Jeep and Angie. But there was something funny about the way Marcia had said it.

"My little girl . . ."

As if her claim to Adrianna were somehow threatened. I remembered that Donna had said how much Marcia wanted children—how Adrianna was a surrogate daughter of some sort, filling that void in Marcia's life. But if she had really filled it now, how could I foul that up? Unless it was anyone who stood in the way of Jeff's conviction for Donna's murder.

But it wasn't vengeance that Marcia was ready to kill for. It was to protect Adrianna. From what? Had Adrianna seen it? Was this four-year-old girl the only witness to this murder?

I sat there for a while, thinking the same thoughts, asking myself the same questions. And underlying all of the questions was the unsettling fact of this death threat, which wasn't the first, by any means. Over the years, several people had threatened to kill me. A few had been punks. A couple had been nuts. Some might have actually done it. But none of those threats had been uttered with Marcia's complete and utter conviction.

She meant it. She'd meant it when she said it. She meant it right now. She'd mean it tomorrow.

24

~m~

I started the car, but when I pulled out of the woods onto the road, I decided to take the long way back to town, a town that was small and seeming smaller.

Tanner and Donnie. Leaman and Tate. Archambault and Albert. And now Marcia.

This town wasn't big enough for all of us. But who'd budge first?

I drove back to Kennebec by making a long loop to the north and then to the east. I drove along country roads, passed people working in their gardens, people riding bikes, guys rumbling along in trucks topped with canoes. Their lives seemed so normal, almost pastoral. I looked forward to the time when I'd do those things again. I wondered when that would be.

When I got back into the downtown it was after noon, but I wasn't hungry. I could duke it out with Jeff and then blithely go have pizza and beer, but seeing Marcia had thrown me. For the first time since I'd come to Kennebec, I felt there was something I didn't know. It was something big, and I didn't know what it was.

I drove along Main Street, my elbow out the window. Downtown was bustling, which in Kennebec meant a UPS truck double-parked. I'd started to pull around it when a guy stepped from between two parked cars and started to cross.

He was holding a paper cup of coffee and a newspaper. He looked at me. I looked at him.

Archambault.

He gave me an uncomfortable sort of frown and I nodded. I kept driving and he continued along the sidewalk behind me and to my right. When a truck lurched out of a parking space, I pulled in. And got out. And waited.

I was leaning against the hood of the car, arms folded on my chest, when Archambault approached. He slowed warily, as if I might step out and clock him. I didn't.

"We need to talk," I said.

He looked surprised and relieved.

"Okay," Archambault said. "I mean, what about?"

"Where'd you get that coffee?"

"The deli."

"Let's go back there," I said. "I could use a cup of tea."

We walked up the block to the deli, side by side, without speaking. When we got there, I held the door for him. When I stepped up to the counter to get my tea, he sat down at a table by the window and waited. The place was empty, and the woman behind the counter got up from reading a magazine to wait on me.

I had the tea black because the cream, like most things in this town, was suspect. As I sat down, Archambault took the plastic lid off his cup. He'd laid that day's *New York Times* on the table. It was the front of the metro section. The lead was a profile of a drunk driver who had killed four people. I knew the woman who had written it.

"You'll learn more from that paper than from anybody in your newsroom," I said.

"And I hear you think I have a lot to learn," Archambault said.

There was an edge of challenge in his voice, but only a faint one.

"I think you need an editor. Your writing isn't bad, and the instincts are there. But you need somebody to tell you when you aren't asking the right questions. A little ethics wouldn't hurt, either. Screw people and it catches up with you in the long run."

"You think I screwed you?"

"Yeah, but I'm minor."

"Who's major?"

"Donna Marchant. You did her a real disservice."

"I heard you quit the paper because of my story."

"Yup."

"What was so bad about it?"

"You took the word of people who have a vested interest in making Donna look bad. Like Tate. She wants to make Donna look like some drunken slut."

"Why?"

"Because Donna came to the court for help and Tate didn't do anything for her. Maybe she wants to ease her conscience, if she has one. Maybe she just wants to keep her job."

"But these are the official sources," Archambault said, sipping his coffee.

I sipped my tea.

"A good reporter doesn't take anything at face value, especially the official word on anything. Your guiding principle should be that people often aren't what they seem. When you try to tie them up in a neat little package, it's usually not true. Life isn't neat. Donna Marchant wasn't a nun, but she wasn't promiscuous. She drank, but she wasn't a drunk. She was a woman and a mother and she'd had some bad luck, but she was trying."

"But I didn't have anybody saying that."

"You didn't ask in the right places," I said.

Archambault looked at his coffee.

"You sent me into that apartment with those lowlifes," he said, looking up. "Was that supposed to be funny?"

"I owed you one. Were they glad to see you?"

"One of 'em took my notebook. But there wasn't anything in it. I thought the guy was gonna take a swing at me."

"Why didn't he?"

"One of the women reminded him about his probation or something. She was screaming and yelling. Jesus."

He paused and stared into his coffee.

"So what's with all the free advice?" Archambault said, looking up suddenly. "What are you after?"

"Information. I want to know if what I'm hearing is the same as what you're hearing."

Archambault thought about that.

"Why?" he said.

"Because if we're hearing different things, then maybe my information isn't as solid as I'd like it to be."

"For what? I mean, what is this information for?"

"You're getting better," I said.

I took a long swallow of tea. It was strong and bitter. Like medicine.

"You're not writing for us anymore, are you?" Archambault asked.

"Nope."

"Then who are you writing for?"

"I'm not," I said. "What are you hearing for a cause of death?"

"Read the paper tomorrow," he said.

"Give me a preview."

It took a few minutes, but little by little Archambault told me what he knew.

He said the state police had let him glance at the medical examiner's report. It said Donna was found in her bed. She'd died of asphyxiation, and her blood-alcohol content at the time of death had been 0.21, more than twice the legal limit for driving. There were broken blood vessels in her eyes, a telltale sign of asphyxia. Bruises on her throat, but no broken bones in her neck.

"Was that seen as unusual?" I asked.

"A little," Archambault said. "At least that's what the cops said. They said they figure somebody started to choke her, then stuck something over her face."

"Was she conscious when she died?"

"I don't know. I mean, I didn't ask that. I don't know. This detective, he made it sound like the thing was pretty much wrapped up."

"So who was it?"

"Which detective?"

"No. Who do they say killed her?"

"Her boyfriend. Jeff Tanner. Off the record, they told me he admitted to trying to choke her."

"Trying?"

"I guess he says it didn't kill her all the way. That's what he said, anyway. The cop, I mean."

"Which one?"

"I'd rather not say," Archambault said. "It was off the record and all."

"Anything else?"

"Not really."

"Why haven't they picked him up?" I asked.

"I heard they're going to," Archambault said. "Tonight or tomorrow morning. I guess they think they know where he is. He's right here in town."

I took a last sip of tea.

"Hey, McMorrow," Archambault said, a smirk easing onto his face. "Why is it you can't find this stuff out? You're the hotshot, right?"

"State police won't talk to me."

"Why not?"

"They say I'm getting in their way," I said, standing up and putting a dollar on the table.

"But they talked to me."

"Then I guess you're not," I said, and I walked to the door and stopped. "You never asked me."

"Asked you what?" Archambault said, getting up from his chair.

"What happened to my face."

"What happened to your face?" he said.

"None of your business," I said, and I walked out of that place, leaving him behind.

So they were about to wrap this one up. Pick up Tanner, call a press conference, then stick Jeff in jail for six to nine months to await trial. Once that happened, it would all be out of my hands. But it wasn't yet.

It was afternoon and I was getting hungry. I stopped at a mom-and-pop and bought yet another tuna sandwich on an Italian roll. I ate it in the car, parked across the street from Foxy's and fifty yards down. And then I waited.

It was interesting to see who went through the door of that dirty little place. A guy with a long lens and an entrepreneurial spirit could probably make some decent money sitting outside Foxy's.

I wasn't in it for the money. I was in it for Donna.

So I sat and then sat some more. I recognized a bank teller and the owner of a Kennebec real estate company. Two guys were wearing ties; one was wearing a blue uniform with his name over the front pocket. My buddy from behind the counter came out four times to smoke. I leaned back in the seat and tried to get comfortable.

Turned on the radio and turned it off. Little kids walked by with backpacks on, throwing rocks at each other back and forth across the street. One of the stones skittered on the pavement and dinged off the wheel of my car. They looked at me and ran. I sat some more.

An older man, stooped and furtive, came around the corner of Foxy's and went inside. I marked the time on my watch and waited for him to come out. How long would it take for him to do whatever it was he did in there? Ten minutes? A half hour? I timed him. Five, ten, fifteen. Twenty, twenty-five, thirty. What was he doing? Rearranging the films in alphabetical order? Come on, man. Get a life. Get—

There he was.

Tanner came around the same corner and slipped inside. I got out of the car and crossed the street and hurried down the sidewalk and up the steps. The door pulled open and the stooped man came out. He looked down at the ground as he passed me. I stopped the door from closing and went in.

My buddy looked up at me and then quickly away. I scanned the first movie room, saw a guy in a suit reading a film package. I went into the rental room and there was a guy with his back to me, hands in his pockets.

Tanner.

I looked at the titles too, circling opposite Tanner as he moved along the wall. He took one package down and flipped it over, then put it back. I did the same. Tanner took another one down and put it back, and then he was moving toward the doorway to the other room. With a last glance, he walked out.

After five or ten seconds, I followed. He was handing my buddy a bill, getting change and tokens back. I hesitated, and he put his money in the pocket of his jeans and walked around the corner into the hall and the peepshow booths. I was right behind him.

Tanner went down the hall almost to the end, where it was so dark I could barely see him. I padded along behind him as he pushed one of the doors open and went in. The door clicked shut and I put my shoulder to it and pushed it back open.

"Hey, sorry, I'm not into any—"

"Shut up," I said, and slid past the door and pushed it closed.

"What are you doing? I told you. Hit the road, ass—"

"Nice hobby, Jeffie boy. Why don't you put one of those nickels in the machine so I can see your face."

"Is that—?"

"*C'est moi.* How's your mouth?"

"You son of a bitch. You've got two friggin' seconds before I—"

"Before I scream bloody murder," I said. "And your reputation as a pervert is further enhanced. Put the money in the machine."

"What for? What the hell are you doing?"

I took a quarter out of my pocket and, in the dim light, shoved it in the slot. The screen turned pale gray and I banged a red button. Naked bodies appeared. Two women and a man. They were moaning, as if in extreme pain.

"This is pretty pathetic, you know that?"

"Who asked you, McMorrow? Get the hell—"

"I'll try not to look," I said. "And I'll try not to touch anything, including you. While we talk."

"I'm not talking. I got nothing to say to you."

Tanner was against one wall. I was against the door. The screen was to our left. The women and the man were still on it, still moaning.

"What a weird job," I said, looking at the screen and then back at Tanner. "I want to know about that night. Everything."

"I got nothing to—"

"Or I make such a ruckus in here that the cops come and, you know, they might get the wrong idea. And word would get around."

"About you too," Tanner said.

"But I don't hang around with homophobes."

"What?"

"Bigots," I said. "Listen. I don't have time to explain it. You want me to start screaming or you want to start talking?"

One of the women on the screen started to shriek.

Tanner hesitated.

"About what?" he said, the flickering light playing off his face. His mouth was still swollen.

"That night. Tell me what happened."

"I didn't kill her, if that's what you mean."

"Let's start at the beginning."

"I did that with the cops," Tanner said.

"And they don't believe you. I want to hear it myself."

"I ought to friggin' kill you."

"Maybe, but not now. Now you ought to tell me what I want to know. Believe me."

Now both women were going into what appeared to be some sort of seizure. The man was feigning pleasure, very badly.

"So ask," Tanner said.

"When did you get there?"

"I don't know. Eight fifteen. Maybe a little later."

"You weren't supposed to be there. Why'd you go?"

"To talk to her. She was blowing me off, you know. I mean, I won't take that from anybody, never mind a—"

"A woman. Right. So what happened?"

"What happened? I don't know," Tanner said. "We got in a fight."

"A fistfight?"

"No. You know. Yelling and shit."

"Yelling what?"

"Oh, man, how the hell am I supposed to remember all of it. Just yelling. I'm telling her she can't just give me the boot. She's telling me I'm nothing and I've got no say and get out now and all this. And I'm saying it's my stereo and she can't just take it and she's saying she'll call the cops."

"Then what?" I said.

Tanner took a deep breath. The film on the screen suddenly went off. I took out another quarter and rammed it in. The threesome popped back on, still writhing like the damned.

"Go ahead," I said.

"So we kind of calm down a little and Donna goes and gets a bottle of Jack out of the cupboard there and she gets a drink and I take the bottle and take a swig and I'm standing there."

"Where's Adrianna?"

"Oh, she's in the living room with the TV on or something. Donna wouldn't let her come near me, since I left, you know? Like I'm gonna kidnap her or something. Hey, I always kind of liked the kid. We used to joke around and shit."

"I'm touched. So what happened?"

"So Donna slams down a couple. That's how she drinks—"

"Drank, you mean."

"Yeah, right. She didn't drink that much, like she'd go weeks without one, but when she did, she'd go right at it."

"And she did that night?"

"Yeah. I mean, she started to. She had two or three. And she's telling me about her rights as a person and stuff, and how I have no right to do this and that, and she says she never should have let me touch her and she wouldn't ever again."

"Uh-huh."

Tanner fidgeted a little. Looked up at the screen, where the film had looped around to the beginning. The two women and the man were clothed, sitting on an orange plaid couch.

"So then she really starts in on me, you know, calling me this and that, and she's met this other guy and he's from the newspaper—that's you, I guess—and he treats her with respect and all this, and I was just a control freak and a drunk and I wasn't worth shit, and I'm standing there listening to this and man, you know you can only take so much."

"What happened?" I said.

"I popped her. But just a little tap, you know. A little slap on the face. She goes friggin' ballistic. She's screaming and swinging at me with both arms and the kid comes out and she's screaming and crying and it's a goddamn nightmare and I'm, like, I don't need this. I mean, I don't want to end up in the joint."

"But you didn't leave?"

"No. I mean, I did. In a few minutes. But she's friggin' swinging at me and I'm backing away, you know. Bumping into stuff in the kitchen and she's calling me this and that and then she friggin' kicks me right in the balls, and I mean hard. I mean, she practically dropped me and there's one thing I won't take from some chick and that's it, you know what I'm saying?"

"I guess I do," I said.

"So I, like, grab her arms and she's still kicking and screaming and she spits in my face and I grab her by the throat, you know? Like, to shut her up. And I guess I sort of choked her a little, but I didn't try to kill her. I mean, I held her like that 'til she calmed down and then I, like, let her go."

I looked at him.

"What do you mean, you 'like, let her go'?"

"I, like, spun her away from me. But she wasn't dead. I mean, she was coughing and crying and shit. I don't know how they can pin this on me. I told those cops. When I left, she was pouring a goddamn drink at the kitchen counter. She was no more dead than you or me. They can't pin this on me. I told 'em. She weren't even hurt, hardly."

"And then you left?"

"Right. I said, 'I don't need this crap.' And I went down the back stairs and out the side door."

"What time was that?"

"I don't know. A little after nine, I think, maybe. I got back to The Mansion and had a few drinks and, like, calmed down, you know? And then I left and went back to the place where I was staying."

"And you didn't go back to Donna's?"

He looked at me. I watched his eyes.

"No way. I'd had enough of that . . . of her. I mean, friggin' A. I don't deserve this. What does she want? A goddamn guy to put his coat in the goddamn puddles or something? Yes ma'am, no ma'am?"

"She doesn't want anything now," I said.

He paused, and I did too. The two women and the man had shucked their clothes and were pawing each other. One of the women was saying, "Oh, yeah," over and over.

"So did you kill her?" I said.

I watched him.

"Hell, no. I didn't even hurt her. I mean, not like some of the other—"

Tanner caught himself.

"So you used to pound on her pretty good, didn't you," I said.

He looked at me.

"She could aggravate a man, I'll tell you. And turn it on and off. When I come home, I want to know what I'm getting, you know?"

"And if you didn't get it, you'd hit her?"

Tanner stared.

"Yeah. Sometimes. But I didn't kill her."

"Hard?"

"Sometimes. But I didn't kill her."

"Ever break bones? Bloody her face? Hold her down and make her cry for you to stop hurting her?"

He looked at me.

"Yeah," Tanner said slowly. "But I didn't kill her."

I looked into his eyes. He looked back.

"I just plain didn't," Tanner said.

No, you didn't, I thought. And as we stood there, face-to-face, chest to chest, the screen suddenly went blank. Tanner looked at me, then took a token from his pocket and dropped it in the slot. The two women and the man were on the carpet, and he glanced at them and then back at me.

"Why do you want to know all this?" Tanner said.

"I just do. And another thing I want to know. Was that you, with the cat on my windshield?"

Tanner's eyes said yes.

"Hey," he said. "She was mine and you were pissing me off."

He looked at me as if he'd done nothing wrong.

"I owe you one for that," I said.

"You were in my face, McMorrow. You broke my window too."

"But you shouldn't have killed that cat."

Without saying another word, I leaned to the right and pulled the door open behind me and left.

25

If not Tanner, then who?

Maybe he had done it. Maybe he was a pathological enough liar to look me in the eye and say he hadn't killed Donna, and to make it believable.

But I didn't think so.

Tanner was a lot of things, very few of them good, but he wasn't devious. In his life in bars, on binges, he seemed to have developed an odd but fairly rigid code of behavior. It was okay to beat a defenseless woman. It was okay to be a cokehead and a drunk. But it was not okay to go around telling lies. To tell a lie betrayed weakness. Lying meant you cared what somebody else thought about you or anything else. And bullish Jeff Tanner didn't. He just plain didn't.

I mulled this over as I inched through Kennebec's six-car rush-hour traffic jam and then crossed the tumbling gray river. Even on this blue-sky afternoon, there was something threatening about the slipping and sliding torrent, something relentlessly lethal in its movement. And there was something—someone—lethal moving around me too. I couldn't give it a name or a face, but I could feel myself getting closer to it. How would I know when I met it? How did I know I hadn't met it already?

I had to keep pushing. Keep moving. Keep talking. Go back to the old woman in the apartment. Keep talking to Lenny. Get Marcia calmed down somehow and maybe even talk to Adrianna. Because Tanner was headed for a murder conviction as slowly and surely as if he had been plunked on a conveyor belt. And then Donna's story would be over. There would be no reason for me to ask, no reason for anyone to answer. The puzzle would be finished and put away, and there I'd be, hunting around the floor for the missing piece.

The sun was at my back as I swung through Albion village and headed for Prosperity. Up ahead, an empty pulp truck rumbled, its chains jingling against the side posts on the truck bed, the driver's tanned arm hanging out of the window. The arm disappeared and the driver downshifted and there was a cough of diesel smoke and then the arm poked out again. He slowed more on an upgrade and the arm waved me by. I passed him, still half lost in thought. Jeff and Leaman. Donnie and Marcia.

Ten minutes later, I pulled into my dooryard and shut off the motor. I sat there in the driver's seat, blackflies buzzing around me, and thought some more.

"I think there's moss growing on you," a voice said.

I looked up. Clair was standing five feet away.

"I hate it when you do that," I said. "You should wear a bell around your neck or something."

"I was about to hold a mirror up to your mouth to see if you were breathing," Clair said.

"So far, so good."

"How's the rest of your day been?"

"Peachy. I went to the porn shop. Saw one of those peep shows."

"Forget I even asked," Clair said.

"And you know who was in the booth with me?"

"How 'bout we talk about the weather."

"Jeff Tanner," I said.

Clair looked at me.

"Yeah, it was the only place I could find where we could talk. He said he didn't kill Donna."

"So what'd you expect him to do? Get down on his knees and confess?"

"Wrong venue. No, really, I believe him."

"Why?"

"Because I looked right at him and I think he was telling the truth. Donnie, too."

"There were three of you in there?" Clair said.

"No, that was out on the interstate in a new Lincoln. Donnie, he's Donna's ex, he said he wouldn't throw away his fancy Jeep and cowboy boots by killing her."

"That would be a consideration, wouldn't it?"

"Yeah. It has a power sunroof and everything," I said.

"Power sunroof?"

"Yeah, but you don't say it right. You have to say it like it's the Holy Grail or something."

"I'll work on it. So you believed him too?" Clair said.

"Yup."

"So where does that leave things?"

"I don't know. Tanner's going down for it. He doesn't know that, but he is. They're just waiting for the last pieces to fall into place. For a tough guy, he's really pretty naive. Like a little kid, sort of."

"The schoolyard bully who never grew up," Clair said.

"No, that's Leaman. Speaking of him, you have to shoot the Fuller Brush man today?"

"Just winged him. Other than that, things were pretty quiet."

"So what'd you do while I was watching dirty movies?" I said.

"Tilled the early spinach under."

"All this clean living's gonna catch up with you."

"I did put real butter on my kale at lunch," Clair said.

"I knew you had a dark side."

"And it's ready for a beer."

"That makes two of us," I said.

"Fifteen minutes. Up at the house," Clair said, and he turned and headed back the way he had come, which was very quietly.

I took the rifle out of the trunk and the cartridges out of the glove box. Standing by the car, I loaded the rifle and carried it as I walked to the door. At the door, I stopped and listened. I heard chickadees in the distance. I opened the door and went through the mudroom to the door to the house. The shed was still, and I waited and listened at the inside door too. I heard the refrigerator click on. I opened the door slowly and walked in, rifle at my side, finger inside the trigger guard.

The house was still.

I put the rifle on the table and went to the answering machine on the counter. The red light was flashing and I pushed the button. There was a whir and then a beep.

Archambault had called but didn't say when.

A woman from the *Observer* had called and asked if I wanted her to mail my check or did I want to come in and pick it up. Right. And talk over old times with the troops.

Roxanne had called and said she'd be late. She was calling from the office, and I could hear voices in the background.

"Hey, Rox, this guy Skip called," a woman was saying. "Oh, I'm sorry. I didn't know you were on the—"

Skip called. I needed a beer.

I looked out the window at the backyard. It was quiet and still and green. For a minute I scanned the edge of the woods, but there was nothing and nobody moving. I went upstairs and stuck my head under the bed. Nothing moving there, either.

Back downstairs, I went to the bathroom and washed my face and hands of road grit and any residue from the porno booth. I brushed my teeth, too, for good measure, and then I took my rifle and went out the door, through the field, and up onto the Varneys' back steps. I unloaded the gun before I brought it inside.

Table manners.

We had our beers in the kitchen. Mary Varney was washing radishes from the garden and Clair was helping her.

"In the bowl, not your mouth," Mary said.

"Yes, dear."

Mary's hands were brown and lithe and strong, rounding the knife over the radishes. Clair's hands were big and blunt, like paws.

"Jack, you could wash the asparagus," Mary said.

I took the bundle of stems from the counter and put it in the big slate sink and ran the water.

"How's the crop?" I said.

"Not bad," Clair said. "It'd be fuller if we'd had more rain earlier in the spring. But asparagus is dependable. It's a vegetable with strong character. You have to admire asparagus."

"I admire asparagus on my plate."

"You should respect and be thankful for something like asparagus. This country has lost the quality of reverence. I always think of American Indians, giving thanks for everything," said Clair.

"I'd thank you to not eat all the radishes," Mary said.

"Like I said, we've lost the quality of reverence. A wife's reverence for her husband . . ."

"A husband's reverence for the wife who puts up with him," Mary said. "If you eat one more radish, I'll show you some reverence."

She picked up the colander and came over to the sink. I took the asparagus out of the sink and put it on a towel on the counter. Mary ran water on the radishes, then put them in a wooden bowl with lettuce and spinach. I lopped the bottom half inch off the asparagus and dropped them in a pan of boiling water.

"Careful with that knife," Mary said. "It's sharp. And how's your face, anyway?"

"Better," I said. "I could take the bandage off, but I don't want to scare small children."

"That's a shame. You should see somebody about that scar."

I shrugged and smiled.

Mary took a paper-wrapped package from the refrigerator and brought it to the counter. She unfolded the paper and lifted out two rosy salmon fillets. The white wine in the pan was starting to simmer. She laid one fillet in and it hissed.

"How late did Roxanne say she'd be?" Clair asked, getting up from the table.

"She didn't."

"I'll wait on the second piece of fish," Mary said. "And I'll save some asparagus. When she gets here, we can cook everything up fresh for her."

"I hope she won't be too late," I said. I thought of Skip and winced.

"You two can set the table and pour me a glass of wine," Mary said, prodding the fish with a fork. "Not necessarily in that order."

So we set the big oak-plank table for four. Clair poured Mary's wine, which was some kind of a sauterne, and in a minute or two everything was ready. Mary pulled a tray of rolls from the oven and put them in a bowl, and we sat and loaded our plates with pink and green. Then Clair raised his beer glass and gave thanks for radishes, asparagus, and salmon. I raised my glass too, but something reminded me of Donna and I felt momentarily ashamed, as if I shouldn't be giving thanks for anything.

Not yet.

After initial bites, we pronounced everything delicious. Clair put butter on his roll, but Mary did not. I ate the salad and asparagus, sipped my beer. Mary asked me how Roxanne liked her job in Portland, and I said she did, that she liked to help kids and there was a lot of help needed. Clair asked when I was going to get my truck back from the state police and I said I didn't know.

"What's going on with all of that?" Mary asked, cutting a piece of asparagus.

"They're probably going to arrest her boyfriend," I said.

"Well, that's some compensation, I guess," Mary said.

"I don't know," I said.

Mary, direct and strong and smart, looked across the table at me. "Why don't you?" she said.

"Because I don't think he did it."

"Well, why not?"

"Because I asked him and he said he didn't do it, and he said it in a believable way. I mean, I believe him."

"Could they convict him?" Mary asked.

"Probably. He grabbed her by the throat. There were bruises on her throat and she died of suffocation at about that time."

Mary ate a piece of fish. I did too.

"So he tried to kill her?"

"He says no."

"Well, he would, wouldn't he?"

"Yeah, but he admits everything else. And this old lady next door, she says she heard the fighting, saw him leave, and then heard dishes clinking in the apartment like everything was normal. Or at least Donna was alive."

"Unless it was the little girl doing the dishes," Clair said suddenly. "Maybe she thought her mother was asleep. Decided to clean up."

I remembered my stoned buddy from the apartment across the alley. He'd said Adrianna washed the dishes. Would she, if she thought her mother was asleep? Had it been Adrianna rattling the plates?

Mary sipped her wine.

"Of course, if this man is wrongly convicted of this, someone else will have gotten away with it," she said. "Who might that be?"

"I don't know," I said. "Her ex-husband hated her, but he says he didn't do it, that it wouldn't have solved his problem with her, which was child support."

"You believe him too?" Mary said.

"I think so."

"Maybe you're too trusting," she said, her fork sliding under her fish.

"But I'm not. That's the problem."

Mary was warming to this and I was warming to her. It was the kind of conversation I could have had with Roxanne, if Roxanne had been here. I wished Roxanne would come.

"But it's very obvious, don't you think?" Mary said. "The little girl was there, wasn't she? She must have seen it happen. She must know who was there. What did she tell the police?"

"I don't know," I said. "The people in the building saw her leaving with the sister earlier."

"Depends on when it happened," Mary said.

"Maybe she was asleep," Clair put in. "What was it, nine, ten o'clock at night? Normally, a four-year-old kid would be zonked right out."

"But if there had been all this ruckus, she'd be wide awake, wouldn't she?" Mary said. "The things kids have to live through. How is she?"

"I don't know," I said. "I haven't seen her. She's with her aunt, and her aunt is pretty protective. She calls her 'my little girl.' She said if I tried to come near her or hurt her, she'd kill me."

Mary's eyebrows rose over her wineglass.

"Does she have children of her own?"

"No. Always wanted them but couldn't have any, I guess. Her husband works a million hours a week at the mill in Kennebec. They probably have a couple hundred thousand in the bank. But no kids."

"They do now," Mary said.

The words floated there for a moment, hovering over the table. I had my glass raised and it stopped. Clair looked at his wife, then at me. Mary sipped her wine, then put the glass back down and reached for her fork.

"Stranger things have happened," she said quietly. "You know that, Jack. With the things you've seen."

Marcia?

It wasn't possible—that she could be that twisted, that is. Did she want a child of her own—did she want Adrianna so badly that she would kill her own sister?

"I don't think. . . . I mean, I can't imagine that she'd . . ."

Would she think that she was saving Adrianna from something? Could there have been an argument between the two sisters? Over Adrianna, maybe. What if Marcia had laid into Donna about the way she was living? What if Marcia had come to the apartment and found the place messed up, Donna drunk, Adrianna uncared for? What if they'd fought somehow and things had gotten out of hand and Marcia had strangled her? In a moment of rage? Was it possible?

"What's she like, this Marcia?" Mary asked.

"Tough," I said. "Efficient. She's in accounting or something. Self-made type. Married this steady Eddie kind of guy, I guess. Very protective of her sister, who was sort of a screw-up by comparison. Or just unlucky. Donna's husband was abusive. A real jerk. They had this girl, but he couldn't care less about Adrianna. That's the little girl. Boyfriend is a bar brawler. Beat her up. When she got up the courage to kick him out, he hounded her. If Jeff turned up dead, I'd bet on Marcia in a second."

"But this sister had the one thing Marcia couldn't have."

"A child?" I said. "Yeah. She was sort of a surrogate mother, though. When things got rough, Adrianna went to Marcia's."

"Maybe she decided that things were too rough for the girl," Mary said.

I thought some more. Clair got up and went and got another beer. He poured half in my glass, half in his.

"I don't mean to be cheap, but I don't think this is the time to let your guard down entirely," he said.

"Probably not," I said. "Probably not."

We finished dinner slowly. The asparagus was perfect, the salmon moist and sweet. I was distracted.

It hadn't occurred to me. Not once. Was that the explanation for her reaction when I came to her house? Was she protecting Adrianna, or was she protecting herself?

I helped clear the table and Clair made coffee. Mary served slices of pound cake with fresh strawberries and Clair poured. I had a small piece of cake and my coffee black. Outside, dusk had fallen and it was growing dark. I wondered about Marcia. I worried about Roxanne.

The rest of the talk was about the Varneys' daughters, their two grandchildren. Mary talked about how different their daughters were from each other, how much of our character is determined by our genetic imprint. It was an interesting topic, and Mary had read magazine articles on it. Another time I would have listened more closely.

But I was only half there.

It was after nine when we picked up the cups and brought them out to the kitchen. Clair said maybe I'd better call and see if Roxanne was still home. Mary looked worried.

"Maybe she called your house and left another message," Mary said, rinsing the cups at the sink. "I used to worry about the girls, driving up here at night. If you have car troubles, you can be stuck out in the middle of absolutely nowhere. That's why I think these car phones are a good idea."

"I told you I'd get you the antenna," Clair said. "I don't need one. I don't go anywhere. But these young women, driving alone at night. And you know what kind of people are out there these days. Jack's certainly run into his share lately. It's scary."

And I was beginning to get a little scared.

We finished putting the food away and Mary said she was going to go make up the guest room. I walked outside with Clair and we stood in the backyard in the dark and listened to the drone of birds and bugs.

"I'm going to walk down and check the machine," I said.

"I'll go with you," Clair said. "Hang on."

He walked to the back door, opened it, and reached in and took out his Mauser. Holding it up to the light from the kitchen window, he slid the bolt open and then closed.

"Be prepared, as the scouts say," Clair said. "I still don't like the sound of this jailbird pal of yours. I don't like a man who's got nothing to lose."

We walked behind the row of cedars that shielded Clair's yard from the road. It was cool and hazy clouds had moved in, putting a gauzy mask over the moon. We'd gone fifty feet, no more, when we both stopped. Then trotted ahead and stopped again.

"Oh, Jesus," Clair said. "Take this."

He shoved the rifle into my hands and turned and ran toward my house, fast. I ran too.

The smoke was an odor and then stronger, and then, when I came out of the field and around the end of the shed, it was billowing out the door like steam.

I stopped ten feet from the mudroom door and heard a rushing, crackling sound from inside. As I stood there, flames flashed along the wall where the mudroom connected to the house. The flames disappeared, then flashed again and crept up the wall. I ran past the front of the house to the outside faucet. The hose was in the shed. I ran back to the shed, and now the flames had climbed the wall to the roof and the crackling had turned to a soft roar.

I ran around the end of the shed to the glass door to the deck. The door was locked, but I punched a hole in the window with the rifle butt and reached in and opened the door. The inside of the house was dark and smoke was moving along the ceiling. I leaned the rifle on the deck and ran through the room and up the loft stairs and yanked open the top drawer of the bureau. Papers. Records. Photographs. My arms full, I tumbled down the stairs and back outside, dumping the stuff on the ground thirty feet from the house.

Back inside, I loaded up again.

More papers. A small box of stuff from childhood. Pictures of my parents. What to take? What to leave?

Clair came through the back door, a bandanna over his mouth.

"What else?" he called, his voice muffled, his figure hazy in the smoke.

"Money. In the freezer. Blue plastic container behind the ice cubes. The stereo. Records and tapes and CDs."

He ran to the refrigerator and opened the door and the light went on, showing the smoke to be thick and dense. I ran back up the stairs and yanked the bureau drawers out and dropped them over the railing. They landed with a crash, and I ran down and grabbed them and heaved them out the door, one by one.

Back up the stairs, I went to the wardrobe and grabbed an armload of shirts. Those went out the door too, and then I went to the bookcase and started pulling. My bird books. Books from my father.

The smoke was gagging me and I was getting dizzy. Clair came and leaned down beside me and yanked books and ran to the back door. Over and over. When the bookcase was nearly empty he came back again, but this time grabbed me by the shoulder and pulled me back. A burst of flame came through the wall to the shed and we both ran out the back door and into the cool night air, stumbling on books and clothes and the cord to the tape deck. I sprawled on the ground and looked back, and the flames were running along the ridgepole near the shed.

"The car," Clair said, and we ran around to the front of the house. The shed was blazing and there were bursts of bright, hissing flame as paint and varnish ignited. I opened the door and rammed the key in the ignition; it started, and I put it in reverse and tromped on the accelerator.

On the road I could see a truck approaching, slamming hard over the ruts. Then more headlights and more after that. The pickups had small red flashing lights on their dashboards and grills, and the trucks skidded as they stopped on the gravel road.

Guys got out and pulled on raincoats and boots and hats, and the red flashing lights of a fire truck came off the dump road, sirens blaring. I recognized some of the guys from the store and the post office, and they nodded as they jumped on the truck, grabbing axes, unhooking hoses. In a few minutes, there were twenty or thirty men around the house and a plume of water was cascading toward the flames.

I stood helplessly and Clair appeared beside me. The firemen nodded to me and gave a terse "Hey, Clair" to him.

"Your rifle," I said suddenly.

"I got it," Clair said, and then we watched the house, the flames licking and caressing and the smoke billowing up, a gray cloud against the sky.

Mary came down and we watched grimly. All three of us were standing there when a silver-haired guy with the word CHIEF on his helmet trotted up.

"Your house?" he said, shouting against the roar of motors, the snarl of radios.

"Yeah," I said.

"You home when it started?"

"Nope. I was up the road. At the Varneys'."

He looked to Clair.

"Eating supper," Clair said.

"Well, the place was torched," the fire chief said. "I'd say gas was poured all over the inside of that shed, along the wall. Who'd want to do that?"

I looked at the flames and smoke.

"They'd have to take a number and get in line," I said.

"You in law enforcement or something?"

"No," I said. "I'm a reporter."

He looked at me curiously and then a ball of flame burst through the roof and the firefighters were shouting and then another voice was calling and I turned.

"Jack," Roxanne said, running toward me.

She grabbed me and held me, her left arm around my chest.

"Your tardiness was fortuitous," I said.

"But I saw them. I followed them. It had to be. They were throwing clothes out of the car. And boots."

"What?"

"A car. I was turning into the road and this old car came out and just about hit me and I saw these two guys and something didn't seem right. I mean, they didn't belong here, and they looked really wound up."

"So what happened?"

"I followed them. I followed them and they were headed for Albion, but then they turned. It was a left and they went up this long hill, and I was catching up to get their license-plate number."

"Did you get it?"

"Yeah," Roxanne said, her face flushed in the flashing lights. "And I got their boot. It smells like gasoline."

We found the fire chief and told him the story and he had a portable radio and he called the state police. The state police dispatcher in Augusta took the information and then we heard it broadcast to state police in Waldo and Kennebec counties. A couple of minutes later we heard that the registration had come back to a 1984 Monte Carlo registered to a woman in Kennebec. Not ten minutes after that, we heard the state police dispatcher tell patrol cars that the car had been stopped by Winslow police.

There were two male occupants, the Winslow police reported. One wasn't wearing shoes.

26

———∞———

Roxanne had her salmon, but not until almost midnight. We waited and watched while the firefighters slowly beat down the flames. When the fire finally surrendered, a little before eleven, the house was a sodden, blackened, stinking mess.

With three walls standing.

Around eleven, Roxanne went back in Clair's truck with Clair and Mary and my stuff, stacked in the back. I hung around the house for another hour or so, watching as the volunteers packed up their hoses and airpacks. I helped another guy lift a generator onto the back of a pickup truck. The other guy was in his forties and very strong, in that quiet, capable Maine way. He eased the generator down and then turned back and reached for his cigarettes.

"You own this place?" he said.

"No, I rent it. Owner's in New Mexico. Millie. Hasn't been here in a couple of years. Totaled, don't you think?"

"Oh, hell, yes. You got walls, but that'll just give the 'dozer man something to shoot for. Somebody got an ax to grind with you or what?"

"Appears that way, doesn't it," I said.

"Coulda been worse. You could've been asleep. Or your wife there."

"We're not married. But it still could've been worse."

He drew on his cigarette thoughtfully.

"That's what I always tell people when their house burns. If everybody's out and you're standing outside with me watching, count your blessings."

He headed back to the crew and the fire trucks. I stood and counted. Up to one. Roxanne.

I told the fire chief that I was heading back to the Varneys'. He said he'd be there a while longer, that he didn't expect the fire investigator from the state to be there until the next morning, at the earliest. But he said the cause was pretty cut-and-dried.

"They took your gas can there and they doused the wall and lit it," the fire chief said. "And that was all she wrote. Who was it, anyway?"

"I don't know yet. I'm going back to call and see if they'll tell me."

"Seems like you'd have a right to know," the chief said.

"Seems like it, doesn't it."

But it wasn't that easy. When I got back to the Varneys', Roxanne was sitting at the table as Mary cooked the salmon and peas and asparagus. Roxanne was sipping a glass of white wine. She looked very tired, but even when she was very tired, she was beautiful. I went to her and gave her a squeeze around the shoulders.

"I'm sorry, Jack," Roxanne said.

"I'm not," I said. "Like one of those firemen was telling me, if you're on the outside watching it burn, you should count your blessings. I'm counting right now."

"Amen," Mary said.

Clair came into the kitchen, smelling of smoke.

"You call?" he asked me.

"Not yet. I'll try state police first."

The dispatcher in Augusta had just come on. He said he'd call Winslow and his own unit to see who was handling the investigation.

I gave him my name and the Varneys' number and said I wanted to know who had burned my house down. In that unflappable tone that cops have, he said he'd do his best.

So we waited. Clair said he'd unloaded my stuff in his barn but the cash was in his safe.

"If I'd known you had a safe, I would have treated you with more respect," I said.

"It's never too late to start," Clair said. "You want a drink?"

"Can we let our guard down now?"

"Does lightning strike twice?"

"I'll wear my rubber-soled shoes," I said.

Clair got two Budweisers from the refrigerator. He handed one to me and we both leaned against the counter and opened them.

"To life," I said, raising my bottle. "And Roxanne Masterson, private investigator."

Mary put a loaded plate in front of Roxanne.

"I can't believe you did that," Mary said. "What if they'd stopped and jumped out and tried to stop you or something?"

"I wouldn't have stopped," Roxanne said.

"Maybe there's a reward," Clair said.

"I think we just got it," I said.

So we leaned and drank while Roxanne ate. Mary got out crackers and pepper cheese and dilled green beans and put them on a plate. We nibbled as Clair told me about a guy he knew who would take down the house and shed. He asked if Millie the artist would rebuild. I said I doubted it. Clair asked if I'd rebuild here on the road. I said I thought so. I didn't say I had no idea how I'd pay for it.

And then the phone rang.

Mary answered. "It's for Jack," she said.

I took the phone. "McMorrow," I said.

"McMorrow, this is Detective LaCharelle."

"You're calling to apologize for keeping my truck."

"No, but you can have it back now."

"You know who did it?"

"Nope."

"What's the good news, then?" I said.

"I heard your name on the radio tonight and I thought I'd help out. That's what. Winslow PD apprehended the two individuals."

"I heard that."

"Well, the two subjects were interviewed here at the Winslow Police Department. They didn't want to cooperate at first, but when we told them they'd been seen on your road out there, one of them implicated the other for setting your house on fire. It's a situation where one's fingering the other. I think we'll get pleas out of both of them."

"Who are they?"

"The one doing the talking is a Byron Blaisdell. He's twenty-three—not a major scumbag, but no stranger to the police around here."

"And who's the other one?"

"I think you know the other one. Name's Leaman. He's got warrants, a probation hold. He's going bye-bye for a long time if this one sticks."

"So what did Blaisdell say they did?"

"Went looking for you, but you didn't answer the door. He says Leaman saw the gas can and started sloshing it all over the house there. Put a match to it and boogied. I guess they were leaving when somebody spotted them and called it in. Who was it, one of your neighbors?"

"Yeah," I said. "You could say that."

"Well, I'll need a statement from him and a statement from you. Your history with Mr. Leaman. I understand you've had an earlier altercation."

"Sure did," I said. "The guy's psycho."

"And that's his friggin' good side."

"When do you need this?"

"Tomorrow morning would be fine. How 'bout Kennebec PD? They'll be in Kenhegan County Jail until Monday. Arraignment in Fourth District Court."

"Tate?"

"I guess," LaCharelle said. "Why?"

"Nothing," I said. "We just didn't exactly hit it off."

"From what I hear, that happens with you."

"It's a gift. I don't have to work at it."

"Yeah, well, how 'bout you meet me at the PD by eight o'clock. Can you get in touch with your neighbor, give him that message?"

"I think so."

"Okay, then. Hey, listen. Sorry about your house."

LaCharelle's condolences were stiff and awkward, but seemed sincere. I sensed an opening.

"Thanks," I said. "What can you do, you know? At least they didn't come at three in the morning."

"They would have if they'd thought about it," LaCharelle said. "You're just lucky they're dummies."

"Very lucky," I said. "Hey, while I have you, what about Donna Marchant? You close to an arrest?"

"This off the record?"

"Very."

"Yeah, we're close. A day or two maybe. AG would like one more piece, but if we don't get it, we'll go without it."

"I ran into him today," I said.

"Who?"

"Tanner," I said. "He says he didn't do it."

"No shit," LaCharelle said. "Stop the presses."

"I kind of believe him."

"I don't," he said.

"But what if he's telling the truth?"

"Hey, you want to lose sleep over it, go ahead. What we've got is—this is off the record—we got a guy who admits to being at the scene, admits fighting with the deceased, admits trying to strangle her at the approximate time of death."

"But he says she was alive when he left."

"Hey, there's a defense," LaCharelle snorted. "'Yeah, I was the only one there. Yeah, I tried to kill her, but I didn't try hard enough.'"

"What if there was a witness who said she heard the fighting and then saw Jeff leave and could still hear dishes clinking and stuff after he was gone."

"You mean the old lady, right?"

"Yeah," I said.

"Hey, he walks out, he walks back in. His alibi sucks. Five or six drunks who couldn't remember what day it was when they last saw him, never mind the time."

"What about the bartender?"

"Won't help Tanner. She says she remembers he was there at some point, but he didn't stay long. He could have gone back to the apartment and killed Marchant ten times that night. Just because some old lady only saw him beating on her and leaving doesn't mean anything. He could have gone around the block and come right back."

"What about the little girl?"

"Hey, McMorrow. That's enough. You got me going, but that's all off the record. Don't screw me, or you'll live to regret it."

"What about the sister?"

"What about her?" LaCharelle said.

"She was there. What'd she see?"

"Jesus, McMorrow. You're so interested, come to the friggin' trial."

"It's not the trial I'm interested in, it's the defendant. I hope you get the right one."

"We've got the right one. We've got the only one. We've got the guy who killed her."

"I'm not so sure," I said.

"Well, then we'll be sure you're not on the jury," LaCharelle said. "Tomorrow. Eight o'clock. And tell your neighbor."

I told her and she said she'd be there. We talked with Clair and Mary a little bit more and then the adrenaline drained from all of us and we decided to go up to bed. Mary said we'd be in the guest room, which was in the ell of the house, to the rear. She said we could stay there as long as we wanted. And she meant it.

The room was cozy, with eaves and a big double bed with fresh white sheets, lots of pillows, and a white down comforter. Roxanne put her overnight bag on the floor and just stood there by the bureau, her eyes closed, her hand rubbing her forehead. I came over and put my arms around her, and she pursed her lips and a tear leaked onto her cheek.

"It's okay," I said. "We're here."

"Oh, I know. It's just—I don't know, it's just a lot. It's just too much."

"I know."

"I'd like to just shut out the world," Roxanne said.

"So let's go to sleep."

Roxanne slipped out of her dress and her underwear and was beautiful and naked for a moment before she dropped a nightshirt over her neck. It was pale pink and short and feminine and, on another night, in another situation, might have led to more than sleep. But she slid into the bed and pulled the blankets up to her chin.

"I'm cold," Roxanne said.

I took off my shirt and jeans and realized they stunk of smoke. My shorts did too, so I took them off and put the whole pile outside the door in the hall. I slipped into the bed, unfolding the comforter over both of us. Roxanne turned her back to me and nestled closer. I draped an arm over her and felt her exhale and almost shudder.

"I'm sorry about the house," she said quietly.

"There are more where that came from," I said.

There was a moment of silence, of just Roxanne's breathing, her back nudging against my chest.

"You know what I'll miss?" she said.

"What?"

"Making love there. We made love well there."

"We make love well everywhere."

"But now that's just a memory."

"Everything's just a memory eventually," I said. "That's what life is. Piling up memories."

"We'll have some good ones, won't we?"

"Already do. And we'll be together tomorrow. We'll wake up together. Have breakfast together. Go to the state police and give the detective a statement together. Go try to talk to Marcia together . . ."

"Talk to Marcia?"

"I need to talk to her. To Adrianna, too."

"Why?"

"I want to know what they saw. Because I want them to know that I don't think it was Jeff. So that if Jeff is found guilty, they know, or at least have been told, that they still might not be safe. But then,

Mary suggested that Marcia did it. Killed Donna so she, Marcia, could have Adrianna."

"Kill her own sister?"

"It happens. But they seemed pretty tight. I don't know. Marcia would be a perfect parent to do an adoption, wouldn't she? Stable. Steady income. But she has this thing about Adrianna."

"The drive to have children can make people do some pretty crazy things," Roxanne said. "Maternal instinct gone haywire. Like those women who steal babies from hospitals."

"Why don't men do that?"

"I don't know. But what if she *did* do it? Like Mary was saying, to have her own child."

"Then maybe that will show through."

"I don't think you should go there," Roxanne said. "And I don't think I should go there either."

"You're probably right," I said, my head beside hers on the pillow.

"But you'll go anyway," Roxanne said.

"You're probably right about that too."

And then Roxanne was quiet and, in a minute or so, her breathing took on a gentle rhythm and I felt her legs twitch as they relaxed and she slept. That made one of us.

I heard the Varneys' mantel clock strike two. Then three. I was sorting the names and faces and picturing Jeff with his hands on Donna's throat, then Marcia with her hands there too. I thought that maybe Jeff was just a good liar and I was a chump, and then I thought that maybe Marcia had found Donna unconscious and had just finished her off. And then the clock was chiming again and the light was streaming into the room and my eyes opened to see Roxanne against the white sheets, the sunlight on her hair and her nightshirt draped over her breasts.

"Damn," I said.

I lifted my arm and turned it to see my watch. It was a few minutes before seven and Kennebec was a good half-hour drive, even on a Saturday morning. I leaned over and kissed Roxanne on the cheek, once and then again, and she stirred and smiled. She pulled the comforter up and I let her enjoy the moments before the memories would flood in. I watched and they did and the smile turned to a frown.

"We're late," I said. "It's almost seven."

"So?" she said, still groggy.

"And we have to be at the police station by eight."

"Okay. Just let me . . . just let me . . . wake up."

I got up and went to the dormer window facing the barn. Clair walked out of the barn dressed in jeans and a red chamois shirt and boots. Downstairs I could hear the rattle of dishes and the clank of pans. Roxanne flung back the covers, showing a lovely stretch of legs.

"Yikes," I said.

"You going to take a shower?" she said.

"With you, I would."

"I feel like that was in another life," Roxanne said, and she slipped by me and into the bathroom. I heard the door close and the water hiss.

Another life, indeed.

We had English muffins and juice standing up. Mary poured our tea and coffee into those conical mugs they use on boats. Roxanne said her friend Skip had a cupboard full of them. Mary told us to drive carefully and we went out, walking down through the field to the charred remains of the house. It stood there, stinking in the sun, like a nightmare that should not have been there when we woke up. I stood and stared.

"Come on, Jack," Roxanne said. "We can look it over when we get home."

So we drove past the rubble, black against the green foliage, and out onto the dump road and up to the highway. We were quiet until we got to Albion village, slowing as we drove down Main Street past the stores and the church, and speeding up as we moved out into the farms and fields.

"You nervous?" I said, breaking the silence.

"I don't think so," Roxanne said, her legs crossed, a tan espadrille suspended in the air. "I've testified in court so many times. Talking to a detective doesn't seem like much. Of course, the cops are usually on my side when I go to court. Why don't I get that feeling in this one?"

"Because I haven't picked a side," I said. "And they're not sure where I fit in."

"You don't fit in."

"You finally noticed?"

"No, I noticed the first time I laid eyes on you," Roxanne said.

"Too late to back out now."

"Yup."

So we whizzed along, past the munching cows, the sagging barns and manure-spattered tractors, the mobile homes with their hay-bale skirts, drawn up like wagon trains against some faceless enemy. When we dropped out of the fields and woods and into the Kennebec valley, the river was moving slowly, as if hungover.

I sped across the bridge and pulled into the police-station lot and parked. There was a row of blue Kennebec cruisers, one white cruiser from Winslow, and LaCharelle's black unmarked Chevy. I shut off the car and started to say something, but Roxanne was already getting out. As she did I glimpsed her face, and it was hard and resolute. It was her business face, and I realized I'd never seen it before.

"You ready?" I asked as we walked to the door.

She looked at me with the same expression, unyielding with a hint of impatience.

The hallway was dark and cool. We stopped at the window and waited for the dispatcher to look up from the radio. Roxanne looked at the posters for missing children.

"Can you imagine?" I said.

"I don't have to," she said. "I've got three now who've disappeared."

"Kidnapped?"

"Not yet," Roxanne said. "But maybe soon."

The dispatcher, a very pleasant, very made-up young woman, looked up and recognized me and smiled.

"We need to see Detective LaCharelle," I said.

"They're in the detectives' offices," she said, eyeing Roxanne curiously. "I'll ring them."

"That's okay," I said. "We'll let ourselves in."

We went down the hall, Roxanne in her jeans and white linen blouse, me in my jeans and dark green polo shirt. We looked as if we might be a happy couple, off to spend a Saturday browsing for antiques.

As Roxanne had said, in another life.

The door was half open. I nudged it open the other half and there was LaCharelle sitting at a desk, his feet up on the blotter, arms behind his head. A Winslow patrolman, a young guy with big, tanned biceps, was leaning against a file cabinet.

"So there's blood everywhere," LaCharelle was saying. "I mean everywhere. On the—"

He saw me and stopped. He saw Roxanne and his eyebrows moved involuntarily upward.

"McMorrow," LaCharelle said, swinging his feet off the desk and getting up.

"Good morning," I said.

"This is Patrolman Nicholson. He made the stop last night."

"Many thanks," I said. "This is Roxanne Masterson. The witness."

"Good morning, miss," LaCharelle said. "Nice of you to come in. When McMorrow said he could bring the witness with him, I had no idea why he'd want to bring the witness with him."

Roxanne stepped farther into the room. She nodded at the patrolman, who gave his head a jiggle and looked away shyly. Roxanne held her hand out to LaCharelle. He took it and she shook his hand and looked around.

"So where do you want to do it?" she said.

LaCharelle's eyes rolled, almost imperceptibly.

"This is fine," he said. "Have a seat. Let me get the paper."

Roxanne sat down. I stood and watched the patrolman watch her. She looked incongruously pretty in the drab little room. I knew it. The patrolman knew it. LaCharelle, when he came back with the forms, knew it too. He put the paper on the desk in front of Roxanne and stared at her for a moment.

"Now, Miss Masterson, this is what we call a voluntary statement. I don't want you to be nervous, because there's really nothing to be—"

"I'm not nervous, Detective," Roxanne said. "I work for the state. I'm a Child Protective worker. I've given many statements over the years. This one isn't going to bother me."

LaCharelle's patronizing smile vanished.

"Oh," he said. "Well, good. You're a pro and I'm a pro. Let's do it."

He sat at the desk across from Roxanne and took a pen from the pocket of his sport shirt. He started to date the paper, but the pen didn't work. LaCharelle made a couple of swirls on the paper and then flung the pen into the wastebasket. He took another pen from his pocket and it worked. He asked Roxanne to spell her full name. She did. He asked her where she lived and she gave her address in South Portland.

LaCharelle looked up.

"I thought you were a neighbor of McMorrow's," he said.

"No. I'm a friend of Mr. McMorrow's. I live in South Portland."

"So last night you were going—"

"To visit Mr. McMorrow."

"Oh," LaCharelle said. "Oh, I get it. Oh."

He looked at Roxanne, then looked at me.

I smiled. Eat your heart out, chump.

"Well," LaCharelle said. "That's nice. So, let's see. Tell me what you saw. In your own words."

Roxanne told him she was pulling into the road when the black car was pulling out. As she went by, she saw the faces of the two guys and they looked very nervous. They took off fast, throwing gravel with their tires, and Roxanne decided to follow them.

"Why?" LaCharelle said.

"To get their license number, just in case something had happened."

"You were expecting something to happen?"

"Mr. McMorrow has been threatened and assaulted over the past few days," Roxanne said. "So if something happened, it wouldn't be a big surprise."

"I suppose it wouldn't," LaCharelle said. "Mr. McMorrow seems to have a knack for having things happen to him."

He looked at me. I looked at Roxanne. She was looking at LaCharelle.

"So you followed the car. You got close enough to get the license number?"

"Eventually. But it took a while."

"What was it?"

"The number? It was 16543 A. I wrote it down. Now I've got it memorized."

"And what else did you see?"

"Well, as I was driving behind them, I could see them throwing stuff out of the car. Shoes or something. I had the plate by then, so I stopped and went back and picked up one of the things. It was in the bushes along the road. Not very far in."

"And what was it?"

"A boot. A boot that smelled like gasoline."

"And you're sure it came out of that car?"

"Yes, I'm sure."

"The black car with the license-plate number you just gave me?"

"Yes."

"And what did you do with the boot?"

"I gave it to the fire chief."

"We have it," the patrolman broke in. "It's Leaman's boot. We found the other one this morning. Gas on that one too."

LaCharelle wrote carefully on the form, then turned it over and started on a second. He paused and looked over both pages, then looked up and smiled.

"Well, I guess that'll do it," he said. "We'll see Mr. Leaman in eight or ten years, if he lives that long. Nice work, Miss Masterson. If you ever decide to leave Child Protective, give us a call. We can always use good female detectives."

The patronizing smile returned as he slid the statement over the desk to Roxanne. She scanned it and signed on the bottom of both pages.

"So where's he now?" I said.

"Leaman? Kenhegan County. Who handled your assault by him?"

"Lenny. Right here. Kennebec PD."

"We'll get that report. I'd say Mr. Leaman is soon to be headed for the big house. Score one for the good guys."

Roxanne got up. LaCharelle got up too, and the patrolman looked uncomfortable. We all moved toward the door, but as we got to the doorway, LaCharelle said, "McMorrow" and nodded back toward the room.

I turned. Roxanne stopped around the corner, just outside the door.

"Two things," LaCharelle said, lowering his voice. I took a step toward him.

"One, I hope you understood that what I told you on the phone last night was confidential. If I see it in print, you won't know what hit you."

I looked at him. Big and fleshy. I'd been hit by worse.

"What's two?" I said.

"The apples are in the cart on Donna Marchant. I don't want 'em upset, if you know what I'm saying."

"I know what you're saying. And I think there are a few apples kicking around underfoot. If you know what I'm saying."

"Let 'em lie, McMorrow. We've got him, you hear me? Stay away from our witnesses. Stay away from Tanner. We're gonna nail him, and he's the right guy. If I didn't believe that, I'd still be out there looking. But I'm not. We've got a warrant for Tanner and we're looking for him. He's gone under, but we'll dig him out. You stay the hell away."

I looked at him and smiled.

"But I thought I was one of the good guys," I said. "I was gonna ask for a plastic badge with my name on it."

LaCharelle looked toward the door. I started to turn away.

"McMorrow," he said.

"I thought you said two things."

"One more. With a nice girl like that, what the hell are you doing, hanging around with a slider like Donna Marchant?"

He looked at me with the faintest of leers.

"She wasn't. I didn't. And I'm not," I said. "Better hang on tight to that apple cart, Detective."

I turned and walked out. Roxanne was beside the door, leaning against the cinder-block wall.

"Did you hear all that?" I said as she fell in beside me.

"Yeah."

"See what I mean?"

"Yeah, I do," Roxanne said.

"She didn't deserve this. Believe me."

"I do believe you," she said.

"So what do you want to do now?"

"What do you want to do, Jack?"

"Pick up all the apples," I said. "Every single last one."

27

Roxanne moved easily in the labyrinth of dim hallways in the big apartment building on Peavey Street. She wasn't tentative. She wasn't shy. She had been doing this for a while.

We climbed the stairs, Roxanne in front, me behind. We went to the second floor, stepped over trash bags, walked past muddy boots. I showed Roxanne where Miss Desrosiers's door was, stuck away in the corner, and then I knocked and waited.

There was a shuffling sound, a couple of clicks, then the door crept open.

"Hi," I said. "I'm Jack McMorrow. From the newspaper. We talked last week?"

"Oh, yeah. What? You got more questions?"

"A couple."

"Well, come in, then. I spent thirty-eight years on my feet, and now I like to sit myself down."

The door opened wide and there she was, small and neat in a blue cotton dress, as if, on a Saturday morning at five minutes before nine, she'd been expecting company.

She led the way and we followed, through the narrow hall and into the living room, all sunlight and crochet.

"I'm sorry about the mess, eh?"

You could have lapped milk up off the floor.

"I'm sorry to bother you," I said.

Miss Desrosiers went to the couch and sat down, her feet, in terry-cloth slippers, barely touching the floor.

"This your wife?"

"No, she's my friend. This is Roxanne Masterson."

"Hello," Roxanne said.

She smiled gently. Miss Desrosiers looked her over.

"She's a pretty girl, eh? You better marry her right off. You don't want somebody else coming in, snatching her up, pretty girl like that."

"No, I don't," I said.

"And now you're dragging her around while you do your newspaper work? You better treat her better or she'll find somebody else, eh? Pretty girl like that, they got all the guys coming 'round. Don't you take her for granted there. I got a nephew. He lives out there in Arizona. He come home and he's got this little girl, my goodness, she was a doll. I say, 'When you gonna get married?' He says, 'Sometime. We don't want to rush things.' Rush things? Well, she's married now, all right. To somebody else. He dillydallied and she found somebody who'd just do it, you know?"

Roxanne looked at me and grinned. I smiled back. "Well, you're probably right," I said. "But the reason we stopped by was to ask you about that night again. The night Donna died."

The woman looked annoyed.

"Hey, I talked about that night so much, I'm blue in my face, eh?"

"You did? To who?"

"To who? The detective, that's who," she said. "I told him. I saw that rat there, I saw him come in. I saw him go out. I didn't see him come back, but I wouldn't. Not if he didn't want me to. I said, 'What do I look like, a cat? See in the dark?' I see him come out because the light's on in the hallway and then the door opens and the light comes out. But if he's sneaking around, I'm not gonna see him."

"So that's what they wanted to know?"

"I guess so. He comes in here and he's got a gun. I know he's got a gun because of the way he sits, you know. I think it was in the back of his pants. Some of the detectives on television hold them there. Some of them have them under the arm. Under the sport jacket. But he had on one of those little short jackets. The ones with the red plaid lining."

"But I was wondering about Marcia. The sister. Could you tell me again when she came and went?"

"When she came and went? Why don't you ask her?"

"We will," Roxanne said, startling me. "But she's been away. Taking care of the little girl. It's been very hard on her, I'm sure. Losing her mother at her age."

It was nicely done. Deflect and disarm.

"Oh, a terrible thing. The little baby, she shouldn't have seen any of the things she saw. His drinking. Hitting that poor girl. Oh, I'd like to give that guy the back of my hand. But then he'd probably hit me too. A nasty bully, and that girl there, she was defenseless, you know? Hey, she needed a couple of big brothers, come and straighten him out. I had a couple of brothers, they're dead now, but when I was her age, anybody touched me, hey, there wouldn't be much left of them, let me tell you. Especially my brother Harry. Oh, he was a big man, and a temper? He'd tear them limb from limb, I'm not kidding you."

Good for Harry, I thought. Good for him.

"Well, I know you told me this once, off the record."

"I don't want my name in the paper."

"It won't be. I promise. But you said Marcia came once and left. Then came again."

"Right. With the little girl. I think things must've gotten worse. That guy must've snuck back in or something."

"And she took the girl with her?" I asked.

"That time, yes. The second time."

"And then she came back again by herself?"

"Oh, yeah. That was when the police came. Right after that. She must've found her and called the cops. The lights were flashing and the sirens. I said, 'You'd think somebody'd been murdered.' I felt bad about that."

"I know," I said. "I remember you said that."

I thought for a moment.

"So do you think the little girl was there when it happened?"

"Oh, God no," Miss Desrosiers said, her pale, translucent hands wringing on her lap. "She came and got her."

"And then she came back again."

"Yeah. But the little girl wasn't with her. She was home. She's married, right? The sister?"

"Yeah. Her husband works at the mill."

"That's good. So he must've been taking care of her."

"I'm sure," Roxanne said. She smiled soothingly.

"So was it a long time between when she picked up the girl and when she came back?" I said.

"Oh, I don't know. I mean, I don't remember. A little while. I can't remember, exactly. But it was after the news when she got the little girl. Hey, I don't know. A half hour. I was finishing my tea, and I made that as soon as the news was over. I think he waited out there in the alley until the sister and the little girl left, and then he went back in and strangled her. Well, he'll burn in hell. See how tough he is then, eh?"

"Probably not very," Roxanne said. "'Did you make that afghan yourself?"

So Roxanne and Miss Desrosiers talked about afghans and crocheting for a few minutes. I half listened, thinking about that half hour of opportunity, about Tanner saying he hadn't killed Donna, that she'd been just fine when he left.

Beaten up. Drunk. Crying. Just fine.

When I tuned back into the conversation, it was winding down. Roxanne had made a friend. She could come by anytime for tea and cookies, chat about the old days in Kennebec. When we left, Miss Desrosiers took Roxanne's hand and told me to marry her while I had the chance. I wasn't the only one who succumbed to Roxanne's charm.

"So what do you think?" I said when we got in the car.

"I think I'm going to find a man who doesn't dillydally."

"Should we go find a justice of the peace?"

"How 'bout we start with a cup of coffee," Roxanne said.

"And talk about our wedding plans?"

"How 'bout we start with a cup of coffee."

She smiled. Barely.

We went to the Donut Shop, a clean, well-lighted place on Main Street, a two-minute drive from Peavey Street. The store with the lunch counter and X-rated movies was closer, but I couldn't picture Roxanne in that setting. But then, maybe I'd have to start.

"You're good at this, Roxanne," I said as we settled into our Formica and plastic booth, with its panoramic parking-lot view.

"Good at what?" she said.

"At talking to people."

"It's what I do. I talk to people about their problems, try to figure out if something's wrong."

"Do you think something's wrong here?"

Roxanne picked at the plastic half-and-half container, then dribbled the stuff into her coffee.

"I think something's strange about it," she said. "That there was such a short period of time for Donna to be killed. If Marcia came and got the girl—"

"Adrianna."

"—Adrianna, a little after ten, and Donna was okay then. But she was dead by eleven."

I sipped my tea.

"But what if she was already dead? What if she was dead in her bed but Marcia thought she was asleep?"

"Then why did she come back?"

"Maybe she just came by to check on both of them," I said. "'Found Adrianna in bed and Donna passed out. Or she *thought* she was passed out. So she took Adrianna home. When she came back to check on Donna, see if she was okay, she found she wasn't passed out. She was dead."

"But you say Tanner says he didn't do it."

"And I believe him."

"Just like that?"

"That's how juries do it. They listen and go with their gut."

"And you're a jury of one?" Roxanne said.

"Yup."

"So who did it, then?"

"Marcia?" I said.

"Police don't think so, according to what that Detective What's-his-name said."

"Maybe they haven't asked her," I said.

"And you want to?"

"It's either that, or let the whole thing drop right here."

"And you won't do that," Roxanne said.

"I have to know what happened."

She looked down at her cup.

"I don't like this," Roxanne said. "I feel like you're being sucked down a drain or something, swirling closer and closer. What if you get too close?"

I smiled.

"Clair'll protect me."

"Clair's fifteen miles away, Jack."

"No plan is perfect," I said.

So there really was only one thing left to do, and that was to go to Marcia and try to talk to her, to divine something from her words, her eyes, her attitude, her niece.

I knew it. Roxanne knew it. Neither of us wanted to say it, so we sat in silence and watched the traffic going by, the English sparrows skittering in the gutter for crumbs. An old man, a hard drinker by the looks of him, walked by in shoes that were three sizes too big. A woman came out of the parking lot, holding a little girl's hand. The little girl's sundress was too small. The woman, stocky in her sneakers and jeans, was weathered and grim. Nobody would stop to let them cross, and they stood there and waited on the curb in what seemed to me to be a humiliating exercise.

"That's what I can't stand," I said.

"What?" Roxanne said.

"To see somebody humiliated like that."

"Like what?"

"Like that woman there with the little girl. Why don't they let her cross, the sons of bitches? Why didn't they leave Donna alone? It's like they see somebody at a disadvantage and they harass them and peck at them and torment them until they can't stand it anymore. I can't stand cruelty. I really can't. She ought to step out in the street with a baseball bat and start smashing windshields."

Roxanne looked at me thoughtfully.

"Sorry," I said. "Must be the caffeine."

I smiled.

"Let's go," Roxanne said.

She got up and I followed.

We headed back across town, with Marcia rising like a specter in the backseat. Neither of us spoke, except when Roxanne asked me to stop at the natural-foods place. I pulled the Olds in beside the Volvos and Saabs and waited as Roxanne went inside. She came out with a big paper bag.

"Some nice bread," she said. "For Clair and Mary. It's really nice of them to let us stay with them."

"They enjoy the company."

"It's still nice."

"And it's the least they'd do. Clair would do anything for us. It's really kind of amazing."

"I know. Maybe you should bring him to the sister's house."

"So he can cover me if she comes to the door with an Uzi?"

"It's no joke," Roxanne said.

"Who's joking?" I said.

The rest of the ride home was somber. I drove slowly, one eye on the temperature gauge. We saw an immature bald eagle coming up the Kennebec as we crossed the bridge, but all I could do was point halfheartedly.

Roxanne nodded. We kept going, past the mini-malls and convenience stores, past the farms, out into the woods, which seemed remote and deep and forbidding. And twenty dark minutes later we pulled up in front of the house, its blackened beams sticking out of the rubble like some charred skeleton, something for the forensics people to puzzle over.

And they did, late in the afternoon. Roxanne was out in the perennial gardens with Mary. I was in the Varneys' kitchen, trying to reach Millie on the phone. The number I had in Santa Fe had been changed to another number in Santa Fe. That number was answered by a machine that played what sounded like Gregorian chants. I left a message telling someone that Millie's house in Prosperity had burned and that I needed her to call me. She probably was in Ecuador. Or Sierra Leone.

But I'd done everything I could. I hadn't been able to say that too often lately.

Clair came into the kitchen from outside as I hung up the phone. He got two glasses from the cupboard and a pitcher of iced tea from the refrigerator.

"I don't even know if Millie had insurance," I said.

"Millie? Insurance? Are you kidding?" Clair said.

"Then how would she get a mortgage?"

"Mortgage? Millie? Are you kidding?" he said. "The fire marshal's office investigator is down there. She went by and I told her you'd come over."

"Shouldn't be too tough. There's the gas can. There's the house."

"They have to prove it for court. This guy gets a good lawyer, they'd better have all their ducks in place."

"You know, it could've been a double murder," I said.

"Triple if I'd caught up to him. Heck with taking any license-plate numbers."

"You'd do that, wouldn't you?"

"If he'd killed you two?" Clair said. "Without question."

"I may have another favor to ask you."

"I'm here."

"I appreciate that," I said.

"Don't get all mushy on me now."

"Do you think this is male bonding?"

"Oh, God almighty. I should've known better than to open my door to somebody from away."

"Too late," I said. "We've got squatters' rights."

"Speaking of which, you gonna rebuild on that same spot? I bet Millie will just give you the land. She'll think it has bad karma now."

"She'd be right. But what do I know about building houses?"

"As much as I can teach you in a summer," Clair said.

"As long as we don't start tomorrow."

"Why not?"

"That's where the favor comes in," I said. "What are you doing after church?"

The fire investigator was quiet and professional. She wanted to know the layout of the rooms, what I had stored in the shed, which no longer existed. I showed her what had been the kitchen, what had been the loft, what had been the front room. She took notes on a clipboard, pictures with an automatic Minolta. We finished the tour out front and stared at the rubble.

"And the gasoline was in the shed?"

"Yeah. A two-gallon can. For my chain saw. It's under there somewhere, I guess. The saw is, too."

"Good thing they got the guy," she said.

"Better than the alternative, I suppose."

She looked at me curiously.

"So why'd this person do this, anyway?"

"It's a long story," I said. "I guess it started when I wrote something about him in the paper."

"Oh, yeah?"

"And then he wanted me to give him the number of my bank card." She listened.

"And I wouldn't give it to him."

"So he burned your house down."

"Yup," I said.

She shook her head.

"Good thing you weren't in it."

"But he didn't know that. I guess planning isn't his forte."

"Forte," she said. "Right."

She turned back toward her car, which looked like a police cruiser but was white.

"You know, things like this don't happen too often around here," she said, turning back to me. "It's not like it's New York or Florida or something."

I looked over the mess that had been a house.

"That's what people keep telling me," I said. "But I'm beginning to wonder."

The investigator shook my hand warily and left. I walked through the mess one more time, picking at the rubble. A couple of picture frames: glass broken, photographs gone. Winter clothes in a soggy mess. My books and binoculars under there somewhere. All my music.

I sighed and then headed back up through the field. Mary and Roxanne met me on their way in from the garden, their arms laden with white and yellow flowers.

"Asters," Roxanne said. "And forget-me-nots."

"They're like the phoenix; beauty rising from the ashes," Mary said. "We have to remember to be thankful that you're both okay."

I looked at Roxanne. Her skin was flushed from the sun. Tendrils of hair had slipped forward on her temples. She looked at me and her eyes glowed.

"We are thankful," I said.

I walked with them back to the house. It was almost five. A late-afternoon breeze had come up, chasing away the mosquitoes and blackflies. Mary said we'd eat on the back lawn. Grilled chicken and baked potatoes with rosemary, done on the coals. The salad would be a meal in itself.

But first we had drinks, sitting out on the white Adirondack chairs. Clair came over from the barn, went in to wash his hands, and came out with a Budweiser for himself and a Ballantine for me.

"You know I had to look all over for this stuff," he said.

"It's for discerning palates," I said, taking the can.

Mary came out with two glasses of white wine. Roxanne brought up the rear, with a plate of cheese and sliced fruit and crackers. We stood for a moment and raised our glasses.

"To good fortune," Mary said.

"And dumb luck," I said.

"The only kind," Clair said.

"Take it when we can get it," Roxanne said. "Cheers."

Glasses clinked, and they sipped. I took a long swallow, but it didn't taste quite right. Clair caught my eye and seemed to be thinking the same thing.

It tasted premature.

28

—m—

Sunday morning was overcast but not raining. I stood alone in the kitchen, where a nearly empty bottle of white zinfandel was the only remnant of dinner the night before. Roxanne had fallen asleep early, coming down after all the stress of the fire and the police. Clair and Mary had gone to bed even earlier, in a somewhat awkward attempt to give us privacy. I sat up alone, considering what to do this morning. It was eight thirty and I was still alone.

Roxanne was in the shower. Clair and Mary had stopped by the store in Albion to get the Sunday paper. I dialed the phone and stood by the counter as it rang.

Once. Twice.

Three times.

"Hello," a suspicious voice said.

"Marcia?" I said.

"Who is this?"

"Jack McMorrow."

I waited for a click. It didn't come.

"I need to talk to you. For your own good. For Adrianna's."

"I don't need to talk to you, McMorrow. I'm calling the police."

"No, please, this is important. I'm not—"

The phone clicked. Then clicked again. Then I heard the dial tone. The house was quiet.

I waited fifteen seconds and dialed again. The phone rang, but Marcia didn't answer. But then, she wasn't calling the cops, either. I hung up the phone.

Upstairs, the shower stopped. I put water on for tea and coffee and went up to see Roxanne. She stepped out of the bathroom wrapped in a towel.

"Make yourself right at home," I said.

"They're gone, aren't they?"

"Yeah, but what if the plumber showed up? Or the furnace man?"

"Or the butcher or the baker or the candlestick maker?" Roxanne said.

"Them too."

"They'd have to avert their eyes."

Ordinarily, I would have attempted to parlay this into a joke. Not this time.

"What time do you want to go?" I said.

"I'll be ready in fifteen minutes," Roxanne said, walking toward the bedroom.

"When Clair and Mary get home?"

"Okay," she said.

I hoped it was.

We had coffee and tea in nervous silence. I toasted half a bagel and put peanut butter on it, but only for something to do. I ate two bites and left it on the plate. At 9:05, I heard Mary's Jeep pull into the drive. Two doors slammed and then the back door opened and they came in. Clair had the *Maine Sunday Telegram* under his arm. Mary was carrying a plastic jug of orange juice.

They stopped.

"You ready?" I said.

"I'll follow you," Clair said.

"So you are going to do this?" Mary said.

"Oh, we'll be home before lunch," Clair said. "Keep the coffee water on."

"I hope you understand, Mary," I said.

"Clair explained it to me. I suppose I do. I just have this feeling that I used to get when the girls would be going off on dates. I knew they had to do it, but I couldn't wait for that car to pull in the driveway and they'd be home, safe and sound."

"So we can't tell you not to wait up," Roxanne said, smiling.

"I'll be here by the phone," Mary said, and then she turned away and opened the refrigerator to put the juice away. We moved to the door.

"I'll be behind you guys," Clair said. "But not too close."

We stepped out into the dooryard.

"Just cover my rear end," I said.

"So what else is new," Clair said, and he walked off toward the barn.

We got in the truck and I started it, wheeled around, and headed out the drive and down the road. Roxanne idly played with her hair.

"You sure you want to have anything to do with this?" I said.

She answered looking straight ahead. "When's the last time you had a meaningful conversation with a four-year-old?"

"I don't know. Probably when I was four."

"I rest my case."

"But I remember it like it was yesterday," I said.

"For me it was the day before yesterday and the day before that. The case still rests."

When we pulled up to the intersection of the dump road, I stopped and watched the mirror. After a moment, Clair's big four-wheel-drive pickup came into view. He flashed his headlights once and I pulled out. When I got up to the main road, he was still back there. I headed for Albion.

We drove in silence through Albion village and well into the farms of East Winslow. I pointed skyward at a turkey vulture and Roxanne nodded, then looked out the window on her side.

"What if her husband is home?"

"Sundays are double time. I don't think this mythical spouse will be around. If he is, well, it'll be interesting to meet him."

"So you think Adrianna might come outside?"

"It isn't raining and she has to go out sometime, right? If not, I'll see if I can get Marcia to let me through the door. She talked a little last time, and she didn't hang up on me right away this morning."

"How long did it take?" Roxanne asked.

"Ten or fifteen seconds."

"Poured her heart out, did she?"

"Progress is made in small increments," I said.

"Or not at all," Roxanne said.

"That's the spirit," I said.

When we came into Winslow, I could feel my breath quicken. Roxanne was quiet. I watched for Clair's truck in my rearview mirror but didn't see it.

Semper Fi, don't fail me now, I said to myself.

Marcia's road appeared too soon, and once we were on it, it seemed as though it had shortened. We came around the corner and there was Marcia's house, sitting in its half-acre square of pasture. Her car was in the driveway, but the truck was gone. I went by once and continued on for a quarter-mile, pulling in and turning beside a run-down hay barn. As I pulled out, Clair's truck came into view. As he went by, he gave me a crisp salute. In the mirror, I saw his brake lights come on.

"Well, here goes," I said.

I pulled the car into the driveway and parked at the end by the road. There was no sign of activity in the front windows, but I could see a few neon-orange and yellow toys in the fenced-in area out back. So Adrianna did play sometimes.

Roxanne reached over and gave my hand a squeeze.

"See you in a sec," I said. "Watch to see if any of those toys move."

I got out of the car and walked up the flagstones to the front door. The gauzy curtains were down in the windows and the inside door was closed. I climbed the steps and listened. Thought I heard something. I pressed the bell.

Waited.

Reached out to press the bell again—

—when the door squeaked. Shuddered slightly and then drew open, very slowly. Four fingers reached out and pulled it open wider. The fingers were very small.

"Hi," Adrianna said through the screen.

"Hi, there," I said quietly. "You're Adrianna."

"Uh-huh."

"Do you remember me?"

"Uh-huh."

"You do?" I said.

"'Yeah, you're Jack in the Beanstalk."

"Right," I said. "We met before, didn't we?"

"Uh-huh. With my mommy. My mommy's not here. She went to heaven."

"I know she did," I said. "I'm sure she's very happy there."

"Uh-huh. My aunt said she can hear us. And someday we'll get to go see her there."

I looked at her. Big dark eyes. Curly hair. Very small hands and wrists and arms. A lot of trust.

"Is your aunt home now?"

"Yes," Adrianna said.

"Can I talk to her?"

"She's pooping."

"Oh," I said. "I'll wait, then."

"Okay. I think she can come soon. I already knocked on the door. She said she was coming."

We stood there for a moment and looked at each other.

Roxanne was right. I didn't know what to say. I half turned and was starting to signal for Roxanne to come up when I heard a door bang inside.

"Adrianna, honey. I told you not to open that door. Close it and come in now, honey. You don't need to—"

Marcia appeared behind Adrianna. Her eyes opened wide.

"Get in here," she gasped, yanking the little girl by the shoulder. Adrianna disappeared from view. Marcia faced me, her face hard and taut and furious.

"What are you doing here? What were you talking to her for?"

"She answered the door. I had to talk to her. She told me you'd be here in a minute."

"You son of a bitch, you have no right to talk to her. What gives you—don't you get it? Stay away from us, McMorrow. You are not a part of our life."

"Well, we were just chatting—"

"About what?" Marcia shot back. "What did she say to you?"

"Well, she said—"

Adrianna appeared at Marcia's thigh.

"Aunt Marcia, I need a drink. I don't want that cranberry stuff, 'cause it tastes like—"

"Just a minute. Just go. Honey, just go and play. I'll be with you in a minute."

The little girl vanished again.

"What did she say to you?" Marcia demanded. "What did she say?"

"I don't know," I said. "She said she remembered me. She said her mother was in heaven, that you said she would get to see her someday. Or something like that. She said—"

"Did you ask her about that night?"

"Did I ask her?"

"About that night?"

"No, I didn't really ask her anything."

"Don't you know how painful this is to a child?" Marcia said through the door. "A child her age. Can't you understand that? My God—"

"Yeah, I understand that. But I need to talk to you. You don't think so, but I really was very fond of your sister. I know you blame me for what happened, and I blame myself, too. God, I do, but I wasn't there that night. I didn't do it. Somebody did, and—"

"And they've got him. And they're going to send him to prison, and we're going to get on with our lives. Mine and hers and my husband's. You've got nothing to do with this. So go before I—"

"Aunt Marcia, I really need a drink. And that cranberry tastes—"

I glimpsed the head of blonde curls.

"Honey, not now. Just go. Go watch TV."

"I don't want to watch TV. I want to go out back and play."

"So go," Marcia sputtered.

The curly head disappeared. I heard a door hiss open, thought I felt a puff of cool air.

"Fine," I said, moving between Marcia and the car. "But just let me talk to you once. I feel responsible. And I'll feel even more responsible if something happens to that little girl or to you because I didn't get five minutes to talk to you. That's all I need. Goddamn it, I liked your sister. I thought she was trying very hard. Really. She had bad luck, and she was overcoming it."

I paused. Marcia hesitated.

"Five minutes. It's for you and Adrianna. How can you not give her that? Why would you not give her that? I'm not a monster."

She looked at me, then pushed the door open. I went in.

Marcia was dressed in khaki shorts and sandals and a dark blue sweater. She was wearing makeup, but underneath it she looked thinner, with hollow cheeks like someone who had been ill.

I stood five feet inside the door, beside an end table. There was an eight-by-ten color photo of Adrianna on the table and a much smaller, older photograph of Donna behind it.

"Five minutes, McMorrow," Marcia said from the middle of the room, her arms folded across her chest. "The clock's ticking."

My cue.

"It's like this," I began. "There's a warrant out for Jeff for Donna's murder. They haven't found him yet, but they're looking for him."

"So?"

"But I talked to him. Have you seen him since this happened?"

"Are you out of your mind?" Marcia said, wrapping her arms around herself tighter. "What are we gonna do? Chat about old times?"

"No, I guess . . . I guess you wouldn't. But, I don't know, I thought maybe he would've tried to call or contact you somehow."

"Yeah, that son of a bitch called. And I hung up on him. My husband hung up on him. You know what he did one time? He called and asked for Adrianna. I couldn't believe it. Like I'm gonna say, 'Sure. Hang on while I go get a four-year-old.'"

"Well, I—"

"I've got one reason for living right now, McMorrow. And that's that little girl. Nobody hurts Adrianna. Nobody. You get to her over my dead body. Nobody is going to hurt that little girl. And I hope that son of a bitch dies in prison. I hope he gets what he gave Donna. Times ten."

I waited for her to pause to take a breath.

"But I don't think he did it," I said.

Marcia gave a little gasp, as if she'd just felt a spasm of pain.

"You've got to be—"

"No, I'm serious. I don't think he did it. I talked to him and he told me he didn't do it. What he said was that Donna was okay when he left. She was drinking and upset, but she was standing by the counter. That's what he said, and I believe him. I really do. I'm sorry, I guess."

As I spoke, Marcia shook her head slightly and bit her lip. She gave a little sigh of disgust.

"So? I mean, who gives a shit what you think, McMorrow? I don't care if you think the moon is made of green cheese. I mean, who the hell are you?"

"I'm somebody who needs to know what happened."

"So read it in the paper. Leave us the hell alone."

"But don't you understand? They get Jeff for this and he didn't do it, and that leaves somebody who did. Walking around."

Marcia looked at me passively, as if suddenly bored.

"And not only do I want to know who did it, and want them caught, but I don't want the person who did it coming back to get you or Adrianna. Where was Adrianna when it happened? What if she saw something? What if whoever killed Donna decides to get rid of all the witnesses? Are you going to follow five feet behind that little girl the rest of her life? Are you—"

"Adrianna is my responsibility, McMorrow, not yours. You've done enough to ruin her life, so why don't you take your asinine bullshit and stick it where the sun don't shine. And leave us the hell alone."

Marcia turned to her left and backed up a couple of steps, craning to see out the window. "So why don't you just—"

She stopped.

"No," Marcia said, and she bolted into the next room. I followed and could hear her saying, "Oh, my God, oh, my God," over and over.

She tumbled down a short flight of steps and slammed open a sliding-glass door. It was still shaking as I came through it and saw Roxanne leaning over the short wire fence around the play yard.

She was smiling.

She was talking to Adrianna.

On a full run, Marcia grabbed the girl under the armpits and swung her up on her hip, like a Cossack taking a prisoner on horseback.

"Hey," Roxanne called out. "Careful with her."

But Marcia had both arms wrapped around Adrianna, and she swung around and ran back toward me. The girl's shirt was pulled up, exposing a narrow, pale back.

I could hear her starting to cry, a high-pitched, gasping whimper.

"Are you nuts?" I said, and I started to step aside, but Marcia stumbled and lurched toward me and they both looked as if they were going to fall, so I reached out to grab them.

"Let go of me," Marcia shouted into my shirt, and then we were all falling and I could see Roxanne jumping over the fence and she was shouting too.

"Get up—he's coming!" Roxanne was yelling. "Get up! He's got a knife! He's got a knife!"

Adrianna was screaming. Marcia scrambled to her feet, holding the girl by one arm and looking toward the field. I saw her eyes lock with fear and I rolled over and looked and saw Tanner running through the grass, the knife in his hand plain as day at fifty yards.

29

He was slogging through the high grass, the knife held low.

"Get her inside," I said, and I shoved Marcia and Adrianna toward the door. Roxanne followed, two steps behind them, and I looked at Tanner and then around the play yard for some sort of weapon.

Everything was small and safe and plastic.

"You tell 'em," Tanner was calling. "I got witnesses. You tell 'em."

He was thirty yards away and closing. I looked in the sandbox, around the yard, and finally picked up a pink plastic tricycle and held it in front of me.

Tanner was close and I could see his eyes and mouth open, panting, and the long blade of the knife jabbing the air.

"You'll tell 'em, you bitch. I'm gonna rip your guts out, you lying bitch," he said.

He said it over and over, and then there was a roar and Clair's truck slammed around the corner, ripping ruts in the lawn and sliding to a halt twenty feet to my right. The driver's door exploded open and Clair was out and his rifle was raised to his shoulder and he was shouting, "Drop the knife! Drop the knife!" Tanner slowed, almost stopped, and looked at Clair. Then he broke into a trot again and was almost to the fence.

The rifle boomed and Tanner stopped. I heard the clack of the bolt and then Clair's voice.

"Drop the knife or the next one puts you down," he said.

His voice was chillingly calm. Tanner hesitated. He looked at me and then back at Clair.

"Friggin' A, man," he said. "Gimme a break, will ya?"

He looked at me. Flipped the knife onto the grass.

"She's got to tell you," Tanner said. "I didn't kill nobody. They can't do this to me. When I left, she was fine. She's got to tell you. I'll friggin' kill her for this."

I put my tricycle down and hopped the fence and walked toward Tanner.

"Were you planning on riding that thing to safety, or what?" Clair said, walking slowly toward Tanner, the rifle still leveled.

"Only if you didn't show up," I said.

"I was watching the road. I didn't expect Ranger Rick here to come out of the woods."

He motioned to Tanner, who was standing there, sweaty and disheveled.

"On your belly on the ground," Clair said. "Hands behind your neck."

Tanner looked at him dully.

"I didn't kill nobody," he said.

"You're gonna be on the receiving end if you're not down there when I count three. One, two—"

Tanner flopped down heavily, his knife sheath empty on his belt. I picked up the knife and held it in front of me. Clair handed me the rifle, too, and then whipped off his belt. He bent down over Tanner, lifted his boots up over his buttocks, wrenched his arms down, first one, then the other. The belt snaked around and between wrists and ankles, and then Clair cinched it tight.

"Where'd you learn to do that?" I said, looking at Tanner, hog-tied.

"Cub Scouts," he said.

"But can you start a fire with a magnifying glass?"

"As long as I have matches."

Tanner grunted and tried to roll over on his side but couldn't.

"I didn't kill nobody," he said again.

"Not for lack of trying," I said.

I looked at him, then handed the rifle back to Clair.

"I'll go in and call the cops," I said.

I hopped the fence and went to the door. It was ajar, and I slid it open and went in and up the stairs. The house was oddly quiet, and I wondered if they'd all gone out the front. I walked into the living room, but no one was there. I pushed the bathroom door open and there was no one there, either. I held Tanner's knife tighter, the blade along my thigh.

The bedrooms in the house were to the left of the living room. I crossed the room and started down the short hallway. Both doors were open. From the one on the right, I heard the sound of a throat clearing. I walked to the door and looked.

Roxanne was sitting on the bed, alone. I followed her eyes to the corner to the right of the door and stopped.

Marcia was standing against the wall, next to a bureau. She had a revolver in her hand and Adrianna in front of her legs.

"It's okay," I said. "We got him. I just have to call the police."

Marcia didn't move. The gun was pointed at Roxanne, whose face was still, her legs crossed. Slowly, the gun moved, until it was pointing at me.

"It's not okay, McMorrow," Marcia said. "It's not okay at all."

I glanced at Roxanne. There was something strange about her expression, something almost sympathetic.

"But we've got him. Clair's got him tied up. Why . . . What's with the gun?"

Marcia smiled wistfully. Adrianna looked from me to Roxanne, her eyes stretched wide, her mouth clamped shut.

"What's with the gun?" Marcia said. "I don't know what's with the gun. I really don't know."

But she didn't put it down, and the barrel still pointed at my chest.

"You want to tell him?" Marcia said. "You know, I don't even know your name."

"It's Roxanne."

"Well, Roxanne, you tell him. And then I'll decide what to do. I'll decide what to do."

I looked at Roxanne.

"I talked to Adrianna," she said. "Outside. Just for a few minutes. That's a pretty name, Adrianna."

The little girl smiled.

"I think you're a pretty lady," she said.

"Thanks. Your mother was pretty too, wasn't she?"

"Yeah, but she's in heaven. Do you stay pretty in heaven?"

"I think so," Roxanne said softly.

I looked up and saw that Marcia had begun to cry. The tears were running down her cheeks, like streams during spring runoff. The gun slowly dropped until it pointed limply at the floor.

"Adrianna, do you know Jack?" Roxanne said. "Do you remember him?"

"Yeah. Jack in the Beanstalk. Mommy's friend."

Marcia suddenly broke in, tears still running down her face.

"Adrianna, can you tell Jack about the night Mommy went to heaven?"

"You won't get mad?"

"No," Marcia said. "'You can tell him. Just like you told this nice lady, Roxanne.'"

"My mommy's sleeping up there, right?"

"Right."

"And she's happy, and she isn't crying anymore?" Adrianna said. She looked up at Marcia.

"No, she isn't crying," her aunt said.

"Can I have some chips?"

"Sure, honey," Marcia said softly. "In a minute. But tell Mr. McMorrow about that night, could you, hon? When Auntie Marcia came over. Tell us what happened."

Adrianna looked up at her for reassurance.

"It's okay, babe," Marcia said.

"Mommy was having whiskey," Adrianna said, her tiny voice giving the word an odd resonance.

"And she was laying on the couch. And then Jeff came and they made me go to bed."

"So did you go to sleep?"

"No."

"And what did you hear?"

"Them fightin'."

"Was Jeff hitting your mommy?"

"Yeah."

"And what else?"

"Yelling," Adrianna said. "At each other. He was calling Mommy bad names."

"And then what happened?"

"Daddy called. My real daddy."

"Yeah?"

"How do you know that?" Marcia said.

"Because he said he wanted to say good night to me."

"Did your mommy let him say good night to you?"

"No, she said he didn't really want to say good night, he was just playing games."

"What kind of games?"

"I don't know," Adrianna said.

Marcia stroked the little girl's curls.

"So then what happened?"

"What?"

"What happened after that?"

"Jeff and Mommy started fighting some more."

"What were they doing?"

"Yelling, and he was hitting her."

"How do you know that?"

" 'Cause I could hear it. The hitting sound. I think they were tummy hits. 'Cause they sound different from face hits. And Mommy was crying. She was saying, 'No, don't hit me.' "

"And then what?"

"Then Jeff kept hitting her, and then he left."

"What did your mommy do?" Marcia asked.

"She didn't do anything."

"Where was she?"

"She was crying."

"Where?"

"On the couch. But then she went to bed."

"And what did you do?"

"I got up."

"Why?"

" 'Cause Mommy had a bad cough. From drinking her whiskey."

"And she was in her bed?"

"Yeah."

"So what did you do?"

"I went to climb in with her, but she was coughing. Yucky-sounding coughs."

Marcia took a deep breath.

"So what did you do?"

"I went and got a bag for her to do throw-ups in."

"That was nice of you. What kind of bag was it?"

"A bag from the kitchen."

"A paper bag?" Marcia said slowly.

"No, I couldn't find one of those kind, so I got a plastic one from the drawer. The bag drawer."

"And what did you do with it?"

"I put it so Mommy could do her throw-ups."

"Where did you put it?"

"On Mommy's face. So she could do her throw-ups."

"Did she do her throw-ups?"

I waited for the answer.

"No. I guess she falled asleep."

"Did you wait for her?"

"Yes. I held up the bag for her."

"On her face."

"Yes. I kept it right there so she could do—"

"Her throw-ups. I know, honey. And then Mommy was asleep."

"And she wouldn't wake up, so I got scared, so I called you."

Marcia blinked back tears. So did Roxanne. I wiped mine with a finger.

"And where's Mommy now?" Marcia said.

"She's in heaven. And we're gonna go see her."

"That's right. Someday we'll go see her."

"Can I have some chips now?" Adrianna said.

"Sure you can, honey. I'll get them in a minute."

Adrianna trotted into the other room and *Mister Rogers* came on. It was a beautiful day in the neighborhood, Fred Rogers was telling her. A beautiful day in the beauty wood.

Marcia looked at me. I looked at her. Then at Roxanne. I wiped my eyes.

"So what do you think, McMorrow?"

"I don't know. Does anybody else know this?"

"Just you and me and her. Roxanne. And my husband."

"Cops don't know?"

"No, they don't. I told them I took her home the first time I went there. They asked Adrianna about the fighting and she told them. And that's all she told them."

"When did she tell you?"

"As soon as she got here. She was all wound up, and when she's wound up, she likes to talk. She told me the whole story."

"Why did you go back alone after you got Adrianna out of there?"

Marcia gave a little shrug.

"I got panicky. I thought I'd left something that would tell them . . . tell them about her, about what happened. So I went back again."

"And called the police?"

"Yeah."

I thought for a moment.

"Tough one," I said.

"Yeah," Marcia said.

I thought some more. Turned around and looked out to where Adrianna was kneeling in front of the television. There was a bowl of chips in front of her on the carpet and she was eating them, three bites to the chip. *Crunch, crunch, crunch.*

If it got out, her life would be changed. She'd know she'd accidentally killed her mother. The world would know that she'd killed her mother. She would have a social worker. She might have a foster home. The story would come out in the paper. For the rest of her life, she would carry this enormous, crushing burden.

I looked at her, at her small feet curled up underneath her. What would Donna want? What did Donna want for her? Up in heaven. I walked back to where Marcia was standing, the gun still hanging irrelevantly in her hand. I was still carrying the knife.

"We need to talk," I said to Roxanne.

She followed me out of the room. I turned and our eyes met.

"You're thinking what I'm thinking, aren't you," I said.

"Yeah," Roxanne said, looking over at Adrianna. "Yeah, I think I am."

"She may realize it someday."

"Maybe. Maybe not. I don't know. Maybe if she's older she'll deal with it better."

"At least she'll have a chance to have a normal childhood," I said. "But you know we'll have to carry this one with us too."

"Yeah," Roxanne said.

She swallowed. I sighed and took both of her hands in mine.

"Okay?" I said.

"Okay."

"Let's do it."

We walked back into the bedroom. Marcia hadn't moved.

"Raise her well," I said.

She looked up at me, then at Roxanne.

"I'm going to try," she said. "What about the police?"

"I don't know," I said. "I'd say Jeff Tanner is in very serious trouble."

30

The police came, many of them. A couple of them untied Jeff and handcuffed his hands behind his back. He protested as they crammed him into the back of the cruiser. I turned and walked away.

There were several cops at the scene, both Kennebec and state. The local cops took statements from me and from Clair. They looked curiously at Clair's big Ford four-wheel-drive, examined his rifle, and when they were done, treated him with deference, which was deserved.

I went up to the house where Roxanne and Marcia were talking to a state trooper. The trooper was waiting for a detective. The detective, when he arrived, was LaCharelle. He took me out in front of the house, alone.

"What'd I tell you, McMorrow?" he said.

"I stand corrected. What happens now? Off the record."

"We go to grand jury, just to keep things nice and neat. Terrorizing, reckless conduct with a dangerous weapon. Attempted assault. And, of course, murder. He won't make bail and he'll sit in a cell for nine months or so until we bring it to trial. Then we do our best to make sure he spends a long, long time in a place where there are no women to beat on."

"What about a plea for manslaughter?"

"No way. This boy's going bye-bye big-time."

He looked at me and gloated.

"So much for reporter's intuition, huh?"

As we were standing there, a black Pontiac roared up and slid to a stop. Tate got out, glanced grimly at me and LaCharelle, and hoofed it across the grass toward the house in her high heels.

LaCharelle gave her a small salute.

"Counselor," I said, nodding.

"McMorrow," Tate said, striding toward and past me. "I guess we'll be seeing more of each other."

"Good. Say hello to Fluffy."

Tate glared and continued walking.

"Fluffy?" LaCharelle said.

"Her cat. What brings her out on a Sunday?"

"Probably heard the TV people'll be here. She tips 'em off and then beats them to the scene. Hey, you know your buddy Danny Leaman?"

"Alphonse?"

"He's telling everybody Tate made him a deal to chase you out of town."

"Anybody listening?"

"You kidding? It'll take more than one dirtbag to tear down what she's got built. Tate'll chew him up and spit him out, cross her like that. He won't see daylight for twenty years."

"So she's still the prosecutor on him sticking me in the car?"

"Yup."

"Seems like a conflict of interest, doesn't it?"

"Yup."

"So what else is new?"

"Yup to that too," LaCharelle said.

We rode back to Prosperity in silence, our hands clasped between the seats. Mary had put out fruit salad and cheese for a late lunch. Clair made a chicken sandwich for himself and we all ate, but not heartily.

When Clair told Mary what had happened with Tanner and the knife and the gun, Mary just shook her head.

"That poor little girl," she said. "Poor little thing. What's the matter with people?"

When we'd had our coffee and tea, I maneuvered Clair over to the barn. Above us, barn swallows were whipping in and out of the open loft door.

"What a piece of aeronautical engineering," Clair said, watching them plummet toward the opening.

"Thanks for what you did," I said.

"Buy me a beer sometime. Buy me two."

"It's a deal. But I have something to tell you."

I did, standing there by the barn door, and Clair listened to all of it. Marcia's story. Adrianna's story. When I was finished, he looked up again at the birds.

"Not an easy call," I said. "I hope you can live with it too."

"Jack, I've done things in my life I never wanted to do. But 'none of the above' wasn't an option at the time. You consider the options you have and you choose the best one. That's what you've done."

"It doesn't bother you?"

"No. Hey, I remember a day in the war. A very long day. We lost two kids that day. Just kids. And I remember this lieutenant; he was pretty green. Toward the end they were bringing in just about anybody. But anyway, that night, they'd brought in the choppers and saved what was left of our butts, and we're sitting there and I was eating, I think, and he says to me, 'Varney, how can you just sit there and eat?' I guess I was supposed to be cutting my wrists or something. Who knows? I said to the guy, I remember this, I said, 'Lieutenant, there were a couple of choices we could have made today. The one we made cost us two kids, the nicest kids in the world. Good, decent kids. The other choice would have cost us a couple hundred. So I'm sorry, but I'm giving thanks.'"

Clair looked up at the swallows, then suddenly back at me.

"You deal with the hand you're dealt, you know? The hand you were dealt today left you with two choices, too. One was to give up that little girl. The other was to give up that scumbag. Way I look at it, if he didn't kill Donna that night, maybe he would have finished her off the next week. Next month. These guys don't just go away, Jack."

"This one is," I said.

"No loss," Clair said.

That evening was spent quietly. Clair puttered in the barn, tinkering with his saw, fiddling with his tractor, dodging the moths that beat themselves against his workbench light. I watched him for a few minutes, then went out back and looked up at the stars, which were gathering against the blue-black velvet. I stood there with my head tipped back and thought of Adrianna and Donna and heaven—that it would be great if there was one.

When I came in, Mary was reading in the living room. She looked up from her book to tell me a David Archambault had called twice from the paper and wanted me to call him. I thanked her and asked her where Roxanne was. She said she had gone to bed. I said good night and went up the stairs.

"If he calls again, you're out?" Mary called after me.

"If you don't mind," I said.

Roxanne was in bed, turning toward the window. The light was out and the stars showed through the glass. I lay down on the bed and put my arm around her shoulder.

"You okay?" I said.

"Not bad, considering."

"Are you going to be okay tomorrow?"

"And the day after that, and a year from now?" Roxanne said. "Oh, yeah. It was the right thing to do. But it's kind of hard, not telling the truth. The whole truth and nothing but the truth, and all that."

"It is hard," I said. "But I figure I can live with that easier than that little girl can live with the truth for her whole childhood. It would be a nightmare for her. It really would."

Roxanne was quiet. I could smell her hair. I pulled us tighter together.

"David Archambault's been calling," I said.

"That isn't going to make it any easier. Reading about it in the paper every day."

"It'll make it harder."

"Let's go," Roxanne said.

"Where?"

"I didn't tell you, but Skip offered us his boat. He's away on business for a week."

"You sure he didn't offer you and him his boat?" I said.

"Yeah, I'm sure. He's gay. He's really a great guy. You know what he does? He has this venture investment company and he gives most of the profits to charities. I guess he's given a huge amount to AIDS research."

"God, and you're stuck with an unemployed reporter who drinks too much beer and has a scar on his face."

"I don't feel so stuck," Roxanne said, her voice soft in the dark.

"Well, I am getting better with my spring warblers."

"My man of many talents."

"But I don't know how to sail," I said.

"Who said anything about sailing?" Roxanne said, taking my hand in hers.

"You mean we'll spend the week in the fo'c'sle?"

"We could."

"But what if we get scurvy?"

"We'll live dangerously," Roxanne said.

"Something new and different," I said.

"Yeah," Roxanne said. "Something new and different."

ABOUT THE AUTHOR

Gerry Boyle is the author of a dozen mystery novels, including the acclaimed Jack McMorrow series and the Brandon Blake series. A former newspaper reporter and columnist, Boyle lives with his wife, Mary, in a historic home in a small village on a lake. He also is working with his daughter, Emily Westbrooks, on a crime series set in her hometown, Dublin, Ireland. Whether it is Maine or Ireland, Boyle remains true to his pledge to send his characters only to places where he has gone before.